Gabriel Harrison

John Howard Payne

His Life and Writings

Gabriel Harrison

John Howard Payne
His Life and Writings

ISBN/EAN: 9783337340636

Printed in Europe, USA, Canada, Australia, Japan

Cover: Foto ©Raphael Reischuk / pixelio.de

More available books at **www.hansebooks.com**

JOHN HOWARD PAYNE,

DRAMATIST, POET, ACTOR,

AND AUTHOR OF

HOME, SWEET HOME!

HIS LIFE AND WRITINGS.

BY

GABRIEL HARRISON.

WITH ILLUSTRATIONS

REVISED EDITION.

PHILADELPHIA:
J. B. LIPPINCOTT & CO.
LONDON: 15 RUSSELL STREET, COVENT GARDEN.
1885.

Dedication.

TO MY PERSONAL FRIEND,

THOMAS J. McKEE, Esq.,

(COUNSELLOR-AT-LAW, NEW YORK,)

A GENTLEMAN OF LITERARY RESEARCH AND OTHER NOBLE QUALITIES,

THIS VOLUME

IS RESPECTFULLY DEDICATED

BY THE AUTHOR.

PREFACE.

In 1875, almost immediately after the "Faust Club" of Brooklyn, Long Island, had erected the monument to the author of "Home, Sweet Home," in Prospect Park, I wrote "The Life and Writings of John Howard Payne." For over twenty years I had been gathering everything that in any way related to Mr. Payne's life. I looked through old files of the New York, Boston, Philadelphia, and Baltimore newspapers, the chief places which Mr. Payne when a boy, "the young American Roscius," had visited. I then sent to London for monthly magazines that contained records of the stage, running back as far as 1813, that I might follow authoritatively and accurately the career of Mr. Payne while a resident of London for twenty years. I also possessed myself of Payne's first publication, a little pamphlet entitled "Juvenile Poems, Principally Written between the Age of Thirteen and Seventeen Years. Baltimore, 1813." Then I obtained a copy of another pamphlet entitled "Lispings of the Muse," published by Payne himself while in London, 1815, printed, as he stated, "In testimony of regard from the author to his personal friends,"—a republication of the Baltimore edition, 1813. Following these, there came into my hands a complete copy of the valuable little paper of which he was the publisher when only fourteen years of age, known as "The Thespian Mirror," New York, 1805 ; also a copy of an octavo volume of a hundred pages, to which was prefixed a stippled head of Mr. Payne in the character of *Hamlet* and entitled "Memoirs of John Howard Payne, the American Roscius, with Criticisms on his Acting in the Theatres of America, England, and Ireland. Compiled from Authentic Documents. London, 1815." Evidently all the matter contained in this book
5

was furnished by Mr. Payne himself, if not put into form for the publisher by his own hands. After this I had the good fortune to discover a copy of the "Opera-Glass: a Weekly Magazine for Peeping into the Microcosm of the Fine Arts, and more especially of the Drama." This periodical was edited and published by Mr. Payne in London, 1826. It was quarto in size, of eight printed pages, containing criticisms, essays, and dramatic biography. For the two last-mentioned invaluable works I was indebted to Thomas J. McKee, Esq., of New York City. Following the possession of these, I purchased of an old bookworm two pamphlets with the following titles: "Sketch of the Life of John Howard Payne, by an editor of the New York Mirror, as published in the Boston Evening Gazette. Boston, 1833"; and the other, a printed "Prospectus of a New Periodical, 'Jam Jabam Nina,' by John Howard Payne. New York, 1833." My next hunt was for the autograph letters and correspondence of Mr. Payne, a large supply of which I had the gratification of finding in the possession of his nearest relative living, and among which I found letters of the highest importance for biographical purposes, letting me into the secrets of his relations with managers, actors, friends, and enemies, with many manuscript poems by Payne, and by others, that had never been published, viz.: by Washington Irving, Miss Croly, J. K. Paulding, William Pinckney, B. W. Proctor, John Alsop, and Charles Phillips. Those separate from Payne's were introduced in the Appendix of my volume, 1875. This correspondence covered the whole of Payne's life while abroad and at home, from 1813 until the time of his death, 1852, furnishing me authentic material to present to the public twenty-two years of his eventful life that had never before felt the impress of printer's ink. After finishing the manuscript, I looked for a publisher; but all to whom I went refused the matter, stating that they "did not deem John Howard Payne of more than enough consequence than to warrant a magazine article," though it must be added that these gentlemen knew nothing about Mr. Payne beyond the fact that he had written the song of "Home, Sweet

Home!" I thereupon entered into a contract with Mr. Joel Munsell, publisher, of Albany, New York, who published the book,—a
small private edition of two hundred and fifty octavos and fifteen
large paper copies of four hundred pages. This he did in the
most liberal manner, and gave to the public one of the finest
specimens of American typography that has ever refreshed the
eyes of bibliographers. The work was so handsomely done, and
the expense attending its execution so large, that neither publisher nor author was remunerated for his trouble. In fact, the
publication was more a matter of pride and justice than any desire
to make money. However, the edition was soon exhausted.
Publisher and author both lived long enough to see the octavos
which had been published at *five dollars* sold at *ten dollars*, and
the large paper, published at *fifteen dollars*, sold at *twenty-five dollars*, anxiously looked for by gentlemen who feel an admiration
for scarce publications. Mr. Thomas J. McKee, of New York, a
gentleman of fine culture, found enough interest in the book to
inlay and illustrate it with no less than three thousand engrav-
ings, letters, and play-bills, increasing the one large paper copy
to ten volumes, of four hundred pages each, for which, as completed, one thousand five hundred dollars have been refused.
Since the publication of the first issue, many applications have
been made for a popular edition, but the writer always refused to
listen to these solicitations, seeing no particular necessity for it
until recently, when Mr. Payne's remains were about to be exhumed and brought home to this country, and when others were
about to publish his life, which, if in any way authentic, would
and must be drawn from my work, the only complete life of Mr.
Payne ever published. I have, therefore, been persuaded to give
this second edition to the public, containing a full description of
the removal of Payne's remains from Tunis, their reinterment in
his native land, and especially as it introduces much additional
matter that will give a deeper insight into his peculiar characteristics as a man. This matter has recently been discovered in a
large number of letters, journals, and manuscripts of Payne's,

now in the hands of a gentleman who, at one time, was consul at Tunis. Much of this material for biographic purposes was long since given up as lost to the world. The biographer feels constrained to state that it would have been far better if much of this private correspondence had met with that fate. But, as Mr. Payne, with scrupulous care, put together in bound volumes all the secrets of his heart, which could not fail to meet the eyes of others, we do not see any good reasons why the mention of the fact should not appear here. And especially so in the possibility of their being made public in the future.

Among this mass of newly-discovered manuscript matter was a bound volume, containing play-bills representing every night Mr. Payne performed while in Europe. Also many MS. plays of his, never published, and memorandum-books dotting the incidents of his travels while abroad. This full statement of the circumstances attending the publication of this second edition is made to satisfy the reader that all it contains is not only authentic, but is adequate to serve as a permanent memorial of a remarkable man.

CONTENTS.

CHAPTER XI.

LIFE AND WRITINGS

OF

JOHN HOWARD PAYNE.

CHAPTER I.

" An honest tale speeds best, being plainly told."

To write the life of such a man as John Howard Payne is a task that requires much forbearance and a good judgment of human character. His varied talents, and his constantly changing disposition to follow this object and the other, causes the writer some difficulty in finding a climax to any of the many vocations which Mr. Payne attempted throughout his life. Yet with all the perplexities of his kaleidoscopic sort of mind, that at the least touch or turn of thought would lead him off to another form as unlasting as the one that had gone before, we cannot fail to see something to admire, and to make his life highly interesting to the reader. Of one thing we are certain, Mr. Payne had good blood in his veins, coming as he did from ancestors of fine intellect and industry. Although none of them reached the highest accomplishments, still they rose far above mediocrity. John Howard Payne's paternal ancestors were of English blood, and some of them date back among the earliest settlers of Eastham, Massachusetts, in 1622.

His grandfather was a settler of this place, and, prior to the Revolution, was a provincial officer of high rank.

Robert Treat *Paine*, of Boston, a judge, and one of the signers of the Declaration of Independence, and Robert Treat *Paine*, Jr., a poet of marked ability, were of the same family.

About forty years after the arrival of the Mayflower at Plymouth, there came from Portsmouth, in the south of England, and landed at Eastham (Cape Cod), in Massachusetts Bay, three brothers named Paine. One of these brothers went to Virginia, and from him descended Miss Dolly Payne, who married President Madison. Another one settled in the Middle States. The third remained at Eastham. He there married for his second wife a Miss Osborn, and there, three months after his father's death, his son William was born, who became the father of John Howard Payne.

While William was quite young, Mrs. Paine married her second husband, a Mr. Doane, of Connecticut, and moved away with him, leaving little William in charge of the Rev. Mr. Crooker, a Presbyterian clergyman.

When a youth, William lived as tutor in one of the wealthy old Boston families. In this position he found time to study for the profession of physician, under the famous General Warren, who perished at the battle of Bunker's Hill. He soon, however, gave up his first choice of profession, and selected that of school-teacher. While on a visit at Barnstable, he met a Miss Lucy Taylor, who became his first wife, but died a short time after marriage. He then went to the West Indies, on commercial business which took him, on his return, to New London, Connecticut. Here he met with a Miss Sarah Isaacs, of East Hampton, Long Island, who was on a visit; they became attached to each other and were married. The father of Miss Isaacs, a convert from the Jewish faith, came from Hamburg, Germany, many years before the Revolution, and settled at East Hampton. He was a man of education and wealth, but difficulties in his own country and the Revolution in his adopted country reduced his wealth to a mere competence. His wife was a Miss Hedges, daughter of a lady whose maiden name was Talmage. Her uncle Talmage was the Earl of Dysart, a Scottish English nobleman of wealth. The earl died unmarried. Upon his death, an agent was sent to this country to notify the brother, but, after a long voyage, it was found that the brother had died but a few weeks after the earl. The brother having left a family of daughters only, the estate reverted to the crown.

Immediately after the marriage of William Payne to Sarah Isaacs, which was about 1780, they removed to East Hampton, Long Island, where Governor De Witt Clinton caused to be erected an academy, and placed Mr. Payne at the head of it. The Rev. Dr. Buel was also concerned in the management of this institution.

Mr. William Payne remained the principal of Clinton Academy for several years. He then moved to New York, and in 1796 he moved to Boston to hold the position of master in the Berry Street Academy. His wife, Sarah Isaacs, died in Boston, June 18th, 1807. After her death, the family once more returned to New York, where Mr. William Payne died on the 7th of March, 1812. Mr. Isaacs, the father of Mr. William Payne's wife, died and was buried at East Hampton, where his tombstone may now be seen, bearing the simple and truthful eulogy,—

"An Israelite indeed in whom there was no guile."

Mr. William Payne had nine children, the dates of whose births and deaths have been taken from the family record:

LUCY TAYLOR, b. 1781, m. in 1816, Dr. John Cheever Osborn, of N. Y. She was the mother of two boys who died in infancy; d. in Brooklyn, N. Y., 1865.

WILLIAM OSBORN, b. at East Hampton, Aug. 4, 1783; d. March 24, 1804.

SARAH ISAACS, b. East Hampton, July 11, 1785; d. Newburg, on the Hudson, Oct. 14, 1808.

ELOISE RICHARDS, b. East Hampton, March 12, 1787; d. Leicester, Mass., July, 1819.

ANNA BEVEN LEAGERS, b. East Hampton, April 9, 1789; d. Newport, R. I., Oct. 11, 1849.

JOHN HOWARD, b. *New York, June 9,* 1791; *d. Tunis, Africa, April 9.* 1852.

ELIZA MARIA, b. in New York, Sept. 19, 1795; d. New York, May 25th, 1797.

THATCHER TAYLOR, b. New York, Aug. 14, 1796; m. in New York, in 1833, to Mrs. Anna Elizabeth Bailey; d. in Brooklyn, Dec. 27, 1863.

ELIZABETH MARY, b. in Boston, Mass., ——; died there, aged about 2 years.

We have been thus particular in giving the above family record that we may be accurate as to where and when John Howard Payne was born and died. There have been so many misstatements made regarding the place of his birth and the time of his death, that we feel, if for no other reason than that of truth, the matter should be made right.

In addition to this, we desire to allude to several other members of the family who were remarkable for talents. While looking over a large number of manuscripts, letters, and poems of John Howard Payne, for the purpose of preparing this book, we came across a dramatic criticism evidently written in a part of an old journal kept by Eloise Richards Payne, and dated 1802, when she was only fifteen years of age. The criticisms showed excellent judgment, and presented the celebrated Cooper's fine acting in *Hamlet*. *Richard*, and other characters, with great discrimination for one so young. She was a lady of extraordinary genius and accomplishments.

At the early age of fourteen, she underwent the questioning, after eight days' study in the Latin language, of the first professor at the Harvard University, and is said to have displayed an almost incredible proficiency in construing and parsing. To more solid attainments, she added so remarkable a skill in penmanship, that some of her productions have been preserved in the library of Harvard University. In the latter part of her life, she became highly distinguished as an amateur artist. None of her literary compositions have yet been published, but her various writings, especially her letters, are spoken of by some of the first belles-lettres scholars in this State, as among the most favorable specimens extant of female genius, in America. The two last years of her life, during which she was often contemplating the probability of an early termination of her broken health by the grave, were distinguished by a peculiarly religious cast of thought, of which she is said to have left some invaluable memorials in her manuscripts.

After a long illness she departed this life full of Christian fortitude, and her remains lie buried in an old cemetery at Lancaster, Massachusetts, beneath a large white marble tablet supported by six stone pillars, which stand upon a red sandstone base. The monument was erected by John G. Palfrey, who was her schoolmate, and it bears, besides her name and age (thirty-one years), these inscriptions: "She will be talked of but little while, and forgotten by society, will survive only in a few hearts, where the memory of such a being is immortal." "Sink into dust, frail covering of a purified spirit! Parent earth, receive thine own! God in heaven, take her soul to thee!"

Thatcher Taylor Payne, who died in Brooklyn in 1863, was for many years a prominent member of the New York and Brooklyn

bar. Those who still live and knew him, as a practitioner of the
law, speak of him as a man of deep research in his profession,
eloquent in his pleadings, and a gentleman of perfect integrity.

The above record of the places, births, and deaths of the Payne
family is taken from the family record as given to the writer by
the nearest living relative of John Howard Payne. All statements that have appeared in the encyclopædias and elsewhere
have been wrong. Even the record on his tombstone at Tunis is
wrong in stating that he was born in *Boston* in *1792*, and died on
the *1st* of *April*, 1852. He was born in *New York, 1791*, and died
on the *9th* of April. Family records might and can be wrong,
but nine times out of ten they are more likely to be correct, and
are, at least, entitled to more respect than any verbal statement
made by even the very person whose birth it concerns. We admit that Mr. Payne himself, on several occasions, furnished the
materials for his own biography, in which he stated that he was
born in *1792*. Although he did make this statement, still it is
more than likely that he was wrong, and the *family record* was
right. In looking over the intervals of the births of the children
of Mrs. William Payne, we find that the mother gave birth to her
children at two years apart. Therefore, if Anna Beven Payne
was born *April 9th, 1789*, and John Howard Payne was born June
9th, 1791, we find her habit of birth-giving about the same time,
viz., two years. The next question that arises is, what cause
was there for Mr. John Howard Payne stating that he was born
in '92 instead of '91? He himself may have had no ground to
make a misstatement, yet others may have had a motive for so
doing, perhaps for purely sinister purposes. It has been frequently the case that when precocious children have been placed
before the public for attractive interest they have been falsely
represented as younger than they really were, and, to sustain
this argument, the writer could name several persons who have
resorted to like tricks for like purposes. Every stage manager
knows that this is very frequently the case with actors, and more
especially so with actresses. Payne began his public career very
young, when he was entirely in the charge of others, and they
may have thought that it was well to make him a year younger
than he was, for the purpose of making him more of a marvel.
We write thus fully as to the year of his birth for the reason that,
should there be any more monuments erected to his memory, the
record may be made correct, and to satisfy the natural inquiries

as to the proper date of his birth. We have been asked, through many communications, to furnish evidence that he was born in the city of *New York*, and not in *Boston*, as is stated on his gravestone at Tunis. This we can do to the perfect satisfaction of all readers. The family record says New York. Every biographical notice of Mr. Payne furnished by himself states New York. The best and most authentic sketch of his life, as published in the "New York Mirror," 1832, immediately on his return to this country, after an absence of twenty years, not only names New York, but in addition names the location: "He was born on the 9th of June, in a house *lately pulled down for new buildings*, near the junction of Pearl and Broad Streets." In 1832, Macdonald Clark, a man of genius and styled the "Mad Poet," from the fact of his eccentricities, brought to my father's house, Charles P. Harrison, artist, No. 3 Reade Street, New York City, John Howard Payne. My father and Payne became fraternal friends, and I frequently saw Mr. Payne, Clark, Dr. Francis, Fitz-Greene Halleck, George P. Morris, N. P. Willis, Charles C. Ingham, Henry Inman, Bass Ottis, Colonel John Trumbull, John James Audubon, the ornithologist, Rev. John Frederick Schroeder, and others of renown at my father's house. As a boy, then fourteen years of age, I was wild for the stage, and was a member of the New York Histrionic Association, where I had made a success as an amateur actor in the character of *Carwin*, in the drama of "Thérèse, the Orphan of Geneva." Hence when my father told me Mr. Payne wrote plays, and had been an actor, and was the author of the above-named drama and the tragedy of "Brutus," which I had seen Mr. Forrest so grandly play, I was wonder-stricken, and used to observe Mr. Payne with wonder and awe.

From that day to this, I have never forgotten John Howard Payne. On one occasion when my father was walking with me on Pearl Street,—I remember it distinctly, for the reason it was in the cholera time, 1832,—he pointed it out to me, and said, "That is the house in which John Howard Payne was born." The said house was then undergoing demolition. It presented an old-fashioned red brick front, with small panes of glass, white trimmings, with an arched fan-light over the door, containing a small tin sign with the figures "33." The building adjoining had been taken down, and one of the side foundation-walls begun. This accounts for the remark in the "New York Mirror" of "Lately pulled down for new *buildings*," which obviously meant that more than one building was to be erected. I have not the slightest doubt that John Howard Payne himself pointed out the very house to my father when strolling with him for a walk on the "Battery," which was the fashion in those good old days in good old New York. In my former volume there was a misprint, giving 33 *Broad* Street instead of 33 Pearl Street.

The engraving here presented is from a sketch made from mem-

PAYNE'S BIRTHPLACE.

ory, by the writer, and we feel as much satisfied with its truthfulness as if it had been made on the day the place was first pointed out.

In my efforts to obtain correct information in regard to the dates of John Howard Payne's birth and death, I wrote to his nearest and dearest relative living, Mrs. E. E. Luquer, daughter of Thatcher Taylor Payne, John Howard Payne's brother. This lady, when a child, was the favorite of John Howard Payne, and she was equally fond of him. His letters to her when a child are marvels of pen-printing and affection. In answer to our inquiry we received the following statement:

"BEDFORD STATION, N. Y., May 12th, 1873.

"GABRIEL HARRISON. EsQ.

"DEAR SIR,—I am able to give you what I consider the best authority to prove that Uncle Howard was born in New York, June 9th, 1791. I take it from a record signed as follows:

"'A true statement.

"'Attest,   WILLIAM OSBORN PAYNE, September 15th, 1795.

"'John Howard Payne, born in New York, June 9th, 1791.'

"This William Osborn Payne was an older brother, who was born in 1783, and was a man noted for great exactness in all other matters. I also find in an older family record a statement of the same dates. The date of Uncle Howard's death is from the official document notifying the government at Washington of the death of the American consul, and which was sent to my father as the official notification of the fact, and reads as follows:

"'TUNIS, the 9th of April, 1852.

"'I hasten to have the honor to bring to your knowledge the decease of our consul, Col. John Howard Payne, who drew his last breath this morning at six o'clock.

"'GASPARY.'"

The reader will notice that the date of the despatch is 9th of April, while the context of the same states that he died *on that morning at six o'clock.*

The above statement should satisfy a reasonable mind. but, as there has been so much cavilling as to where John Howard Payne was born and died, we desire to end all controversy on the subject, and put the matter to eternal rest with his body.

It has been claimed that John Howard Payne was born at East Hampton, Long Island. Whatever arguments we have read on this point have been too much of a hearsay character to require much attention: record, only, should or can substantiate so important a fact. We have no preference as to where Mr. Payne's birthplace may have been. It would suit us just as well to have him born at East Hampton as in New York City; but we must take sides with the strongest proofs.

PAYNE'S TOMBSTONE AT TUNIS.

Determined to clear up the gross error on his tombstone at Tunis, which states that Mr. Payne was born in Boston instead of New York, and that he died on the 1st of April instead of the 9th, we, after diligent research, found the gentleman who worded the Tunis tombstone and had it placed over the grave of Mr. Payne. This gentleman is the Hon. William Penn Chandler, of Philadelphia, an ex-consul of Tunis, who filled the place of consul, commencing two years after Mr. Payne's death,—others having acted as consul until the government made the appointment of Mr. Chandler to fill the vacancy caused by the death of Mr. Payne. We here give Mr. Chandler's answer to our letter of interrogation as to the origin of the mistake. The honesty of Mr. Chandler's statement is admirable. His letter is highly interesting from the fact that he was the first one at the consulship who had any authority to investigate Mr. Payne's effects, and, if possible, put his matters in proper order.

"2110 Spruce St., Philadelphia, February 26th, 1883.

"Mr. Gabriel Harrison.

"Dear Sir,—Yours of yesterday is at hand, and I proceed immediately to reply to the interrogatory you make.

"The mistake as to the birthplace of 'poor Payne' which appeared on his gravestone occurred from the simple fact of *ignorance.*

"In 1855 or '56, when I obtained leave to place a monument over his grave at the expense of the government of the United States of America, it was not so easy as at present to obtain information in reference to the deceased, his life and history.

"The subject had disappeared from the public journals and public notice for years. Something led me to believe that he was born in Boston.

"You will remember he went there very early with his father and family, and the very few incidents recorded of his infantile years referred to his residence in that city. However, I think I did the best I could under the circumstances.

"Upon taking charge of the consulate at Tunis, in July, 1854, I found his grave in a shamefully neglected condition, unmarked, unhonored, and liable very soon to become unknown.

"This became more conspicuous from the fact that the last resting-place of U. S. Consul-General Heap was covered with a fine, large, white marble slab, bearing the arms of the United States, and a labored notice of his life, services, and death sculptured upon it was directly alongside of it.

"Under this state of affairs I applied to our government for permission to cover and mark the grave of Col. Payne with a suitable monument. Hon. Mr. Marcy, then Secretary of State, who during his life had been a warm friend of Payne, promptly directed me to place a monument over his remains, which I did.

"A young gentleman in the foreign correspondence branch of the State Department, whose name I have long been endeavoring to recall, furnished me with the very appropriate and touching quatrain which I subsequently had cut on the edge of the covering slab. The reason why this did not appear on the face of the slab was because the copy was not received until after the slab was placed and covered entirely with the inscription I had devised for it and with the armorial bearings of the United States.

"There is one word in this inscription which would have been altered had the desirability of so doing occurred to me earlier. I would have used the word 'appreciative' instead of 'grateful' in connection with the word 'country.'

"It seems to me in so polyglot a community as Tunis, until one has been long a resident there, one too frequently forgets to speak his own language with accuracy before acquiring a correct knowledge of any other.

"Had I been able to remember the name of the author of the quatrain herein referred to, I would have addressed a letter to the public explaining the manner in which the error as to the birthplace of the consul occurred, as well as correcting other errors which have been floating about for some time in the public press, but the name of the gentleman has entirely escaped me.

"An examination of the Blue Book for 1854 and '55 would show it. I had a copy of it, but long since it found its way to the junk-shop, when my library underwent one of its periodical 'weedings.'

"Should there be any other point upon which you desire information in my possession, it will be readily furnished.

"Some twenty years since, more or less, I was applied to to state how Col. Payne's effects came to be sold by his creditors, or some matter of that character.

" That subject is fully and laboriously set forth in my despatches to the State Department, with abundant exhibits at the time.

" Should you desire information on that point, it is suggested you could well pass a few hours looking it up from those sources in the State Department, or I could give you an abstract from memory only : the former mode would be preferable. Perhaps, however, you might come to the conclusion that that subject had as well rest where it is. One thing I may be allowed to add, that the whole of the relics (including his library), which existed untouched at that time, was rescued by me and placed at the disposal of his late brother, provided he would pay the few hundred dollars remaining due to his creditors ; but this was not done, and the prohibition placed upon the proceeding was ultimately withdrawn and the creditors permitted to reimburse themselves, they having already possession of the effects.

" The United States government once gave an order to the commodore in command of the Mediterranean squadron to take the remains of Col. Payne home (this was during our economical days), and the order was coupled with the most stringent provision *that no expense whatever should be incurred* by the government in connection with the matter. I think I appealed to his brother in this case also without success, so the order had to remain unexecuted.

" I remain.

" Very truly yrs.,

" W. P. CHANDLER."

John Howard Payne, sixth child of William Payne, was born in the city of New York, (old number) 33 Pearl Street, on the 9th day of June, 1791. Although he was born in the city of New York, yet the larger part of his early childhood was spent at the old homestead, East Hampton. Long Island. It was there his young heart drank its first inspirations from the beautiful nature that surrounded him, and where *the lowly cottage. and the birds singing gayly, that came at his call*, made the lasting impression which recurred in after-years when, *An Exile from Home*. he wrote the song that will live forever. It was in Boston, however, that Howard Payne received the early part of his education. It was at this time also, 1804, when only thirteen years of age, that the precocious boy organized the little military association which attracted so much attention that it made his name in the city a household word. On one occasion, while parading on the Boston Common, Master Payne's company, of which he was captain, was presented with a standard by a young and beautiful girl, who afterwards became the wife of one of our foreign ambassadors. Major-General Elliott, who was also at the time on parade with the military of the city, heard of the presentation, and immediately thereon extended to the young volunteers an invitation to join them in the line of march. For their discipline they received the congratulations of the general and the huzzas of the crowd.

Among the branches of education for which young Payne's father obtained the greatest renown was that of elocution. His mode of teaching it was peculiar, and succeeded far better with a larger number of his pupils than any who at the time professed the same branch of education.

Young Howard benefited by it very rapidly; and, having suffered severely from a nervous complaint which incapacitated him two or three years from applying to deeper studies, his attention was principally confined to this. This exercise of declamation was supposed to do his health good service; and from an earnest scholar in his class he soon became assistant instructor. In the school exhibitions, where scenes of plays were acted, he always took the lead from the superior merit he showed both in acting and in elocution. Just as Master Payne began to be noticed for these evidences of dramatic talent, the fame of Master Betty, the Youthful Roscius of England, had reached this country, and the press everywhere resounded with his praises. This had a powerful influence over young Payne's mind; it wholly absorbed his attention, and his great ambition was to be the Betty of America. He thought of nothing else, he talked of nothing else, he devoted all his leisure moments to the reading of plays and the study of characters, he already felt himself bedecked with the sword and shield of *Young Norval*, and heard the thunders of applause that greet *Octavian*, when in rags, and staff in hand, he rushes from the dark cave to seek the first rays of the morning's sun. He sought every opportunity to assist and perform in private theatricals. On one occasion, a member of the Boston Theatre, who held quite a high position as an actor, happened to be present at a performance in which Master Payne took a prominent part, and was so much struck with the young man's personal beauty and remarkable dramatic talents that he conceived that Payne might be made the young Roscius of America.

He at once called on young Howard's father and offered to take charge of the son, and give him all the instructions in his power for one-half of the emolument that might be derived from a two years' engagement. The offer was at once refused by the affrighted parent, who was a strict church member, and who had never for one moment thought that his son desired to dedicate his talent to the theatre. The friends of the father and of the youth became alarmed. Every method was immediately employed to discourage Master Payne's wish to be an actor. " *The guards were doubled*," as they say in the play; every entrance and exit of the boy was watched. They would listen at his door to discover whether he was reading the dramatic poets aloud, as hitherto he frequently had done; his play-books were secreted from him. Shakspeare was tucked away from his sight, Beaumont and Fletcher were hidden among the cobwebs on the rafters of the garret, Congreve was lost, and the engraving of Kemble as *Hamlet*, which had adorned the side wall of his room, and created new eagerness for dramatic fame every time the youth's eyes beheld it, suddenly fell upon the floor and was destroyed by the merest accident in the world. But all this availed nothing. It was in his blood to be an actor; it was his nature, and no power could change his love and desire for the profession. His dramatic Etna was smothered but for the time, and was destined to break forth with irresistible flame, and to illuminate his name.

Thus, as he was not permitted to act at the time, young Payne became a critic upon actors, and by some adroitness he found his way into the theatre to see the principal performers of the day. The papers always indulged him with the use of their columns; his essays on the drama attracted so much attention that he was encouraged to become a contributor upon general subjects in the local periodicals.

Mr. Fay, who at one time was the editor of the " New York Mirror," in a short biography of Mr. Payne, published in that paper in 1832, immediately after Payne's return from Europe, says that at the time young Payne was with his father in Boston, in 1804, he became acquainted with Samuel Woodworth, the poet, then himself a boy in a printing-office, where he published a child's paper of his own, called " The Fly." The assistance of young Payne was encouraged by Woodworth, whose affection for the friend of his youth strengthened with the lapse of years.

It so happened about this time that his elder brother, William Osborn Payne, suddenly died. He was a merchant in the city of New York, the favorite and the pride of the firm of which he was a member. The shock of his death was terrible to his mother, whose health was then declining, and from this she never recovered. With this loss the spirit of his father also seemed to bow, and his life became ever after a gloom and a fatigue.

William Osborn Payne left his partner in possession of the business. It was thought desirable to remove young Howard from the associates and pursuits which had riveted his attention to the stage; and equally important to place him in the way of being qualified, ultimately, to take the place and the business of his deceased brother. He was accordingly sent to New York, to assume the position of a clerk in the counting-house of which his brother had been a member, and with a strict understanding that his propensity for theatricals was to be *watched and crushed*. This was perhaps attempted by modes unsuited to his temper, and which, by making him uncomfortable, increased the very attachment whence it was meant he should be weaned. As we may conjecture, such errors are sometimes committed from the best and the kindest of motives. We have it in our power to say, only, that the next we know of him is his being engaged, soon after he entered the counting-house, in the clandestine editorship of a little paper in the city of New York entitled "The Thespian Mirror." Boy-like, he undertook this work without the remotest view to any consequences, for the only object the little editor proposed was to indulge his favorite pursuits as a relief from those to which he went with a heavy heart. His solicitude was not for notoriety, but concealment. With much alarm, therefore, he read in the "New York Evening Post" a notice from the editor, Mr. Coleman, promising the communication of *Criticus*, from the "Thespian Mirror," in his next paper. A boy's terror at being detected in forbidden sports haunted his imagination with visions of his master's frowns and short words, for this was the tender point; in this he had sinned. He felt as if he had unintentionally pulled upon his head a ruin under which he and his little world must all at once be crushed. In his horror he wrote to the editor of the "Post," for the purpose of deprecating any remarks which might involve an exposure; and the singularity of the note, "written." observes Mr. Coleman, "in a beautiful hand, though evidently in haste," and the mention in it of the writer's age, strongly excited the curiosity of that gentleman to whom it was addressed.

Upon this subject, however, we let Mr. Coleman speak for himself. "I perused the note," says he in the "Evening Post" of January 24th, 1806, "a second time, and it will not, I think, be considered strange or harsh that I was incredulous as to the story of the writer's youth. I turned to the paper, and my credulity was by no means lessened.

"It was difficult to believe that a boy of fourteen years of age could possibly possess such strength and maturity of mind, but, to take up the story again, I wrote him a note, inviting him to call in the evening. He did so, but his occupation in the counting-house had detained him till so late an hour that I had gone out. In the morning he returned, and I saw him. I conversed with him for an hour; inquired into his history, and the time since he came to reside in this city. He told me that he was a native of New York City, but had resided in Boston, and a portion of his earliest life at East Hampton, and his object in the publication in question. His answers were such as to dispel all doubts as to any imposition, and I found that it required an effort on my part to keep up the conversation in as choice a style as his own. I saw him repeatedly afterwards, and had not only the circumstances of his extreme youth confirmed, but, what was more astonishing, that three years of his little life had been, as it were, blotted out of his existence by illness, so that he really could be considered scarcely more than ten years of age. He was introduced to some of the first circles in the city of New York, and there he was looked upon as a prodigy."

Mr. Thomas J. McKee, of New York, possessing a large collection of valuable material relating to the stage, and among which he has a perfect copy of the "Thespian Mirror," has kindly furnished the following interesting history of this miniature periodical, and a copy of young Payne's introduction to his publication, and farewell address on leaving the editorial chair of the boy-journal.

"The 'Thespian Mirror' first appeared December 28th, 1805, and was issued weekly, on every Saturday evening. It was of octavo size, well printed and on good paper. It appeared anonymously, and was printed for the editor by Southwick & Hardcastle, No.

2 Wall Street. The paper contained well-written memoirs of Cooper, Hodgkinson, and other contemporaneous actors, with criticisms of their performances and the plays they performed in, besides various items of interesting dramatic and literary news from the London, Boston, and Philadelphia periodicals, showing considerable research, extensive reading, and good discrimination. Each number also contained a portion of a story which ran through several numbers to its completion, together with poems, which, though generally attributed to correspondents, were no doubt written by the editor himself. He seems to have been on the best of terms with his contemporary editors, for there are frequent acknowledgments of the receipt of exchanges, and thanks for courtesies extended.

"Having before us a copy of the 'Thespian Mirror,' we introduce the youthful editor's salutatory to the public, as presented in the first number of his journal:

"'THE THESPIAN MIRROR.

"'SATURDAY EVENING, DECEMBER 28, 1805.

"'TO THE PUBLIC.

"To wake the soul by tender strokes of art,
  To raise the genius and to mend the heart,
  To make mankind in conscious virtue bold,
  Live o'er each scene, and be what they behold ;
  For this the Tragic muse first trod the stage,
  Commanding tears to stream thro' ev'ry age ;
  Tyrants no more their savage nature kept,
  And foes to virtue wonder'd how they wept!"

POPE.

"'In presenting the present sheet to the enlightened citizens of New York, as a specimen in matter and manner of a work which on sufficient encouragement will be issued in this metropolis, the Editor would observe that it is proposed to comprehend a collection of interesting documents relative to the Stage and its performers, chiefly intended to promote the interests of the American Drama, and to eradicate false impressions respecting the nature, objects, design, and tendency of Theatrical Amusements.

"'It cannot be denied that the Stage is calculated for purposes at once the most laudable and useful. From its gloomy and impressive representations the Tyrant is induced to relax his wonted severity; the hand of Avarice is opened to the generous influence of Benevolence; the wantonness of the profligate is succeeded by philosophic thoughtfulness; the asperity of misanthropy is softened into charity and cheerfulness; the conscience of the criminal is struck to repentance, and those absurdities and follies which pervade the

" ' Living manners as they rise,'

and are not immediately cognizable by the criminal or canon laws, are made to shrink and retire before the lash of dramatic satire:

" ' Safe from the bar, the pulpit, and the throne,
Yet touch'd and sham'd by ridicule alone!'

Under these impressions, the Editor of the Thespian Mirror ventures to present his work to the public eye; and though it comes forward unintroduced, and without any other recommendation than its own merits, he is induced to hope that the little stranger will be received with civility, judged with candor, and (if consistent with its deserts) be rewarded by the cheerful beams of public patronage.

"'Having said thus much, the Editor respectfully submits the publication and its plan to the candid examination of the community at large, anticipating (while he espouses the cause of the Stage as the epitome of men and manners, and the teacher of virtue and morality) his reward in the encouraging patronage of the citizens of New York, to whom the publication is respectfully dedicated by

" ' THE EDITOR.'

" There were rumors at the time that the editor of the 'Mirror' was about to appear in character upon the Park stage, and as there was a general curiosity and desire to see him, the theatre was filled upon the occasion of his rumored appearance. There is no doubt that Payne then intended a series of performances after the manner of Master Betty, but was prevented from so doing by his friends.

" Payne learns of the rumors, and seems to have rather enjoyed the publicity thus given his journal, and in number VI. of his 'Mirror' he says, 'The editor of the " Mirror" was not a little amused on hearing it whispered throughout the boxes on this occasion that he was to personate *Don Carlos* in the "Duenna," and

3

his amusement was somewhat heightened upon the entrance of the expected novice, "a pretty strapping boy," exclaimed one; "pretty tall for his age," said another. The editor begs leave to inform those who still labor under this unfortunate mistake, that he *really was not* the *Don Carlos* of Monday evening.'"

The "Mirror" ran through fourteen numbers, the last appearing March 22d, 1806. In his farewell address in this number, his name appears for the first time as editor. This address is so neatly expressed that I give it entire, and from it you can form an idea of the style of his articles generally, and understand how it was that there was a general doubt of the editor's being but fourteen years of age.

" *To the Public:* The editor of the 'Thespian Mirror' respectfully acquaints his friends and subscribers that, in consequence of circumstances that have transpired since the publication of the fourth number of this miscellany, he has resolved to relinquish the editorial duties of that work, in order more particularly to devote himself to studies which may promote his future usefulness in life, and mature, strengthen, and extend a disposition for literature which has grown with his earliest years. When the 'Mirror' was commenced in this city, it was under circumstances which have since materially altered. From the interest which some warm-hearted friends (perhaps injudiciously) took in the editor, the work was brought forward, and enthusiastically ushered into public notice. Various were the sentiments of the community respecting it, and as various was popular conjecture on the effects of the misdirected exertions of its juvenile editor. From a wish to render himself useful rather than ornamental in society, plans were agitated for placing him in the full possession of advantages with which he might cultivate a literary taste and direct his views to objects which promise benefit to his country, satisfaction to his friends, and utility and honor to himself.

" The work which he had heedlessly commenced, was considered by the judicious as the fruit of an itch for scribbling, the materials for which, without a more extensive stock of ideas drawn from the pure fountains of classical learning, would be soon exhausted. The patronage of one to whom he *feels* obligation which he cannot express has placed within his reach advantages, the rejection of which would be the height of folly and ingratitude. A collegiate education will, therefore, be the object of his present pursuits, and the study of the law the *goal* of his future exertions. And, determined exclusively to devote himself to these important objects, he now declares his design of discontinuing the 'Mirror' after the publication of this number (which completes the original term of engagement), and of waiting patiently the laurels *of fame* until *science* shall expand his mind, and crown his labor with lasting and deserved celebrity. He begs leave to express his warmest acknowledgments to those friends who have encouraged him by their assistance in the advancement of the 'Mirror,' he is convinced that, feeling for his real welfare, they will approve the step which he has taken, and he assures them that, cherishing the most grateful sentiments, he will never feel himself more happy than in the opportunity of expressing the esteem with which he is

" Their much obliged,

" And very humble servant.

" JOHN H. PAYNE."

That we **may** enjoy the astonishing precocity of our youthful critic, we introduce from page 21 of his " Thespian Mirror" his remarks on the performance of "The Wheel of Fortune" and " The Romp" :

"THEATRICAL REGISTER.

" MONDAY EVENING.

" ' 'Tis with our judgment as with our watches. . . . None
Go just alike, . . . but each believes his own.'

" *The Wheel of Fortune and The Romp.*

" Our avocations were such as to prevent our attendance sufficiently early on this evening to observe the whole of the play. From what little we saw of it, however, we were not induced to regret not being earlier at the house.

" Mr. Fennel's second appearance, since his late return to the stage, in *Penruddock* did not strike us so forcibly, perhaps, as it might have done, had we not before seen Cooper (who is very great in the part) in the same character. It is probable that long disuse has somewhat blunted Mr. Fennel's dramatic talents : for we observed throughout that where Cooper wholly absorbed the spectator in the passion he would express, Mr. Fennel gave us time (if we may be allowed the expression) to see him feel. In short, candidly speaking, we did not consider Mr. Fennel's abilities so well adapted to *Penruddock* as to many other characters which we can name. We must, however, in justice add that, although Mr. Fennel's representation was somewhat cold, his conception of the part was distinguished for its justice, chastity, and correctness.

"Mrs. Barrett's *Mrs. Woodville* was frequently interesting, but in many points inaccurate. *Emily Tempest* found a fine representative in Mrs. Johnson, who always excels in parts of this nature. Messrs. Tyler and Johnson were very good, particularly the latter. Martin's *Sir David Daw* was much applauded.

"Robinson was uncommonly dull and inanimate. His repetition of this character

"'And the death of a dear friend
Would go near to make a man look sad.'

"With the after-piece we were much more gratified than with the play. Mrs. Jones in *Priscilla Tomboy* reminded us of our well-remembered Mrs. Hodgkinson. She was animated, natural, and easy. 'The Romp' was never more justly represented. Mrs. Jones' songs were very fine, particularly that of

"'My husband and, may be,
A sweet little baby,' etc.,

which was repeatedly encored.

"Mr. Hogg's *Watty* was excellent, and, without the disadvantage of a bad person for the character, would have been perfectly natural. *Watty*, though an overgrown lad, is not yet one of those whom Cooper calls

"'Children of a larger growth,'

and we are induced to think that the appellation of ' Little Watty' was misapplied.

"Mr. Johnson was very excellent in the old uncle, and Mr. Tyler was pleasing in the *Captain*. Misses Graham and White were tolerable. We would recommend more animation and energy to the former, and to the latter we think more attention to her part than to the audience would be an improvement. Glancing over the boxes has no good appearance, however well it may be done."

Mr. Coleman thought it advisable to make the adventure public, and through the nobility of his heart, and an active interest in the boy's behalf, formed and carried out a plan to have the youth sent to college. Mr. Seaman was thereupon introduced to young

Payne, and was at once captivated with the boy's beauty, smartness, and manliness. This gentleman was always busied in doing kindness to others, and he at once looked into young Payne's situation, and here he found room for his philanthropy. He consulted Payne's friends and his father by letter, who was at the time in Boston. He proposed to pay the expenses of his education at Union College, Schenectady; the offer was accepted. Young Payne left the counting-house forever. It was at this time that Joseph D. Fay, the father of one of the editors of the "New York Mirror," became the intimate friend of John Howard Payne, and so remained through his life. Charles Brockden Brown, the celebrated American novelist, also became deeply interested in Payne, and was very active in his behalf. Payne had now become the charm in the learned circle of New York; every one seemed to feel that the boy's future was no longer in his own hands; each and all strove to monopolize the youth and crowded upon him all sorts of advice; he was trotted from house to house, and completely covered with flattery. Brown seeing this over-officiousness in its right light, more than once expressed his regret, and feared that the youth's regard for good advice would be endangered by its too frequent intrusion, when his mind was too young to admit of it, like doses of physic thrust upon men when well, to prevent them from being sick. The hour, however, had now arrived for young Payne to take his departure for college. Mr. Seaman, Mr. Coleman, and Mr. Brown frequently talked the matter over. Brown was selected to conduct the youth to the seat of learning, at Schenectady, New York, of which the well-known Dr. Nott was the president. In those days we had not the iron horse to dash us with electric speed up along the banks of the Hudson, nor had we floating steam-palaces, that, like things of life, swiftly glide over the waters at the rate of twelve knots an hour. It was either by the dull rocking and plodding stage over the rough roads, or by the sloop that would at times only have speed enough to raise a white foam along its bow, but which more frequently would lie at perfect rest for hours, awaiting the whims of the winds. However, they took passage upon the sloop Swan. Charles Brockden Brown was young Payne's companion. It was in the soft month of June, the weather was beautiful. Thus speaks a letter of young Payne's to his father, dated at Albany, "June 18th, 1806.

"The passage through the 'Highlands' is sublime. I have

never seen anything more striking, and I fail of the power to describe the effect its magnificence had upon my mind. . The winds,
however, are so very precarious, that no calculation can be made
as to how long it will take to make a passage to Albany. We
stopped on our course no less than four times; this gave us a fine
opportunity to look around us, to walk along the shore, to view
the mountains and country about us. Mr. Brown, the celebrated
American author, and myself had many delightful walks along
the hill-sides and over their tops. I found his conversation ex-
cessively pleasing and instructive. I also found Col. Willet and
his lady very agreeable company. There were two other female
passengers equally pleasing."

This extract from Master Payne's letter is a slight evidence of
the boy's mind and style when he was fifteen years of age. As
regards the remark of Mr. Coleman on the peculiar neatness of
Payne's handwriting at those early years, they are fully confirmed by the several letters of Master Payne that now lie
before us.

Young Payne's mind was so fully imbued with the beautiful
and picturesque effects of the Hudson River scenery, when under
the mystical influences of moonlight, that, one night while on his
trip to college, he wrote the following sweet poem in his journal,
that he kept at the time:

"On the deck of the slow-sailing vessel, alone,
 As I silently sat, all was mute as the grave;
It was night,—and the moon mildly beautiful shone,
 Lighting up with her soft smile the quivering wave.

"So bewitchingly gentle and pure was its beam,
 In tenderness watching o'er nature's repose,
That I liken'd its ray to Christianity's gleam,
 When it mellows and soothes, without chasing, our woes.

"And I felt such an exquisite wildness of sorrow,
 While entranced by the tremulous glow of the deep,
That I long'd to prevent the intrusion of morrow,
 And stay there forever to wonder and weep."

This journal, containing several other poems and accounts of
the scenery along the Hudson, was handed around when he arrived at Albany, and created quite a sensation among the *literati*.
The following verses were afterwards published in a magazine
edited by Mr. Brown at the time in Philadelphia:

"Sweet face! where frolic fancies rove,
  Where all youth's glowing graces reign,
What art thou? Genius? Pleasure? Love?
  The smiling vision answer'd, *Payne!*

" I thought *Pain* was a spectre dire,
  Was Genius', Love's, or Pleasure's bane;
Thy cheek is health; *thy eye* is fire;
  No, beauteous youth! thou art not *Pain!*

"Ah, gentle maid! if e'er thy breast
  Knew transient Joy, Love's galling chain,
One ray of Genius hadst possess'd,
  Thou wouldst have known they *all were Pain.*"

After a few days' rest at Albany, Master Payne was introduced
to Dr. Nott, president of the college, by Robert M. Sedgwick, of
New York, and Hermanus Bleecker, of Albany. The kindness
of the president to Payne lasted through his collegiate career.
But, after the two friends of the young student had left him at
college, with everything looking bright and comfortable before
him, young Payne soon began to feel that some influence was
bearing too hard upon him. His patrons were advised to keep a
strong hand over him, and not to let him have more money than
was indispensable; his instructors were admonished not to allow
him too much latitude, lest he should contract an appetite for
pleasure, and every word he uttered was watched, and every expression of impatience reported as a proof that he required still
more restraint. The thing had gone so far as to create frequent
uneasiness between Mr. Payne and his friends; letters were even
sent to Master Payne's father, which annoyed Master Payne so
much that he sought other arrangements with the college, and
started a little paper called the "Pastime," the avails of which
were to pay the three hundred dollars a year for his education.
The college-boys became great patrons of the paper. They also
elected him an officer of one of their literary societies. Payne
was also appointed master of ceremonies whenever they gave a
dramatic performance in the college chapel, where he on several
occasions distinguished himself, beyond all others, by his good
acting; and especially so on one occasion, when he performed the
part of the heroine in an original play called "Pulaski." He for
this occasion wrote the epilogue and spoke it in the costume of
the female character, *Lodoiska.* In this part his success was

great, as his beautiful face and sweet voice added much to the deception and the perfection of the character. After this performance of *Lodoiska*, he became the little god and the great everything of the college. He made many strong friends and a few
enemies—the latter always an accompaniment of success. Not a
great while after this, he was invited by his college-mates to write
a Fourth of July ode, of which the following anecdote is told. It
was a somewhat crude, hasty, boyish cluster of rhymes, but it
nevertheless got into the papers, and, as a matter of course, his
enemies were ready to tell its faults to the author, " Only for his
own good, nothing more." Perceiving too much of this spirit
towards him, he determined to combat it, and, having gone for a
few days to Albany, and fully aware of the faults of the ode, he
wrote a critique upon it, which was published in the Albany
papers, and which very pointedly enforced all the bitter warnings
which had been pronounced against him, and very humorously
laid open more faults than even the most voluble of his friends,
for the professed purpose of correcting his vanity, had been industrious enough to point out. On the appearance of this critique, a vast change took place suddenly in the deportment of
many who had before done him honor. Even some who thought
that he ought to be kept from listening to praise, were less forward to touch their hats to him since he had become the theme
of censure.

At a public table where he was a little shunned, a gentleman
proposed for a toast, pointedly addressing young Payne, " The
Critics of Albany ;" a loud jeering laugh followed. The toast
was drunk with acclamation, upon which Master Payne is said to
have returned thanks very good-humoredly, but in a way which
at once left room for the truth to be decidedly inferred, and he
turned the laugh upon those who meant to joke him down.

In a letter now before the writer, dated Albany, September 23d,
1806, addressed to his father, Barry Street, Boston, young Payne
thus alludes to the critique:

" You will receive herewith a newspaper containing a critique
on me and my productions written in the Mitchellian style by
myself. I did it for amusement, and was well repaid. It was
attributed to so many, and it gave rise to so much speculation,
that I would not have lost the pleasure which it afforded for
the injury a real attack could do me ; it was an excellent sham-
fight.

"The cat was so soon out of the bag, 'that embryo answers from Mr. J. V. N. Yates, H. Bleecker, Dr. Finn, Dr. Nott, and Robert Sedgwick lost their effect. It has discovered for me who are not my friends. In the same paper you have an original elegy of mine.' "

By a letter dated February 26th, 1807, we still find Payne at college and hard at work. He said in his letter to his father, that, at his own request, the president had placed him under the immediate instructions and care of Mr. Allen for private preparation for the next commencement, and that, as Mr. Allen was the most learned man in the college, he had attained more knowledge in the past few months than in the whole year before.

The young student certainly had many friends to urge him on through the labyrinthine paths of college study, and as for good advice, there were none who gave it more judiciously than Charles Brockden Brown. In one of his letters dated from Philadelphia, shortly after Payne had entered college, and which we extract from Dunlap's Memoirs of Mr. Brown, page 238, he says,—

"Most sincerely do I rejoice that you find Schenectady so agreeable. I tremble with apprehension when I think how much of the dignity and happiness of your whole life depends upon the resolutions of the present moment. Were it possible for a miracle to be wrought in your favor, and that the experience of a dozen years could be obtained without living so long, there would be little danger that a heart so unperverted as yours would mislead you. The experience of others will avail you nothing. They may talk, indeed, but till you are as old as the counsellor —and have seen, with your own eyes, as much as he—his words are idle sounds, impertinent and unintelligent. Fancy and habit are supreme over your conduct; and all that your friends have to trust to, is a heart naturally pure and tractable, and a taste, if I may so call it, for the approbation of the wise and good. When you write next, I hope you will have both leisure and inclination to be particular on the subject of your studies.

"What are your books and your exercises? What progress do you make? and what difficulties or reluctances stand in your way? I have a great deal more to say to you, but I am afraid, judging from the brevity of yours, that you have no passion for long letters. I will therefore stop, in due season, and only add the name of   Your true and warm friend,
                    "CHARLES BROCKDEN BROWN."

There is a judiciousness of advice in the above that but few friends have the power to give; and, when such impressions are made upon the mind of the young, the effect is lasting.

When we look over the broad lawn, and, by the clearness of the atmosphere, are almost enabled to count the leaves upon the far-distant trees, we seldom think, at such a moment of calmness and brightness, that there lies far off behind the hills, or low down in the horizon, the dark cloud laden with the storm that does not select its path, or stop to pick out the shrub or tree it may destroy, while sweeping onward; but at times the storm is there, and will come, with wild roar through the air, to do its work of devastation; and so it is with our afflictions and sorrows in this world, which often come, when least expected, to darken and throw a gloom over the thresholds of our homes.

The storm for Master Payne now came; suddenly it broke with its worst wrath over his home, and he realized for the first time in his little, busy, sunny life, the gloom of deep sorrow. On the 18th day of June, 1807, his mother died. To a nature like Payne's the blow was overwhelming. He remarked in one of his letters to his father: " To me, now since mother's death, all nature seems speechless; the flowers have lost their colors and their perfume. The heavens are black, and the trees seem motionless, but, when I think of mother's many virtues, there comes a solace to soothe my deep grief. If a life spent in the exercise of all that is pure and noble in female character can lift the cloud from off the bereaved heart, then the dispersion will come to mine. The stranger witnessed her urbanity; the afflicted were solaced by her sympathy, but her family alone knew the extent of her meek and unassuming goodness."

Old Mr. Payne had been severely tried by the death of his elder son, and now the second blow seemed nearly beyond his bearing, and he became too distressed in mind to give that attention to his affairs which an unprosperousness, that had been for some time coming over them, rendered necessary.

" The law accomplished what bereavement and misfortune had begun, and he was compelled to abandon all he had to his creditors." Young Howard Payne looked upon this shipwreck with the philosophy and the calmness of a hero. The ruin must be cleared away, and there was no one else so competent among those who were left as himself; immediate measures became necessary. He at once thought of his dramatic talents, and at last wrung from his father and friends a slow, reluctant, and weeping consent that he should try his fortune upon the stage. The Etna of his dramatic Sicily, that had been so long smouldering, at last broke forth in a blaze. The conduct of his patron on this occasion was kind and beautiful; he stood behind the scene with young Payne's father and Mr. Joseph D. Fay (who composed the introductory prologue spoken by Mr. Twaits on the occasion) during the whole evening of the 24th of February, 1809, when John Howard Payne made his first appearance on the public stage as *Young Norval*, at the Old Park Theatre, New York.

His *début* and the circumstances leading to it were treated in a manner so poetical, at his subsequent appearance in Boston, by his relative, Robert Treat Paine, Jr., that it would seem like neglect not to insert here that portion of it, and, though a little out of chronological order, it will nevertheless be acceptable to our readers :

> " An humble weed, transplanted from the waste,
> Form'd the proud chapiter of Grecian taste.
> Chance dropp'd the weight ; the yielding foliage twined,
> And drooped, with graceful negligence inclined.
> Sculpture a model saw, to art unknown,
> Copied the form, and turn'd the plant to stone ;
> The chisell'd weed adorn'd the temple's head,
> And gods were worshipp'd where its branches spread !
> If in our Norval candid judges find
> Some kindred flower, to grace the stage design'd ;
> If, to the pressure fortune has imposed,
> You owe those talents art had ne'er disclosed ;
> If, like the graced Acanthus he appear,
> Be you Callimachus,—be Corinth here !"

The success of the *débutant* was complete. Mr. Dunlap, the dramatic author, and for a long time manager of the New York Park Theatre, remarks, in his " History of the American Stage," that the applause was very great, and the boy's effort a surprise to all present. The papers of the day following his *début* were extremely warm in his praise, and pronounced his death-scene of *Douglas* a master-piece of dramatic art.

In those days critics and actors were of a more austere character than they are at the present time, and it was not so easy to obtain an opportunity to make a first appearance upon the stage, or to get the critics' praise at any other price than that of real merit. In those days, too, the theatre was the fashion. The opera was not known to us, and frequently the wealthy and the learned crowded into the best seats in the pit and the boxes of the best-managed theatres; this seemed to add importance to the drama, and indeed it was more important than at the present day. Previous to the beginning of the first act of the evening's entertainment, there could be seen in the boxes, here and there, servants of private families, dressed with the most scrupulous care, with a white napkin fixed around the right arm above the elbow, holding the reserved seats until the party they represented came to occupy them, and, long before the performance was over, strings of carriages for blocks up and down Park Place would be in waiting for husbands and wives, the old, the young, the beautiful, and the learned, who had graced the theatre on the occasion. This style of audience would not tolerate such vile trash as the " Black Crook" and the " New Magdalen" of our days.

A supper was tendered to Master Payne and his immediate friends, after the performance, at the residence of the manager, Mr. Price, where the young Roscius in speech and manners appeared as old as any of them.

His engagement was for six nights only; but, having one night to spare, prior to his departure to fill an engagement at Boston, he performed on the seventh for his own benefit, on which occasion the *débutant's* share was fourteen hundred dollars, notwithstanding the rigors of a cold, stormy night. The following we take from a Boston paper:

"Master John Howard Payne has completed his engagement at New York with the most brilliant success; and afterwards, by request, performed an additional night. In force of genius and taste in belles-lettres there are few actors on the stage who can claim competition with him. This is not flattery; and, if it were, it would not be pernicious to him, who has so uniformly been quoted as a rare instance of intellectual precocity. But his successful application even of these thrifty and uncommon properties of mind to the profession of the stage will excite some wonder, when it is known that he has had no dramatic preceptor in the artifice, that his word and his action have been disciplined by his own judgment, and that he steps before the public, full grown, like Minerva, without being indebted to Jupiter's head for his origin. A letter from New York which we have before us, states: 'I have seen Master Payne in *Douglas, Zaphna, Selim,* and *Octavian,*

and may truly say I think him superior to Master Betty in all.
There was one scene of his *Zaphna* which exhibited more taste
and sensibility than I have witnessed since the days of Garrick.
He has astonished everybody.' The writer of this letter, we may
add, had seen all the best actors from Garrick to Kemble. This
account may amaze the incredulous, but it has been truly said by
the poet:

> ' The art of acting its perfection draws
> From genius, more than from mechanic laws.' "

His next success was in Boston, where the boy had not been forgotten as the youthful captain and the boy-editor. His reception
amounted to an ovation, and his success even more pronounced
than in New York. It was here that he accepted highly lucrative offers to appear in Philadelphia and Baltimore. After leaving Boston he went to Providence, Rhode Island, where his
reception seems to have been most affectionate. One of the
newspapers of that city stated: " Up to the present time we preserved an obstinate and stubborn incredulity, and what was said
of young Payne in New York and Boston passed with us for
nothing. But unexpected good fortune at length gave us the
more decisive testimony to our ears and eyes, and from repeated
evidences of this kind, we are happy now to concur in what has
been said elsewhere. Last evening, a small party of friends, with
ourself, heard Master Payne recite Collins's ' Ode on the Passions,' which has been by critics thought, and justly so, the cri-
terion of merit. We were at once caught involuntarily by the
magnetism of his manner; and all the passions delineated in that
delightful ode were as forcibly reflected on our hearts. If, in
such a turmoil of surprise, we should select one stanza in preference to another, it is this, ' Last comes Joy's ecstatic trial,' etc.
His voice and cadence in this portion of the ode were so measured as to leave nothing to wish for in the perfection of elocution."

On his way South he performed a second engagement at the
Park Theatre, with a still greater success than on the previous
occasion. At the conclusion of his second engagement, it was
Master Payne's misfortune to disoblige Mr. Stephen Price, the
manager of the Park Theatre. It was a part of Payne's engagement that he was to be supplied with dresses by the management. The finery of these dresses to him, of course, was a very

great affair. When his wardrobe was sent home to be packed for his journey South, he found all the finery removed. With a childish impetuosity, he called upon Mr. Price with a self-important loftiness. The manager told him that the "ornaments belonged to Mr. Cooper, and had now to be returned for his immediate use." This did not satisfy the young Roscius, and it is very likely that he was too rash to the gentleman, who had been his friend. Price was of a very high-toned nature and looked upon Payne's conduct as ingratitude, and really never forgave Payne, though on many occasions the feelings of the veteran manager were momentarily extinguished. Yet the influence of Mr. Price, with the managers throughout the United States, was of such a character that he could arrange or disarrange engagements at his pleasure. We do not here pointedly accuse Price of interfering with Payne's engagements elsewhere; but Payne was surprised to find, on stating his readiness to perform at Baltimore and Philadelphia, that those theatres seemed on a sudden closed against him. He, therefore, remained unemployed for some time; but at last determined to find out the cause of the coldness of the managers in those two cities. In a sort of reckless disposition he wandered to Baltimore, where, at the time, the Philadelphia company was performing. He arrived there an utter stranger, and, strolling the streets listlessly, to look for the theatre, he chanced to remark the sign of the book-store to which he had addressed some letters. He saw a group of persons there listening to a letter which he had sent to his friend Edward J. Cole, who, as soon as he saw Payne, caught him by the hand, and led him to the group, exclaiming, "This is he!" Jonathan Meredith and Mr. Alexander Contee Hanson stepped forward. They told him they had just heard a letter from a gentleman of New York (the author of "Westward Ho!" can tell our readers something about that gentleman), stating that there was supposed to be a theatrical combination to put him down. They bade young Payne to have no fear of such a combination. The rest may be told briefly. The wanderer was taken at once by Mr. Meredith to his house. Mr. Hanson also espoused his interest with the greatest enthusiasm and effect. Mr. William Gwynne became his fast friend. He was engaged. His reception by the warm-hearted inhabitants of Baltimore forms quite an era in the history of Baltimore theatricals. In a fortnight he had fifteen hundred dollars in his pocket. We cannot in our present opportunity, fail of presenting the following epigram which ap-

peared there the day after his benefit, when the house had been
filled to overflowing:

"THE RETORT COURTEOUS.

" All those who from Payne had experienced delight,
With increased admiration and pleasure each night,
To evince their desire of delighting again,
Attended last night, and gave pleasure to *Payne!*"

From Baltimore he went to Philadelphia, where he made an
impression equal to that in Baltimore. At Richmond, his profits
were great, and it was here that he became acquainted with the
celebrated Mayo family, upon a member of which he wrote some
verses, which were reprinted in many of the newspapers. He then
visited the Charleston theatre, and other theatres in South Carolina. It is stated that the celebrated comedian, Mr. Henry Placide, ·
who for many years was one of the principal dramatic lights in
this country, first became known to the public by the wonderful
imitations he gave of Master Payne in several of his characters.

"Returning to New York, Howard Payne found his father re-
establishing himself in the business of education, and his sisters
independently settled in a boarding-school of the first class in
Rhode Island. He yielded to the always earnest wishes of his
family and friends to endeavor to relinquish the stage, and opened
an institution similar to our present Athenæum, which he pur-
posed to extend into one equal to the Athenæums of Liverpool
and Boston. Now it was that Cooke arrived in America. No
one offered to make young Payne known to him, and he called
without an introduction. In " Cooke's Journal," which Mr. Dunlap publishes, he mentions this call. " I was visited," says Cooke,
" by Master Payne, the American Roscius : I thought him a polite,
sensible youth, and the reverse of our young Roscius." Mr. Cooke
appointed a time to pass an evening at young Payne's, who wished
that his father and friends should see the lion of the day ; and
this evening Mr. Dunlap describes in his life of Cooke : "A party
of ladies and gentlemen met, all anxious to see this extraordinary
creature, and anticipating the pleasure to be derived, as they supposed, from his conversation, his humor, and his wit. Cooke refused an invitation to dinner, and waited for his young admirer
to lead him to the circle of his friends ; but, tired of solitude, he
sent for Bryden (who kept the Tontine Coffee-House, where he
lived) *pour passer le temps* over a bottle of Madeira, and, when Mr.

Payne arrived with a coach to convey him to the tea-party, Cooke
was charged much higher with wine than wit. He was, however,
dressed, and, as he thought, prepared, and it would not do, on his
companion's part, to suggest anything to the contrary; besides,
the effect of what he had taken did not yet appear in its most
glaring consequences. They arrived, and Cooke, with that stiff-
ness produced by the endeavor to counteract involuntary emotion,
was introduced into a large circle of gentlemen, distinguished for
learning, or wit, or taste; and of ladies, equally distinguished for
those acquirements and endowments most valued in their sex. A
part of the property of the tragedian, which had been seized by
the custom-house officers under the non-importation law, had not
yet been released, owing to some delay from necessary form, and
this was a constant subject of irritation to him; particularly that
they should withhold from him the celebrated cups presented to
him by the Liverpool managers; and now his introductory speech
among his expecting circle was addressed to one of the gentlemen
[Washington Irving], with whom he was acquainted, and was an
exclamation, without any prefatory matter, of—'My dear Washington! they have stolen my cups!' The astonishment of such
an assembly may be imagined. After making his bows with
much circumspection, he seated himself, and very wisely stuck to
his chair for the remainder of the evening; and likewise stuck to
his text; and his cups triumphed over every image that could be
presented to his imagination. 'Madam, they have stopped my
cups. Why did they not stop my swords? No,—they let my
sword pass. But my cups will melt, and they have a greater love
for silver than for steel. My swords would be useless with them;
but they can melt my cups and turn them to dollars! And my
Shakspeare,—they had better kept that: they need his instruction, and they may improve by him—if they know how to read
him.' Seeing a print of John Kemble as *Rolla*, he addressed it:
'Ah, John, are you there?'—then turning to Mr. Payne, he, in his
half-whispering manner, added, 'I don't want to die in this country,—John Kemble will laugh.' Among the company was an old
and tried Revolutionary officer [the late Colonel Marinus Willet], a
true patriot of 1776. Hearing Cooke rail against the country and
the government, he at first began to explain, and then to defend;
but, soon finding what his antagonist's situation was, he ceased
opposition. Cooke continued his insolence; and finding that he
was unnoticed, and even what he said in the shape of query

unattended to, he went on: 'That's right; you are prudent; the
government may bear of it.—walls have ears?' Tea was repeatedly presented to him, which he refused. The little black girl
with her tray next offered him cake,—this he rejected with some
asperity. Fruit was offered to him, and he told the girl he was
'sick of seeing her face.' Soon after she brought him wine.
'Why, you little black angel!' says Cooke, taking the wine, 'you
look like the devil; but you bear a passport that would carry you
unquestioned into paradise!'" The company separated early,
and Mr. Payne happily resigned his visitor to the safe-keeping of
the waiters of the Tontine Coffee-House. But, notwithstanding
this irregularity, Mr. Dunlap mentions that Mr. Cooke was by no
means sparing of his admonitions when in company with his
young friend. "He not only did not offer wine to him. but told
him he ought to avoid it." "Once," observes Mr. Dunlap, "when
young Payne was sitting with Cooke at the Tontine, the veteran
taking his glass after dinner, chatting very pleasantly, Mr. Duffie,
formerly on the stage in Dublin, who frequently visited Mr. Cooke,
called in. Cooke received him with a cool kind of civility, desired
him to take a chair, and then continued talking to Master Payne.
'Mr. Duffie, help yourself to a glass of wine,—John, I don't ask
you to drink. Oh that I had had some friend when I was at your
age to caution—to prevent me from drinking! Mr. Duffie, your
good health. Yes, John, I should have been a very different man
from what I am. It's too late now!'"

The Athenæum speculation, projected by Payne, now began to
require greater resources than it produced. Cooke had talked
with him of the expediency of an attempt on the stage in England. His thoughts, by the stress of circumstances, again dwelt
on acting. Just then Cooke's attraction began to decline. Master Payne was invited to act with him. "Notwithstanding,"
says Mr. Dunlap, "the kindness with which he treated Master
Payne, and the terms of approbation with which he spoke of
him,"—"to have a boy called in to support him wounded his
pride so deeply, that he could not conceal his irritation, or its
cause." He was announced to play *Glenalvon* to Payne's *Douglas*,
and afterwards in other parts, but, throughout, affected illness.
On the 1st of March, 1811, however, he performed *Lear* to Master Payne's *Edgar*, for the benefit of the latter,—and this was
the last time, we believe, that our countryman ever appeared at
the Park Theatre. He afterwards went to perform in Boston,

4

and, during his absence there, his father suddenly died. He sub-sequently performed in Philadelphia and Baltimore. During his visit to Baltimore a memorable event occurred. The printing-office of his friend and supporter, Mr. Hanson, who then published a political newspaper there, was levelled to the ground by a mob. Mr. Hanson was absent from Baltimore. The recollection of former services came upon Mr. Payne. Though he never meddled in politics, he felt it to be his duty not to forget friendship. He wrote to offer his aid to Mr. Hanson in re-instating his paper. It was accepted. He was very active in his attentions; but after remaining at his post three days, was desired, on the night of the dreadful scenes which occurred there, to convey a message to Mrs. Hanson. On his return, he found the house besieged and the war begun. Mr. Hanson has included him among those to whom he publicly returned thanks, although his offices chanced to be merely those of kindness before and after the battle. But the gratitude of this gallant and enthusiastic gentleman impelled him to urge and assist the departure of Mr. Payne for the purpose of studying the fine models of the arts in Europe, and benefiting, if he should succeed, by the fame of London. Under the auspices of Mr. Meredith, Mr. Hanson, Mr. Gwynne, Mr. D'Arcy, and others, of Baltimore, Mr. Payne now turned his attention to England, intending to limit his visit thither to one year. He was, on the 17th of January, 1813, accompanied by his brother, Thatcher Taylor Payne, and by his admirer and most particular friend, Joseph D. Fay, to the wharf, in New York, whence he embarked in the ship Catherine Ray for Liverpool. It was not the destiny of Mr. Fay and Mr. Payne ever to meet again.

CHAPTER II.

"If not critical, I am nothing."

HAVING brought the history of our youth to that part of his life where he deemed it necessary to leave his country, in order to seek his fortune abroad, and having given the opinions of many critics and friends on Master Payne's abilities as an actor, all of whom seem to have overpraised his youthful efforts, we think it proper to introduce here a criticism taken from the "Mirror of Taste," published in Philadelphia, 1810. It is the only criticism that we have found on our youthful Roscius that speaks within the bounds of reason, and, therefore, gives a more just idea of his merits, as well as his faults, in his difficult art. In addition to this fact, we present it as a specimen of critical acumen equal to any written by our best critics on the subject of acting. It was written by Mr. S. C. Carpenter, the editor of the paper, and whose criticisms on the celebrated actor, George Frederick Cooke, are the finest ever written on that genius of the English stage.

FROM THE "MIRROR OF TASTE."

"Master Payne, since he has been acting in Philadelphia, has represented the following characters: *Young Norval, Octavian, Fredrick, Zaphna, Hamlet, Rolla, Tancred, Selim,* and *Romeo.* All of the above-named characters are well known, and from the peculiar circumstances attending their performance, they call for a share of particular attention, which would otherwise be superfluous. Where there is something new, and much to be admired, it would be inexcusable to be niggard of our labor, even were the labor painful, which in this instance it is not. The performance of Master Payne pleased us so much, that we have often since derived great enjoyment from the recollection of it; and to retrace upon paper the opinions with which it impressed us, we now sit down with feelings very different from those which, at one time, we expected to accompany the task. Without the least hesitation we confess that when we

were assured it would become our duty to examine that young
gentleman's pretensions, and compare his sterling value with
the general estimate of it, as reported from other parts of the
Union, we felt greatly perplexed. On one hand, strict critical
justice, with the pledge which is given in our motto, imperiously
forbidding us to applaud him who does not deserve it, stared us
in the face with a peremptory inhibition from sacrificing truth to
ceremony, or prostrating our judgment before the feet of public
prejudice; while on the other, we were aware that nothing is so
obstinate as error, that fashionable idolatry is of all things the
most incorrigible by argument and the least susceptible of conviction,—that while the dog-star of favoritism is vertical over a
people there is no reasoning with them to effect, and that all the
efforts of common sense are but given to the wind, if employed
to undeceive them, till the brain-fever has spent itself, and the
public mind has settled down to a state of rest. We had heard
of Master Payne's performances spoken of in a style which quite
overset our faith. Not one with whom we conversed about him
spoke within the bounds of reason; few indeed seemed to understand the subject, or, if they did, to view it with the sober eye of
plain common rationality. The opinions of some carried their
own condemnation in their obvious extravagance, and hyperboli-
cal admiration fairly ran itself out of breath in speaking of the
wonders of this cisatlantic young Roscius.

"But how to encounter this reigning humor was the question:
to render his reasoning efficacious, the critic must take care not
to make it unpalatable. And here the general taste seemed to
be in direct opposition to our reason and experience; for we had
not yet (even in the case of young Betty, with the aggregate
authority of England, Ireland, and Scotland in his favor) been
free from scepticism; the Roscio-mania contagion had not yet infected us quite so much; in a word, we had no faith in miracles,
nor could we, in either the one case or the other, screw up our
credulity to any sort of unison with the pitch of the multitude.
We shall not readily forget the mixed sensations of concern and
risibility with which, day after day, from the first annunciation
of Master Payne's expected appearance at Philadelphia, we were
obliged to listen to the misjudging applause of his panegyrists.
Yet not one in twenty could we find to praise Master Payne
without doing it at the expense of others. 'He is superior
to Cooper,' said one; 'He speaks better than Fennell,' said a

second; these sagacious observations, too, are rarely accompanied by a modest qualification, such as, 'I think,' or. 'it is my opinion.' but nailed down with a peremptory is. This is the mere naked offspring of a muddy or unfinished mind. which, for want of discrimination to point out the particular beauties it effects to admire. accomplishes its will by a sweeping wholesale term of comparison, more injurious to him they praise than to him they slight. Nay, so far has this been carried that some who never were out of the limits of this Union have, by a kind of telescopical discernment, viewed Cooke and Kemble in comparison with their new favorite, and found them quite deficient.

"We cannot readily forget one circumstance. A person said to another in our hearing. at the play-house.—

"'You have been in England, sir? Don't you think Master Payne superior to young Betty?'

"'I don't know, sir, having never seen Master Betty,' answered the man.

"'I think he is very much superior,' replied the former.

"'You have seen Master Betty then, sir,' said the latter.

"'No, I never did,' returned he that asked the first question; 'but I am sure of it. I have heard a person that was in England say so!'

"This was the pure effusion of a mind subdued to prostration by wonder. In England this was carried to such lengths that the panegyrists of young Betty seemed to vie with each other in fanatical admiration of that truly extraordinary boy. One, in a public print. went so far as to assert that Mr. Fox (who, as well as Mr. Pitt. was at young Betty's benefit, when he played 'Hamlet') declared the performance was little. if at all. inferior to that of his deceased friend, Garrick. With the very same breath in which we read the paragraph we declared it to be a falsehood. Mr. Fox had too much benignity to utter such a malicious libel upon that noble boy.

"These considerations naturally augmented our anxiety, and we did most heartily wish. if it were possible, to be relieved from the task of giving an opinion of Master Payne. For. in addition to his youthfulness, we knew that he wanted many advantages which young Betty possessed. The infant Roscius of England had, from his very infancy, been in a state of the best discipline; being, from the time he was five years of age, daily exercised in recitation of poetry by his mother, who shone in private theatricals, and having been afterwards prepared for the stage and hourly tutored by Mr. Hough, an excellent preceptor. By his father, too, who is one of the best fencers in Europe, he was improved in gracefulness of attitude, and nature had uncommonly endowed him for the reception of those instructions. We considered that when young people do anything with an excellence disproportioned to their years, they are viewed through a magnifying medium; and that, being once seen to approach to the perfection of eminent adults, they are, by a transition sufficiently easy to the wondering mind, readily concluded to excel them. Thus Betty was said to surpass Kemble and Cooke, and thus young Payne was roundly asserted to surpass Cooper and Fennell.

"Such were the feelings and opinions with which we met Master Payne on his first appearance, for which the tragedy of 'Douglas' was judiciously selected; and we own that the first impression he made upon our minds was favorable to his talents, in this way: he appeared to be just of that age which we should think least advantageous to him; too young to enforce approbation by robust, manly exertion of talents; too far advanced to win over the judgment by tenderness; or, by a manifest disproportion between his age and his efforts, to excite that astonishment which, however short-lived, is, while it lasts, despotic over the understanding. Laboring, therefore, under most of the disadvantages, without any of the advantages, of puerility, candor and common sense pronounced at once that much less of the estimation in which he was held was to be ascribed to his boyishness, and, of course, much more to his talents, than we had been led to imagine. If, therefore, he got through the character handsomely, and still carried the usual applause along with him, we directly conceived that there would be just ground for thinking it not entirely the result of prejudice, nor by any means undeserved.

"At his entrance he seemed a little intimidated, as if he were dubious of his reception; nor could he for some minutes divest himself of that feeling, though he was received with the most flattering welcome. This transient perturbation gave a very pleasing effect to his first words, and when he said, 'My name is Norval,' he uttered it with a pause, which seemed to be the effect of the modest diffidence natural to such a character upon being introduced into a higher presence than he had ever before approached. Had this been the effect of art it would have been fine,—perhaps

it was,—but we thought it was accidental. The utter impossibility
of a beardless boy of sixteen or seventeen years at all assimilating
to the character of a warrior and mighty slayer of men is of itself
an insuperable obstacle to the complete personification of certain
characters by a young gentleman of the age and stature of Master
Payne. He might speak them with strict propriety ; he might act
them with feeling and spirit ; but, had he the general genius of
Garrick, the energies of Mossop, the beauty of Barry, the elocution
of Sheridan, and the art of Kemble, he could not. with the feminine
face and voice, and the unfinished person inseparable from such
tender years, personate them ; nor, so long as he is seen or heard,
can the perception of his nonage be excluded, or he be thought
to represent that character, to the formation of which not gristle,
nor fair, round, soft lineaments, but huge bones and muscle, well-
knit joints, knotty limbs, and the hard face of Mars are necessary.
If we find, as we do in many great works of criticism, objections
made to the performance of several characters by actors of high
renown merely for their deficiency in personal appearance ; if the
externals of Mr. Garrick are stated by his warmest panegyrists as
unfitting him for characters of dignity or heroism, even to his
exclusion from *Falconbridge, Hotspur,* etc. ; and if we find that
the greatest admirers of Barry considered the harmony and softness of his features as reducing his *Macbeth, Pierre,* etc.. to poor,
lukewarm efforts, how can it be expected that a boy just started
from childhood should present a true picture of a warrior or
philosopher ? We premise this for the purpose of having it understood that what we are to say of Master Payne is to be subject
to these deductions, and that in the praise which it is but just to
bestow upon him, we exclude all idea of external resemblance to
the characters. Of the mental powers. the informing spirit. the
genius. the feeling which he now discloses, and the rich promise
they afford of future greatness,—of these it is we profess to speak.
Further we cannot go without insincerity, untruth, and manifest
absurdity.

"As might have been expected from Master Payne's limited
means of stage instruction. he several times discovered want of
judgment. In the speech in which *Norval* tells his story, he tres-
passed on propriety in his efforts to throw an air of martial ardor
into his expressions, by suddenly changing the key and raising
the tone of his voice, and speaking with increased rapidity the
words that more immediately related to fighting, erecting them

into a kind of alto-relievo above the level of the rest, particularly in, 'I have heard of Battles,' etc. 'We fought and conquered,' etc., all which is a narrative that should be delivered with humility and a strict avoidance of anything like vainglory, or egotism, studiously softening down, with modest air, those details of his own prowess which the author has necessarily given to the character. Had Master Payne had a Hough to instruct him, or a Cooke for his model, he would have escaped the error into which he fell in that part of the fourth act in which *Norval* describes the Hermit who instructed him; he would have known that acting what he narrates is highly improper,—indeed absurd; as it is acting in the first person and speaking in the third at one and the same time. While he repeated the words,—

> ' Cut the figures of the marshall'd hosts,
> Describ'd the motions, and explain'd the use
> Of the deep column, and the lengthened line,
> The square, the crescent, and the phalanx firm,'

Master Payne cut those figures and described the square and the crescent with his hands,—a great error! A better lesson cannot be offered to a young actor on this subject than may be found in the novel of ' Peregrine Pickle,' in which Doctor Smollett ridicules Quin, the player, for acting narrative in ' Zanga.' Master Payne would find it to his interest to avoid as much as may be, long declamatory speeches. till his organs are enlarged and confirmed. But in those parts in which *Douglas* discloses his lofty spirit, and no less in all the pathetic parts, he far exceeded expectation, and deserved all the applause he received.

> ' Oh ! tell me who, and where my mother is ;
> Oppress'd by a base world, perhaps she bends
> Beneath the weight of other ills than grief,
> And, desolate, implores of heaven the aid
> Her son should give. Oh ! tell me her condition !'

There was in his delivery of these lines an expression of tenderness which appealed forcibly to the heart, and was rendered still more striking by the abrupt transition to his sword,—

> ' Can the sword—
> Who shall resist me in a parent's cause ?'

Which he executed with a felicity that nothing but consummate genius could accomplish. Again he blazed out with the true spirit in the following lines:

> 'The Blood of Douglas will protect itself—
> Then let yon false Glenalvon beware of me.'

"That part, however, in which he disclosed not only exquisite feeling, but a soundness of judgment that would do honor to an experienced actor, was where Glenalvon taunts him, for the purpose of rousing his spirit to resentment. In that speech particularly which begins,—

> 'Sir, I have been accustom'd all my days
> To hear and speak the plain and simple truth.'

The suppression of his indignation in this and the succeeding passages,—the climax of passion marked in his face, his tone, and his action when he says to himself,—

> 'If this were told!'

The gradation thence to,—

> 'Hast thou no fears for thy presumptuous self?'

Till at last he flames into ungovernable rage in,—

> 'Did I not fear to freeze thy shallow valor,
> And make thee sick too soon beneath my sword,
> I'd tell thee—what thou art—I know thee well!'

was altogether a string of beauties such as it rarely falls to the lot of the critic to commemorate. Had age and personal hardihood been added, it would have defied the cavils of the most churlish criticism, and deprived even enmity of all pretence to censure.

"The next striking beauty he disclosed was in his reply to *Randolph,* when the latter offers his arbitration between him and *Glenalvon:*

> 'Nay, my good lord, though I revere you much,
> My cause I plead not, nor demand your judgment.'

The cold peremptory dignity he threw into these words was beautifully conceived, and executed in a masterly manner; nor

was he less successful in the transition to an expression of poignant but smothered sensibility in the next line:

> ' I blush to speak ; I will not, cannot speak
> Th' opprobrious words that I from him have borne.'

His delivery of this, and all the other lines of the speech that
followed it, deserved the thunders of applause with which it was
greeted,—it was, indeed, admirable.

"In impassioned feeling lies Master Payne's strength. Hence
his last scene was deeply affecting, though we could well have
spared that Kembleian dying trope,—his rising up and falling
again. It is because we seriously respect Master Payne's talents
that we make this remark: clap-traps and stage-trick of every
kind cannot be too studiously avoided by persons of real genius.
It would be injustice to omit one passage :

> ' Just as my arm had master'd Randolph's sword,
> The villain came behind me—But I slew him !'

In the break, the pause, and the last four words he was inimi-
tably fine.

"In Master Payne's performance of this character we perceived
many faults, which call for his own correction. They are, we think,
such as he has it in his power to get rid of. As they are general,
and pervade all his performances, we reserve all our observations
upon them till we close the course of criticism we are to bestow
upon him, when we mean to sum up our opinion of his general
talents. Meantime, we beg leave to remind him that Mr. Garrick
himself, after he had been near forty years upon the stage, often
shut himself up for days together restudying and rehearsing parts
he had acted with applause a hundred times before. *Sat sapienti*,
nature has bestowed upon this young gentleman a countenance
of no common order. Its expression has not yet unfolded itself,
but we entertain no doubt that when manhood and diligent professional exercise shall have brought the muscles of his face into
full relief, and strengthened its lines, it will be powerfully capable
of all the inflexions necessary for a general player. At present
the character of his physiognomy is perfectly discernible only
upon a near view. When he advances towards the front of the
stage, the lines may be perceived from that part of the pit and
boxes which are near the orchestra ; even the shades are so very

much softened by youth, and the parts so rounded, and so utterly free from acute angles, that they can. as yet, but faintly express strong. turbulent emotions, or display the furious passions. In a boy of his age this. so far from being a defect, is a beauty, the reverse of which would be unnatural; and if it were a defect, every day that passes over his head would remedy it. What is now wanting in muscular expression is in a great measure supplied by his eye, which glows with animation and intelligence, and at times speaks the language of a soul really impassioned. Upon a close view, when apart from the factitious aids and incumbrances of stage-lights, costume, and paint. he must be a shallow-sighted physiognomist who would not at the first glance be struck by Master Payne's countenance. A more extraordinary mixture of softness and intelligence never were associated in a human face. The forehead is particularly fine ; Lavater would say that genius and energy were enthroned there ; and over the whole, though yet quite boyish, there is a strong expression of what is called manliness; by which is to be understood. not present, but the indications of future manliness.

"Of Master Payne's person we cannot speak (nor do we hope) so favorably as of his face, and we much fear that he will not be allowed to undergo the pain of mending it by abstinence from indulgence. Early hours, active or even hard exercise, particularly of the gymnastic kind. and diligent. unremitting study, are as indispensable to his fame, if he means to be a player, as food or drink are to his support. In general his action is elegant. his attitudes bold and striking; but of the former he sometimes uses too much, and in his appropriation of the latter he is not always sufficiently discriminating. This was particularly observable in his performance of *Frederick* in ' Lovers' Vows.'—a character in which we shall have occasion to speak of him, and with great praise, in a future number. His walk, too, which in his own unaffected natural gait is not exceptionable, he frequently spoils by a kind of pushing step. at open war with dignity of deportment. It would be well for this young gentleman if he had never seen Mr. Cooper. Perhaps he will be startled at this, and flatters himself that he never imitates that gentleman. We can readily conceive him to think so, even at the moment he is doing it. To imitate another it is not necessary to intend to do so. Every day of their lives men imitate without the intervention of the will. The manners of an admired or much-observed individual insensibly

root themselves in a young person's habits,—he draws them into
his system as he does the atmosphere which surrounds him. We
doubt very much whether Mr. Cooper himself would not be surprised if he knew how much he imitates Kemble. Though seemingly a paradox, we firmly rely upon it. Mr. Cooper may be
aiming at Cooke, when he is by old habitual taint really hitting
Kemble. On the subject of imitation much is to be said. Kemble
rose when every bright luminary of the stage had set. Being the
best of his day, in the metropolis he has become the standard of
acting to the young and inexperienced. More from pride than
want of judgment he goes wrong. His system of acting is radically vicious; but as it makes labor pass as a substitute for genius,
by transferring expression from its natural organs to the limbs,
and making attitude and action the chief representatives of the
passions and the feelings, it not only fascinates because it catches
the eye, but is adopted because extremely convenient to the
vast majority of young adventurers on the stage, who, possessing
neither the feelings fit for the profession, nor the organs, nor the
genius to express them if they had, are glad to find a substitute
for both. Hence the system of Mr. Kemble has spread like a
plague,—infected the growing race of actors, mixed itself with the
very life-blood of the art, and extended its contagion through
every new branch, even to the very last year's bud. Thus Mr.
Kemble is imitated by those who never saw him. Let us tell
Master Payne that it is the very worst school he could go to, this
of the statuary. It is as much inferior to the old one—to that of
Garrick, Barry, Mossop, and nature—as the block of marble from
which the Farnesian Hercules was hewed is to the God himself.
Of its superiority we need urge no further proof than that of Mr.
Cooke, who, though assuredly inferior to several of the old stock
and groaning under unexampled intemperance, has, in spite of
every impediment which artful jealousy and envy of his talents
could raise against him, risen so high in public estimation, that
even when just reeking from offences which would not have been
endured in Garrick or Barry, his return is hailed with shouts, as
if it were a national triumph. And why? Because he is of the
old school, and scorns the cajolery of statue-attitude and stage-
trick. We speak thus freely to Master Payne because we think
he has talents worth the interposition of criticism, and if we
speak at all, must speak the whole truth. The praise we give him
might well be distrusted if from any false delicacy we slurred

over his defects and errors. The most dangerous rock in his way will be adulation. Sincerely we wish him to be assured that those who mix their applause with a proper alloy of censure are his best friends. Indiscriminate flatterers are no better than the snake which besmears its prey with slime, only to gorge it the more easily. On reviewing what we have written, we find no observation on Master Payne's voice, in which nature has been very bountiful to him. We heard him a few times, with no little pain, strain it out of its compass. He need not do so; since, judiciously managed, it is equal to all the purposes of his profession. Those are dangerous experiments, by which he may spoil a voice naturally clear, melodious, and of tolerable compass. His pronunciation is at times hurtful to a very nice ear. He is not to imagine that he has spoken as he ought when he has uttered words as they are pronounced in general conversation. There are some, and high ones too, who will say 'good-boy,' when they mean 'good-bye;' and it would not be at all impossible to hear a very fine lady say that she was daown in taown to buy a gaown. We do not accuse Master Payne of this; but at times a little of the *a* cheats the *o* of its good old round rights; so distantly, however, as not to be noticed except by a very accurate ear; but he ought not to let any ear discover it. To the correct orthœpist, several persons on the stage give offence in the pronunciation of the pronoun possessive *my*, speaking it in all cases with the full open *y*, as it would rhyme to fly, which should only be when it is put in contradistinction to *thy*, or *his*, or any other pronoun possessive; in all other cases it should be sounded like *me*.

"Of the characters represented by this young gentleman, those in which he evinced the greatest powers are *Douglas*, *Tancred*, and *Romeo*, while that in which he is least exceptionable is *Frederick*, in 'Lovers' Vows.' In his *Octavian*, which followed next after *Douglas*, some of the pathetic passages were finely expressed. Mrs. Inchbald, in her prefatory remarks to the play of the 'Mountaineers,' says, 'This true lover requires such peculiar art, such consummate skill in the delineation, that it is probable his representative may have given an impression of the whole drama unfavorable to the author. Nor is this a reproach to the actor who fails; for such a person as *Octavian* would never have been created had not Kemble been born some years before him. But notwithstanding the difference of their ages, it is likely they will both depart this life at the same time.' While the

difficulty of delineating *Octavian*, and the merit of a living performer of it are such that it is scarcely possible to think of the
play without thinking of Kemble, it has so happened that scarcely
any character has been attempted by so many actors of all qualities,—nor is there one in which so few have come off with
actual disgrace. Men who could scarcely be endured in third or
fourth-rate parts have selected *Octavian* to figure in on their
benefit nights. One man, who was laughed at in every other character, was supposed by a misjudging audience to play *Octavian*
well; nay, to our knowledge, was preferred to Hodgkinson and
Cooper in it. The reason is plain: to the portraying of madness
the injudicious can imagine no limits. The more a madman raves
and roars the better; rags, slovenliness, and matted hair, and
beard too, are the usual associates of awkwardness and vulgarity.
Any man, therefore, who can rant and play the extravagant, no
matter how ungracefully, may pass with some audiences for a
very natural *Octavian*,—an abominable absurdity! For these two
reasons *Octavian* is a very hazardous part for a performer who
aims at substantial fame to attempt. In Master Payne's performance of it there was no extravagance to censure; nothing that
had the least tendency to enrol him among the bedlamite butchers
of the character; nor was there, on the other hand, a complete
uniform delineation of *Octavian* to afford him the same rank in
that which criticism willingly allows him in some other characters.

"In the characters selected by Master Payne there are but four
which we can think judiciously chosen. For the whole selection
we should find it difficult to account if we did not know that they
had before been chosen for Master Betty, by thus closely walking
in the steps of whom Master Payne has, in our opinion, wronged
himself. It is evident that in choosing characters for the infant
Roscius of England his instructors had it more in view to exhibit
the boy as a prodigy, than the characters well acted. The people
were to be treated to an anomalous exhibition, and the greater
the anomaly the better the treat. What but a determination
to inflame public curiosity to the highest pitch by a contrast as
absurd as unnatural could have induced them to put forward a
little boy of twelve years old in the formidable tyrant Richard?
Like modern composers of music, their object was not to produce
harmony or natural sweetness, but to execute difficulties. As the
actor was a boy loitering on the verge of childhood, the plan,
if not correct, was at least politic. But the public do not look

on Master Payne in that light, and, therefore, he ought to have selected parts more suitable to his time of life and talents,— parts calculated to aid, and not to depress him. What judicious actor is there now living who would not think it injurious to him to be put forward by a manager in *Selim* or in *Zaphna?* The united powers of Mossop in *Barbarossa*, and Garrick in *Selim*, could barely keep that play alive. We have seen Mossop play it to a house of not ten pounds, though aided by the first *Zaphna* in the world, Mrs. Fitzhenry. From either of those char- acters Master Payne could not derive the least aid. His *Hamlet* we put out of the question,—we did not see it. On his *Tancred* we can dwell with very different sensations; considering the ma- terials he had to work upon, his delineation of the character was highly creditable to his talents. For the love part little more can be done by a good actor than by a good reader; as poetry, it is soft, and sweet, and flowing; as a practical representation of that passion, it is mawkish; yet, in the performance of Master Payne, it was not entirely destitute of interest. In all the rest, in every scene with *Siffredi*, particularly in his warm expostula- tions with the honest, but mistaken old statesman; in his subse- quent indignation and despair; in his lofty bearing and menaces to *Osmond*, and thence onward to his death, he was truly ex- cellent, seemed perfect master of the scene, and in depicting the tumult of passions which struggle in the bosom of the lordly *Tan- cred*, evinced that he possesses the legitimate genius and true spirit that should inform the actor. For his benefit he personified *Romeo*. The house was so crowded, and in all places that were accessible after the doors were opened there was so much press- ing, confusion, ill-mannered noise and struggle and rudeness, that few but those who had places taken in the front boxes could see or hear the play out. From the upper gallery, where with diffi- culty we at last got a seat, we indistinctly saw what passed on the stage, and could hear a little by snatches. What we did hear and see induced us to lament our not hearing and seeing more, and to wish that we may speedily have another opportunity of witnessing a performance respecting which there is but one opinion, and that highly favorable to Master Payne's reputation."

CHAPTER III.

"Use every man after his deserts, and who shall 'scape whipping."

PAYNE ABROAD.

We introduce Mr. Payne to our reader again with his arrival at Liverpool, after a passage of two-and-twenty days.

At that time the United States and Great Britain were at war. Although the ship had a cartel, and he bore the list of letters, our young friend and all his companions on their arrival were marched to prison. But Payne states in a letter written at the Liverpool Borough Jail, February 11th, 1813, that "on Wednesday, after all the British subjects were discharged, at the special intercession of some of the most influential of the inhabitants, 'His Worship' the mayor, who is a very gentlemanly man, treated us with great politeness, and indulged us with permission to be removed to our present lodgings, which are delightful, and for which we are permitted to pay five guineas a piece weekly. 'We are seven' in number. The only thing that interferes with our comfort is the confinement within our massy gates, but our apartments within the house of the governor are as pleasant as can be wished for. When our passports have been examined in London, and returned, we shall probably be set at liberty, and permitted to visit the great metropolis."

Mr. Payne remained in confinement for fourteen days, and, on the 28th of February, he left Liverpool for London, by the way of Chester. On his arrival there, he met several of his old New York friends, and the first of them that he dined with were the brother and sister of Washington Irving. Here, too, he met Mr. Brevoort, who was staying, the most of his time, at Edinburgh, and who was hand and glove with Walter Scott Jeffreys, and all of the *literati*. Brevoort was overjoyed to meet the young American of so much promise, and for two or three days devoted his attention to him in showing him around London.

A few days after his arrival, Payne presented his letter of introduction to Roscoe, who received him most cordially, at once be-

THEATRE ROYAL, DRURY-LANE.

This present FRIDAY, JUNE 4, 1813,
Their Majesties Servants will Act the Tragedy of

DOUGLAS.

Norval, by a YOUNG GENTLEMAN,
(*Being his first appearance in London*)

Lord Randolph, Mr. HOLLAND,
Glenalvon, Mr. RAYMOND,
Stranger, Mr. WROUGHTON,
Donald, Mr. COOKE,
Officer, Mr. FISHER.   Servant, Mr. MADDOCKS.
Matilda, Miss SMITH,
Anna, Miss BOYCE,

After which (*for the 26th time at this Theatre*) the Grand Musical Romance of

LODOISKA.

With the ORIGINAL MUSICK (from the Scores of the late Mr. STORACE,
And with entirely New Scenery, Dresses and Decorations.

POLANDERS.

Prince Lupauski, Mr. POWELL,   Count Floreski, Mr. PHILIPPS,
Baron Lovinski, Mr. RAYMOND,   Varbel, Mr. LOVEGROVE,
Adolphus, Mr. J. SMITH, Gustavus, Mr. WALLACK, Sebastian, Mr. Buxton,
Casimir, Mr. FINN, Michael, Mr. MILLER, Stanislaus, Mr. EVANS,
OFFICERS—Messrs. MARSHALL, HARTLAND, BARNS, BROWN BUXTON,
First Page, Miss CARR,   Second Page, Master SEYMOUR,
Princess Lodoiska, Mrs. MOUNTAIN.
POLISH GUARDS.—Messrs. Aberdeen, Newman, Chappel, Blower, Bynam, Jamieson,
Billet, Staples, West, T. West, Seymour, Wilson, Hanly, George, Dean,
Miller, Reece, Shade, Tulip, Read, Melvin, Jacobs, Douglas, Appleby.

CAPTIVES.

Mrs. Pyne, Miss Vallancy, Miss Ruggles, Mrs. Scott,
Mesdms. Chatterley, Minton I. Boyce, Jones, Caulfield, Lyon, S. Dennett, A. Scott,
F. Jones, Carlyle, Henly, Corrie, Cooke, E. Cook, Horrihow, Barrett, Lettin, Johannot, Barnes,

TARTARS.

Kera Khan, Mr. DE CAMP,   Ithorak, Mr. PYNE,   Khor, Mr. COOKE,
Japhis, Mr. BELLAMY,   Kajah, Mr. I. WALLACK,
Tamuri, Mr. CHATTERLEY,   Camazio, Mr. FISHER.
CHIEFS—Messrs. KIRBY, PACK, MADDOCKS, WEST, LEE,

THE HORDE

Messrs. Danby, Caulfield, Whilmshurst, Ebbertson, Wallack, Cook, Jones, Dibble, Clarke,
Oddwell, Mead, Wilson, Bennett, Dixon, &c.
PRINCIPAL COMBATANTS.—Messrs I. WALLACK, HARTLAND, CHATTERLEY,
KIRBY, WALLACK, I. WEST, PACK, LEWIN, APPLEBY, BARNES,
MATHEWS, HOPE, COST. BROWN, HORRIBOW, H. SEYMOUR.

To-morrow, a Grand Performance of SACRED MUSICK.
On Monday, (for the last time at this Theatre,) the Operatick Romance of The DEVIL'S BRIDGE,
with the Farce of HONEST THIEVES.
On Tuesday, (2nd time at this Theatre) the Operatick Drama of The PEASANT BOY.
The Publick are respectfully informed that Mr. SOWERBY's Performance of the
Character of JAFFIER was on Saturday night received with the highest applause,
and that the Tragedy of VENICE PRESERVED will, in conseqence, be repeated *on
Wednesday.*
On Thursday, (First Time at this Theatre) the Serio-Comick Opera of The MANIAC;
or, the SWISS BANDITTI, the part of Henry Cleveland by Mr. BRAHAM.
On Friday, will be produced A NEW COMEDY in Three Acts, which has been sometime

A fac-simile of the old London Play-bill of 1813.

came his personal friend, and introduced him to John Philip
Kemble, Campbell, Coleridge, Southey, and other magnates in the
world of English learning.

After waiting for a long time, and using every means of influence to obtain a hearing upon the stage of some one of the London theatres, he at last wrote a letter himself to the celebrated
Mr. Whitehead, who was then chairman of the Drury Lane
management. The result was a promise of an immediate interview, which shortly followed. resulting in arrangements for a'
series of performances at the old Drury. He was admonished
not to appear so near the end of the season. but Payne had
become impatient, and his *début* before an English audience was
fixed on, and his *entrée* was to be in the character of *Zaphna.* but
Douglas was finally substituted. At the same time, it was proposed by the *débutant* and acquiesced in by the management, that
there should be no mention in paragraphs or play-bills of his name
or history. He was desirous to stand or fall by the unbiased
judgment of his hearers. It was consequently announced that
on "Friday evening. June the 4th, 1813, the tragedy of 'Douglas'
would be performed, the part of *Douglas*, by a young gentleman,
his first appearance."

At the only rehearsal summoned, and this not until the day of
the performance, Miss Smith (afterwards Mrs. Bartley), who was
cast for *Lady Randolph*, was not present. Our young aspirant
called on her and talked over the business his part had with hers,
but she was haughty, and did not agree with Mr. Payne, on the
ground that his mode of performing the part would take the
attention of the house from her, and. with a cool, low courtesy, she
bid the young actor "Good-day," with the wish that he would
succeed.

At night, as Payne entered the green-room dressed for the part
of *Norval*, the stage manager informed Payne, for the first time,
that he had a new *Lady Randolph* for him, that Miss Smith was
sick, and that they had borrowed Mrs. Powell from Covent
Garden. "There she stands. on the stage; come; it is time for
us to begin," and this was his first introduction to the lady with
whom his part had so much important stage business. and his
entrée upon the boards of an untried stage in a strange country!
Although he had no opportunity for a moment's conversation,
the interest expressed by his theatrical mother was throughout
kindly, and perfectly maternal. While the house was ringing

5

with the thunders of approbation at the triumph and power of his death-scene, the great Mrs. Powell, as she leant over him, was exclaiming in an exulting whisper, "There! do you hear that? do you hear the verdict?" His performance throughout was crowned with unbounded applause.

The next day Payne sent a letter to Mrs. Powell, in which he thanked her for her sympathy and attention, and lauded her excellent performance of *Lady Randolph*, to which she replied: "If you saw any merit in my performance of the part, it was entirely owing to a son that I felt proud of." On his next appearance, which was not till Monday, June 14th, Miss Smith appeared in her part, but the audience resented her conduct. The managers were now more explicit in their announcement, and stated, on the bills of the Monday following, that the "Young Gentleman" was Master Payne from the New York and Philadelphia theatres. The papers spoke of the young gentleman as having made a hit. The "Morning Herald" remarked that his angry scene with *Glenalvon* had the marks of genius in it, and that he maintained the meaning of his author with spirit, particularly when he exclaimed, "*Hast thou no fears for thy presumptuous self?*" and concludes, upon reconsidering the whole of his performance, "We have never seen a finer representation of *Young Norval*. Nature has endowed him with every quality for a great actor, and, to reach that position, all he requires is more time and study. He possesses all the simplicity and purity of style that in the end must tell with great force, and this seems to be the result of his own natural taste. He speaks at once to the sober senses, to the feelings, and to the heart; in passion he is never noisy. His own discretion is his tutor. But, when he comes to contend with *Glenalvon*, he bursts forth in all the fire of indignation and anger, arising from wounded pride, and, when he found he was to '*perish by a villain's hand*,' his remark '*had slain him*' was not delivered in a loud, boasting voice, but in the mild accents of a dying hero, modestly conscious of his courage. Such is the character of this young gentleman, who makes a fairer promise than any juvenile adventurer we have ever seen."

The theatre was now about closing for the season, there remained time for only one attempt more. *Romeo* was selected for the occasion, although it was not Mr. Payne's choice of character, yet he succeeded in the part. At that time he was very handsome, and looked Romeo in this respect to the very life. It is

worth recording, as a marked event in the history of the stage
and theatrical revolution, that Mr. James W. Wallack, one of the
finest actors the British stage has ever produced, that evening
represented the trifling character of the *Prince*, and his brother,
also famed on this side of the Atlantic, that of the servant
Abraham.

The success of our young countryman in the city of London
caused many offers from the provincial managers. "Their eagerness was not in the least shaken even by an attempt, probably
emanating from stage-jealousy, to get up a prejudice against him
upon the assertion that he was "an illegitimate son of Tom
Paine."

After his performances in London, he next appeared at Liverpool, where his success was far beyond what he experienced in the
city of London. Gore's "Liverpool General Advertiser" of July
15th remarks : " His performance of *Hamlet*, on Tuesday evening,
being his fourth appearance here, was received with even more
enthusiasm than either of those which preceded it. The management at the close of the play-scene was hailed with loud cheering,
and the curtain dropped to applause." In the "Liverpool Mer-
cury" we find the following : "Mr. Payne's benefit, on Friday
evening, was attended by one of the most elegant audiences which
have graced the theatre this season. At the close of the interlude,
Mr. Payne unexpectedly appeared in *propria persona* before the
curtain, and made the following spontaneous address : 'Ladies and
gentlemen, I should think myself wanting in gratitude and candor
could I quit this place without emphatically acknowledging the
warm welcome with which I have been honored by the inhabitants
of Liverpool, and those particularly concerned in the direction of
the theatre. It has been everything which could be hoped from
hospitality, and has forced me to forget that I was a stranger.
Under existing circumstances, ladies and gentlemen, I must feel,
and feel sensibly, the magnanimity of that spirit which, disdaining
national distinctions, can hail even the humblest member of the
family of literature and the arts, in whatsoever clime accident may
have thrown his birthplace, as a brother and a friend !' The applause at the end of this address was protracted." Mr. Payne performed with equal success in Birmingham, Litchfield. Walsall,
Tamworth, and a great number of small places ; and especially in
Manchester, where the following curious comparison was made
between him and Mr. Betty : "This gentleman has a figure not

imposing, but well-proportioned; a face almost too beautiful for a
man; and a voice the clearest and most bell-like we remember ever
to have heard. His acting is quite equal to that of Mr. Betty at
the time of public admiration and enthusiasm in his favor. In
graceful attitudes, and the pantomime of the art, they are nearly
equal; in expression of countenance and conception of character,
Mr. Payne has by far the advantage, but in treading the stage, the
palm must be given to Mr. Betty." The next visit of our countryman was to Dublin. Here he was received with very great kindness, both in public and private, and formed an intimacy with the
celebrated Mr. Daniel O'Connell, Charles Phillips, and others. It
was while here that young Payne was made a Freemason, in company with O'Connell and Phillips. This fact Payne states in MS.
notes. He appeared in "Rolla." He was so well received in it, that
the play was instantly repeated. He was supported throughout
his engagement by the since so highly celebrated Miss O'Neil.
The "Hibernian Journal" noticed his engagement thus: "The
departure of Mr. Payne from our boards was marked by an incident of deep interest, which riveted his claims upon the best
feelings of our countrymen. His extemporaneous parting address
on that occasion was one of the best-conceived efforts of the kind
we remember ever to have heard, and certainly nothing was ever
received with greater fervor and delight. The impression created
by this gentleman's performances, especially his *Hamlet*, has been
of such a nature as to excite the warmest wishes in every quarter
for his speedy return, which will be hailed, whenever it may happen, with all the warmth which Irish liberality never fails to exercise towards public talent and private worth. The following is a
faithful report of the address which was alluded to: 'Ladies and
gentlemen, the unusual circumstances under which I have appeared before you will, I trust, explain and justify this unusual
mode of acknowledging the politeness with which my theatrical
efforts have been received in Dublin. It is not my object to thank
you for having buried national hostilities in your generosity to an
individual. The want of a disposition to do this is illiberal, but
there is no liberality in possessing it. I have too much respect
for those whom I have the honor to address, to incur the risk of
offending them by offering thanks for so negative a kindness.
But permit the wanderer, who has been warmed by the sunshine
of the Emerald Isle, in the plain sincerity of gratitude, to declare
that, in whatever clime or circumstances accident may place me,

it will ever be my glory to hail the Irishman as a brother, and to proclaim to my own countrymen and the world that the stranger may make friends in other lands, but in Erin he shall find a home!' This address was followed by a round of prolonged applause."

It was on this occasion that the greatest compliment (perhaps a little whimsical in its way) was paid to Mr. Payne that a Dublin audience can pay an actor. After the first piece was over, there was still to be performed a comic song and a farce, but the audience were so well pleased with the young American, that, immediately after Payne had retired from his speech-making, many of the people, on the spur of the moment, cried out "Home! Home! Home!" The hint was taken by the rest of the audience, and in a few moments more the house was closed and in darkness.

After this engagement, he played with the same success at Waterford; here the great Miss O'Neil joined in with Payne, and for the first time appeared as a star, he having induced her to leave the stock-company for starring purposes. This was the starting-point of her brilliant fame. She was then quite young and very beautiful. Payne, too, was very handsome, and, when they appeared as *Romeo* and *Juliet*, they suited the characters so perfectly that they carried the house by storm. They next appeared together at Cork, where Miss O'Neil performed for the last time, prior to her success as a star upon the London stage, at once seeming to fill, as a tragic actress, the void made by the retirement of Mrs. Siddons. While Mr. Payne was performing with Miss O'Neil at Cork, he was very handsomely eulogized in a speech, relating to some political row in the theatre, by Mr. O'Connell. On his benefit-night, Miss O'Neil performed the parts of *Lady Randolph* and *Katharine* to his *Norval* and *Petruchio;* and he spoke an address, written for the occasion by the celebrated Charles Phillips. Here, after extending his engagement by playing for several benefits of the company, which he did gratuitously, Mr. Payne went with O'Connell and Phillips to Killarney and its neighborhood, and shared the honor everywhere lavished upon the party. It was on this occasion that they witnessed the stag-hunt upon the lake, described by Phillips in his fine poem of "The Emerald Isle," and it was at a dinner on Innisfallen Island, in reply to a toast given with reference to the two strangers, Phillips and Payne, and the countries to which they belonged, that Phillips made his celebrated speech on Washington and America, which became celebrated on this side of the Atlantic and was spoken in all our colleges and schools. Phillips in his remarks on this occasion said, "To be associated with Mr. Payne must be, to any one who regards private virtue and personal accomplishments, a source of peculiar pride, and that feeling is not a little enhanced to me by the recollections of the country to which we are indebted for his qualifications."

On the return of Mr. Payne to London, the war having terminated, every one who could flocked to Paris, anxious to see and to be in the midst of the world of fashion, and also to enjoy the acting of the great Talma, and for the last-named purpose, especially, Payne went thither. The period proved a most interesting one for Payne. It was that of Bonaparte's return from Elba. Payne was captivated with the brightness, whirl, and bustling of the great city, and remained beyond the *hundred days.* Here Payne met Washington Irving, and for some time they were room-mates. A few days after his arrival, he was introduced to the great actor. His reception by Talma was affectionate in the extreme, and always afterwards Payne and Talma were intimate and personal friends.

The theatres in France were, and are, under the control of the government, and all civilities extended from them to strangers are looked upon as a national compliment. The National Theatre of Paris extended to Payne, through Talma, an invitation to the freedom of the house. Payne returned his thanks in an elegantly written letter in French, which gave so much satisfaction to the committee and Talma that it was published in the papers, with a short biographical sketch of Payne. The following is a translation of Payne's letter:

"GENTLEMEN,—I certainly would be insensible to the value of the high compliment which you have paid me, by offering me the freedom of your National Theatre, did I not, on the instant, acknowledge the receipt of your communication. I am too conscious of the humbleness of my personal pretensions not to esteem the kindness as a tribute paid more to my country than to myself, and to the progress of the new world in a branch of the liberal arts of which no representative but myself has yet appeared on this side of the ocean, and I shall deem it a duty to excite in my native republic, to which the compliment properly belongs, the feelings of respect, gratitude, and admiration for the elegant hospitality I have had the honor to receive on behalf of my native land.

" I remain,

" Your obliged and obedient servant.

" JOHN HOWARD PAYNE.

" PARIS, March 27th, 1815."

This regard on the part of Talma and the committee of the National Theatre presented the subject of our biography with a fine opportunity to study the best French models both of acting and dramatic writing, and although Mr. Payne was a good French scholar at the time he arrived there, he at once devoted himself to a still further study of the language, and became an almost constant reader of the best French dramatic poets.

By one of John Howard Payne's letters, June 5th. 1815, it appears that he had been holding a correspondence with Talma, as to the best school for instruction in acting, to which Talma returned the following answer:

" PARIS, June 7th, 1815.

"MY DEAR PAYNE,—I cannot point out the principles better than Shakespeare has, in a few lines he has laid down as the basis and true standard of our art. Therefore I refer you to what *Hamlet* says (Act III., Scene II.) respecting the means of personating the various characters which are exhibited in human life. It will unfold to you my own principles, and at the same time my veneration for that most wonderful of all dramatic writers and instructors."

In another letter to Payne, he remarks:

"If you take any lessons from the gentleman you speak of, they should be given upon the stage, and not in the room, that you may give a full scope to your steps, and to your motions; but, my dear friend, the first rule is to be deeply impressed with the character and the situation of your personage, and all his surroundings, until your imagination is fully imbued with the character, and your nerves agitated to a proper condition, the rest will follow; your arms and legs will properly do their business. The graces of the danseuse are not requisite in tragedy; choose rather to have a noble elegance in your gait, and, if it is a historical character you propose to represent, know well the history of

the man, and the events of the times he lived in, even before and
beyond the period of the dramatic action of which he is one of
the figures. It is only by this thorough acquaintance with your
subject that you can gain the over-confidence, as it were, which
enables us to paint with a bolder brush and to give that broad
and grand effect necessary to impress the mind and captivate our
hearers. . . .

                    " Believe me ever,
                    " Your true and affectionate friend,
                                        " TALMA."

This advice, from one of the greatest artists of the stage, should
be of inestimable value to those gentlemen of the dramatic profession who too frequently think that the mere committing of the
words of the author is all that is required to make an actor, while,
in fact, there is no profession that requires more culture and careful study than that of the actor.

It is not always possible to keep strictly in the path of biographical incidents, and especially so in a biography of such a
man as Mr. Payne, who, all through his life, was deviating from
one thing to another; a more unsettled man never lived, like a
bee that seems to care not as to which flower it alights upon so
long as it extracts a sweet from each. The man of genius may
do several things well, but, if he gives his entire attention and
industry to some one thing, he is sure to excel, and such would
have been the case with Mr. Payne, either as an actor or dramatic
writer. Mr. Payne would also have excelled as a critic; the evidence of this will at once be perceived in the following remarks
of Mr. Payne's, which we extract from a letter of his, written to
his sister. She had written a letter to him in which she requested
that he would send his opinion as to how Kemble and Kean compared with her great favorite, Cooper.

To us Leigh Hunt is the best of all dramatic critics. Any one
who has read his critical essays on the great actors of his day,
enumerating Kemble, Siddons, Pope, Raymond, Bannister, Mun-
don, Fawcett, Liston, Mathews, Powell, Jordan, Mattocks, and
hosts of others, cannot fail to be impressed with his sound judgment, fairness, and honesty of purpose; and we perceive these
same qualities in the following extracts from Mr. Payne's letter
on the comparative merits of the celebrated actors above mentioned :

" LONDON, June 19th, 1817.

"DEAREST ELOISE,—A letter which I send to brother Thatcher, by the same opportunity which carries this, will fully explain the causes of my silence, and the nature of my pursuits, for the last two years. Upon the future I cannot speak distinctly, because the necessity for daily labor to produce daily resources greatly impedes the soarings of ambition, and prevents one from doing many grand things, merely because nature forces us to follow the fashion of eating and drinking, and both cost money. As soon as I can reconcile my plans to my means you shall know what I propose, but were I to tell you all the schemes which have crossed my mind. so different are they, you would at once say my madness lacked a method. Something. however, shall shortly be decided to regulate the movements of my future life,—some goal, —some point for the attainment of which my efforts shall be concentrated ; 'but of this more anon.' Why should we strive to see disagreeable things in the past, through a sacrifice of precious moments which might be devoted to fine fancies of a bright and pleasant future ?

"You ask me for my opinion of Siddons and others of the British stage, and how Cooper. your favorite actor, compares with Kemble and Kean.

"I have seen Kean in several of his characters, but oftener in *Shylock* and *Richard* than in any other of his representations. and in these always with increased delight. If I may use comparison, he does not seem to me calculated to produce, like Kemble, a powerful first impression ; there is nothing in him to dazzle the senses ; but he steals upon the judgment. captivates and satisfies it. The recollection of Cooke was vivid in my mind when Kean appeared in London. If Kean never saw Cooke, and he tells me he never did, the similitude in certain parts of their acting, as well as the conception of the true character, seems to me to be still more wonderful. Their leading features of resemblance in *Shylock* and *Richard* exhibit so marked a correspondence in their genius that it almost proves that both modelled themselves upon similar views of nature. I say 'similar views of nature' for this reason. Two persons of equal talents may see the same thing in very different lights. Hence spring the innumerable varieties of judgment. Kemble is a profound investigator, yet Kemble takes a view of *Richard* totally unlike Kean's. and Kemble's *Richard* to me appears radically false in design, and in execution stupefying and tedious. Yet even Kemble's *Richard* has its admirers in opposition to that of Kean. But I look upon *Richard* as Kemble's worst effort, and I conceive it to be rather unfair to institute a comparison between the worst production of one rival and the best of another. The anxious labor and the long-suffering, by which Mr. Kemble has won his laurels, deserve a better reward than he now receives from the ingratitude of a nation of whose fame, in one branch of the fine arts, he has so many years been a principal and an illustrious supporter. Mr. Kean has often failed of obtaining that power over my feelings with which Mr. Kemble almost invariably held them captive. Compare Kemble and Kean in those characters, of which each gentleman is admitted by the whole world of criticism to be a master. Is Mr. Kean's *Richard* or his *Shylock* equal, on the whole, to Mr. Kemble's *Cato, Coriolanus, Hamlet, Anthony,* or *Macbeth?* Or is there any individual excellence in either of the efforts of Mr. Kean, which is not superseded by some individual excellence in each one of the efforts of his competitor? Is Kean's ' *What do they i'th north'*—' *Off with his head!*' —' *I'll not trust thee,*' with the residue of that scene which chiefly delighted me, equal, in the electricity of their effects, to 'By Jupiter, forgot,' 'Alone I did it,' or the whole of any one impassioned scene of Coriolanus? I think, my dear sister, that, when you ask me to tell you which is the greatest actor, the only way to get at it is by a liberal mode of comparison. Give full scope to each man's genius, and comparison of each man's mind, when each is in his glory. Deciding by such a system, I am inclined toward Kemble. The latter gentleman is more even through his whole performance of a character, and for the study thereof, the evidence of the patient, hard-working student is decidedly with Kemble. He, in every scene of the play, sends out a steady, burning light, that fascinates you from the moment he appears before you. Kean, by flashes, like Etna, always is emitting the evidence of a hidden fire, one which at times flashes forth to astonish you. With Kemble, the eye and the intellect are both filled and satisfied: the ear wishes for something; with Kean, the eye and the ear is pleased, but the intellect is not satisfied. I can never forget Kemble's *Coriolanus,* his *entrée* was the most brilliant I ever witnessed. His person derived a majesty from a scarlet robe which he managed with inimitable dignity. The Roman energy of his deportment, the seraphic grace of his gesture, and the movements of his perfect self-possession displayed the great

mind, daring to command, and disdaining to solicit, admiration.
His form derived an additional elevation, of perhaps two inches,
from his sandals. In every part of the house the audience rose,
waved their hats. and huzzaed. and the cheering must have lasted
more than five minutes; and at the same time, a crown of laurels
was thrown before him from one of the private boxes, and he
wore the laurel in the following triumphal procession. while the
house shook with the thunder of the populace. A similar enthusiasm was manifested in all his future touches, throughout the
play, but most emphatically in two clauses, the first, where *Coriolanus* is made welcome, the audience instantly made it a personal
application:

> 'A hundred thousand welcomes! I could weep,
> And I could laugh: I am light and heavy.—Welcome!
> A curse begin at every root of's heart,
> That is not glad to see thee!'

Here was a general 'Huzza! Bravo!' and loud and long clapping.
The end of the speech—

> 'Yet, by the faith of man,
> We have some old crab-trees here at home
> That will not
> Be grafted to your relish'—

produced a loud laugh, 'Huzza!' and applause. At the fall of
the curtain, there seemed to be but one mind that actuated the
whole house; it was as if the audience had been tranced by the
effect. They all at once got up and cheered until the actor came
before them; another 'Huzza!' and so ended Kemble's triumph,
every night he performed.

"Mrs. Siddons, unfortunately, did not burst upon me, when she
first came upon the stage, as Kemble did. I was present the
first night of her return to the stage, when she acted for the
benefit of the theatrical fund. I risked my limbs to see her, as
the rush and the crowd was so great; but got a most excellent
place. She acted *Mrs. Beverley*, and I was not only charmed and
every way interested, but at times astonished. The grace of her
person, the beauty of her arms, the mental beauty of her face. the
tragic expression of her voice, and the perfect identification with
the character, left nothing for me to wish for. In these she was
so great, that even her unwieldy figure. which at first somewhat

annoyed me, was soon forgotten. I never saw, nor could have conceived, an effect so sublimely agonizing as her attitude; the rapid glancing of her eyes for nearly a minute, then their sudden stop, and the riveting of them upon her insulter, *Stukely*, when he first shocked her with dishonorable advances. I cannot tell you in this letter all I saw and all I felt in this one performance of Siddons. If, at her present time of life, she could so affect us, what would she have done, and what did she do with her hearers, when her figure and her voice were in the full vigor and freshness of her perfect womanhood.

"When she left the stage this night with the understanding that, more than likely, she would never again appear before the public, a feeling of great sadness came over me, which took hours for me to shake off; the melancholy thought that she should ever disappear from the public, before the whole world had seen her, and felt her great power, still lasts with me, and I have no doubt always will, whenever I think of her. I fear, dear sister, that she has spoiled me for the enjoyment of all other actresses in the future.

"As regards Cooke, I was at the first performance of Cooke in America. He made a different impression upon me from any other actor I have ever seen; there was something so exclusively unique and original in his dramatic genius. He always presented himself to me in the light of a discoverer, one with whom it seemed that every action and every look emanated entirely from himself; one who appeared never to have had a model, and who depended entirely upon himself for everything he did in the character he represented. Cooke reminds me of no one but himself, and I have never been able to recognize the real *Richard* in any other actor than Cooke. Kean reminds me of Cooke, and Booth of Kean. The two seem to have absorbed something from the great former, but Kean more from Cooke, and Booth from Kean. Besides, Cooke's genius covers a broader field. He was just as great in dialect-parts as he was in the English heroic. His Scotch parts were wonderful. Indeed, I think Cooke (if there is anything in originality) the genius of the English stage; but why ask me about Cooke? You saw him when I had the honor of playing *Edgar* to his *Lear*. I deem it a glory for my country to have his remains resting in its soil.

"I have mentioned the name of Booth, and, in my last letter to you, stated that there was a little man of that name to appear at the Covent Garden. When I described him to you, as standing upon the steps of the Theatre, awaiting the event of his first appearance in the city of London. little, indeed, did I then imagine that the little man would drive great London mad before I should communicate to you again. Such, however, is the truth, and, as far as the history of his career has yet transpired, I will make it known to you.

"On Wednesday, Feb. 12. Mr. Booth, 'of the Brighton and Worthing Theatres,' was announced to play 'Richard the Third' at the Covent Garden. Nothing was known of Mr. Booth, but that he had performed the last season at the Covent Garden in the humble capacity of message-carrier, and had subsequently distinguished himself at Brussels, Brighton. Cheltenham, and elsewhere, in all Kean's characters. When he appeared, the house, I think, was thinner than I ever saw it. He was greeted with an enthusiastic welcome by the few that were present. His figure was more *petite* than Kean's and thinner; his voice, manner. everything, are of the most perfect and extraordinary imitations that can be conceived. You would have declared it was Kean playing the part, so faithful was the resemblance throughout, far closer, as a copy, than Vandenhoff's, and copied with better taste. Opposition showed itself early, but so evidently it was opposition for opposition's sake, that the honest good sense of John Bull was roused to take the young man's part, and every attempt at hissing called forth unprecedented applause and shouting, so that the intervals between the acts were filled up with acclamations. When the curtain fell, the applause was beyond all parallel. Abbott came on to announce 'Midsummer Night's Dream' for Thursday night, but there was a general cry, 'No! No! "Richard the Third," Booth as *Richard!*' to which the managers were not reluctant to accede, and, of course, Abbott, after walking to the stage-door for orders, came back and said, 'Ladies and gentlemen, by your desire, Mr. Booth will repeat *Richard* to-morrow evening.' This satisfied the ladies and gentlemen, who blistered their hands for a few minutes longer. The next night the house was far better, and Booth received even a greater applause than on the night before, and the curtain fell amid loud cries of 'Repeat *Richard!*' but Mr. Booth was stated to be too unwell to repeat it the next night. and it was consequently announced for Monday. On Saturday, however, Mr. Booth called on Mr. Harris, and had a long conversation as to terms. Booth had been getting in the towns a little over two pounds a week. The managers thought that he would measure his salary in London by what he had been getting in these small places; to this Mr. Booth would not agree. He knew his price better. The Drury Lane management, hearing of this disagreement, laid a plan to bring Booth over to their house, and Kean was appointed to carry the project into effect, and the result is that Kean and Booth have performed together at Drury Lane. I saw Booth in the part of *Iago* to Kean's *Othello*. The house was packed from pit to gallery; it was a great performance and a grand sight. The new little man behaved himself like a great hero. Kean seemed to feel the force of the newcomer and performed up to the full height of his wonderful powers. In the jealous scene, their acting appeared like a set trial of skill, and the applause that followed the end of each of their speeches swept over the house like a tornado. The effect was almost bewildering. At the end of the play, both of the actors appeared to be exhausted from the extraordinary effort they had made. Kean appeared to take much delight in bringing Booth before the curtain. He seemed to enjoy Booth's success just as much as the audience did, and as he brought him through the proscenium door, you could see, by the intelligent glitter of his piercing eyes, and the smile through the copper color of the Moor's face, a sort of fatherly feeling, as if dragging an over-modest son to receive the honors of his success. The whole house seemed to feel it in this spirit, and, when Kean conducted Booth back to the door, and then made one step forward to acknowledge the compliment offered to himself, I thought the applause would never stop. 'This much of the new actor can I tell thee, and nothing more.' I think, however, that he is destined to fill a large place in the future history of the English stage.

"As regards Cooper in comparison to Kemble, Cooke, or Kean, he is not so great an actor as either of the three, and must take his position as fourth on the roll. But in placing him there, he must not be taken from among the first-class stars. Cooper is of the Kemble school; not that he is a copy of Kemble, as Booth is of Kean, but is of the heroic style, and becomes such a part as *Othello* better than that of *Iago*. He resorts, too, to less tricks of the stage than Kemble, who enlarges his legs and arms by pads, and consults pictures and artists, to produce personal effects. I don't object to this on the part of Kemble or any actor, when he produces the desired result. What I mean is, you see nothing but

what belongs to Cooper; he is more natural, while Kemble is more
artistic. In natural grace. Cooper is far beyond any actor I have
ever seen, and he is, too, the best *Hamlet* on the stage, he is even
more scholarly than Kemble, and, if not so startling as Kean, or
so grand as Kemble in the part, he is certainly far less rude than
the former, and more natural than the latter. Cooper was the
first actor of note I ever saw. It was in Boston, on the 11th of
March, 1805, eleven years ago, when I was a mere boy. The
circumstances of his *début* were peculiar. After his return from
England, he, on his starring expedition, came to Boston in the
middle of the season, without invitation or engagement. The
performers combined to prevent his appearance, assigning as a
reason that their benefits were just about to commence, and that
his strong attraction would, to a great extent, interfere with their
success. But jealousy was doubtless at the bottom of it. The
beaux esprits of the town embodied in a phalanx, and threatened
the banishment of the company unless Cooper was brought forward. The manager immediately closed the theatre. A com-
promise ensued at once. Cooper engaged to act alternately for
the house and the benefits. The theatre re-opened with Cooper
in *Hamlet* after a week's interregnum, and Cooper cleared, by the
arrangement, three thousand five hundred dollars in thirteen
nights. His reception was very ardent. My young mind was
enraptured; he enchanted me, though at the time I could not tell
why. His deportment to me is always full of natural dignity;
his action and whole manner is chaste, vigorous, and characteristic, and his enunciation always fine. I shall never forget
his finished style of bowing to the audience. It acted like a mysterious magic over all, and at once made the audience his personal
friends."

Mr. Payne's acting career in England was of short duration.
From his folio book of bound play-bills, representing every performance he gave while in Europe, we here mention the characters and theatres he performed in. His first appearance was at
Drury Lane Theatre, on Friday evening, June 4th, 1813, in the
character of *Young Norval.* His second appearance was in the
same character. On Monday, June 14th, and Monday, June 21st,
he performed the part of *Romeo* to the *Juliet* of Miss Smith.
These three nights ended his performances at Drury Lane.
He next appeared at Liverpool, July 2d, in the character of *Norval;*
July 6th, as *Ashmet;* July 7th, *Romeo;* July 13th, *Hamlet;* July

15th, *Rolla.* From here he went to Birmingham, and appeared as *Tancred* on July 22d; July 23d, *Frederick*, in "Lovers' Vows; Liverpool, July 28th, as *Tancred;* August 3d, at Stourbridge, *Norval;* August 4th, Birmingham, *Romeo;* 5th, *Hamlet;* Stourbridge, August 6th, *Hamlet;* 9th, *Octavian.* He then returned to Liverpool for three nights, and performed the part of *Zaphna.* At Tamworth he performed seven nights, at Lichfield four nights, at Walsall, six nights, performing *Alexander the Great* for two nights. March 7th, 1814, he commenced an engagement of six nights at Manchester. Monday, May 2d, he made his first appearance at Theatre Royal, Dublin, and performed six nights. Here he performed *Hastings* and *Romeo* to Miss O'Neil's *Jane Shore* and *Juliet.* It was during this engagement he first met and performed with this lady, who was at that time a member of the stock company. He then performed for seven nights at Waterford, supported by Miss O'Neil. From here the two young stars went to Cork, and there made their first appearance August 15th, 1814. During this engagement he added *Jaffier, Count Lunenberg, Reuben Glenroy*, and *Biron* to his list of characters. In this engagement Miss O'Neil's success was unequivocal, and sent her name on the wings of fame to London, where soon after she became the great star of the English stage. She at once almost filled the place of Siddons. whose star was glimmering above the horizon just before its setting forever. Miss O'Neil had the great combination within her of beauty and genius, which the public could not withstand. And as soon as she appeared before a highly-cultured audience. she grasped fame and fortune. Payne and O'Neil parted at Cork for a while. His next appearance was not until April 8th, 1817, when he appeared at Bath for six nights. Here he performed in England, for the first time, the character of *Venoni*, by M. S. Lewis. Payne next appeared for one night at Shrewsbury, on October 8th, 1817, on which occasion he performed *Jaffier* to Miss O'Neil's *Belvidera.* He did not perform again until May 27th, 1818, which was for two nights at Birmingham, performing the parts of *Norval* and *Hamlet.* This was the last appearance of Mr. Payne upon the English stage, or any stage. While in Europe he performed in all one hundred and six nights, and represented twenty-two different characters. His greatest success was at Liverpool, in 1813. As an actor he did not grow with his audience, and lacked the genius to hold a place as a star upon the English stage.

PARTS PERFORMED BY PAYNE.

1. *Young Norval*	in	" Douglas."
2. *Octarian*	in	" Mountaineers "
3. *Frederick*	in	" Lovers' Vows."
4. *Zaphna*	in	" Mahomet."
5. *Hamlet*	in	" Hamlet."
6. *Rolla*	in	" Pizarro."
7. *Tancred*	in	" Tancred and Sigismund."
8. *Achmet*	in	" Barbarossa."
9. *Romeo*	in	" Romeo and Juliet."
10. *Edgar*	in	" King Lear."
11. *Alexander*	in	" Alexander the Great."
12. *Lord Hastings*	in	" Jane Shore."
13. *Orestes*	in	" Distressed Mother."
14. *Lothair*	in	" Adelgitha."
15. *Venoni*	in	" Venoni."
16. *Count Lunenberg*	in	" Adelaide."
17. *Jaffier*	in	" Venice Preserved."
18. *Reuben Glenroy*	in	" Town and Country."
19. *Petruchio*	in	" Katharine and Petruchio."
20. *Biron*	in	" Isabella."
21. *Wyndham*	in	" Royal Oak."
22. *Charles De Moor*	in	" The Robbers."

NOTE.—From one to fifteen were played in America by Master Payne before leaving for England; they were all repeated there, and in addition those subsequently numbered.

In considering the cause of Mr. Payne's leaving the stage and changing his pursuits of life, we are forced to go back to the early days of our hero, and thence trace upward the solution of our inquiry.

Criticisms on what are styled precocious children, like Master Betty, John Howard Payne, and Master Burke, are generally characterized by a praise far beyond their deserts. This fault arises in many cases from an over-sympathy for the age of the child, often forgetting that the child has been under obligations for instructions to older and abler minds. Master Payne had a father of high culture, who was for many years a prominent teacher in New York and Boston. and was at one time at the head of a college. He professed elocution and rhetoric, and finding in his son Howard a disposition that naturally leaned towards those branches of education, took special care to nurse his taste,

6

which soon developed to a demonstration of absolute talent. It
was the same with Master Betty, for his father was a man of independent means, and had the ability to teach him fencing and
elocution. After taking his son to the theatre several times, to
see the celebrated dramatic artists of the day, among them Sarah
Siddons in the character of *Elvira*, and John Philip Kemble, her
brother, as *Rolla*. Mr. Betty expressed surprise that his son should
have the taste. the talents, and should evince the desire to become
an actor. This boy made his first appearance at Belfast, when
only twelve years of age. He was born in 1791, the same year as
Master Payne. He went to London in 1804, and appeared as the
tenth " Wonder of the World." at Covent Garden Theatre. The
people at once went mad over him. and the critics seemed bereft
of common sense in their wild and ridiculous comparisons of the
child to Siddons, Kemble, and Young. Many pronounced him
equal to Garrick, in their remembrance of the great artist " when
he was in the brilliancy of his best days." So great was the enthusiasm over the boy, that for a while the three above-named
apostles of the stage were almost set aside by the public, or else
forced to perform to empty benches, while Betty was performing
to houses filled to suffocation, men and women fainting away for
want of air. The fashionable and profound vied with each other
in all their splendor and perfumed habiliments, and ladies of the
court rolled this " Child-Wonder" around in their gilded equipages.
He was called before the king and treated with marked honors.
On one occasion, when he was to play *Hamlet*, the House of Com-
mons. on a motion made by the great Pitt. was adjourned and went
to the theatre in a body to see him. In one engagement of twenty-
three nights. the receipts amounted to nearly sixty thousand dollars. But in two or three years all this tumult about the boy-
wonder died away. He left the stage, and entered Christ's College,
Cambridge, as a fellow-commoner. He never rose to a higher
rank than captain of the North Shropshire Yeomanry Cavalry.
The tree bore no more fruit. The flaming torch soon burned down
to a dim flicker.

   When Master Payne made his *début* in New York City he was
nearly eighteen years old, with rather a tall, manly figure, as his
picture in the character of *Norval* represents him. Whatever talent
he displayed, it was not received with that wild and ungovernable
enthusiasm that greeted Master Betty. It is too often the case
when precocious children are placed before the public, that the

parties in charge of them over-estimate their ability for the sole
purpose of making money. This desire so preponderates that
their advocates say anything in excessive praise of their talents,
even to the sacrifice of artists who have long been in every sense
their superior.

It is a singular fact that there is not a single case on record of
any youthful actor who in his manhood improved constantly and
advanced to a high position in his art. It was so with Payne, and
Betty, and Burke. To a certain extent, this may arise from an
over-satiety with the attractions of the stage before they reach the
age to appreciate justly the more subtile and captivating beauties
of the noble art; or, most probably, destitute of true genius, they
depend while young largely upon the instructions of others, which
makes them admirable only at the time. It stands to reason that
had Betty, Payne, or Burke been possessed of an inborn great
ability for acting, it would have continued through life, and would
have elevated them to higher attainments in their profession.
True genius is a fire that does not exhaust itself any more than
the sun ever wanes in its brilliancy of light. If genius exists in
the youth it must inspire the manhood; it can be seen and felt
more forcibly in manhood than in youth, provided the efforts to
express it are proportional. Genius, like the tide, will find its rise,
and carries upward with it public favor as the tide uplifts the bark
upon its surface. Betty, Payne, and Burke were not boys of
genius. They possessed large faculty of imitation, which, aided by
instructions, caused them to accomplish their work so well that
it was mistaken for genius; Betty's power, as we have stated,
soon died out, and by the time he was of age he was so little
heard of that many thought him dead, though he lived on in retirement, and did not die till over sixty years after his first appearance upon the stage. Mr. Payne when performing in London
did everything in his power to get the public to acknowledge
him as an actor of great merit, but he failed. He then wisely
left the stage, and took to dramatizing, for which he had far more
natural ability than for acting.

Master Burke, with all his musical and dramatic precocity,
soon disappeared from the public gaze and applause, and now in
his old days can be found playing the second violin in some orchestra. Such was not the case with Garrick, Kean, and Forrest.
They were all men of *genius*, and from the moment they first
touched the stage they swept onward and upward with a talis-

manic power that controlled public acknowledgment to the hour of their death, and enrolled their names highest upon the scroll of dramatic fame. Garrick was but a little older than Payne when he first struck his London audience with astonishment. The storm of public approbation began with his *début;* and he almost simultaneously brings the very court and genius of the time to his feet. He held the world captive till the hour of his death, and then was laid away to rest, followed by a funeral cortege that would have done honor to a king; genius alone could do it!

Edmund Kean, of unknown parentage, with a heartless mother, at whose vagabond side he wandered about to serve as her pack-horse; with no refining influences to lift him to a moral worth, no remarkable education to expand, refine, and intensify the remarkable action of his mental powers and in manhood to console him with the thought, "I know that I am right;" with no friends, with but little prestige, and penniless, yet finds his way at last, when less than twenty-five years old, to the doors of a London theatre. Thither he had tramped through slush and snow to his first night's performance, with only the sixth of a house in size of audience to see him perform the character of *Shylock.* The curtain falls on that performance with the occupants of pit and boxes standing waving their handkerchiefs and shouting their approbation. For weeks, for months, and for years he held spellbound the intelligent and refined wherever he went, and died full of fame! Only genius could do it!

The distinction of genius marked Edwin Forrest for a great future at an earlier age than Garrick or Kean, when less than twenty-one years old he arrested the public attention by his dramatic power, and they at once endorsed his genius, irresistibly applauding his efforts, and sustaining him through a long career, till he died an artist at sixty-seven years of age, so full and ripe in the perfection of his sublime art that his bitterest enemies were forced to admit his greatness, and to write in letters of gold upon the curtain when it dropped for the last time upon his eventful life, "Genius alone could achieve it!"

This great actor was more antagonized than any other man that ever trod the stage. He was the first prominent dramatic artist of a new nation; a nation still largely tainted with foreign influences, and with rank prejudices against art in whatever form emanating from American genius. It was thought by many Americans to be next to impossible for a new nation three thousand miles away from the art treasures of the old world to find a man who could produce anything great in art. The press of the country was overloaded with dramatic critics, English by birth, who were prejudiced against American actors, and, indeed, two-thirds of the managers and actors of our theatres were Englishmen, who labored under the idea that all dramatic talent, at least, must come from the mother-country. But as soon as Edmund Kean, the genius of the English stage, saw and heard young Forrest perform the part of *Iago* to his own *Othello* at Albany, he pronounced him full of ability, and in a speech, at a dinner given to him at Philadelphia, he predicted that Forrest was the forthcoming tragedian of the republic. In spite of all vulgar spleen of the press and the uncalled-for sarcasm such as was hurled at him by Fanny Kemble and others, he was not at all deterred, but ascended steadily to a higher excellence in his art, that has emblazoned his name forever as among the greatest actors of the world.

In making these comparisons we do not mean to detract anything from whatever talent Mr. Payne may have had for acting, but simply to place him among a host of other actors who, while considered good in their profession, had not the ability or the requisites to place them high among the first. Had he possessed any great talent, the theatre would not have shut him out. Managers will encourage all who have the ability to attract full houses, because their object is money. Mr. Payne took a wise course for himself when he resorted to dramatic writing, since it was the best thing he ever did and the best thing he could do.

The method used in the introduction of young Payne to the stage was the worst that could have been planned. The act of constantly presenting him to the public for the purpose only of assisting a father's broken fortunes, as if it were something of a crime to be an actor, could not fail to impress the public that he was somewhat more an object of charity than a performer of great merit.

CHAPTER IV. .

"There's a divinity that shapes our ends."

PAYNE AS A DRAMATIST.

DURING Mr. Payne's visit to Paris, he became particularly acquainted with Sir John Cam Hobhouse, the celebrated friend of Lord Byron. The suicide of Mr. Whitbread had made a change of the directory of Drury Lane Theatre. Some of Sir John's most intimate friends had got into power there. The Hon. Douglass Kinnaird was chairman of the managing committee, and Byron was one of the leading and most influential members. Payne was already acquainted with Byron, and Sir John gave Payne a very earnest introduction to Mr. Kinnaird. It happened that, during Payne's abode in Paris, the well-known melodrama of the " Maid and Magpie" appeared there. As an exercise in his study of the French language, and without dreaming of ever turning his attention to dramatic writing, Payne made a free version of the piece in question. He took it with him to London, and, by the merest accident, while in a conversation with Mr. Kinnaird, he mentioned that he had been making a translation of the " Maid and Magpie." Mr. Kinnaird was delighted with the idea, looking it over, and regretted that they had one made which was far inferior. Mr. Kinnaird also congratulated Mr. Payne on the hopes of his re-appearance at Drury Lane. The chairman decided, however, that it was expedient to secure the advantage of a more favorable moment than that selected on the former. In the course of the conversation, the general interests of the theatre were discussed, questions were asked about Parisian novelties. The " Maid and Magpie" was naturally a subject of very anxious inquiry, especially as Drury Lane had obtained a translation, and meant to bring it out almost immediately. Mr. Kinnaird was so much enlightened by Mr. Payne's knowledge of the French stage, that he told Mr. Payne that he might be of great advantage both to the theatre and himself by returning to France and remaining there. with an eye to Parisian novelties for Drury Lane, until there should be an opening to bring him out as an actor in a way that might do him justice, and advantage to the object. Under a promise to Kinnaird, in the name of the committee, Mr. Payne agreed to return to Paris, and send over French pieces for Drury Lane till its directors could promote his interest as an actor, with the same zeal they promised to exercise towards him as an author. Meanwhile, Mr. Harris, of Covent Garden, having heard of Mr. Payne's version of the "Maid and Magpie," called upon him, and offered a hundred pounds for it, with leave to make every change in it the theatre might think fit. The bargain was struck, and Mr. Payne now went back to France upon the affairs of Drury Lane. From this time his career as a dramatic author commenced. That the theatre might receive every possible advantage from his exertions, Mr. Payne was so thoughtless as to listen to one of those literary adventurers who are ever on the lookout for prey in crowded cities. This person had introduced himself to Mr. Payne, who was touched by the picture he drew of his wretched fortunes, and gratified with a talent he displayed for music. He thought he might at the same time serve a neglected genius and benefit the establishment which seemed to be so warmly espousing his own interests. Indeed, he spared no trouble or expense for the purpose of gaining advantage to Drury Lane over the rival house. The first play he sent over was "Accusation," a melodrama. in three acts; in the manuscript of which the stage business was so thoroughly defined that, notwithstanding its complexity, the drama was produced in the unprecedentedly short time of ten days following its arrival in London. The circumstance is mentioned as a remarkable one in the reminiscences of Dibdin, who was then stage manager. But he does not state whence the celerity arose, and takes the credit of it to himself. Indeed, a system was organized by our new-fledged dramatic author, through which any work might be transferred to London, with all its original beauty and finish, as soon as the news could arrive there of its first performance in the city of Paris.

In the mean time, the "Maid and Magpie" had been produced by Mr. Harris, and had proved a great success.

The drama of "Accusation" was produced for the first time, at the Drury Lane Theatre, February 1st, 1816. We have taken the following remarks on its first production and its plot from "The European Magazine." The story of the drama is a pretty one and will interest our readers:

" Feb. 1. 'Accusation ; or, The Family of Anglade.' This drama is an historical tale of domestic suffering, recorded in a French work entitled 'Causes Célébres.' It abounds in the pathetic ; and is dramatized with considerable ingenuity of plot, as well as scenic illusion. *Valmore* (Wallack) is the impetuous representation of a guilty passion which he desperately cherishes for *Madame d'Anglade* (Miss Kelly), upon whose spirited rejection of his infamous suit, he resolves on the destruction of her husband (Rae). To this end he employs the agency of *Hubert* (S. Penley), who is his valet, and a most ready scoundrel. The plans of his confidant are materially assisted by his accidentally discovering an old friend in iniquity (Barnard) disguised as an Italian strolling musician ; who, at his instigation, meditates a political robbery on *Madame Serval* (Mrs. Glover), the aunt of *Valmore*, resident in the same hotel with the *d'Anglades*. It happens, meanwhile, that a mysterious stranger (Bartley) obtrudes unceremoniously into the presence of *M. d'Anglade*, avowing himself to be the rightful heir of certain estates inherited by *M. d'Anglade* under the supposition of his decease. The demands of this stern visitor are peremptory : he not only claims restitution of his lands, but insists on instantly receiving their past revenues. *M. d'Anglade*, the soul of honor, had devoted much of his income to the claims of humanity ; whence he is compelled to yield, under his ill fortune, to the endearing solicitations of his beloved wife, who urges him to sell her jewels, and satisfy his unexpected creditor. This circumstance coming to the knowledge of *Hubert*, he commits the preconcerted robbery that night, and his associate, the following morning, personates the jeweller who was expected to purchase the *d'Anglade* diamonds. The transfer having taken place, *M. d'Anglade* unconsciously becomes possessed of £4500 of stolen notes ; and the jewels, together with the pocket-book of *Madame Serval* containing the remainder of the robbery, excepting five hundred pounds, are insidiously placed beneath a sofa pillow in the study. The police almost immediately enter to search the house ; and having made the *arranged* discovery, *M. d'Anglade* is torn from the embraces of his distracted wife and committed to the city prison. Previously, however, to this latter event the stranger re-appears, professes himself the friend and advocate of his injured kinsman ; manfully denies the possibility of *M. d'Anglade's* guilt ; and offers to purchase his release to the extent of his immense fortune. *Madame Serval*, with equal magnanimity, releases her claims ; but the law will be obeyed. At length, through the villany of the confederates, who are desirous each to cheat the other of the secreted five hundred pounds, notes to that amount are found upon *Hubert.* Suspicion likewise attached to a sailor ; he is taken up, and recognized as the pretended jeweller. While in separate custody, these wretches are lured into mutual recrimination, and the whole secret is disclosed. *Valmore,* to avoid an ignominious death, becomes a suicide ; and oppressed virtue gloriously triumphs in revealed innocence. The performers all excelled in their respective parts ; insomuch that it would be difficult to point individual merit. There are, however, two scenes, of which we must particularly speak. The first relates to the introduction of the police to *M. d'Anglade's* study. At this moment, we lost all recollection of the public theatre. Our feelings domesticated with the agonized family, we participated in the fulness of their distress ; reverencing the calm dignity with which the devoted *d'Anglade* sustained his conscious integrity, and repelled the vile suspicion levelled at his honor ; but, above all, we hailed the animated tenderness with which he repaid the conjugal affection so exquisitely expressed by Miss Kelly ; because we have been accustomed to see unmanly suffering superior to the claims of female attraction. This scene cannot be called acting ; it is a natural unfolding of the human heart, free from assumption, and spontaneously eloquent. The other is the scene in which *Madame Serval,* reluctantly convinced of her nephew's guilt, undertakes to probe his conscience, and to urge him, as he values her peace and his own honor, to a vindication of her injured friend. Mrs. Glover gave consummate pathos to this high-wrought passage, and Mr. Wallack's agonies were finely descriptive of a mind tortured by the conflicting emotions of remorse and personal safety. This is the finest acting we have ever seen this gentleman do. When we consider that this play was publicly exhibited on the tenth night after its translation was received from the author at Paris, we are at a loss to comprehend the elegance of the new scenery, classically adapted to its representation. The gradual decline of evening, with advancing clouds to usher in the night, was admirably executed, and the returning gondolas with Chinese lanterns were beautifully effective. *M. d'Anglade's* study was in the true spirit of French decoration ; and the opening of his window to gardens illuminated by the effects of a meridian sun was a novelty deservedly approved. If 'La Pie Voleuse' had never been represented in this country, we are

ready to believe that 'La Famille d'Anglade' would have excited
unmixed and universal sympathy; unfortunately, they produce
similar interests. although the latter confessedly claims priority.
Let not cavillers sneer at a casual introduction of foreign imagery
to our would-be classic boards.

"Be it remembered, that Attic salt seasoned the banquet at the
Roman schools; and although French sentiment may not irradiate
to the splendor of our native muse, we see no good reason why it
should not be permitted to dazzle, without prejudice to the greatness of our native drama."

The drama was so successful that it had a run of many consecutive nights during its first season, and for several seasons afterwards it was frequently repeated. Notwithstanding all Mr.
Payne's devotion to the interest of Drury Lane Theatre, an un-
looked-for and strange difficulty started up in his path. He had
warmly praised to the committee the manner in which his associate's share of an opera had been executed. Mr. Kinnaird echoed
the praise, and accepted the opera. The man's vanity was now
excited to supplant the master. It happened, unfortunately, that
the theatre was getting into embarrassment. No offer of indemnity
for the vast expense Mr. Payne had incurred had been tendered.
He sent a sketch of his outlay. An *éclaircissement* followed, which
hurried Mr. Payne forthwith to London again. The instant remuneration was asked, numerous works which had been eagerly
accepted were sent back. An opposition to Mr. Kinnaird in the
committee endeavored to shift entirely upon his shoulders the
engagement of Mr. Payne. Mr. Kinnaird, at the same time, as far
as possible to get rid of the consequences, and keep our countryman in check, encouraged the faithless agent we have mentioned,
who, wishing to get the employment into his own hand, had in-
veighed not only against his employer's talent, but his industry
and his demands. Even the pledge to produce him as an actor
was subtly shunned, by the specious offer of a line of characters
it was privately known he would not accept. The result was, a
loss of not only his time but of upwards of two thousand dollars
expended for the interest of Drury Lane Theatre. For all the
labor he had done he received about two hundred guineas sterling
(one thousand dollars). That amount having been the sum regularly accruing from the performances of "Accusation," could not
be avoided. Further compensation would have been awarded had
there been an appeal to the law; but Payne was too much dis-

gusted and annoyed at this tissue of sordid and paltry intrigues not to be glad that the affair should drop. Indeed, he felt himself too unfriended and alone even to dream of further struggling; and it so happened that another opening immediately arose which withdrew his attention from the ill treatment of old Drury and her myrmidons.

In the midst of this dilemma. Howard Payne had a visit from Mr. Harris of the Covent Garden Theatre; that gentleman expressed his regret at the conduct of the rival house, and offered him an engagement at Covent Garden, both literary and theatrical, and said that he would put it in so specific a form as to render disappointment impossible. For these services he offered three hundred guineas for the general attention of Mr. Payne to the benefit of the establishment during the season, and stipulated to bring him out as an actor, with further and independent compensation, and allowing him, also, to select his own plays and characters. This was satisfactory to Mr. Payne, and he was secured. For his literary aid there was a still further provision. He was to acquaint the management with all the novelties which might appear abroad. Should a free translation be required, he was to make it and receive fifty pounds, and should the management then have him make an adaptation of it, he was to obtain a further recompense to the full extent regularly paid to authors, viz., about the rate of one thousand dollars a play. This engagement, which could not have been dictated by any but a liberal spirit, was forthwith accepted, and it led to great intimacy between the manager and Mr. Payne. Unfortunately, however, they were known to be daily closeted upon the affairs of the theatre. The nature of the engagement was not understood, but Payne was suspected of having great influence and to be dangerous. *Favorites have no friends.* The first discontentedness was brought about by the interference of the hack writers about the establishment with a right implied in the literary clause of his contract. Versions of his were given to others to work up. Some of his pieces, thus obtained, became stock plays. A second source of disquietude originated in the postponement of his announcement to act. It chanced unluckily that Macready had been engaged just before him. To Payne was intrusted much of the machinery of this actor's success at the time. That being secured, the manager was reminded that the season was wearing away. Mr. Harris, at length. determined to keep his word. "Adelgitha" was the play fixed for his *début*. We have now before us the bills of Covent Garden, in which the play altered by our author is cast as follows:

Guiscard .	. .	Mr. Young.
Michael Ducas .	. .	Mr. Macready.
Adelgitha . . .	. .	Miss O'Neil.
Lothair . . .	. .	John Howard Payne.

This announcement was on the bills of the 20th, 22d, 23d, and 24th of February, 1817, and the bills of the 25th, 26th, 27th, and 28th; it is promised to be positively performed on the following Tuesday, but, on Saturday, March 1st, and Monday, 3d, it is changed again to the Saturday following, and then never mentioned more. How, it may be asked, did this happen? Those who are versed in green-room mysteries can perhaps answer. There are no leading men of any profession who like to be leading objects more than actors. It is a great fault in the profession everywhere. In Payne's case with "Adelgitha," every time the tragedy was announced for performance some one of the three leading actors named in the cast was suddenly taken sick. In the interim, Passion-week put in its appearance. On that occasion the London theatres were usually closed, but those elsewhere continued open. Payne was now invited to perform during the week at Bath, where he was received with great enthusiasm, and could have played another week with equally great success, but other engagements of stars in the theatre prevented him. On his return to London, unluckily, in springing from the coach he sprained his ankle, which laid him up for several weeks. Now that he was unable to appear, all the other actors announced that they were ready for "Adelgitha." Too plainly was advantage taken of his accident. Besides, the envious about the theatre, during Payne's confinement, embraced the opportunity to cool the manager against him, by persuading the withdrawal of "Adelgitha" on the sole ground of ridiculous superstition.

Mr. Harris then offered to bring out Mr. Payne in all of Mr. Charles Kemble's parts, with whom at the time Mr. Harris was at variance. But then to oppose an actor so well liked and upheld by the public, would have been an act of madness on the part of Payne; and he, therefore, in the most manly manner, refused to do anything of the sort. Angry communications followed, in which Mr. Harris upbraided Payne for complaining of his treat-

ment as an actor, when, as an author, he had received from the
theatre that season more than he had brought to it. Mr. Payne
protested against the unfairness of the charge, because he had
been bound down to act under the dictations of the manager.
"Shall Mr. Harris blame the instrument, because he did not know
how to work it, and would not be instructed?" Of this it was
not long before Payne convinced Mr. Harris.

At this time, Payne observed that the great Kean was somewhat languishing in public favor from more than one cause, and
that the Drury Lane required some new attraction to lift up its
then declining fortunes. The idea struck Payne that a new five-
act play, suiting the peculiar powers of Mr. Kean, would revive
the business of Drury Lane and the fortunes of the tragedian.
He had read several plays on the subject of "Brutus" in as many
languages, and concluded that it was just the subject. He at
once constructed his new tragedy, and concluding that it was in
good shape, although not finished to his perfect liking, he took it
to the chairman of the Drury Lane management, by whom it was
read, he in turn immediately sent for Mr. Kean, who at once took
hold of it with avidity, and said that he did not conceive it capable of improvement. It was decided to produce it. Mr. Payne
was sent for, but declined producing it without a little more pol-
ishing, which he did in a few days. It was accepted, and the
production of the tragedy was placed in his hands. He made all
the plans for the scenery and stage sets, overlooked the making
of the properties and costumes, and placed the piece upon the
stage with such historical accuracy as had very seldom been seen
upon the English stage. The tragedy was produced for the first
time on Thursday evening, December 3d, 1818. The play at once
met with the most marked success, and was performed to crowded
houses for twenty-three consecutive nights, and would have continued without abatement had it not been for other arrangements
of the management, and the holidays, stepping in for the purpose
of pantomime and such other performances as were imperative
with all theatres at such seasons. However, the holiday season
over, "Brutus" was reproduced on January 13th, and was that
season continued up to fifty-three nights. The cast of the play,
the costumes, and the scenery were spoken of by the press in the
highest terms. As we have in our possession an original play-
bill of the eighteenth night, we here insert a *fac-simile*, which is
worthy of preservation.

Last Night of the Company's performing till the Holidays

Eighteenth Night of the New Tragedy.

THEATRE ROYAL, DRURY-LANE.

This Evening, WEDNESDAY, December 23, 1818,

His Majesty's Servants will perform, (18th time) a New Historical Tragedy, entitled

B R U T U S;
Or, The Fall of Tarquin.

With new Scenery, Machinery, Dresses and Decorations.

The SCENERY by Mr. GREENWOOD, and Assistants.
The MACHINERY by Mr. LETHBRIDGE, and the DECORATIONS executed under his direction,
by Messrs. Murphy, Morris, and Assistants.
The DRESSES by Mr. BANKS and Miss SMITH.—— DECORATRICE, Miss ROBINSON.
The MUSICK, incidental to the Piece, by Mr. T. COOKE.

Lucius Junius,	Mr. K E A N,
Titus, Mr. D. FISHER,	Sextus Tarquin, Mr. H. KEMBLE,
Aruns, Mr. PENLEY,	Claudius, Mr. COVENEY,
Collatinus, Mr. BENGOUGH,	Valerius, Mr. HOLLAND,
Lucretius, Mr. POWELL,	Horatius, Mr. YARNOLD,
Tullia, Mrs. GLOVER,	Tarquinia, Mrs. W. WEST,
Lucretia, Mrs. ROBINSON,	Priestess of Rhea's Temple, Mrs. BRERETON.

In Act the First,

The Procession of Tarquinia to the Temple of Fortune.

In the course of the Tragedy, the following NEW SCENES, designed by Mr. GREENWOOD,
and painted by him and Assistants, will be exhibited.

A STREET IN ANCIENT ROME.

Roman Encampment before Ardea,

The TENT of SEXTUS, with distant View of the CAMP before ARDEA.

The Equestrian Statue of Tarquinius Superbus.

The Forum.

The Court Yard and Palace of Tarquinius Superbus.

RUINS IN ANCIENT ROME.

Temple of Rhea & Monumental Statue of Servius Tullius.

APARTMENT IN THE HOUSE OF BRUTUS.

VIEW in ROME taken from La Thierre's celebrated Picture of

The JUDGMENT of BRUTUS.

††† The *Romance of* BARMECIDE, *as it is performed, may be had in the Theatre: and of*
R. WHITE, 11 Brydges Street.

After which (10th time) a new Dramatick Romance, in 3 Acts, called

B A R M E C I D E .

Principal characters by

Mr. H. JOHNSTON,	Mr. H. KEMBLE,	Mr. WATKINSON.
Mr. COWELL,	Mr. BENGOUGH,	Mr. SMITH, Mr. COVENEY.
	Mrs. ORGER.	

In Act I. (Incidental to the Piece).

A PAS DEUX, by Miss VALANCY and Miss J. SCOTT;
And a PAS SEUL, by Miss TREE.

Vivat Rex !   *No Money to be returned.*   *Rodwell, Printer, Theatre Royal, Drury Lane.*

The New Historical Tragedy of

BRUTUS, or The Fall of Tarquin,

Having now attained the utmost height of popularity and universal approbation, producing on every
Evening of performance a vast overflow from all parts of the Theatre very shortly after the doors are
opened;—its representation being nightly accompanied by torrents of the most loud and rapturous
applause, and its announcement for repetition constantly hailed by the unanimous cheers and acclamations of the whole House, will be acted *this Evening;* after which its performance must be
suspended on account of Mr. KEAN's absence from London to fulfil a provincial engagement,
but on Mr. K.'s return, the representations of that unprecedentedly successful and popular Tragedy
will be immediately resumed.

R° NO ORDERS CAN POSSIBLY BE ADMITTED.

Mr. KEAN

Whose representation of *Lucius Junius,* in the New Tragedy, has been productive of the most powerful
effect on the feelings of delighted and admiring audiences, will repeat that character this Evening.

On *Saturday,* (December 26) Lillo's Tragedy of GEORGE BARNWELL.
George Barnwell, (1st time) Mr. H. KEMBLE, Trueman, Mr. HAMBLIN, (his first appearance)
Millwood, (first time) Mrs. W. WEST
With (never acted) A new COMICK PANTOMIME, called

HARLEQUIN and the DANDY CLUB

JOHN HOWARD PAYNE. 89

It was originally intended that Mr. Payne himself should perform the part of *Titus*, but this was opposed by Stephen Kemble at the time, on the ground of his thinking it indelicate for the author to appear in his own play. Kemble was the stage manager of the theatre, and Mr. Payne, in his good nature, gave way to Mr. Kemble's idea. This was a great mistake on the part of Mr. Payne, as the long run which the tragedy had would have been the means of introducing Mr. Payne more frequently to the public as an actor, and thereby giving him an opportunity to become a favorite as such with the public.

The tragedy of "Brutus" was a wonderful success; Kean made a great hit in the part of Brutus. The fortunes of the theatre and the actor were redeemed, the great theatre was packed every night, while Covent Garden was nightly performing to almost empty benches. Harris now fully discovered that he had not valued Payne as highly as he deserved, and regretted that he allowed himself to be prejudiced against him, and did not make better use of the materials he had placed in his hands. The tragedy was spoken of in very high terms by the press, with the exception of one or two papers, which, not able to find fault with the construction of the tragedy, etc., set up a plea that Mr. Payne had made a very large use of materials belonging to other dramatists. The person who started this assault upon the originality of the tragedy is the same elsewhere alluded to in former parts of this work. The first accusation was, that Mr. Payne had taken the most of his plot and language from a manuscript play by the then late Mr. Cumberland. But the "London Literary Journal," in which this ridiculous statement first appeared, on the week following the first production of the play, contradicts the whole matter by the following statement:

(*Literary Journal, Saturday, December 12th*, 1818, *page 602.*)

"The tragedy of 'Brutus' was repeated on Wednesday evening for the sixth time, before a crowded audience and with great applause. We have great pleasure in finding ourselves authorized to contradict the statement to which we referred last week, and in which the late Mr. Cumberland was represented to have been the real author of this play. 'Brutus' is undoubtedly the production of Mr. John Howard Payne. The construction of the subject differs thoroughly from any former treatment of the story, and the present production is exceedingly creditable to the poet."

The "European Magazine and London Review," one of the best critical authorities of the day, remarked thus: "The new tragedy of 'Brutus' attracts nightly such audiences as it so well merits. It is from the pen of Mr. John Howard Payne, a young gentleman of much actual merit and of great future promise. He has followed his story in the Roman history with a judicious softening of the more austere features of the monstrous act. The play opens at the camp of Ardea, near Rome, after the return of *Brutus* from Delphia, still wearing his idiot's guise. *Tullia*, the tyrant's wife, who drove her chariot over the dead body of her father, is disturbed by dreams and predictions. 'The fall of Tarquin shall be effected by a fool,' such was the prophecy that roused her fears, of which the object is *Lucius Junius Brutus*. She sends for him, but is quieted by his seeming imbecility. The memorable wager is now made at the camp, and *Collatinus* and the younger *Tarquin* set out instantly for Rome, to make trial of the excellence of their wives. They visit *Lucretia; Sextus Tarquinius* becomes enamored, returns the next night alone, and by the infamy of his crime provokes the genius of Roman liberty and justice. *Sextus* on his return meets *Brutus*, relates to him his infamous adventure. The latter throws off the mask, starts forth into his real character, and assails the wretch with indignant curses. *Brutus* swears upon the reeking dagger to revenge her, and give Rome freedom. The people join him; shut the gates against the tyrant, and tear down the palace. *Tullia* is condemned by *Brutus* to be imprisoned in *Rhea's Temple*, which contained her father's tomb. She is brought there, horror-struck, and dies, at the side of the monumental statue of her father, which in her frenzy she fancied was his spectre. The consular government is now formed, and the conspiracy of the young nobles of Rome is discovered. The son of *Brutus* (*Titus*) is among them. He had been won by his love for *Tarquinia*, the tyrant's daughter, who had saved his life. Now comes the trial of the soul of *Brutus*. The consulate condemn to death all of the young nobles, but *Titus*, whom, out of respect for the deliverer of Rome, they place in his hands for judgment. *Brutus* could not fail in the cause of justice, and is, therefore, forced by the example of the consulate to mete out the same punishment to his own son as had been given to others. He judges and condemns his own child to death, gives the signal for his execution, sees it done behind the scenes, loses the Roman in the father, when the axe gives the fatal blow, and falls into the arms of his brother-consul when the curtain falls.

" The unity of time, it will be observed. is wholly disregarded by the author of the play, but Shakspeare has done the same thing in all of his historical plays. Mr. Payne, however, has observed the simplicity of the action, and even the unity of place is not very palpably violated by the change of scene between *Rome* and *Ardea* and *Collatinus.* The author of the play has taken some advantage of Lee's play on this subject, and is somewhat indebted to Voltaire. The traces of Lee may be observed in the early scenes, which are made use of more in the light of suggestion than literally. There are several plays on this subject ; *but the structure of the tragedy before us* has not been taken from any of them. We should judge, on the contrary, that the author took the subject as he found it in Livy, one of the most eloquent, and decidedly the most dramatic, of historians, that he sketched out his play on his own views, and, in completing his work, has given us a successful tragedy on the subject of *Brutus,* which none of the other dramatists have done with the same subject. The character of *Brutus* was performed with great ability and effect by Mr. Kean. The transitions from seeming idiocy to intellectual and moral elevation were powerful, natural, and unexaggerated. There was, perhaps, some want of the antique classic grandeur which we associate with the elder *Brutus,* but, on the other hand, there were fine touches of energy and pathos. All the other characters were subordinate. *Titus,* the son of *Brutus,* and *Sextus* were respectably played by Mr. Fisher and Mr. H. Kemble. Mrs. Glover represented the remorse and frenzy of *Tullia* with great force, and Mrs. West produced some fine effects in *Tarquinia.''*

It might have been supposed that the overwhelming success of "Brutus" would have turned the tide of fortune in Mr. Payne's favor, for, as his career had been a baffled one, a little bit of sunshine here might have been looked for. but it was not his fate, and, however gratifying its numerous performances may have been to the author, still the fact of having been accused of appropriating the ideas of others without acknowledgment was like a wreath of thorns to his over-sensitive mind, which no measure of success could relieve of the sting. The tragedy of "Brutus" was placed before the public in printed form in ten days after its first

7

performance. In the preface, Mr. Payne says, "There are seven plays upon the subject of *Brutus*, which are before the public; only two have been thought capable of representation, and those two did not long hold possession of the stage. In the present play, I have had no hesitation in adopting the conceptions and, in some slight instances, the language of my predecessors, whenever they seemed likely to strengthen the plan I had prescribed. Such obligations, to be culpable, must be secret."

At last. however. all admitted that Mr. Payne had large claims on the public for having wrought and combined into a fine tragedy a Roman story over which all previous dramatists had failed in producing a successful result. "We maintain," says a London reviewer, "that old and new parts combined constitute a new whole. If new parts are added to an old machine and thereby cause it to produce new results, the whole machine is a new one."

The attack on the score of want of due acknowledgment soon died away. It was discovered to have originated with the person who had taken the place of Mr. Payne at Covent Garden, and the reason of its being so pertinaciously urged no longer ceased to be a wonder. It is said that Thomas Moore asked Washington Irving what all this bustle was about Payne and "Brutus."

"Why," replied Irving, "Payne has given credit for his play to six authors from whom he has taken hints; but, because he has included a seventh, from whom he has borrowed nothing, they have raised against him a hue and cry for plagiarism." A London paper answered the censors in an epigram: "That the ancients leagued with *Brutus* to turn out oppressors, but the moderns now turned out to oppress *Brutus*."

The attacks, however, were not made to be refuted. The object was, if possible, to destroy Mr. Payne's standing with the committee, one of whom testily told him that the Lord Chancellor would be applied to for an injunction to prevent the performance of "Brutus," which it was feared would be granted, and when he inquired into the origin of the impression, it was answered that the Right Hon. Sir William Scott (afterwards Lord Stowell) had complained to his brother, the Lord High Chancellor (Lord Eldon), that the play of "Brutus" was unconstitutional and ought to be suppressed; upon which the Chancellor, it was said, promised to read it and decide, and was expected to decide unfavorably, upon which Mr. Payne immediately wrote to that learned jurist, and

obtained the following candid and circumstantial reply in explanation :

" To John Howard Payne, Esq.

" Sir.—I have no right whatever to complain of the mode in
which you attempt to do yourself justice; and I shall be truly
sorry if I have unintentionally done you any injustice. It was
far from any purpose of mine, in a conversation to which you
allude, the whole of which I most unreservedly submit to you, as
far as I recollect it.

" Living upon terms of the most unguarded familiarity with
my brother, I certainly did mention to him incidentally what I
had heard in several companies, that the play of ' Brutus' did contain passages calculated to produce democratic impressions ; but
I added, that I had neither seen nor read the play, and therefore
could say nothing of it but what was conveyed to me in common
report. I was not at that time talking to the Chancellor in his
official capacity, or in the way of complaint, but to my brother,
in the idle style of private gossip, meaning neither to express
any opinion of my own, nor that what I said should go beyond
himself and some other person who happened to be in the room.
The subject was not started by me, nor pursued by me any further. I think my brother said he had heard similar reports of
strong passages in the play. The matter dropped there entirely,
and I am grieved that any such consequences as you describe
have resulted from it. It never could have occurred to my
thoughts that such a conversation so qualified could have produced them. If any such use has been made of it. it is a very
unjust one, and for which I cannot consider myself as at all
morally answerable, though I regret very much the having accidentally given the slightest and remotest occasion for it.

" I am, sir, your most obedient servant,

" (Signed)   Wm. Scott.

" Grafton Street, Jan. 22, 1819."

A copy of this letter was laid before the sub-committee, who
generally expressed their satisfaction at the course adopted, but
the particular member whose remonstrance had led to the appeal
spoke of it with much chagrin. It then came out that it was
with that member himself Sir William had conversed. By *him*
the subject had been started. So much for the intrigues even of

the wealthy and the wise when they get into a green-room. The committee, however, loved the author none the better for showing them that he had been wronged among them. The proof soon appeared. "Brutus" was bringing thousands to the treasury. Even Kean was gaining fifty pounds a week extra for performing in it. But the author had been lured into an improvident bargain. He had consented to be paid by benefits. But he consented upon an over-statement of the average of the season, and an extravagant estimate of charges. It chanced, too, that the weather and other drawbacks rendered the houses on his nights thinner than on any other. There were four: the first, December 5th, yielding a profit of £48 2s. 6d.; the second, December 9th, £14 11s. 6d.; the third, December 12th, £86 2s. 6d.; the fourth, January 15th, £34 9s. 6d.; in all £183 6d.: being twenty pounds less than the established recompense for a successful afterpiece. This was so utterly inadequate, that Payne was advised to apply to the committee for a reconsideration of the agreement. Whereon Mr. Payne sent the following communication:

"To the Committee in Management of the Theatre Royal, Drury Lane.

"Gentlemen,—It has been stated to me in knowing quarters, as coming from a member of your committee, that I had gained a *thousand pounds* by the tragedy of 'Brutus.' This is a very wide and injurious mistake, and I beg leave to state (which you must know as well as I do) that the full amount I have received is *one hundred and eighty-three pounds six shillings*. There was an agreement that I should have the surplus of four nights' benefits, as the amount to be paid for the tragedy. This agreement I acknowledge has been faithfully fulfilled. It was not my wish to have given the play on such terms. My own proposals in writing are in Mr. Kemble's hands. But I was led to understand that no other terms would be accepted.

"I am aware that all theatrical speculation is peculiarly uncertain; still, from the beginning, I indulged an expectation that, even if my benefits failed, I should not be suffered to lose. I was impelled to this belief by knowing that there is no recorded case of great success which has not met with a corresponding consideration from the theatre, whether previously agreed upon or not. Performers are always paid in some proportion to the increased profits arising to the house from their engagement, and authors

are rewarded for extraordinary attraction upon the same principle. Though four hundred guineas is the established sum for a
five-act play which runs twenty nights, yet it is an equally established custom to present any person who furnishes the theatre
with a play which produces great advantages an *additional* remuneration, which has varied, in different cases, from one to five hundred guineas. A farce is usually rated at two hundred guineas
for twenty nights. Hence it appears that 'Brutus,' which has
now reached its forty-first representation, has brought me twenty
pounds less than the regular recompense for a successful after-
piece.

"It is an object of some consequence to me to ascertain what
chances of emolument I may find, to fix my attention upon dramatic authorship. The present play has enjoyed a popularity as
great as can be wished for any like production, and allow me to
refer you to your own bills for your own impression of its attractions. The mind is unnerved for further great exertions when it
is not suffered to derive adequate advantages from present success.
If the greatest good fortune to the theatre confers no encouraging
reward on him who causes it, even hope itself is deprived of incentive. Payment by benefits is, at best, precarious. When the result to the one party proves of such high importance, something
further is naturally to be expected by the author.

"If I advert to the copyright of 'Brutus,' it can only be to say
that it did not bring me a sum by any means commensurate with
its acknowledged popularity. Mr. Kemble has undoubtedly apprised you. gentlemen. that the most indefatigable attention was
paid by me to the getting up of this tragedy. I spared neither
pains nor expense. I may safely say that it cost me, in various
ways, far beyond one-third of the sum received for it from the
theatre. In the arrangement of the costumes, the scenery, the
processions, all of the stage business, you will discover, upon inquiry from the directors of every department, that I was active
and unceasing in my exertions, these labors absorbed the whole
of my time while the tragedy was in preparation, and their effect
is obvious in the unqualified approbation with which they are
honored nightly. Even the construction of the play-bills, and
most of the preparatory paragraphs for the newspapers, were referred to my care. These circumstances will prove that I have
not been wanting in ardor to the cause.

"Having now fully submitted the case to your consideration. I beg leave to sum it up in a few words: *I have received from your treasury* ONE HUNDRED AND EIGHTY-THREE POUNDS SIX SHILLINGS for the tragedy of ' Brutus.' Permit me, gentlemen, to ask you if this sum, in your opinion, is a sufficient recompense for my exertions and the service which the tragedy of ' Brutus' has rendered your theatre.

" I have the honor with the highest respect to be

" Your very obedient servant,

" JOHN HOWARD PAYNE."

The committee admitted that the return was not liberal enough, and the manager was authorized to offer Mr. Payne another benefit, but the terms were fixed so high and the season so far gone, that Mr. Payne was forced to decline it, as the result would most assuredly bring him into debt. Mr. Payne understood the small practice of managers in putting up the expenses so high that it forbade the possibility of the beneficiary receiving one cent. The tricks of the green-room and the box-office had before given him a sad experience. Thus, instead of being bettered by his success as a dramatic author, he was made the victim of every sort of dirty animosity. The very management was stirred up against him by a report that he was intriguing for the pasteboard crown. Kean, whom he had so largely served, treated him with marked neglect, and, to the astonishment of all the performers, publicly presented Mr. Stephen Kemble, the stage manager, with a gold snuff-box, bearing the last scene of " Brutus" engraved upon its lid, but took no notice of the author, notwithstanding the author had previously presented Mr. Kean with the very toga he wore, and showed him how its folds should be adjusted to the true Roman style. Kean carried his coldness still further. He had induced Payne to prepare a play on the subject of " Virginius," which, when finished, and after much labor and loss of time, he cast aside. Meanwhile, the subject of his new tragedy got abroad among the members of the different theatres, and the first thing that Mr. Payne knew was, that the same subject had been worked into a five-act play by a particular friend of Mr. Kean's, which was accepted and handsomely paid for, but it had a run of only thirteen nights, and then was lost sight of forever. The subject of " Virginius" being a first-rate one, James Sheridan Knowles took hold of it and produced a fine play, which, although it did not have a long run at the time, still holds possession of the stage.

I take the greatest
Pleasure in bearing my strongest
testimony as to the competency
of my worthy friend R.J.H. Payne,
for the management of your
Theatre, if he should be so
fortunate as to obtain it.
His Dramatic Qualities
have been tested in the
Severest, and also in the

most successful manner in the production of his Tragedy of Brutus, which has had such ample, and almost unexampled success at Drury Lane Theatre.

If any thing which I can say in favour of Mr Payne can be useful to him, I shall be most happy

I have the honor to be Gentlemen, with the highest respect your most obedient

Edmund Kean

Feb 12th 1819

It is fortunate for the stage that Mr. Knowles was encouraged and treated with more kindness than Mr. Payne, for it has been the means of producing one of the greatest English dramatists.

The "Virginius" of Payne never appeared; parts of it, however, were quoted in the "London Magazine" and highly commended. No further transactions occurred between him and the Drury Lane Theatre that season, except the following, which is scarcely less singular than the rest that has gone before. A piece upon a French basis was sent to the committee and returned as "being admirable for its incident, but deficient in its dialogue." Payne took it back, rewrote the dialogue in the inflated style then current, and returned it to the committee, before whom it was read by the celebrated Mr. Oxberry. The decision now was, "That its dialogue was admirable, but it was deficient in incident." The French drama which had supplied the story for this twice-returned drama was almost immediately afterwards brought out both at Drury Lane and Covent Garden Theatres, and was successful. As he found that so much advantage was being derived to others by his hints and works, he began to think that the only way was for him to turn manager himself, and produce his own pieces upon his own stage. He saw the Birmingham theatre advertised to let, and at once made application for it. The proprietors caught at his proposals and desired him to call instantly, but circumstances which he could not control forced him to delay his visit for over a week, and, when he did call, he was informed that the house had been leased to the person who had so attacked his "Brutus." But, though circumvented, Mr. Payne did not give up his purpose. Ere long, "The oldest and most respectable minor theatre in London" was to let. The proprietors at once closed with Mr. Payne. The great Edmund Kean had so high an opinion of Payne's abilities to be a manager that he did not hesitate to give him the following recommendation contained in the *fac-simile* letter which we here present, for the double purpose of his opinion of Payne and to show the spirit and the dash of the great actor's pen. He entered upon a hazardous speculation, without fully knowing the ground upon which he ventured. Sadler's Wells Theatre had always been a summer play-house; regular acting was never thought of there, indeed, never permitted by law, but Mr. Payne thought a new interest could be given to it by changing its character, and, although the idea was a good one, still it required more money than Mr. Payne had to carry it through. It

turned out, too, to be a bad time, as there was a great excitement
concerning the queen of George IV. The play-goers remained at
home to avoid the mobs; this and death in the royal family subjected him to further loss, as the London theatres on such occasions are always closed for several days. He incurred still greater
disadvantages for disobliging the court-party by upholding her
majesty's cause in allusive plays. Even the proprietors of the
house became alarmed, and remonstrated with him for endan-
gering their license. The success of the house afterwards was all
the better for the boldness of Mr. Payne. The next season, the
queen rewarded the attention her interest had received by commending a certain play, but her highness did not know that the
management of the house had changed hands. By similar good
luck, the new management received from the royal treasury for
opening the house gratis on the coronation-night more than Payne
lost by closing it for the royal death. The new management,
by the seed Payne had sown the season before, reaped a fortune,
while our adventurous author was brought to great wretchedness
by his losses of over seven thousand dollars, and was besides
lodged in a debtor's jail. While here, in this wretched plight, and
pondering over his hard situation, one morning he received a
parcel sealed in black and inscribed "Octavius." He opened it, and
found it to contain two French pamphlets, the first of which was
a play that had been translated and acted on the opening of his
late theatre. He thought that the parcel was meant as an ill-
intended banter, and flung the pamphlets aside. But in an hour
or so afterwards, wanting something to interest his mind, he picked
one of them up again, and on reading a page or two, he became
interested and ran it through. He saw at once that it had material for a most admirable drama, and would just suit the wants of
Drury Lane, which had now been abandoned by the old "Brutus"
committee, and was under the direction of Mr. Elliston. In three
days the new play was finished and presented to Elliston, who
read it and immediately accepted it, and in ten days afterwards
it was acted upon Drury Lane stage, when the bills and the press
pronounced it the best and most successful melodrama that had
ever been produced at Drury Lane. The drama in question was
"Thérèse, the Orphan of Geneva." His success even here, however, was destined to be made a source of opposition. The managers of the minor theatres caused the piece to be taken down in
short-hand from the pit, and it was brought out at one of the

other houses, but was forced from the stage by an injunction from the Chancellor. Covent Garden also produced a rival version, and with great pomp of scenery and other effects, but was not successful, it being performed for only a few nights, while the people rushed to see Payne's drama at Drury Lane. Miss Kelly made a great hit in the part of *Thérèse*, while J. W. Wallack added fresh leaves to his dramatic laurel in the part of *Carwin*. Payne, while the piece was in rehearsal, managed by some influence to obtain leave to go from his temporary confinement to the theatre for the purpose of directing its production. He disguised himself as best he could, and by the assistance of a friend, a coach, and the by-streets, he not only produced the piece, but attended the theatre on the first night of its performance. We extract the following from Mr. Payne's own journal which lies before us, to show the difficulties under which he produced the drama :

" On Tuesday, January 16th, a parcel was brought to me without a letter or explanation. On it was written Havre, January 18th, and bearing a black seal inscribed ' Octavius.' The parcel contained two productions of M. Victor. ' Calas' and ' Thérèse.' The uncommon merit of ' Calas' the British public had already been made familiar with. I at once read ' Thérèse,' the new production of its ingenious author, and could not hesitate a moment in fitting it for the English stage. I went to work, and on Thursday night, January 18th, the adaptation was finished, on the Monday following it was placed in Mr. Elliston's hands, he accepted it on Friday, January 27th, and produced it on Thursday evening, 2d of February, 1821.

" I am indebted to M. Victor for the compliment which he paid me in so mysterious a manner. I beg to return my thanks for it, and at the same time ask his indulgence towards some alterations in the construction of the drama, especially so in the third act.

"Tuesday, February 1st. I could not attend rehearsal of ' Thérèse,' Purification Day no court sits, and a pass must be signed by the court every morning.

" Thursday, February 2d, a scampering rehearsal, and Miss Kelly wanted to be excused from attending on account of illness, but was persuaded by a note from me. Heaven help ' Thérèse !' everybody in a bad humor; Elliston——and the Pavilion scene not finished. In the third act, Miss Kelly got out of temper, and told the management that it was shameful in undertaking to produce a piece without giving time to the performers to learn the words in a drama; that, if proper time were given, fine effects could be produced; that it was trifling with the dramatists and the little reputation she had acquired, and that both were to be sacrificed to an unnecessary precipitation. We got through the rehearsal late in the afternoon. All the company parted with little or no hope for the success of the piece. Distracted myself, I was too sick and prostrated to leave the theatre, was invited to dine in Elliston's room, where I remained 'till 'twas time for the theatre to open; increased headache. At the performance, I got into the upper private box with Mrs. Edwin, Georgina, and Phillis. There was evidently an unfriendly feeling before the curtain drew up; the overture (one of Mozart's, which had been mistaken by the audience as something new) was hissed. The setting of the first scene was applauded, and the interest of the audience soon began to be excited. The applause was frequent, and increased at every step, 'till, when the act-drops fell, it became tumultuous, and was repeated in three or four rounds.

"There was a long pause before the next act began. The people got impatient; I ran down to the stage, alarmed for the consequences. To this act there was not so much applause as might have been, until the close.

"The third act, especially the scene between *Fontain* and *Thérèse*, was tremendously applauded. Miss Kelly's acting in that scene was one of the most impressive pieces of acting I have ever seen. The play went off to my utter astonishment. The third act was the triumph. I was congratulated by the performers, and the performers congratulated each other. The Hon. George Lamb came up, shook hands with me, and expressed his pleasure at the great success of the piece; he also congratulated Miss Kelly for her fine acting.

"Before the piece began, I stopped for a moment or two in the green-room. They all asked me how I felt. On my asking Wallack the time, he answered, 'Don't be afraid, Payne (laughing), I shall be dressed in time, and things will go well.' His ease of manner gave me some hope, for Wallack was always honest in his opinions, and would never give encouragement unless he had just cause.

"February 3d. Well, 'Thérèse' has succeeded triumphantly, and splendidly, and I am enjoying my triumph with a box of pills before me, a bowl of gruel, my feet in hot water, no fire, and a terrific headache. Yet I cannot help remarking the contrast in the manner of my reception by the actors and others upon the stage last evening to the dreadful coldness with which I was treated on the same stage when 'Brutus' was produced. Miss Kelly thanked me for the little stage-business I showed her, and Wallack thanked me heartily for naming him for the part of *Carwin.*"

This interesting drama of 'Thérèse' was, shortly after its production at Drury Lane, published, and its first edition of one thousand copies, the usual number for theatrical purposes at that time, was consumed, by the general public, in less than one month.

Mr. Payne, in his preface to his first edition, after complimenting the ladies and gentlemen of the company who first acted in the drama, says, "One word to my friends the critics, and I have done. They have honored me with more attention than I ever coveted, but I wish them to understand that this, like former publications of mine, is a work planned for stage-effects exclusively, and printed for managers and actors only. It is so necessary in the production of the modern drama to consult the peculiarities of leading performers, and not offend the restive spirit by means of situations almost pantomimic and too impatient to pause for poetical beauty, that it seems almost hopeless to look to the stage of the present day for a permanent literary distinction. An actable play seems to derive its value from what is done, more than from what is said, but the great power of a literary work consists in what is said, and the manner of saying it. He, therefore, who best knows the stage, can best tell why, in the present temper of the audience, good poets should so often make bad dramatists. Should my better stars ever give me leisure or independence to devote myself to literary work, which I may hope to render worthy of being recollected, I shall select something in which the imagination may be less fettered than it must be by the necessities of the stage. I am not, nor ever *have* been, so unprincipled as to claim what does not belong to me, and I have only to desire, as a point of common courtesy, that if my excellent good friends should ever do me the honor to censure, or to quote, any of the trifling remarks I have ventured to offer upon the present occasion, they will enhance the obligation by first reading them.

"J. H. P.

"LONDON, February 11th, 1821."

The clouds sometimes gather around us so thickly that we become hopeless as to their ever clearing away. Such was the case
with Mr. Payne at the crisis when the mysterious parcel was sent
to him by M. Victor. At no period in the whole of Mr. Payne's
life was he more seriously situated than immediately after his
management of Sadler's Wells Theatre, and when he wrote
"Thérèse." The sunshine came when least expected. It came,
too, in the hours of his deepest gloom, and he was lifted out of
his darkness. The profits of "Thérèse" soon brought him enough
to relieve his personal wants and to satisfy his creditors. His
affairs were quickly adjusted, and in less than one month after
the first production of "Thérèse," Mr. Payne was in a situation
to be asked by Elliston to return to France, and there watch for
the interests of Drury Lane Theatre. The new lessee assured
him that he would now find different persons to deal with from
those who managed the theatre when his tragedy of "Brutus"
was brought out. On these assurances he returned to Paris, and
watched for the announcements of all new plays. When a new
piece was mentioned, he at once sought and became acquainted
with the author, and frequently obtained the privilege of reading
the manuscript drama before it was produced upon the stage.
This done, he would immediately notify Elliston of the fact, and
send him a full description of the plot, scenery, dresses, etc., and
then anxiously await Elliston's answer, as to whether he should
go on with the translation and adaptation. To this effect, some
of Mr. Payne's letters are highly interesting, containing as they do
several pages showing in every sense his industry and devotion
to his employer. But Elliston was too slow ; he was not the man
to be associated with such a quick mind as Payne's. He had
neither discernment nor determination,—he hesitated too long,
and lost the golden opportunity of transplanting some of the
finest and most successful Parisian novelties. During all this
delay on the part of Elliston, Payne's expenses were going on.

Meanwhile, a person by the name of Burroughs, who had been
in this country, took the Surrey Theatre, a large minor house in
London, and immediately on securing it, he packed off to Paris
to obtain the services of Mr. Payne to supply him largely with
manuscripts ; but Burroughs was not a man of means, nor prompt
when he had them, nor decided in the production of the dramas
that Payne would send him, sometimes holding the new piece for
three or four months before he would produce it, while he was

losing his valuable time by reproducing old hackneyed pieces, that cost him quite as much for new scenery, dresses, etc.. as it would have done for Payne's novelties of the French stage. Payne did a great deal of hard work for both him and Elliston. But both concerns, through bad management, were hanging on the rugged verge of bankruptcy, while Payne received little or nothing for his hard work and large outlay.

The amount of correspondence that Payne did with Elliston, to induce him to produce certain pieces, is remarkable, and especially so on one piece, which he saw performed at the *Panorama Dramatique*, which struck Payne as just the thing for the Drury Lane stage and a London audience, but Elliston could not be convinced as to what was best. In this case, Payne invited Washington Irving and Thomas Moore, who were at that time in Paris, to go and see the performance. Irving could not attend, but Moore and others did. all of whom were delighted with the play, and predicted for it a great run, if placed upon the Drury Lane stage. Mr. Irving sent the following letter on the subject to Payne, and Payne in turn sent it to Elliston. hoping that it would induce the tardy manager to a speedy conclusion:

" PARIS, May 1st, 1821.

" R. W. ELLISTON, Esq.,—Mr. Irving has this moment sent me a note on the subject of the play which I so much desire you shall produce upon the Drury Lane stage. I hope his letter, which I here transcribe, will induce you to say 'Go on with the work.' I have every faith in the success of the piece if properly done.
" J. H. P."

" DEAR PAYNE,—I did not get to the *Panorama Dramatique* on Saturday evening, as I expected, but I have seen Mr. Moore and others of the party, who express themselves highly pleased. Moore seems to have been quite struck with the piece. He thinks the story very interesting and affecting, and the getting up of the piece quite ingenious and picturesque. He thinks that it would appear to even greater advantage on the large stage of the Drury Lane Theatre, where the machinery, decoration, and properties are superior. He was very much delighted with the last scene (the apotheosis), though it seemed to have shocked one of the ladies a little. That scene, it appears to me, will be a critical one : it may mar the piece, or it may give it an extraordinary

attraction. Moore says the scene was rather defective. ' It seemed
to be beyond the scope of their art; excepting the representation
of the atmosphere.' I presume the whole scene could be managed
better upon the London stage, and from the good report of Moore
and others, I would advise you to do the work, whether Elliston
desires it or not. Perhaps some other theatre, at some future
time, may take a fancy to it.

" Yours very truly,
" WASHINGTON IRVING.

" RUE MONT THABOR, No. 4, April 30th, 1821."

The communication did no good. Elliston still hung fire, and
likely lost a great success. The capricious notions of Elliston,
the delay of Burroughs in producing what Payne had sent him,
and the receiving of little or no money from either of them,
now placed our dramatist in an unpleasant position. We feel it
of sufficient value to relate here an interesting anecdote which
transpired between Payne and Elliston. It was shortly after
Payne's arrival in England, and during Elliston's last season at
Birmingham, that he met John Howard Payne, the American
Roscius, as he was then called, and with whom he had some intimacy. Elliston, at this time greatly pressed by a variety of un-
dertakings, was advertised to play the part of *Richard III.* on a
certain ensuing evening, and was on his way to the rehearsal
when he encountered his friend Payne.

" My dear Payne," said Elliston, " I well know your readiness
in conferring favors, and in the present instance you can oblige
me much. I am on my way to the theatre. We have a rehearsal,
—' Richard III.' A rehearsal must be had for the sake of the
company, who are a little wild in the play. You know not, my
dear fellow, the whirl I am in at this present moment. Country
theatres in a state of insurrection, and no solid loyalty at home.
Oblige me,—run to the theatre,—go through the rehearsal with
my people,—you know the business,—put them to their work, and
relieve me from this morning's annoyance."

" Why, 'tis so long since I played the part," replied Payne,
" that really——"

" No man living could have presented himself more capable of
serving me than you,—only put 'em right for Wednesday night,—
show them how they flog us at New York," added he, with one
of his slyest twinkles.

After a little further expostulation on the one hand, and amicable contention on the other, Howard Payne consented. On entering the stage, Elliston introduced his friend to the principals in attendance, and bidding the prompter immediately call the rehearsal, once again whispered "New York!" into Howard's ear, and vanished.

The manager now took the opportunity of gliding into an obscure corner. He noticed all that was in progress on the stage. Having witnessed the very able manner in which his friend was conducting the rehearsal in one or two scenes, he left the house with extreme precipitation, and, making the best of his way to his printers, set the compositors at work in striking off two or three hundred bills, of an extraordinary size, announcing, "The arrival of the celebrated American Roscius, Mr. Howard Payne, who would have the honor of appearing, on Wednesday evening next, in the part of *Richard III.*"

The bills were printed and nearly posted, in various parts of the town, before the termination of said rehearsal. When, at three o'clock, the actors were returning from their morning task, and with them, of course, Howard Payne himself, their eyes were saluted at the corner of almost every street with the "American Roscius for Wednesday evening!" Payne was thunder-struck and became furious; refusing, of course, to play a part into which he had been so thoroughly entrapped, and went in search of the manager. Arriving at Elliston's lodgings, he there learnt that unexpected business had called the manager suddenly away to Leicester.

Poor Payne now retraced his way to the theatre, where at every step "The American Roscius" in *Niagara* type assailed his gaze. The actors here gathered about him, for, should Payne still refuse to act, the theatre on Wednesday night would be closed. Payne, who had but lately arrived in England, knew that he had the public to conciliate; and it was now forcibly represented to him that, should he fail to perform, the Birmingham people would naturally enough suspect Payne of some breach of contract with Elliston, and thus look coldly on him for the future. The whole company with one common effort entreated him to play. Their prayers and other considerations finally prevailed. Payne consented; Wednesday arrived. "The American Roscius" was flattered by crowded boxes and pit, the actor was highly applauded, the receipts great, and Elliston, true to the Wednesday, returned to Birmingham before the first act was over, when all grievances were forgotten in the triumphant result of "Richard III." But, better than this for Payne, at the end of the play, Payne was loudly called before the curtain, and a repeat demanded by the whole house, which Elliston had to assent to; Payne, consenting, performed three nights, and received ten pounds per night.

But to return to Payne at Paris. After Elliston and Burroughs had placed our dramatist in an unpleasant position by their delays, he did not have to wait long before he received the news that a change had taken place in the management at Covent Garden Theatre. Mr. Charles Kemble now succeeded Mr. Harris. This gentleman had scarcely assumed the management before he sent to secure the services of Payne. His means being exhausted, no time was to be lost, and he at once put together a batch of manuscript plays, sent them to Kemble, setting the price of two hundred and fifty pounds upon the whole. Among this collection of plays was one which afterwards appeared under the name of "Clari." This drama had long previously been sent to Burroughs under a different name, but he, failing to see its merits, did not produce it. Payne got it back from Burroughs through the instrumentality of his old friend Sir Henry Bishop, the composer, who had hitherto arranged all the music for Mr. Payne's pieces. Payne, in his communication to Mr. Kemble, stated that it would make a good opera, and if he would accept it at once for the sum of fifty pounds, he would make the necessary alterations and get Bishop to arrange the music for it. Kemble instantly accepted the proposal, and sent Payne fifty pounds on account of the two hundred and fifty pounds for the batch of plays, of which the drama of "Angioletta," now changed to the name of "Clari," was one. At this very juncture, however, Burroughs, hearing of what Payne intended to do, produced "Angioletta" at the Surrey, without the least intimation to Mr. Payne, but withdrew it on the third night at the requisition of the author.

Mr. Payne changed the plot somewhat, and introduced several songs and duets, after which it was immediately brought out as an opera at Covent Garden with prodigious success. Miss M. Tree (the sister of Miss Ellen Tree, afterwards Mrs. Charles Kean) performed the part of *Clari* to crowded houses for the larger part of the season. It is said that her exquisite performance and singing of the part won for her a husband, the wealthy Mr. Bradshaw. It is in this opera that Mr. Payne introduced his immortal song of "Home, Sweet Home!" This song has had a more universal circulation than any other song written before or since. It is a fact that upwards of one hundred thousand copies were issued by its publisher in London in less than one year after its first publication. The profit yielded over two thousand guineas. It at once became so popular that it was heard everywhere. Whether in the streets or the concert or the theatre, it was always welcome to the ear. It has been heard in the cottage and the palace, it has been sung constantly by the humblest peasantry, and sanctified by the sweet warblings of a Pasta and a Malibran. "It has been quoted in sermons, and sung, with slight alterations, in places of divine worship. It is a favorite song of the exile, and is not unfamiliar in the desert wilds of Africa." This one effort has so much of the "touch of nature" in it, that the whole world becomes akin in acknowledgments and love for its author.

Still, with all the success of the opera, and the publication of the song, Mr. Payne was the least benefited of all concerned. The publisher of the song did not even place Mr. Payne's name on the title-page as the author of the words. or compliment him with a presentation-copy of the music.

Of late years, there has been some doubt expressed as to who was the composer of the music of "Home, Sweet Home!" But the title-page of the original and earlier edition of the sheet-music expresses the matter so clearly, that further cavil on the subject is in every sense unnecessary, and, as we have now before us one of the editions published while the opera of "Clari" was performing, we copy the title-page below :

(Fourth Edition.)

HOME! SWEET HOME!

SUNG BY

MISS M. TREE,

IN

CLARI

THE MAID OF MILAN,

COMPOSED AND PARTLY FOUNDED ON A SICILIAN AIR [1]

BY

HENRY R. BISHOP.

Composer and director of the music to the Theatre Royal, Covent Garden.

London, published by Goulding, D'Almaine, Potter & Co., 20 Soho square, and to be had at 7 Westmoreland St., Dublin.

[1] The Air alluded to is from Mr. Bishop's collection of "Melodies of Various Nations."

8

On the fourth page of the same publication is the original Sicilian melody from which Bishop arranged the music of "Home, Sweet Home!" This fourth page, also, has a title, as follows:

"'MID PLEASURES AND PALACES!"

The additional stanza, sung by

MISS BEAUMONT IN THE EPISODE."

The additional stanza is identical with the first verse of the song, commencing with the words of " 'Mid pleasures and palaces," with a more frequent repetition of " There's no place like home." The change in the melody from the original Sicilian air is but slight, and the writer regrets that he has been unable to discover the name of the composer of the original Sicilian air. Donizetti wanted an English air for the last scene in his opera of " Anna Bolena," and selected for this purpose " Home, Sweet Home!" thereby unknowingly returning the air to its native language.

We have elsewhere stated that the publisher of the music of " Home, Sweet Home!" did not, on the title-page, credit the words to Mr. Payne; this is accounted for in the fact that Goulding & Co., the publishers, very seldom in those days placed the name of the poet on the title-page.

Mr. Payne, on one occasion in 1835, while at New Orleans, when questioned on the subject of the music of the song of " Home, Sweet Home!" told his personal friend Mr. James Rees, of Philadelphia, that the air was not wholly original with Mr. Bishop, and related the following pleasant anecdote concerning it. He said, " I first heard the air in Italy. One beautiful morning, as I was strolling alone amid some delightful scenery, my attention was arrested by the sweet voice of a peasant-girl who was carrying a basket, laden with flowers and vegetables. This plaintive air she trilled out with so much sweetness and simplicity, that the melody at once caught my fancy. I accosted her, and after a few moments' conversation, I asked for the name of the song, which she could not give me, but having a slight knowledge of music myself, barely enough for the purpose, I requested her to repeat the air, which she did while I dotted down the notes as best I could. It was this air that suggested the words of ' Home, Sweet Home!' both of which I sent to Bishop at the time I was preparing the opera of ' Clari' for Mr. Kemble. Bishop happened to know the air perfectly well, and adapted the music to the words." This statement is fully sustained in the following letters of Mr. Payne to Mr. Bishop, which we here introduce for the sake of historical accuracy, and also to prove that the words of the song were written in Paris, and not in London, as has been frequently stated. The opera of "Clari" was first produced May 8th, 1823, at the Covent Garden Theatre.

"PARIS, February 12th, 1823.

" HENRY R. BISHOP.

" MY DEAR FRIEND,—I sent off 'Clari' by the diligence on Sunday morning. You will find I have done what I could to improve it by your suggestions. The hint about the melody I sent you is so vague that I can only give you something approaching the measure of the 'Ranz des Vaches' without much reference to the air, which, of course, you desire to make as near original as you can. Besides the duets, I have given the *Prince* three songs, and do not see where more music can be introduced without overloading the piece. In the songs, I have endeavored to give as much variety as possible. There was not time to have polished them as I wished. 'Home, Sweet Home!' as a refrain will come in nicely. I think that in the duet between *Rose* and *Nimpedo* it would be well to introduce some playful business, which the little laugh I have inserted evidently requires. I have written very largely about the business of the piece, and the acting of *Clari*, and hope Miss Tree will not deem it impertinent.

" I am indebted to you for the prompt interest you have taken in my affairs with Mr. Kemble, and desire that you will express to him my thanks for the thirty pounds I received yesterday, making, in all, eighty pounds of the two hundred and fifty for the three dramas.

" Your ever obedient friend,

" JOHN HOWARD PAYNE."

There have been many ridiculous statements made as to the circumstances under which Mr. Payne wrote the words of his celebrated song. Some have stated that he was residing in London at the time, without a shilling in his pocket; others have stated that, " on one stormy night, beneath the dim flickering of a London street-lamp, gaunt and hungry, and without a place to shelter his poor shivering body, he wrote his inspired song upon a piece of ragged paper, picked from the sidewalk." This was not so. The letter of Mr. Payne above quoted proves directly the contrary. We see, by his acknowledgment to Bishop of the receipt of eighty pounds, that he was comfortably situated when preparing " Clari" for the stage. We admit that Mr. Payne never, at any period of his eventful life, accumulated any considerable amount of wealth, but those who knew the state of his circumstances knew that he never was a street-pauper. In a still later communication to Bishop is another acknowledgment for fifty pounds on the sum of two hundred and fifty which he was to receive for the three dramas, entitled " Ali Pacha," " The Two Galley-Slaves." and " Clari," all of which were produced at the Covent Garden Theatre, under the management of Mr. Charles Kemble.

Mr. Payne has never been "let alone"; almost everything he ever did has been doubted, and it is somewhat surprising that his consulship at Tunis has not been denied him, but what of that? fools have been found who doubted that Shakspeare wrote his own plays, and that Poe was not the author of the " Raven," and, with all their mooting of the question, they never could find any one else who did perform the works. As at one time it was stated that Mr. Payne did not write the words of " Home, Sweet Home!" the assertion called forth inquiry. Washington Irving was applied to on the subject, and his reply was, that he " had been unable to discover who else did, and he could see no reason for doubting the authorship."

Pierre M. Irving, in his excellent biography of his uncle, Washington Irving, often alludes to his uncle's acquaintance with Mr. Payne while the two were in Europe. He states on page 3, vol. ii., that Mr. Irving was employed by Payne to assist him in a slight literary job of altering a French play entitled " Richelieu." Mr. Irving made the venture with Payne while waiting for other matters to turn up. The play was produced in London, and, as a literary effort, it was successful, but was forced from the stage on account of some political expressions which the play contained. He states that at this time Payne had fitted up a cottage at Versailles in very handsome style, which he had occupied, but was now living, as Mr. Irving found, at Paris, " in a sky-parlor at the ' Palais Royal.' " This was in 1823, when Payne produced " Clari," and is another proof that Mr. Payne was not starving in the street when he wrote the song of " Home, Sweet Home!" Washington

Irving in one of his letters at this time mentions that Mr. Payne had made handsomely by the success of some of his pieces.

Nowhere has Mr. Pierre M. Irving mentioned in his life of Washington Irving that his uncle had anything to do with the writing of the song of " Home, Sweet Home!" as has been hinted by some few, who begrudge Mr. Payne the due credit for his own work. It is more than likely that had Mr. Irving written the song of " Home, Sweet Home!" he would have left some evidence of the important fact in his correspondence, which Mr. Pierre M. Irving would have been only too happy to have made known in his biography of his famous uncle. There are some people who would at any time rather steal the laurel from off the brow than add a single leaf thereto. The several attempts that have been made to deprive Mr. Payne of the authorship of "Home, Sweet Home!" have in every case proved fruitless,—proved fruitless for the reason that they have excited others to make the deepest research on the subject, as it has the author of this work, who has looked everywhere for some one other than Payne as the author of the song, and have so far completely failed.

Several have hinted that Thomas Haynes Bayly was the author of " Home, Sweet Home!" This could not have been, for the reason that Bayly did not begin to write for the public until 1833, while Payne's song of "Home, Sweet Home!" was written and known all over the world ten years previously. Bayly wrote a song entitled " My Home is the World," a beautiful poem in itself, but there is not one line in it suggesting Payne's "Home, Sweet Home!"

The Hon. W. B. Maclay, of New York. an old and personal friend of Mr. Payne, took a great interest in this question, and addressed a letter on the subject to Mr. Amos Perry, consul at Tunis, who knew something about Payne, and who, at the time Mr. Maclay wrote to him, was on a visit to the city of London, where he could thoroughly investigate the subject; he did so, and could not find the slightest cause for attributing the authorship to any other than Payne. On the receipt of Mr. Maclay's letter, Mr. Perry called on Mr. Miller, the publisher, who knew Mr. Payne perfectly well, and who purchased the copyright of the opera of " Clari," and published its several first editions. Anxious to learn what Mr. Maclay could say on the subject, we sent a letter asking for the information in his possession, to which inquiry he sent the following interesting reply :

"New York, Oct. 2d, 1873.

"Gabriel Harrison, Esq.

"Dear Sir.— . . . I was first introduced to Mr. Payne in Washington, many years before his death. His name having been familiar to me from boyhood as the author of 'Home, Sweet Home!' awakened my particular attention toward him, and led me to observe him closely. In stature he was below the ordinary size. He was quite bald. His complexion was florid. His eyes blue and large, and full of expression. There was something extremely winning in his manner, an air of refinement, more easily recognized than described. He always possessed an ease of manner, a collectedness, a certain quality of propriety of bearing, hitting the just medium between reserve and familiarity, apparently spontaneous, but in reality the fruit of culture, and a varied intercourse with many of the finest minds of his time both in Europe and America. Payne afforded the social circle in which I often met him no little amusement by the stories of his experience as an actor in England, and the rich collection of anecdotes he had stored away in memory's safe-keeping. . . . In answer to the doubts that have sometimes been expressed, whether he was the author of the popular song of 'Home, Sweet Home!' attributed to him, I send you an extract from Mr. Perry's letter on the subject.

"'London, Sept. 19th, 1865.

"'My dear Mr. Maclay,— . . . Mr. Miller has done me the kindness to show me the first printed edition of the opera of "Clari," with the song of "Home, Sweet Home!" interwoven with the play. In reply to my remark that the authorship had been called in question, Mr. Miller stated that he entertained not the slightest grounds for doubt; that Payne was introduced to him by Washington Irving, and knew Mr. Payne intimately well; that he purchased the copyright of the opera, and that Payne read the proof-sheets at the time of its publication. . . .

"'Very truly yours,

"'Amos Perry.'"

As will be seen by the reader, we shall introduce no less than *three* different arrangements of the words of "Home, Sweet Home!" which are copied from Mr. Payne's own manuscript journal in possession of the writer at this present moment. His first arrangement of the words will be found among the poems of "his later days," and identified by the words "as originally written." It was this version that Mr. Payne altered to suit the music of the natural Sicilian air. The third "Home, Sweet Home!" with the two additional verses he wrote for Mrs. Joshua Bates, of London, England, are still somewhere extant in the music-sheet which Mr. Payne presented to Mrs. Bates, who was a distant relative of his, and whose fortunes, while abroad in Europe, were widely different from Mr. Payne's, which fact is the burden of his poetic strain, and is as beautifully expressed as the accepted words which are set to the music of the song. We deem it unnecessary to say anything further as to the true authorship of "Home, Sweet Home!"

PAYNE AS A DRAMATIC WRITER.

Mr. Payne, in all of his dramatic writings, shows a superior knowledge of the human passions. He knew how to color and present them to his audience without the wild bombast of words so frequently used in dramatic productions. His situations, his entrances, and exits, are always admirable, and at the same time perfectly natural. His characters never lose much time by reviewing the past, or talking about what is to happen in the future of the play. The action is there and then. The passions are immediately presented to intensify the situation, which affords the actor a full opportunity to express his dramatic power, and thereby to grasp the sympathy and attention of his audience.

The pathos of his characters comes from the heart, and the reader or listener is often excited to tears. The scene in "Clari," between *Rolamo, Clari,* and the mother, is truly fine. The same thing may be said of the scene in "Thérèse," where she relates the story of her persecution to *Fontain.*

In the language of his more classic and heroic characters, such as *Brutus, Virginius, Romulus, Richelieu,* and the *Italian Bride,* there is a dignified simplicity that is seldom met with in pieces of like character. The *dramatis personæ* are cut off from strut and bluster. They are forced down to the facts of nature, and look and speak and walk like human beings. There is perhaps nothing in the whole range of the English classic drama that is superior for intensity to the situation between *Brutus* and his son *Titus,* where the father, through the crushing force of circumstances, is compelled to condemn his own son to death, and particularly the words of *Brutus* in his reply to the reproach of *Titus*. The language seems singularly appropriate—listen !—

" *Ti.* The axe !—Oh heaven !—Then must I fall so basely ?
What! shall I perish like a common felon ?
    Br. How else do traitors suffer ?—Nay, Titus, more—
I must myself ascend yon sad tribunal—
And there behold thee meet this shame of death—
With all thy hopes and all thy youth upon thee.—
See thy head taken by the common axe—
All—if the gods can hold me to my purpose—
Without one groan, without one pitying tear.
                   [*Turns up the stage, as if in agony.*
    Ti. Die like a felon ?—Ha! a common felon !—
But I deserve it all :—yet here I fail :—
This ignominy quite unmans me !
Oh, Brutus, Brutus ! Must I call you father,   [*Kneels.*
Yet have no token of your tenderness,
No sign of mercy ? Not even leave to fall,
As noble Romans fall, by my own sword ?
Father, why should you make my heart suspect
That all your late compassion was dissembled ?
How can I think that you did ever love me ?
    Br. Think that I love thee by my present passion,
By these unmanly tears, these earthquakes here,
These sighs that strain the very strings of life—
Let these convince you that no other cause
Could force a father thus to wrong his nature.
    Ti. Oh, hold, thou violated majesty :   [*Rises.*
I now submit with calmness to my fate.
Come forth, ye executioners of justice—
Come, take my life—and give it to my country !
    Br. Embrace thy wretched father. May the gods
Arm thee with patience in this awful hour.
The sov'reign magistrate of injur'd Rome
Condemns a crime
Thy father's bleeding heart forgives.
Go—meet thy death with a more manly courage
Than grief now suffers me to show in parting ;
And, while she punishes, let Rome admire thee !
Farewell ! Eternally farewell !"

However great, Kean may have been in the part of *Brutus*, and however much " his great acting may have helped the success of the tragedy," still it was these masterly touches of Payne that gave the actor the opportunity to express himself, and it was by these natural and deeply pathetic touches that the story of the *Stoic* was made acceptable to an audience. This was accomplished by Mr. Payne in so high a degree that the audience, like *Titus*, offered no further opposition to the dreadful act of a father condemning his own child to death, but left the theatre with all their sympathy for the father, and with but little compassion for the son.

The tragedy of "Brutus" has stood the test of fifty years, and has been performed by all of the greatest actors that have adorned the stage since it was written. We can never forget the wonderful and perfect picture Edwin Forrest made of the part, and especially so with the whole of the last act. His personification of the fool in the early part of the tragedy was, perhaps, a little heavy. The peculiar physical character of the great tragedian did not seem to suit the portraiture of a fool. But, where he threw off the disguise of the fool and revealed himself as the sane man, the picture was perfect. In the second scene of the play, (before the camp of Ardea) after the exeunt of *Claudius* and *Aruns*, the look that followed them and the stress of contempt Forrest placed upon the words of

> " Yet; 'tis not that which ruffles me, the gibes
> And scornful mockeries of ill-govern'd youth—
> Or flouts of dastard sycophants and jesters,
> *Reptiles who lay their bellies on the dust,*
> *Before the frown of majesty!* All this
> I but expect, nor grudge to bear ;—the face
> I carry, courts it!"

was masterly in the extreme, and then the change that followed immediately after in the towering up of his manly figure, seeming in an instant to grow to an additional height of several inches when he exclaimed,—

> "Son of Marcus Junius!
> When will the tedious gods permit thy soul
> To walk abroad in her own majesty,
> And throw this vizor of thy madness from thee?
> To avenge my father's and my brother's murder!
> . . . Grant but the moment, gods! If I am wanting,
> May I drag out this idiot-feigned life
> To late old age, and may posterity
> Ne'er hear of Junius but as Tarquin's fool!"

His majesty and his fervency here, and the perfect tones of his voice, presented a piece of declamation which left an impression upon the mind like to that from looking upon a mighty figure by Angelo. And then again, in Act III., Scene 1, where the statue of *Tarquinius Superbus* is struck by lightning, and he launches his curse on *Sextus*, after disclosing his atrocious act with *Lucretia*. The intense listening of *Brutus*, the inward struggle pictured upon the actor's face to keep down the passion within him till *Sextus* revealed the result, the blood almost bursting from every pore in his face, and the swollen veins about his neck and temples, in his interrogation of—

> " And—and—the matron ?"—
>
> *Sextus.* " Was mine !"

And then the frenzy that followed in the speech of—

> " The furies curse you then !—Lash you with snakes !
> When forth you walk, may the red flaming sun
> Strike you with livid plagues !
> Vipers that die but slowly, gnaw your heart !
> May earth be to you but one wilderness !
> May mankind shun you—may you hate yourself—
> For death pray hourly, yet be in tortures,
> Millions of years expiring !"

At the end of this speech amazement seemed to sit upon every face in the house, electrical chills crept over all, and so affected the audience that they deemed their applause could not express their admiration for the actor, and gave their expression of approval by turning to each other and exclaiming, " Wonderful !" But, however great Mr. Forrest was in his passionate scenes, he was equally fine in pathos. As an elocutionist, we doubt that he has ever had his equal. Nature had lavished on him every requisite for an actor. She had endowed him with a voice remarkable for sweetness and sonorousness, and a mouth so perfectly formed for speech that articulation with him was as perfect as it would be if expressed by the finest intonations of the violin. His whisper was remarkable. It mattered not how large or how crowded the house might be, it could be heard in every part. The sobbing and choking sounds he produced in sorrowful passages were irresistible in their sympathetic effect, and this was especially so in his last act of *Brutus*, when, with an apparent heart-breaking, he sentences his son *Titus* to death.

"Think that I love thee by my present passion,
By these unmanly tears, these earthquakes here,
These sighs, that strain the very strings of life,—
Let these convince you that no other cause
Could force a father thus to wrong his nature."

At the close of these words the whole audience could be seen wiping the trickling tears from their faces, sobbing was audibly heard coming from several parts of the house, and finally, when he ascends the steps of the tribunal, after the lictors have conducted *Titus* off the stage, and it becomes his sad duty to wave his hand as the signal for his son's head to fall from the executioner's block, the pallor that came over his face, the struggle to lift his arm, and then, when the trumpet's sound proclaims it done, the wrapping up of his head in his toga, as it were to shut out the horrid sound, the sudden relaxing of his whole figure and its heavy fall upon the stage, made the acme of dramatic effect, and one we have no hopes of ever seeing equalled again.

Mr. Payne seemed always to select for his dramas subjects which the mind of sensibility delighted to contemplate. In "Clari," for instance, the subject is *Home*, where the earliest delights of childhood and the attachment of manhood cling with an increasing fondness. The educated and the uneducated are captured by the memories of "Sweet Home." The rough sailor, amid the storm and in the calm alike, turns his thoughts homeward. The soldier, when at night he throws himself upon the tented field, enwreathes his thoughts of home with a long sigh, and, after his eyelids have shut out the starry canopy that hangs over his earthly couch, the spirit of dreams paints her vivid pictures of home "however so humble," and he awakes with the exclamation, "There's no place like home!"

In the first edition of "Clari" the editor thus described the plot of the opera, and as it is not our intention to include the piece in this work, and it is more than likely that all of Mr. Payne's plays will never be collected and published in a compact form, we presume that the plot of this beautiful drama will be acceptable to the reader:

"The opera of 'Clari' at first sight exhibits *Clari*, the daughter of an Italian farmer, in rather a questionable state. She is enamored of the *Duke Varaldi*, who comes by chance to the cottage of her parents. His grace tells her the usual tale of flatterers, promises marriage, and hints at an elopement; a fainting fit comes to his aid; she sees nothing but the smoke curling over the trees, not even the post-horses, that are ready to gallop off with her to the casino! Her village dress is now exchanged for court finery; she is magnificently boarded and lodged, and subjected to just as much of her lover's company as is agreeable to her. In addition to this state of fear and hope, of uncertainty and apprehension, the thought of the home she had left, the parents she had deserted, crosses her mind, and, like Ali Beg, the Persian shepherd, she surveys her rustic garb, 'the sad memorials of her happier state,' with the fond enthusiasm of one who had discovered how much she had lost by the exchange.

"The piece opens with *Clari's* birthday, and preparations for rejoicing. Paris has been laid under contribution to ornament her person, while a troop of itinerant actors are engaged to perform a play for her special entertainment, of which *Jocoso*, the *Duke's* valet, is appointed manager. The plot of the piece exactly tallies with the story of *Clari*. Her agitation increases as the scene proceeds,—when a father, being about to call down the vengeance of heaven upon his undutiful child, she starts from her seat. interposes between the actors, and implores the parent to suspend his curse! The *Duke*, enraged at this public exposure of his villany, throws off the mask ; and, to the remonstrances of *Clari*, who reminds him of his oath, returns answers no longer equivocal. She now awakes to the full sense of her delusion and danger, and, having dispelled the one, secretly resolves to fly the other. Her female sentinel, *Vespina*, who is engaged in a love-affair with *Jocoso*, chancing to slumber at her post, affords the desired opportunity. She ties her scarf to the balcony, offers a prayer to heaven, and, by way of climax, blows out the candles! Her descent, the moonlight scene, the alternate darkness and light, are very skilfully and beautifully managed. *Clari* reaches her native village in safety ; it is on the eve of a wedding between *Vinetta*, the companion of her youth, and a chosen swain, *Nimpedo*. She appears before her friend, and is received with affection and joy. A well-known air, sacred to *home*, strikes upon her ear, and seems to welcome the returning wanderer. An interview subsequently takes place between *Clari* and her parents. The mother, assured of her daughter's innocence, is soon appeased ; not so the father, who refuses to receive her until the entrance of the *Duke* himself, who confesses his crime, implores pardon, demands the hand of *Clari* in marriage. and clears up every doubt. It is not often that the imprudent rambles of a cottage-maid meet with so happy a termination. As we began with a *moral*, so will we end; and what one can be more *appropriate* than the following *just*, beautiful, and affecting picture?—

> " Ah, turn thine eyes,
> Where the poor, houseless, shiv'ring, female lies!
> She once, perhaps, in village plenty bless'd,
> Has wept at tales of innocence, distress'd.
> Her modest looks the cottage might adorn,
> Sweet as the primrose peeps beneath the thorn ;
> Now lost to all—her friends, her virtue fled,
> Near her betrayer's door she lays her head ;
> And, pinch'd with cold, and shrinking from the shower,
> With heavy heart deplores that luckless hour,
> When, idly first, ambitious of the town,
> She left her wheel, and robes of country brown."

In the opera, Mr. Payne has most happily and feelingly introduced his song of " Home, Sweet Home!" He has done it at the moment when *Clari* first begins to realize her situation, and the terrible truth that she had deserted her home. She awakens to this fact one morning, when leaving her toilet-chamber, and entering her new and splendid apartments. The gayeties of the place, the heavy rich draperies at the windows, with their gilded mouldings, the carved furniture, the harp in one corner of the room, the thick Turkish floor-covering and other embellishments of the palatial parlor, at once thrust upon her the contrasts of the lowly thatched cottage and all she had left behind, and in this spasm of melancholy she introduces herself to the audience by singing the song of " Home, Sweet Home!"

It is very seldom that we see the words of this song correctly printed, and we embrace this opportunity of presenting them here as taken from Mr. Payne's original manuscript, and with his own precise punctuation.

"HOME, SWEET HOME!

> " 'Mid pleasures and palaces though we may roam,
> Be it ever so humble, there's no place like home !
> A charm from the sky seems to hallow us there,
> Which, seek through the world, is ne'er met with elsewhere !
> Home, Home, Sweet, Sweet, Home !
> There's no place like Home !
> There's no place like Home !

" An exile from home, splendor dazzles in vain !
 O, give me my lowly thatched cottage again !
 The birds, singing gayly, that came at my call—
 Give me them !—and the peace of mind, dearer than all !
　　　　Home, Home, Sweet, Sweet, Home !
　　　　There's no place like Home !
　　　　There's no place like Home !"

Although this opera was almost entirely original with Mr. Payne, yet he was accused, by some of the English critics, of *plagiarism.* This was done at a time when he was out of the country, and was residing in Paris. There were enough in London who knew of the originality of the play, but none had the firmness to defend the dramatist. Once, when he saw the piece announced at a minor theatre as a " translation from the French," he wrote to the manager and explained that it was not a translation. That there was a ballet-pantomime only upon the same story, which had been performed at one of the opera-houses in Paris, and, had not the story of the ballet been essentially varied, the feet of the dancers could scarcely supply sentences so as to justify the epithet " translation." The manager assured Mr. Payne that he was aware that the drama was original with him, but it was a rule at all minor theatres to endeavor to evade the law by assuming that works were translated, and the drama was too valuable to him to be lost through any delicacy. He therefore declined to withdraw the assertion, and invited Mr. Payne to stop in at his theatre and see how much better it was placed upon his stage at Tottenham Court Road than at Covent Garden or at Drury Lane.

Payne's next success was with the comedy of " Charles the Second." This comedy Payne dedicated to Mr. Charles Kemble. It was sold to Covent Garden Theatre for fifty pounds, one-fourth of the price usually paid for a successful farce. He accepted this paltry amount because the management was too poor at the time to pay more, and he was too hard pressed to wait for a better opportunity to sell it. The comedy was extremely popular at the time, and is yet frequently performed. Its incidents and situations are almost identical with those of " La Jeunesse de Henri V." But the dialogue differs widely, and especially so with the rôle of *Captain Copp,* a character original with Mr. Payne, and the best part in the piece. This excellent comedy was first produced upon the stage of Covent Garden in 1824. The following was the original cast of characters :

King Charles II. . .	. . .	Mr. Charles Kemble.
Rochester . . .	. . .	Mr. Jones.
Edward (page) . .	. . .	Mr. Duruset.
Captain Copp . .	. . .	Mr. Fawcett.
Lady Clari . . .	. . .	Mrs. Faucit.
Mary	. . .	Miss M. Tree.

Mr. Payne, in his preface to the first edition of "Charles II.," remarks, "I understand that the authorship of this comedy has been claimed by different persons in the public papers on the ground of their having produced translations of the French original, which have been performed at the minor theatres. In reply to this, I would observe that I have never seen any of those translations. My play was written last autumn at Paris. It was founded on a printed copy of 'La Jeunesse de Henri V.,' of which a number of editions have appeared. The incidents and situations are nearly the same, but the dialogue differs essentially throughout, especially in the part of *Captain Copp*."

Mr. Charles Kemble made a great hit in the part of *Charles II*. Prince Puckler-Muskau, in his book on England, sketches his performance of the character in contrast with what he had seen at Drury Lane. "Far better," observes the prince, "was the play at Covent Garden, where Charles Kemble, one of the best English actors, gave an admirable representation of the part of *Charles the II*. Kemble is a man of the best education, and has always lived in good society. He is, therefore, qualified to represent a king royally, with the *aisance* that is proper to all exalted persons. He very skilfully gave an amiable coloring to the levity of *Charles the Second*, without ever, even in moments of the greatest *abandon*, losing the type of that inborn, conscious dignity, so difficult to imitate. The costumes, too, were as if cut out of the frames of old pictures, down to the veriest trifle." "So very eminent was 'Charles the Second,' especially among the higher class, that George IV. commanded it to be acted before him. On that occasion he even departed from his usual etiquette. He made his first visit of the season at Covent Garden instead of at the Drury Lane, which was exclusively the 'Royal Theatre,' and where alone performers were distinguished by the title of 'His Majesty's Servants.' 'Charles the Second' is distinguished for another marked incident in dramatic history. It was in this piece that the celebrated Fawcett, whose performance of *Copp* was so inimitable, took his leave of the stage."

"The history of Mr. Payne's career in England is only a history of struggles for petty advantages; often, for the reverse. There was much excitement about a tragedy of his, 'Richelieu,' which followed 'Charles II.' The descendant of *Richelieu* chanced to be the French minister at the Court of St. James. He did not wish his profligate ancestor to face him upon the stage. The Lord Chamberlain was applied to, and, but for firm remonstrances, the work would have been altogether suppressed. On condition, however, of the name being changed and certain mutilations, it was allowed to appear. As might have been expected, however, the strong arm of power being against it, it had the abuse of the papers as immoral, was caballed against in the theatre, and, after five nights' performances, was withdrawn. This tragedy was dedicated by Mr. Payne to his dear friend Washington Irving. It was first produced at the Drury Lane. This play was altered by Mrs. Catherine Farren, and was frequently played in this country as the 'Bankrupt's Wife.' "

Soon after "Richelieu" followed the opera of the " White Lady." The success of this piece was somewhat impeded by the jealousy of Miss Paton, who, at the last moment, gave up her part, apprehensive of being eclipsed by Madame Vestris in *George Brown*. A paper-war ensued, and parties were the consequence. The piece was imperfectly done, but well received throughout, and announced, amid loud cheers, for repetition. It ran about twenty nights.

About this time Mr. Payne made a new venture, and established a new critical paper entitled the "Opera Glass," one of the most popular periodicals of the day. But the fatigue of attending exclusively to such a work, and the annoyances and vexations from the way in which he was treated about his theatrical and literary enterprises, threw him into an illness, during which his life was despaired of. All communications upon business of any description were interdicted; an unlucky event, on one account, for at that period he was offered the management of a theatre in London and one in Paris, which he could not accept. After his recovery he produced plays of various descriptions at various theatres. Those most noted were the comedy of "Procrastination," the farce of "Fricandeau," at the Haymarket Theatre; the interlude of "The Lancers," the opera of the "Tyrolese Peasant," and the play of the "Spanish Husband," were brought out at Drury Lane. The one-act comedy of "Woman's Revenge," which was first produced at Madame Vestris's theatre, had a most brilliant reception. This, we believe, was the last piece that Mr. Payne wrote while in Europe, and the last of his dramatic productions produced upon any stage, although Mr. Payne wrote several other pieces after he returned to this country in 1832. One in particular we here allude to, called the " Italian Bride," a play in four acts, two manuscript copies of which now exist, one in the hands of Mr. James Rees, of Philadelphia, and the other in the hands of the writer of this book. From a letter in our possession, we are inclined to think that Mr. Payne wrote this play for Miss Cushman. The lady had it to read, but returned it to Mr. Payne with many compliments, and declining to accept the play on the grounds that her many engagements would not allow her time to study the leading part. The play is very interesting in plot, and has in it some of the best dramatic passages written by Mr. Payne. Mr. Payne, after his return to this country, made an effort to get Mr. Forrest to produce his " Romulus" and his " Virginius." Mr. Forrest was much pleased with " Romulus," and requested some alterations, but as to Mr. Payne's making these alterations no proofs appear.

In reviewing Mr. Payne as a dramatist, we should keep in sight the history of his life while in England, and the character of the productions he was forced to make, so as to please the notions of the several managers, who seemed to desire "Parisian novelties" only. Those who have looked upon him in the spirit of detraction, and have insisted earnestly upon his having been so largely indebted to the French stage, should not have lost sight of the above fact. When Terence was accused of such a thing, he replied in the prologue to his famous self-tormentor :

> " As to reports, which envious men have spread,
> That he has ransacked many Grecian plays,
> While he composes some few Latin ones,
> That he denies not he has done ; nor does
> Repent he did it ; means to do it still ;
> Safe in the warrant and authority
> Of greater bards, who did long since the same."

And Mr. Payne might quote the mighty example of Shakspeare himself, as Terence has done that of his own exalted predecessors; but our countryman had motives more imperative than either Terence or Shakspeare. It was expressly for the purpose of transferring foreign works that he was first lured from acting to

9

authorship. At the time he began this career, it was the greatest
recommendation of a piece that it was the first English version
of the last French success. This is even yet, in some degree, the
case, though not so much as it was before the minor theatres took
so many liberties. To comprehend how it happened, the difference
between the regulations of the drama in France and those in England must be understood. In Paris there is a theatre set apart
for each particular species of drama, of which new specimens must
continually be produced; and each, of course, brings out its own
in the greatest perfection, and pays for it the best price. For
many years there was no winter-mart in London for the numerous
novelties of these various theatres except the two great houses of
Drury Lane and Covent Garden. If a hit appeared in Paris, it
was important to each not to be anticipated by the other; and
the immense advantages of the immediate transfer of a Parisian
novelty rendered it of the first consequence to seize upon it and
to be earliest in the field. From the necessity of despatch, original works, not being likely to create the same sort of competition,
were invariably postponed whenever a foreign novelty appeared,
sanctioned by a foreign triumph; and he who could prepare such
best and quickest was the best patronized by managers. Mr. Howard Payne had the reputation of being able to accomplish these
transfers with unmatchable celerity. Though his plays from
foreign sources have always been sufficiently varied to have justified a larger claim than has ever been made for them on his account by his best friends, it is not to this fact that he owes his
standing. It is for having done subjects which other dramatists,
and experienced ones, have tried in and failed (although aided by
the identical foreign originals), so well as to secure to his works a
permanent standing upon the stage. This was the case with his
first attempt in "Accusation." Mr. Kenney, one of the best then
living authors, was paid liberally for a piece on the same subject
at the rival theatre. Mr. Kenney himself concurred with the
public and the papers, and owned that his effort was a failure, but
the other triumphant. Mr. Poole also tried the "Two Galley-
Slaves" at Drury Lane against that of Mr. Payne at Covent
Garden. Poole's was damned, while Payne's still continues to be
acted. The rival "Thérèse" we have already mentioned as having
failed at Covent Garden in the hands of Mr. Beazely, also an
author of eminence. Other examples might be adduced, but these
are enough to prove that what our countryman undertook to do

he achieved, and that to its fullest extent. Upon the subject how far he deserves praise on that score, we will take the following opinion of a London monthly reviewer of one of his adaptations: "The author of an original play has, no doubt, a sufficient and allowed claim on public praise; but no estimate seems to have been formed of the merits or of the difficulties of transferring the *chefs d'œuvre* of the foreign stage to our own. The facility of translating French seems to put this operation in the power of every aspirant, and where all may gather the laurel, it is not unnatural that the wreath should be little worth the wearing. But in full contra-diction to this easy fame may be placed that of the able adapter, who, coming to his work with a perfect knowledge of the demands of his national theatre, lays upon himself the task of moulding the incongruous and the foreign, of invigorating the feeble, and inspiriting the dull into the shape and interest that attract the tastes of England. The praise is higher if over this there is thrown the living hue of genius, and the understanding is raised and charmed by beauties unsought for by the original author. Mr. Payne, a writer already known to the public by some excellent productions, has in the present instance increased his literary dis-tinction. He has had all the difficulties of stage-translation to encounter, and has overcome them with singular skill. His ar-rangement of the scene is admirably theatric, his additions are happy, and his language is of a rank entirely above the usual vulgar tongue of translation; it is at once forcible and refined, expressive and elegant."

It would occupy more space than we have a right to engross to go much more largely into his merits. To this praise, however, he has an unquestionable right. That he is the *first* native Ameri-can who, either as an actor or a dramatic writer, ever attracted attention and secured a firm stand on the other side of the ocean. He has not lost that stand either there or here. The liberal spirit of the "old country" has unhesitatingly acknowledged, even though he was known to be a wanderer from the new. that, as he was the first American actor "qui ait vu sa reputation franchir le vaste ocean," so is he the first American author whose plays have been known on the British stage, and adopted there as the stock pieces of the national theatres. Among upwards of half a hun-dred of these, it is owned that he has given to England and to America the most popular tragedy ("Brutus"). comedy ("Charles the Second"), melodrama ("Thérèse"), opera ("Clari"), and song

("Sweet Home"), of the day in which they respectively appeared; and "when," said a London paper, "the Lord Chancellor Brougham asked, in a discussion concerning the patents some time ago, who in the present day had produced plays which might be considered as established, and deserving to be so, the name of Mr. Howard Payne was one of the first quoted in the High Court of Chancery, and several of his works were enumerated as part of the stock dramas which did the most credit to England."

It was these considerations which induced some friends who had become well acquainted with his annoyances abroad to urge Mr. Payne's return to America. They reminded him that his plays had been acted for many years in his own country, and at a great profit to our theatres and actors, without any recompense to him in any shape. As compensation had been often volunteered to foreign writers for the advantage derived from their productions, he was assured he would not be forgotten where Bulwer, Mrs. Hemans, and others had been so profitably remembered. He was promised that if he came he should find the necessity for such struggles as had embittered his life for years no longer pressing on him. But reports had reached him abroad of unkind things which had been said of him at home. He doubted if the zeal of those who wrote to him had not blinded them as to his being recollected so generally; but especially as to his being recollected with so much good will. He thought, if he lingered awhile longer, he might return more independent; and he was reluctant to show himself, after so many years, not quite so well off. as when he went away.

But the thought of home and the love of country prevailed over all his distrust. About two years subsequently to the first invitations which had been sent to him from New York, he landed in that city on the 25th of July, 1832. Yet here his evil star seemed still predominant. He found no one to receive him. His first intelligence was that there was cholera raging and an Indian war. No sooner, however, did the alarm subside, and the city fill, than plans were laid to bid him welcome. A meeting was immediately called for the purpose by the following gentlemen: James Lawson, Duncan C. Pell, Samuel Swartwout, Henry Ogden, J. J. Bailey, Prosper M. Wetmore, Isaac S. Hone, Theodore S. Fay, and George P. Morris. It was publicly resolved, that, as his native country had so many years enjoyed the advantage of his productions without any compensation to him, it was proper she should make some acknowledgment, and that in a form the most complimentary. It was determined to offer him a benefit " in the name of his native city, New York." To give the greatest *éclat* to the festival, the military officers resolved, on the motion of the venerable and public-spirited Major-General Morton, to attend in full uniform. The ladies of fashion determined to sit in the pit (in those days exclusively for men), which was opened to the boxes, and decorated for the occasion. The price of every part of the house was raised to five dollars, excepting the gallery, which was fixed at one dollar, the then usual box-price. The following address, spoken by Mrs. Sharp, was written by Mr. Theodore S. Fay, one of the editors of the " New York Mirror," whose father had written the address for the occasion of Master Payne's first appearance on the same stage in 1809:

" ADDRESS.

" One snowy, winter night, in times of yore,
At least some twenty years ago—or more,
Within these very walls, where now you sit,
A radiant crowd of fashion, beauty, wit,
Together came, like that which greets me now,
Youth's summer head, and age's frosted brow.
Full many a belle was here—and many a beau
Who've flirted—flourished—faded—long ago;
And children, too, perchance—the little elves,
Who now are here, sweet belles and beaux themselves.
Upon the stage, a glowing boy appeared
Whom heavenly smiles and grateful thunders cheered;
Then, through the throng, delighted murmurs ran,
The boy 'enacts more wonders than a man.'
Each word—each look—his loftier nature proved;
The men admired him—and the women—loved.
Not fairer Phaon in the forest stood
And graceful turned, when lovely Sappho wooed.
Round his young brow, the beams of genius shone;
Columbia smiled and claimed him for her own.
Changed was the scene—the boy was here no more—
His footsteps wandered on a foreign shore.
Not here again his boyish beauties played
Not here his voice was heard—his glances strayed:
Yet oft his *spirit* spoke, and all obeyed.
Oft has the listening crowd been hushed to hear
The *Maid of Milan's* song enchant the ear.
In beauty's eyes tears oft have quenched the blaze,
Mourning the sorrow of the sweet *Thérèse,*

Till *Charles*, mad son of an unhappy sire—
To the soft orbs recalled the dangerous fire.
Rome's reverend patriot, too, appears in sight,—
Let traitors shrink—(were traitors here to-night,)
To view him, summoned by the poet's art,
On freedom's altar lay his mighty heart,
Bleeding and torn—fit offering to the laws.
Who drew the picture,—merits your applause.
Again the scene is changed: the poet boy
Pines for his native land with trembling joy;
And, like his *Clari*, ceased at length to roam,
His graver footsteps lead to ' Home, Sweet Home!'
But who shall tell what wonders meet his view ?
Himself is changed, and all around him, too,
The swelling mound and broken marble tell
Where lie the hands that pressed his last farewell,
And friends around him throng, so different grown
Scarcely his eyes receive them for his own.
Oh I let him find, whatever change appears,
Our hearts unaltered with the lapse of years.
Though frequent orbs of foreign genius rise,
Kindling and blazing in our western skies,
And one fair stranger shining from afar,
Like Venus burns—a ' bright particular star'—
Yet let him meet, where first his breath he drew,
Firm friends, to him and to their country true.
So they whom gods in future times inspire
To wake the music of Columbia's lyre,
Shall ever find a grateful nation here,
Their names to cherish, and their toils to cheer ;
And never know, where'er their steps may roam,
More dazzling honors than their welcome home."

A faithful copy of the bill presented on the occasion is given on the opposite page.

A stronger cast was never placed on an American play-bill. The house was filled from pit to gallery, and the audience was the most elegant and intellectual ever assembled within the walls of the Park Theatre, "The Old Drury of America." The receipts of the night were over *seven thousand dollars*. At the close of the performance, there was a loud and general call for Mr. Payne. He responded to the call; the " Evening Post" says, " He was at first embarrassed but presently recovered, and the grace of his manner, the sweetness of his voice, the clearness of his enunciation, affected the audience with a sort of surprise." His speech

GREAT DRAMATIC FESTIVAL AT THE PARK THEATRE.

BENEFIT

Under the direction of the friends of literature and the drama

Sustained by the Volunteered line Talent of the ladies and gentlemen connected with the Stage. In Compliment, from His Native City, New York, to

JOHN HOWARD PAYNE.

On this occasion, in addition to the regular company of the Park Theatre, the following ladies and gentlemen, from various parts of the United States have, in the readiest and handsomest manner, tendered their valuable services:

MISS FANNY KEMBLE,

MISS HUGHES,   MISS ROCK,
MRS. BARNES,   MISS WARING,
MR. C. KEMBLE,   MR. J. W. WALLACK,   MR. G. BARRETT,
MR. T. A. COOPER,   MR. E. FORREST,   MR. C. HORNE,
and MR. J. R. SCOTT,

Of the Arch street theatre, Philadelphia, his first appearance in this city.

Thursday Evening, November 29th, 1832,

Will be performed the Historical Tragedy of

BRUTUS;

Or, The Fall of Tarquin.

WRITTEN BY JOHN HOWARD PAYNE.

LUCIUS JUNIUS BRUTUS,	MR. FORREST.	HORATIUS,	MR. RICHINGS.
TITUS,	MR. SCOTT.	CELIUS,	MR. CONWAY.
COLLATINUS,	MR. BARRETT.	FLAVIUS,	MR. HARVEY.
SEXTUS,	MR. CLARK.	CENTURION,	MR. POVEY.
ARUNS,	MR. BARRY.	MESSENGER,	MR. COLLETT.
CLAUDIUS,	MR. KEPPLLE.	1st CITIZEN,	MR. HAYDEN.
VALERIUS,	MR. BLAKELEY.	2d "	MR. KING.
LUCRETIUS,	MR. NEXSEN.	3d "	MR. JOHNSON.

Senators, Lictors, Guards, etc.,

TULLIA,	MRS. BARNES.	PRIESTESS,	MISS SMITH.
TARQUINIA,	MRS. SHARP.	VESTAL,	MRS. CONWAY.
LUCRETIA,	MISS WARING.	LAVINIA,	MRS. DURIE.

AFTER THE TRAGEDY

MRS. SHARP, will speak an ADDRESS written for the occasion, and MR. JONES will sing the SONG of

HOME, SWEET HOME!

From Mr. Payne's opera of Clari: followed in full chorus, by the Finale to that piece,

WELCOME HOME!

MISS HUGHES will sing THE MERMAID'S CAVE.

Composed expressly for her by C. E. Horn, Esq., words by Miss F. H. Gould, accompanied by Mr. Horne, on the pianoforte.

After which Shakespeare's Comedy of

KATHERINE AND PETRUCHIO

PETRUCHIO, (1st time in America),		TAILOR,	MR. FISHER.
	MR. KEMBLE.	NATHANIEL,	MR. JOHNSON.
BAPTISTA,	MR. BLAKELEY.	PETER,	MR. HAYDEN.
HORTENSIO,	MR. NEXSEN.	COOK,	MR. CONWAY.
GRUMIO,	MR. PLACIDE.	KATHERINE, (1st time in America),	
MUSIC MASTER,	MR. POVEY.		MISS KEMBLE.
BIONDELLO,	MR. RICHINGS.	BIANCA,	MRS. DURIE.
PEDRO,	MR. COLLETT.	CURTIS,	MRS. WHEATLEY.

MR. COOPER has obligingly consented to recite in the course of the evening

ALEXANDER'S FEAST.

To conclude with the Comedy of

CHARLES THE SECOND,

WRITTEN BY JOHN HOWARD PAYNE.

*CAPT. COPP (studied for the occasion),		EDWARD (the page, with songs),	MR. JONES.
	MR. WALLACK.		
CHARLES THE SECOND,	MR. BARRETT.	MARY COPP (with songs),	MISS ROCK.
EARL OF ROCHESTER,	MR. RICHINGS.	LADY CLARA,	MRS. SHARP.

Rules and Regulations. The pit will be handsomely fitted upon this occasion, as an amphitheatre, for the accommodation of ladies and gentlemen. The usual entrance will be closed, and admittance obtained only through the box-doors. The committee of arrangements will see that ladies are conducted to eligible seats, and no more persons will be admitted than can be conveniently accommodated with places. It is requested that carriages approach the theatre from Broadway, and that they be dismissed on arrival. Carriages will be at the door to convey the company home. Suitable persons will be in attendance to take charge of hats, cloaks, etc.

Doors open at 6 o'clock; Performance to commence at half past six.

Price of Tickets: Boxes and Pit, Five Dollars; Gallery, One Dollar.

May be had at the Box-office.

was frequently interrupted by deafening applause. The "Post" reported his speech as follows:

"My honored countrymen, my most valuable friends, I thought I should have been better prepared for the emotions of this moment; but it is long, very long since I stood in person before the public, and so immeasurably is the anticipation of my wildest dream exceeded by what I now experience, that I am compelled to cast myself upon your indulgence, and shall I not do so without apprehension, having the 'beautiful and the brave,' the wise and the wealthy, clustering in one unequalled galaxy of lofty and of liberal hearts; that, for anything, depending upon kindness, it is impossible to look to you in vain? Grant me your pardon, then, if I am incompetent to acknowledge that kindness as I ought; for it is your own goodness that paralyzes the power to thank you, and I am dazzled, surprised, overwhelmed.

"When I think that, in this place, three and twenty years ago, my youthful steps first ventured before the public, feelings and associations rush through my memory, for which my own sympathies will find a language that my tongue seeks in vain. The very theatre in which I stood has been levelled to the ground, and, though I am upon the same spot, there remains no vestige of the stage which the fond fancies of a boy arrayed in all the charms and promises of fairy-land. Since then, the character of my ambition has changed; yet I remember 'Such things were, and *were* most precious,' and the retrospect becomes the more touching to myself, now that I appear on it for the last time, and bid it, formally and eternally, farewell. It is high satisfaction to me that my adieu to the stage, and my return to my home, should be marked by an event which, to all Americans who devote themselves to literature and the arts, will give a glorious lesson. It will show them that they belong to a country, which is incapable of forgetting her sons. Let those sons, whatever their discomforts, toil on, and not despair, for the time *will* come when they shall be nobly recollected. For myself, I do not acquiesce in the testimonial of this night under any vanity regarding my own claims which can mislead me as to its real incentive; but I have a deep sense of the responsibility imposed on me by this unprecedented kindness; and believe me, my excellent friends, believe me, my beloved countrymen, it will be my study and the prayer and the perpetual hope of my future life, to render myself worthy of the present moment and of a country of which I was ever proud,

and now, since I have seen other countries, am yet more proud
than ever, and of a city in whose far-sighted and graceful and
generous and gallant acts, hourly I witness fresh motives for
exulting that it is my distinction to have been born her son."

On the day following a card was sent to him for a public dinner
at the City Hotel, from "a number of his fellow-citizens, uniting
the feelings of personal friendship with those which had actuated
the acknowledgment of his efforts in the cause of literature and
the drama," and who were "anxious no longer to delay adding
their welcome to his native city to the one already so properly
given by its inhabitants at large." In accepting the invitation, he
wrote: " It is superfluous for me to say that I am gratified by your
attention ; and, although a public dinner is by no means a distinction to which my humble labors can have given me any claims,—
as the one to which you do me the honor of inviting me is suggested as the welcome of personal friendship,—I should be sorry to
incur the suspicion of carelessness of your kindness by not meeting
you at the time you mention." On Saturday, December 1st, the
dinner took place. It was largely attended by the first literary
and professional persons in New York, and some from Philadelphia, and spoken of as one of the most entertaining of such assemblies. On Mr. Payne's entrance into the anteroom he was presented
with a letter from the Benefit Committee, officially acquainting him
with the proceedings on that occasion. Isaac S. Hone, Esq., was
in the chair. General Prosper M. Wetmore was the first vice-
president, and Colonel George P. Morris, second. The cloth being
removed, Mr. Hone closed a most eloquent speech with the following toast :

" Our distinguished countryman,—John Howard Payne. The
family of literature welcomes him to the home whose praises he
has so sweetly sung."

As soon as the acclamations with which this toast was received
had subsided, Mr. Payne replied,—

" Since my arrival in America I find, Mr. President, that the
phrases of gratitude are less various than the forms in which my
countrymen display their kindness. Only two evenings since it
became my duty to attempt the acknowledgment of an unique
attention, unprecedented in its elegance and delicacy and munificence ; and now a welcome greets me in another shape, yet I can
only give utterance to my feelings in the same simple assurance of
how deeply I am obliged. Little could I have fancied in the first

hour of my return that I should have had such liberalities to speak
of, that I should have been blest with such friends to make my
native city more than ever dear to me! Sir, the omens of that
hour, and even of days which followed, would have driven a superstitious man back, and he would have returned no more. After
an absence of twenty years—that little lifetime, twenty years!—
when uproused one morning by intelligence that the pilot was on
board and our ship within hail of the shore—I flew on deck. A
tempest raged. The angel of death seemed careering in the clouds,
and flinging around lightnings which almost made each one of us
expect his own last moment in the following flash. But the storm
cleared, and I beheld the fair city of my birth enthroned upon her
beautiful waters, and I rejoiced in belonging to such a mother, and
that my weary pilgrimage had closed at such a home! But this
succession of emotions was but symbolical of deeper ones to which
I yet was destined; for, when my steps sought the spots to which
in earlier life they were accustomed, I found a severer darkness
frowning over them in the pestilence, and houses untenanted, or
most of those which had inhabitants in tears and mourning. When
I asked for many a friend of years gone by, I was pointed to the
tomb. But presently the streets began to brighten into what they
were; many a warm hand renewed the earnest grasp so long ago
remembered : the welcome of many a departed parent smiled on
me in their children; until at length I beheld the memories of a
former day gathering the lovely and the gallant, and the intellectual, and the affluent, in one splendid circle, where I could almost
fancy the spirits of some of the long-buried dead, who would have
united at that moment with the living, hovering o'er a scene which
made me forget the humbleness of my own desert in exultation for
the glorious privilege of once again exclaiming, as I gazed before
me, 'The wanderer *has* a home, and it is *here.*'

"You have alluded, Mr. President, to my long residence abroad,
and I thank you for the opportunity of mentioning those whom
I have just quitted. My career has, indeed, been a very chequered
one, but I am not aware that its infelicities have exceeded those
inherent in a literary life without advantages. In my earlier
ramblings I am bound to remember France and the revered
friendship of Talma ; I should also speak of the hospitalities of
Liverpool and her lamented Roscoe ; and when in Ireland, wel-
comed by her O'Connell and her Phillips, and myriads of the
warm-hearted and enlightened, I said to the people of Dublin,

'My countrymen shall be told from my experience that an American may make friends in other lands, but in grateful Erin he shall find a home,' and I should be glad to know that there are any present belonging to that country, for they would not let it be forgotten that my word to Dublin, eighteen years ago, is now fulfilled with pride and thankfulness to my native city of New York. In the great metropolis, London, I have endured struggles,—bitter, heart-breaking struggles,—but it should be understood that in a place overthronged with so much bustling competition it is hard for any aspirant to escape unbruised. My own country would think me unworthy of her could I deem it any recommendation to her favor to suppress the truth that I have found the land of my birth by no means so undervalued as we are taught to fancy in the land which I for so many years have made that of my residence. I have experienced cordial friendship from every rank, and though sometimes hardly dealt with by little minds from sordid motives, I have been sustained by great ones from the most disinterested. Nay, I must not except some of the aristocracy itself from especial praise for qualities adapted to make members of that order respected even in America, where we do not value them for their rank. When I have been sinking, the support of such men as the Devonshires, the Seagraves, the Mulgraves, has been accorded to me with an elegance and promptitude for which I am aware I am less indebted to my own merits than to their honor for a country which I felt the prouder of when I found it a passport to the kindness of persons with a nobility beyond their coronets. But perhaps there would be required no better testimonial of the good will of that nation toward ours in all matters connected with literature and the arts than the cordial alacrity with which the most distinguished representatives of the British drama last Thursday came forward in support of an American. If I single Mr. Kemble and Mr. Wallack from the rest, it is not because I think the attention of one person on such an occasion less complimentary than that of another, but that it enables me to mention how much my gratification was, under all the circumstances, enhanced in seeing my reception from my native city graced by those who so many years have been the rival managers of the two great theatres of London with which I have been principally connected.

"Mr. President, had I not already detained you too long, I might have attempted to say something upon other points of your address, though I should tremble to approach a subject which had been touched by your eloquence. My feelings for the literature of the drama, and my sense of its importance to the community, must be inferred from my past attention to it, and will, I trust, be obvious from my future efforts to desire a place among those of my countrymen who have shown, and some very recently, the power of achieving great things for our fame to come in this most difficult pursuit. Though, as I believe, the earliest native adventurer in the representative department of the drama, I myself have voluntarily withdrawn from the course; with my young countryman, who so nobly wears the laurels I once so longed to win (need I say Edwin Forrest?), the destinies of native acting rest where they are sure to be borne up proudly. But it is time I should release you, and, if I may still be permitted to pursue my strain of egotism, I would ask you to allow me to close with the mention of the three names which are dear to me,—two as my earliest patrons in this my native city, and one as a warm and most devoted friend,—and I do not know that I ever again shall have so fitting an opportunity of paying them the tribute they deserve from me, as among those who have shown their spirit towards me in later life, though in a different form. I would, therefore, Mr. President, beg leave to propose, without further preamble,

"The memories of William Coleman, John E. Seaman, and Joseph D. Fay."

Mr. Payne no sooner resumed his seat than the following ode, written for the occasion by Samuel Woodworth, Esq., was recited by Mr. J. J. Adams, the actor:

"PAYNE'S WELCOME.

TUNE—"*Scots, wha' hae.*"

" Braid the wreath, the chaplet twine,
Weave the laurel with the vine,
Taste and mirth shall here combine
    To grace our revelry.

" *Native genius* claims our praise,
Tell his worth in tuneful lays,
Crown him with o'ershadowing bays,
    Blooming verdantly.

" Freedom's sons who cease to roam,
    Thus receive a welcome home,
    Here beneath her temple's dome,
        Where her anthems swell.

" List to him whose magic quill
    Moulds our passions to his will,
    Waking feeling's sweetest thrill,
        We the tribute pay.

" List to him, whose classic lyre
    Can the oldest heart inspire,
    With a glow of patriot fire,
        That can ne'er decay.

" Does he not our hearts appall,
    In the despot *Tarquin's* fall ?
    Does not sweet *Lucretia* call
        Tears of sympathy ?

" Does not *Richelieu* impart
    Tremors to the ' Broken Heart' ?
    Do not gems of pity start
        For his *Oswali ?*

" Lo ! the magic wand he waves !
    Kings and courtiers burst their graves ;
    Charles, with all his merry knaves,
        Joins in revelry.

" *Clari* and *Thérèse* are here,
    See the white maid, too, appear !
    ' Home, Sweet Home !' salutes the ear,
        Dear to memory.

" Hail him welcome to the shores
    Where bright Freedom's eagle soars,
    Where her temple's open doors
        Welcome all the free !

" Where in academic bowers,
    Shadowed by her loveliest flowers,
    Once he passed the sweetest hours
        Of careless infancy.

" Bard, beloved by all the nine,
    Minstrel of the lyre divine,
    Fadeless honors shall be thine
        Through futurity.

" Take the wreath from friendship's hand,
    Woven by this festive band,
    Welcome to thy native land—
        Land of Liberty."

The toasts and speeches were very numerous, but the only one we have room to repeat is an exceedingly appropriate one, which was much admired at the time, and was given by Mr. Redwood Fisher:

"*A philosophy more refined than that of the Stoics,*—the PLEASURE of receiving—PAYNE."

In a few weeks after Mr. Payne's grand receptions at the Park Theatre and at the City Hotel, he was invited by some old friends to Boston, where lay the scenes of his childhood. He accepted the invitation, and his reception was most flattering. No sooner had he arrived than plans were laid for a complimentary benefit at the Tremont Theatre, to take place on the 3d of April, 1833; but in a moneyed sense it was a failure. The performance consisted of selections from the various productions of Mr. Payne, viz.: the one-act comedietta of "Love in Humble Life," the drama of "Thérèse," "The Lancers," "Charles II.," and an address by Park Benjamin.

On this occasion the box-tickets were placed at three dollars each, and the rest of the house at one dollar. By some mismanagement a portion of the citizens, who felt warmly towards Mr. Payne, were dissatisfied, and only the higher classes in the city attended. The house, though brilliant, was unexpectedly thin in numbers; besides, other things conspired to injure the success of the undertaking. "The Kembles were announced to appear shortly. The night was unpropitious, preceding, as it did, the general fast, when many families leave the city to unite in social gatherings."

The following address was spoken by Mrs. Barrett:

"ADDRESS.

" Could some enchantress, by her magic spell,
    Fair as Love's Goddess from her ocean-shell,
    Chase the dim vapors that conceal the past,
    And o'er Time's sea a tender radiance cast;
    What various scenes, to gladden and surprise,
    Would to your view, in bright succession, rise!
    Alas! our age has unromantic grown,
    And fancy is the sole enchantress known.

Invoke her aid, and from her starry bower
She may descend to gild the passing hour.
Through the long vista of departed years,
What vision first, in Fancy's light, appears?
See yonder group of happy playmates stand
Round one who seems the leader of the band!
His cheek is blushing with the rose's bloom.
Why o'er his forehead waves a crimson plume?
His form for Cupid's well might be adored.
Why is it girded with the glittering sword?
He speaks—the group disperse—now formed once more,
Behold on air a silken banner soar,
In serried ranks, with measured steps, they come.
Hark! the shrill fife and spirit-stirring drum.
What field is this? Who leads this gallant train?
'Tis Boston Common—Captain Howard Payne.
The scene is changed—lo! in the still midnight,
A lonely student, by his lamp's faint light.
Pale is his cheek—his eye all dim with tears;
Can such deep grief belong to childhood's years?
A son, his tribute of affection pays—
To her whose smile had blest Life's early days.
Can this frail student be the radiant boy
Whose heart so late was redolent of joy?
Ah, yes! immured in Learning's cloistered shade,
Like a caged eagle's, does his spirit fade.
Once more a change of scene—and such a change!
A stage—a theatre—how brightly strange!
A simple lad, in cap-and-tartan dress,
Yet proud his bearing and superb his crest—
'My name is Norval!' Norval! can it be?
Transformed so quickly! that sweet voice—'tis he!
That smile—lip curled in high disdain,
That graceful form—nine cheers for Master Payne!
Let blushing honors gather round his fame—
This 'happy deed shall gild his humble name;'
For the wide stage his youthful footsteps press,
To shield a much-loved father from distress:
And, greeted thus by richly-earned applause,
'Who shall resist him in a parent's cause?'
Loud were the praises that his welcome gave,
In that far land beyond th' Atlantic wave.
There, like a halo, on his young brow fell
The laurel-garland he has worn so well!
Another change—within so brief a span
Has this fair boy become a serious man?
'Tis true—but sacred in his bosom glows
A fire like that which burns 'mid Alpine snows:

Though tempests shatter the volcano's throne,
Though Winter belt him with an icy zone,
Still do the splendors of his lofty head
On regions round a sun-like lustre shed.
So Genius, left to poverty and woe,
Whose rending thoughts the world can never know,
In its lone majesty, all coldly shrined,
Throws its broad gleam along the realms of mind.
A change of scene—the nearest and the last,
We need no spirit to reveal the past;
For, lo! 'tis present and before you now,
The warrior-child, with sword and plumed brow;
The student, bending o'er the written page;
The actor, proudly marching on the stage;
The author, bringing forms to life and light,
Which, here reflected, you may see to-night—
At length has come—Heaven grant no more to roam—
To his own native land, his ' Home, sweet home!' "

At the close of the address, there arose a loud cry for Mr.
Payne. He at once appeared, and spoke to the audience as follows. " The sound of his well-remembered voice," says the
" Commercial Advertiser," " was familiar to our ears, and, while
all the boyish softness has given place to a more manly tone, it
still is as musical as ever."

" MY KIND-HEARTED FRIENDS!—(You will, I know, forgive my
informality in thus addressing you,—called to an interview like
this, how were it possible I should adopt a phrase more ceremo-
nious?)—I little expected ever again to hail the intellectual
beauties, and the graver worth and talent, of this early-valued
city, from the stage; but surely I shall not be regarded as rescind-
ing by it my resignation of a pursuit once so dear to me,—for I
should indeed be unmeriting the warmth with which you bid me
welcome, were I capable of meeting you as an actor now.

" I remember in my rovings among distant lands to have heard
one of the last of the bards, himself in solitude, enchanting with
his harp the picturesque solitudes of his native Wales. 'Three
things restored,' exclaimed the minstrel, 'give back to the worn
and tired of the world the hopes and cheeriness of youth: the food
with which in childhood we were nourished; the climate where
we were in childhood reared; the train of thought by which in
childhood we were amused.' When, amid the inconveniences of
a struggling and a troubled life abroad, recollections of the land I

had quitted were rekindled by our writers, and 'the woods where
I had dwelt pleasantly rustled their green leaves in the song, and
our streams were there with the sound of all their waters,'—even
the idea of HOME,—'fraught with the fragrance of home-dwelling
joys, would reanimate the drooping spirit, as the Arabian breeze
will sometimes waft the freshness of the distant fields to the weary
pilgrim of the desert.' If bare remembrance of such joys could
thus charm away discomfort, how must I feel since I have found
myself in the actual possession of all concerning which I, for so
many years, have only been permitted to dream; realizing that
the promise of the poet of Wales was not a fiction! And where
can I realize it more touchingly than in that spot which, if it did
not give me birth, inspired my earliest impressions? where every
step reminds me of some sweet hour of infancy? where I scarcely
move without being greeted by the smile of some companion of
departed days, or some engaging event of the morning of my existence? Nay, in glancing around me here, it may be that there
can some be found, at this time chieftains of renown, whom, in
the mimic grandeur of military pomp as a boy-warrior, I was myself the first to lead to glory over the old Common, with true
martial valor, never flinching even from the squibs by jealous
urchins flung at us on election-days; and others, who from the
press, the bar, or the senate, have won still greater honors than
those for which we once contended in the school-room or the
college. Indeed, I cannot but exult in the manly and the wholesome feeling which, during my recent visit, regardless of the dif-
ferences since created by fortune or position, has animated numbers in extending to the returning wanderer the hand of cordial
recognition, and of kindness even fraternal. Many, long since
gone from the earth, would have this night brought hither hearts
as warm as the warmest which are now beating here; and there
was one, most nearly and most dearly allied to me, who would
not, could his spirit witness what has passed since my arrival, be
unmoved by the evidence that out of the many, who from him
and from some of his family, derived the first impulse to knowledge, there should yet be those remaining who affectionately, in
me, remember him and them.

"But I trust it is on higher grounds than any merely personal
that I have acquiesced in this opportunity of expressing to you
my thanks. The awakening of public feeling upon such an occasion is only of importance as it proves a dawning enthusiasm re-

10

garding points of national taste and literature. If, by so humble
a pretext as my poor claims, the slightest interest can be excited,
the tendency is likely to rise into something which must, ultimately, elicit genius worthy of every honor. To my high-hearted
and liberal friends in a neighboring city I predicted that the disposition which there so splendidly and so spontaneously displayed
itself towards me would prompt similar encouragement to others,
and it did; and, should such a disposition continue, we may ere
long expect for everything intellectual the bright day when
'delicate spirits' shall never again, like Ariel in the cloven pine of
Bermuda, only be discoverable among the treasures of the new
world by cries of anguish and by supplications for relief. Would
you rival other lands in literature? Give it advantages. Do not
be content with leaving literature, like virtue, to be its own reward. For myself, allow me to repeat my earnest gratitude that,
in my case, another assurance should have been suggested that
my countrymen begin to think upon such matters in a way which
will be sure to rivet all hearts which take an interest in them to
our native land. My own, at a distance, has for many years
gloried in the majesty of our eagle's flight; but my admiration
cannot but deepen into love the more I feel what warmth and
comfort dwell beneath her wings."

It seems that, besides the ill-selected night for Mr. Payne's testimonial, and the fact of the Kembles being announced shortly to
appear, that some invidious person, one of those who seem to live
for no other purpose than to find fault and to stab at the finest
feelings and intelligence of others, saw fit on this occasion to de-
preciate, through one of the papers, the efforts of Mr. Payne as a
dramatist, and also to stigmatize the testimonial offered to him by
the citizens of Boston as an act of charity. On this conduct the
following remarks were made by the spirited editor of the old
"New York Mirror":

"MR. PAYNE'S BENEFIT AT BOSTON.

"The complimentary theatrical festival offered to Mr. Howard
Payne in Boston seems to have been less cleverly managed than
that given in New York. It was attended, however, by a galaxy
of beauty and fashion, represented as exceeding anything of the
kind ever before witnessed in that city; but the time chosen was,
from a variety of causes, unfavorable. The bill had little attrac-

tion, and the audience was not so crowded as every one anticipated. The papers are warm in their eulogies of Mr. Payne, with
the exception, we believe, of one discordant voice, which emits
something about *charity*, very inappropriate to, and quite uncalled
for, by the occasion.

"It is a pity if the friends of Mr. Payne, as an actor, an author,
and a man, and the friends, also, of dramatic literature in general,
may not have the privilege of awarding to him a compliment on
his return to his native country without opposition from people
who, if they do not assist, might at least refrain from interfering.
In regard to the pecuniary profit of the benefits to Mr. Payne,
they are just as much charitable donations as the sums paid to
Walter Scott by his publishers, the subscription-money received
by an editor, the fee handed to a lawyer, or the reward allowed to
any artisan or artist who receives a *quid pro quo.* The 'Boston
Evening Gazette' says, 'Averaging the performance of plays by
Mr. Payne at twenty in Boston each season, it would take more
than one year, acting every night, Sunday not excepted, to have
got through the number of actual representations we have had of
his pieces.'

"For all this the author had been but inadequately paid abroad,
and not at all here. We trust he will not find his praises of 'Home,
Sweet Home' overwrought. Is it *charity*, then, in us to express to
him our appreciation of his various and beautiful productions, and
to put that expression in a form which will be as useful as it is honorable to him? A number of physicians rendered services to the
people in this and other cities during the prevalence of the late
epidemic. Some of them have been presented with complimentary
tokens of regard, and a few with money. Is this charity? On the
death of Dr. Dwight, his works were collected and published, and
the proceeds of their sale appropriated to the use of his family.
Was this charity? It must be remarked, also, that Mr. Payne
was *invited* from London to receive in this, his native country, the
identical compliments, the conferring of which is now beheld so
enviously by certain individuals."

It is a relief to know that there was but one paper in Boston
that had the littleness to assault Mr. Payne, and to accuse him of
having appealed for public charity, while it found fault with him
for not having been born in Boston. "He had better go back to
London," it said, "where he has spent so many years of his life,
and there seek the compensation for his labors which he now de-

sires to obtain from our fellow-citizens." To this gratuitous tirade
of the "Atlas" the "Boston Transcript" made the following reply:
"We may set it down as a general rule that no man can receive
notice without provoking enmity; for, as Shakespeare says, 'It is
the bright day which brings forth the adder'; and in reference to
our own country, the idea has been amusingly amplified in a manner which may not be inapplicable: 'The same sun whose plastic
power decks the blooming temples of Flora with chaplets, and
bows the broad shoulders of autumn with luxuriance, quickens
from the chrysalis the spleeny race of musquitoes, and operates
like galvanism on the torpid venom of the rattlesnake.' For
shame! charity, forsooth! Here is, an early townsman of our
own, himself and his family well known and highly respected
here for years, and whose youthful connection with Boston, while
abroad, whenever he was spoken of advantageously there, has
uniformly been most pompously paraded. Well, this townsman
produces a vast number of plays, which are uniformly successful.
These plays are caught at by our managers with avidity. For
sixteen years they constitute stock pieces on our stage. Averaging the performance of plays by Mr. Payne at twenty-five in
Boston each season, it would take more than one year, acting
every night, Sundays not excepted, to have got through the number of actual representations we have had of his pieces. The average is doubtless much beyond our statement; for, even since his
present short visit to Boston, pieces from his pen (*not* including
the three on Wednesday, which would swell the sum to fourteen)
have been acted eleven times. To one of these, the 'White Maid,'
brought out even under his very eyes, the managers had no right
whatever. They acted it against Mr. Payne's wish. It was never
published. The manuscript was clandestinely obtained from London. Mr. Payne might have legally prevented its appearance, or
forced the managers to *pay* him thrice as much as his benefit has
been said to have yielded. But he allowed the Tremont managers
to reap the advantage, which *they* regarded as sufficient to justify
them not only in paying three 'stars' and extra choristers and
musicians, but in complimenting Mr. Sinclair with a magnificent
gold watch and chain and other appendages (costing nearly two-
thirds as much as, after the house-expenses of the festival are paid,
the benefit will produce), and which Mr. Sinclair displays at parties as the tribute to him from the theatre for the success of his
acting the principal character in an opera by Mr. Payne. What

is done for Mr. Payne all this time? Do the managers show *him* any attention? They do. They *allow* his friends to take the theatre on paying a much greater sum than could be brought into it by any other means at such a time, and to give him a benefit as some remuneration for what his countrymen have enjoyed in gratification, and the theatre itself in profit, for sixteen years from his labors. The benefit is given. The gentlemen who give it, following the high example of New York, handsomely offer any praise to be derived from so proper a tribute to the city generally. All things, where the many are concerned, must originate with the few, and in such matters the few necessarily represent, in the first instance, the many. The elegance and fashion of Boston turn out, but the pecuniary result is unworthy of such a city, unworthy of such an occasion. What follows? Mr. Payne is represented as a supplicator for public charity and an undeserving one! We have scarcely patience to repeat an imputation so disgraceful to the maker! At the very moment that we write we see a man sticking play-bills all over the town for Mr. Pelby's benefit on Monday evening, announcing John Howard Payne's tragedy of 'Brutus,' probably for the hundred and fiftieth time in Boston, as the great attraction, and yet, while this is doing, we have to screen Mr. Payne from the dirt thrown at him in our 'literary emporium' as accepting a charity in accepting a benefit welcome for himself! *Had* it been a charity, it would have been rather an unchristian thing among a religious people, and rather an ungracious one among a polite people, to have spoken of it as such; and, looking at the amount, it would have been somewhat of a reflection upon a liberal people to have shown themselves incapable of a better. But being a civility, and a civility not claimed by Mr. Payne, but offered to him by the patrons of the theatre, is it not rather hard that it should be rendered only a source of insult and of discomfort to a gentleman whose deportment during between two and three months that he has been among us has been uniformly such as to secure him not only respect but friendship? And that, even of many who have been influenced against him by the petty tricks which are always set in motion by the malignant to depress the popular, and who have been astonished at their prejudices the moment they have been favored with his acquaintance? Let our countryman be assured that such is not the feeling of our city, nor is there any one among us who enters at all into the paltry slurs attempted to be cast upon him for having remained so long abroad. Let those

who go to see his 'Brutus' on Monday evening say whether, since
he has been away from us, his writings have not upheld those
principles most dear to us as Americans, and judge whether we
ought not to value him even almost as much as we are expected
to do some who have remained among us to display feelings of
which we have every reason to be ashamed. No; let our distant
friends be certain that Boston people disclaim with indignation
such a course of conduct as has been attempted to be ascribed to
them on this occasion, although, we are sorry to say, there are
now and then one or two to be found among us who get something like our east wind in their heads and their hearts, which
blows no good to themselves or to anybody else. But, as to the
question whether the leading people of Boston had anything to do
with the complimentary part of this affair, that will, we conceive,
need no further answer than this: one of its first recommenders
was a Boston representative to the legislature, one of its first committee was another Boston representative to the legislature, one
of its last committee was also a third representative, and one of
our wealthiest citizens, too, to the Boston legislature. Those
present, without an exception (unless perhaps some one who may
have taken a gift of two tickets and then set to work abusing it),
were persons from our most fashionable and wealthy families, and
all long and thoroughly known in Boston. So large an assemblage
of persons exclusively of the high fashion of Boston has never before been seen. We state this merely for the information of those
at a distance. To all here it is, of course, known thoroughly."

And now we proceed to the reply of the committee of arrangements, which is copied from the " Transcript :"

"The committee of arrangements of the Payne festival who
have 'humbugged' the public, cannot allow the article in the
' Atlas' to pass without a comment. As the friends of Mr. Payne
never admitted the word or feeling of charity to enter into their
views in the management of the benefit, nor wished aid to it under
such impressions, they pass over in silence that part of the article
reflecting such an imputation on the true friends of Mr. Payne
and of dramatic literature. The members of the committee concur entirely with the ' Atlas,' that the benefit was not given by
the city of Boston, but by the friends of Mr. Payne. It would
have been unkind, even to his enemy, if he have any, and we have
not yet realized the fact, had the committee prefaced their bill by
saying they only expected or invited the particular friends of Mr.

Payne to be present. They wished to give the city of Boston the opportunity of proving whether it had any feeling for such an evidence of Mr. Payne's merits or not. The sequel has proved that, independent of a very attractive bill, it had not the feeling in question. We cannot allow that one solitary paper, among so many, should be an evidence of the feeling of the community at large. We place the matter entirely on the ground that the 'Atlas' has done, so far as regards those who gave the benefit, and we are happy in saying that the Tremont Theatre never was more graced than by the bright galaxy of fine faces and intelligent minds that were assembled on that occasion.

"A better representation of the feeling of a community could not have been chosen, and we are confident in saying that had the theatre had it in its power to afford as attractive a bill as was brought forward at New York, the house would have been filled not only by the personal friends of Mr. Payne but by the mass of the people."

Shortly after the Boston *fiasco* he returned to the city of New York, where he had been so handsomely received, and resided with his brother, Thatcher Payne, who then had risen to eminence as a lawyer. Here he constructed the ground-work of the "Life of our Saviour," which he had prepared in the manner of a harmony of the four Gospels. It was said to have been beautifully executed, on the common theory of the three years' duration of the ministry of Jesus. But after consulting a friend on the subject of its publication, he concluded not to have it printed, from the fact that a similar work by Mr. Ware had preoccupied the market. This given up, he soon after issued a prospectus for a weekly periodical, which was to be published in London, and conducted on an international basis, its contributors to be both English and American. The idea was a novel one, and at that time could not have failed to make the English better acquainted with our progress in all things pertaining to a high civilization, as well as to modify a national feeling of conflict between the two people.

Mr. Payne said in his "Prospectus," "Literary labor in America can only be rendered a source of sure and permanent benefit to its followers and others through some connection with the periodical press. Even abroad this is widely, though less exclusively, the case; Byron himself knew it, and was ambitious of establishing a magazine with Shelley and Hunt. Scott was for a long time at the head of an 'Annual Register,' and to the last was more or less concerned in less ponderous publications of the same class; and Campbell, Bulwer, Lockhart, and numbers equally eminent in England, besides Jouy, Durval, and others in France, and many who might be quoted in various parts of the world, look for their least precarious resources and means of usefulness, notwithstanding their popularity as makers of books, to their editorships of periodicals.

"But there is no country where works of that nature form so essential a portion of national literature as ours, or where their power of doing good or evil can be so widely and so suddenly diffused. It was, therefore, the first thought of the writer of this to associate himself with some establishment already in existence here, or to create upon the spot a new one of his own.

"He has found every place, however, in the enterprises now existing, not only filled, but ably filled. He has found, too, that the country already contains as many dailies, weeklies, monthlies, quarterlies, and annuals, upon the established system of such productions, as it appears to require, and no opportunity seems open for a new undertaking of the sort which might not be an interference with those already popular. To the enlightened persons connected with works of this description throughout the United States the undersigned is indebted for many civilities, and so large and liberal has been the kindness with which they have sustained him equally through good report and evil, that he would not for a moment entertain a thought of any speculation, which could scarcely be successful without disturbing the arrangements of some one who, though a stranger, may have been a friend.

"But, in the course of his examination, he has remarked how largely some of our papers draw upon materials from abroad, and so prevailing is the desire for European extracts and information, that papers are not only liberally patronized expressly for these alone, but republications made in London journals as they stand, and even some of the best of our own, establishing a strong claim to patronage upon the correspondence of agents, whom they employ abroad. Thus the voice of Europe is heard incessantly in every corner of the North American Republic.

"In the mean time, who hears of our own Republic in Europe? Who knows anything of the innumerable improvements we are hourly making in the application of science to the useful arts,—of the many valuable works which are constantly issuing from our press,—of the numberless displays of high intellectual power in every department among us, which, from circumstances, are never wrought into books;—in short, of how much we are laboring in the great cause of universal good, which, even when the effect is felt in other climes, is felt without any recognition of its source?—And who, in America, is not aware—even while the press of Europe is so much courted in America—through what distorted mediums it leads us to look upon productions and events, or how seldom, even when fairly represented, they are exhibited in those points of view which would be, to us, the most interesting or instructive?

" These reflections have suggested to the undersigned a project which, though venturous, appears to supply the only stand never yet taken for extensive usefulness in periodical literature. It is an enterprise which could only proceed from a country situated like ours, and it appears to him equally a desideratum for both sides of the Atlantic. The work in question is an original American journal, to be published every week in London, supported by the united talent of both countries, and containing the most accurate information from both upon every subject—excepting politics —which can have interest or importance either in America or Europe.

" The proposed title of this Journal has been hinted by the story of the magical cup, so much the theme of Eastern poetry, and to us rendered peculiarly interesting from the impression among certain of the Scripture commentators, that, in the sack of Benjamin, some cup with such a story must have been placed to have impelled Joseph's servant to ask his brethren, ' Is not this it whereby my Lord divineth?' It is scarcely necessary to add that the allusion is to that famous cup supposed to possess the strange property of representing in it the whole world and all the things which were then doing, and celebrated as *Jami Jamshed,* the cup of Jamshed, a very ancient King of Persia, and which is said to have been discovered in digging the foundations of Persepolis, filled with the elixir of immortality. The name given to this cup by the poets of Persia is the one thought of for the present purpose, and if the work in contemplation should be attempted, it will probably bear the eastern title of 𝕵𝖆𝖒 𝕵𝖊𝖍𝖆𝖓 𝕬𝖎𝖒𝖆, which means, in English, the goblet wherein you may behold the universe.

" On each side of the Atlantic the intended journal is expected to afford distinct advantages, which may unite to assist objects of vast interest to the world at large.

" To America it can be serviceable thus :

"I. By providing a depository where original literary productions from the writers of America and England may appear side by side, a competition may be created tending to most favorable influences upon our literature, while its effects, exhibited before so large a mass of readers on both sides of the ocean, will afford evidences in our favor better than the best of arguments. Nothing overcomes mere prejudice more effectually than acquaintanceship, and there is a sort of remorse mixed up with the sense of having been unjust through ignorance, which almost always changes those who were once embittered, by want of knowledge of each other, into the most earnest friends. The closer intercourse of England with this country, by means of literature and the arts, has done more to wear away bad spirit than all the negotiations of all our political ambassadors.

"II. It will supply a vehicle in which the intellectual interests of America may be upheld. As our political relations call for a political ambassador,—and our commercial intercourse causes the establishment of houses of commerce,—and our fashionable world keeps up its envoys at the courts and coteries,—is it not equally desirable that some mode should be created for extending attention to the moral and mental, as well as to the physical and mercantile, strength of this vast republic? for steadily representing the reading and the writing and the thinking portion of the people of America in the great parliament of European letters which taxes them so largely?

"III. It will give Europe a *catalogue raisonnée* of all the original books issuing from the American press; and prompt inquiry after, and knowledge of, many of which otherwise nothing might be known beyond the limited sphere of their publication.

"IV. It will circulate the names and powers of numerous writers of the first-rate merit, whose reputation is now merely local, and who seldom seek an outlet for their productions of wider range than a magazine or newspaper. Our business habits, and the large influx of English works, concur to check original publications among themselves; and while booksellers can supply the market with sufficient novelty from abroad, which, to the advantage of being obtained without cost, adds that of bringing along with it an established fame, many who can write admirably write only for themselves. A magazine of the sort now described would draw them out and circulate their treasures. It would, at the same time, make foreigners familiar with some now entirely hidden from observation by the very limited number of book-makers, compared with the number of those among us capable of making books.

" V. It will communicate most readily and extensively every discovery we hit upon in science and the mechanical arts.

" VI. It will enable misrepresentations of our country to be answered ere they have time to take root.

" The service it can render on the other side of the Atlantic may be :

" I. To provide opinions upon productions and events entirely uninfluenced by party or local prejudice. It has often been remarked that we are, with respect to Europe, a sort of cotemporary posterity. Towards England our intellectual relations are altogether unprecedented in the history of nations. Our mutual influences exceed those of other nations, because we do not only think upon the same topics, but in the same language; and our understanding of each other never suffers through those distortions often inevitable from the different shades of signification growing out even of the clearest communication in any language not our own. As to their earlier master-minds, that country is identified with ours ; and we have only been rendered a separate nation by having realized the inspiration upon the subject of national liberty for which some of these mighty teachers became immortal. But, though divided from the rest as the peculiar people who went apart to preserve the right principles of national happiness, we have continued as one and the same people in every thing relating to literature, to science, and the arts. The identity of our interests in these matters is strengthening with time ; and as the vast increase of readers of works from England goes on increasing (as it has done ever since Pope complained that he could only be ' read in one island'), the desire to stand well with this new literary public becomes more vivid with the British literati. But if we contribute so largely to their fame, we are entitled to a voice in the legislature of their taste ; and a work which shall speak the sentiments of a clear-headed republic will not be heard without interest, and probably not without courtesy and profit, by those who are gratified with that great republic's sanction."

Any one will admit that Mr. Payne's proposition for an international journal was full of excellent ideas. He made a strong effort to start the journal. He applied to many of his best friends throughout the Union, and none did more to assist him than S. H. Jenks, a gentleman of Boston of high literary culture, and for many years connected with the press. He was also a companion of Payne's in their boyhood, and was one of the officers of the military company of which Payne was captain in his youth. S. H. Jenks was the father of F. H. Jenks, at present one of the editors of the " Boston Transcript," and who for many years has been devoted to the culture and progress of music in Boston. The following letter of Payne's, sent us by F. H. Jenks, will show Payne's anxiety to get the journal under way, and show too that he did not receive the encouragement his noble enterprise deserved :

"Boston, July 24, 1834.

"My dear Sir,—I have been here some time fruitlessly endeavoring to obtain subscribers for my work, of which I send you the Prospectus and list. Pray oblige me by saying whether I could do anything by a trip to Nantucket for some two or three days. Would the land of whales assist me with oil for the enlightener of the two hemispheres? If I can hope for anything I will come forthwith, but I am weary of laboring for empty professions and smiles, which cost more than they come to.

"Perhaps you will oblige me by answering this by return post. I shall go to New York at once else, instead of going to Nantucket. Old associations will lead you to forgive me for thus troubling you, and I can only add, trouble me in the same way as much and as often as you like.

"Yours, my dear sir, most truly,

"John Howard Payne.

"S. H. Jenks, Esq."

Mr. Payne travelled through many of the Western and Southwestern States to obtain subscribers at ten dollars each, in advance, which appeared at the time to be too large a sum, and the amount of money required to start the enterprise—fifty thousand dollars—was harder to accomplish than he at first supposed, and after spending more money to obtain subscribers than was subscribed, he quietly abandoned the project.

In 1835, while on his way through the South, he stopped at New Orleans, where he was at once received by the press and the citizens with much consideration, and, shortly after his arrival there, a large number of citizens offered to give him a testimonial at the

"Camp Street Theatre." The event took place on the evening of March 18th, 1835. The bill offered for the occasion consisted of "Charles the Second" and "Thérèse,"—two of Mr. Payne's own dramas,—a "Prize Address," together with an "Olio" and the farce of "More Blunders than One." The stars of the occasion were the celebrated Irish comedian, Mr. Tyrone Powers, Mr. Holland, Mr. Keen, the singer, Mr. Finn, Miss Placide, and Mrs. Knight.

The committee who had the matter in hand, offered as a prize for the address a silver cup, which was awarded to Mr. James Rees, of Philadelphia, a gentleman who had written many dramas, and is now better known to the public as a dramatic critic, over the signature of "Colley Cibber." The latter part of the address is finer than any other that has been on any occasion offered as a graceful tribute to Mr. Payne.

"ADDRESS.

" When classic Greece first reared the infant stage,
And to the drama gave her title-page,
Æschylus caught the all-inspiring flame,
And sent the volume down to future fame.
Then Shakespeare with a radiant beauty bound
The mighty work which Genius' self had crown'd,
Until the world, the sceptic world approved
What all admired, what all so fondly loved.
The volume opens, on whose varied page
The spirits shine of a departed age:
Richard, Macbeth, Othello, glide along,
Raised by the magic of that prince of song.
But, hark! another sweeps the glowing strings
Of nature's harp—'tis our own Payne that sings,
And see! stern Brutus panoplied appears:
Himself all marble; kindred, friends, all tears.
Then Carwin, hid beneath his cloak of crime,
Seems the dread angel of destroying time.
Again—but lo! what brighter visions rise,
Each sense enthralling in a glad surprise,
' Whose wings, like heaven's vast canopy, unfurled,
Spread their broad plumage o'er the subject world,'
Around whose form young Genius proudly clings,
And ' *Jam Jehan Nima*' glitters on their wings!
'Tis Learning's arch extending o'er the main,
Raised by the talisman of gifted Payne.
But what reward for him, whose midnight lamp
Emits its ray from chambers cold and damp ;

Whose cheerless looks and dreary aspect seem
The spectred portrait of some horrid dream ;
Whose mind, replete with lore, profusely gives
Food for the million, while himself scarce lives ;
Who decks creation with a brighter gem
Than ever sparkled on a diadem ?
Thus Genius pines, his stores display in vain,
Thus bards have languished, steeped in grief and pain :
No showers of gold, by speculative art,
Dispel the gloom, or warm the aching heart.
What star is that, whose bright, increasing light
Breaks on his soul, and cheers the gloom of night?
His country's star ! it comes to the bard to cheer;
The exile has a home—*he finds it here !"*

Music—" Home, Sweet Home !"

" What sounds are these, what pleasing, heavenly strains,
Whose echoing sweetness wanton o'er the plains ?
Hark ! (music) now on airy wings they float,
And angel voices catch the inspiring note,
'Tis the warm welcome,—' Wanderer, cease to roam ;
Thrice doubly welcome to thy ' Home, Sweet Home !' "

(Curtain fell to music of " Home, Sweet Home !")

Immediately after the benefit the following correspondence occurred between the committee and Mr. Payne. The letter of Mr. Payne is of the most highly interesting character, as it shows him to have been one of the strongest and earliest champions of international copyright law, and the argument is so pertinent that it would be an injustice to the interests of literature to omit it :

"CORRESPONDENCE.

"JOHN HOWARD PAYNE, ESQ.

" DEAR SIR,—Enclosed we have the pleasure to hand you a check for one thousand and six dollars and fifty cents ($1006.50), being the net proceeds resulting from the performances at the American Theatre for your benefit on the 18th inst.

" We regret that the inauspicious state of the weather should have caused the amount of the receipts to be less than was anticipated. We trust, however, that, viewed as a compliment to you as an American author, it will be acceptable, and be considered as an evidence of the good wishes of the gentlemen under whose management the benefit was presented to the notice of the public.

"We avail ourselves of the occasion to convey to you the expression of our distinguished consideration, and remain most respectfully,

"Your obedient servants,

"JAS. SAUL, *Chairman,*
"NATH. DICK,
"J. FOSTER, JR.,
"*Committee.*

"NEW ORLEANS, April 2, 1835."

"GENTLEMEN,—I am this moment honored with your letter, enclosing the sum of $1006.50, being the amount remaining after payment to the play-house managers for one evening's performance at the American Theatre, volunteered for my advantage, on Wednesday, the 18th of last month, by my countrymen at New Orleans. In return, I beg you to make my grateful acknowledgments to all who have promoted this attention, and to accept for yourselves, and for the other gentlemen composing the various committees, my especial thanks. Apart from any considerations personal to myself, I believe the evidence of a disposition for such actions will inspirit the literary of our land, by showing that neither time nor distance can cause their labors, however humble, to be forgotten or entirely fruitless.

"As, however, there may be some who are not altogether apprised of the peculiar position of writers for the stage, and to whom the unique one in which I myself have stood may not be familiar, I take the liberty of naming my reasons for having acquiesced in this and previous civilities of the same nature. I scarcely need mention why I have deferred this representation until now. Had it been made earlier, by some it might have been regarded as a sort of electioneering stratagem to promote my pecuniary interests; but now, I trust, there is no one who will not do me the justice to take it as it is meant, to understand it as emanating entirely from a wish to make the deplorable state of patronage to the literary portion of the drama understood among us, that all may see, for the advantage of authors in general, the necessity for a speedy reform.

"Dramatic authorship in the English language—although the most vexatious, while it is the most widely influential branch of literature—has always been the least protected by the laws both of America and England. The authors of France have a permanent interest in every representation of their plays, and this property descends to their families,—the law obliges theatres to pay them. In England, until very lately, dramatic writers were sustained by no law but that of custom, and custom only entitled them to claim the profits of the third, sixth, ninth, twelfth, twentieth, and fortieth performance of any play from the theatre in which it first appeared, but from no other; and no sooner had it appeared than it was at the mercy of the prompters, who made vast perquisites by supplying early copies to all the provincial theatres of England, and by forwarding them to the managers of this country. When published, the author had no power to screen his interest from the cupidity of gain in managers; his play, even against his expressed wish, as in the case of Lord Byron, could be impudently wrested from him before his eyes, and acted without recompense, and without even thanks. This enormity was, for some years, a theme of unregarded remonstrance in the newspapers and magazines. I myself wrote quires to call the attention of the British legislature to the injustice, and to invite them to imitate the law of France. At length the subject was brought before the Parliament of England by Mr. Bulwer. A law was very recently passed, securing to the author (or if the copyright were sold, the proprietor[1]) of any play appearing in the English

[1] This was not the original intention of the act. The act meant to secure the rights of authors, exclusively, to a species of profit which can never be calculated in the outset; for nothing is more uncertain than the future fortunes of a play, and that which has promised the least, and under such a doubt has often been sacrificed for a trifle to managers or publishers, has very frequently turned out the most lucrative in the end. But, from being loosely worded, the act has since been perverted from its original purpose. Indeed, its framers did not see the necessity of providing for the difference between publication by printing and publication by performance, which has always perplexed the question of dramatic copyright, until it has been recently forced upon them through this perversion of their purposes by the grasping spirit of managing and bookselling speculators. When the decision was pronounced in favor of the latter, and against authors, in the court of King's Bench, the court, though compelled to adopt the literal construction, advised a remodelling of the statute, which had evidently defeated itself by the carelessness of its phraseology, and notice has been given that an explanatory law will be submitted. It was, of course, intended to prevent authors from becoming the victims of circumstances, and to insure them all the advantages of greater success with the public than they expected.

language, whether published or in manuscript, a right to enforce compensation, during some five and twenty years, for every performance of that play, wherever it may appear, within the jurisdiction of the British government. So impressed was the legislature of England with the inadequacy of theatrical payment, as it stood previous to the reform I mention, that they made the new law revert to productions which had been brought out within seven years. I myself might have gained largely by this enactment; but, never looking for such a law, I had sold most of my copyrights, during the first run of each play, to publishers who are at this moment reaping incomes from them; and such as remained my property, and are still constantly acted as stock-pieces, were produced on the wrong side of the seven years' limitation.

"What are our own laws upon this subject? We have none. Dramatists are at the mercy of managers. The now obsolete law of custom in England still remains feebly imitated with us; not in four benefits for a success, but in one alone; and even that one is usually proffered under circumstances so hopeless that authors seldom avail themselves of the opportunity. Present a new play to a manager, and he delays its production till the season is withering, and then flings it upon the forlorn hope; or, if you ask a certain compensation, he replies, 'We are glutted with plays from England, which we must produce, because they bring with them a fame which will excite curiosity; and for these we have only to pay the prompters, who are salaried to smuggle over all the novelties.' Within a few years some opportunities have been afforded to a few, employed by certain popular actors, travelling as stars, to write under their patronage and direction. and for their own personal aggrandizement; but such a market is very soon supplied, and perhaps not always the most desirable. To me it has never been offered. On the contrary, when I was abroad, and new productions have occasionally been wanted from England for any particular purpose in America, I have seen myself passed over, and the commission tendered to others, not American ; and since I have been in America, play after play have I presented for performance, and have uniformly been answered, 'We can get new plays from England, and for nothing.'

"It will be unnecessary. after this explanation, to state why the market which pays must be the one resorted to by the person who is not wealthy enough to labor without pay. It will explain, also, why I have taken my productions to the theatres of England.

11

I had no other means of deriving profit from them. I had no other means of getting them before the public of my own country. In this manner I manœuvred myself, as it were, into opportunities of being heard, and from the frequency with which my plays were announced all over America, and from the praises of them in the papers, I naturally imagined that I had been heard with favor. To confirm this, invitations were sent to me to return, and to receive from my countrymen testimonials that, if managers would not reward me, the public would; that many plays of mine, which had been acted for some nineteen years, would be acknowledged by a benefit in each town where they had been acted, and that, having thus shown that the past was not forgotten, I should find an equal alacrity to make the future prosperous. It was known that much prejudice had been excited against me by a party in England for having so strongly asserted my American principles, as to endanger the license of certain plays and to bring down the vengeance of certain critics, and I was promised that my own land would sustain me against what I have suffered from the support of sentiments to which I trust no persecution will ever make a citizen of our country false. It was known, too, that my most fortunate efforts had been made when the theatres were so much embarrassed that they could never pay me one-fourth of the prices usually paid, although it was publicly stated that these very efforts had averted the bankruptcy, first, of Drury Lane, and afterwards, of Covent Garden, and many enthusiasts fancied I should find better opportunities and better rewards at home.

"My return, however, was delayed by business till two years subsequently to the invitations of which I speak. I was reluctant to comply with a request which might have exposed me to the imputation of having been brought to America only to court notice and attention. I waited until other matters rendered a visit to my native land desirable; but, when I did return, I found the professions which had been made to me from New York were not forgotten. My native city gave me the welcome which had been tendered.

"From various parts of the United States I was invited to receive similar testimonials. I never understood these as public honors,—of such I never had the vanity to dream. I considered them as a mere compensation from those who had often expressed approval of my labors, and never before had an opportunity of offering that sort of acknowledgment for them which no writer,

in any language or in any nation, ever deemed himself dishonored
in receiving; which your divine receives, your lawyer receives,
your doctor receives,—and why should not your author? Nor
could I feel that an acceptance from any theatre—after the performance in it, times innumerable, of many plays during some
nineteen years—of the profits of one night, under the title of a
benefit, could be less a simple recompense, in the straightforward
way of business, than the acceptance of the profits of one similar
night, after merely a couple of performances in such theatre of
any single play. How could I, unless I could be convinced that
hundreds of representations degraded that return into the stigma
of charity, which only two could elevate into the dignity of compensation? How could I, unless I could discover that payment
long deferred must necessarily be construed as alms bestowed,
merely because the sum total of that payment had dwindled by
delay and come without interest? And still less, when not only
Mr. Irving and Mr. Cooper, the novelist, but even writers much
their inferiors, can secure for their publications, through the press,
an equal property on both sides of the Atlantic by a protective
law,[1] still less could I see any impropriety in receiving advantages

---

[1] Colonel Hamilton, in his work on our country, thus alludes to this point:
"Copyright, in the United States, is not enjoyable by a foreigner, though an
American can hold it in England. The consequence is, that an English
author derives no benefit from the republication of his work in America,
while every Englishman who purchases the work of an American is taxed in
order to put money into the pockets of the latter. There is no reciprocity
in this; and it is really not easy to see why Mr. Washington Irving or Mr.
Cooper should enjoy greater privileges in this country than are accorded to
Mr. Bulwer or Mr. Theodore Hook in the United States. There is an old
proverb, 'What is good for the goose is good for the gander,' which will be
found quite as applicable to the policy of Parliament as the practice of the
poultry-yard. It is to be hoped this homely apophthegm will not escape the
notice of the government, and that, by an act of signal justice (the aboli-
tion of American copyright in England), it will compel the United States to
adopt a wiser and more liberal system."—*Men and Manners in America*, p.
201, Cary & Lea's 8vo edition

What would the colonel have said had he been aware that for the particular
branch of literature whose rights I am asserting even our own countrymen
cannot secure the only profitable copyright of their productions,—that of publication by representation, if these productions happen first to have appeared
in England, the only country where, under existing circumstances, they can
be made first to appear with profit and fame. Perhaps, were our theatres in
the hands of Americans, the interests of Americans might suffer less. But

of correspondent character, though inferior value, from the publication performances of my efforts, when my countrymen were disposed to atone for the want of a similar protective law by what they
deemed an act of voluntary justice,—no compassion—no charity—
but justice, simple justice,—though a justice deriving peculiar elevation from the grace and lustre of having been unforced, unasked,
unlooked for. Nor would I insist on limiting this sort of justice
to the works of natives of our country, especially as the law
of England involves no exclusion to the detriment of Americans,
but renders the manager who produces any play in the English
language responsible to its author, no matter to what country
that author may belong. If we can pay the actors of England
for entertaining us, we can pay their authors too; and if it were
necessary to pay both equally, it would save us from much foreign
trash and force advantages for writers of our own. But their
first-rate authors ought to be paid. It would make them love
our country and respect its lofty principles,—and the respect of
the intellectual is thought lightly of by none but fools. Our countrymen think entirely as I do upon this head, for we are at this
very moment paying one of their most estimable and distinguished
dramatists, Sheridan Knowles, and, by doing so, we do ourselves
honor in honoring a great genius. But, if there must be an exclusion, let us not exclude any native of our soil, especially while our
literature and arts are yet so much in the difficulties of their dawn
that they need extra encouragement from those partialities which
have ever been regarded as a duty towards the first steps of timid,
faltering infancy. But to return to the case in question,—my own
case. It is not on the quality of my labors that I would expatiate.
They were even, most of them, produced under circumstances
which forbade much excellence; circumstances which might have
paralyzed far greater powers than any I can boast of. But it is the
principle of deeming any work from an American, which has been
thought worth often listening to, at least worth once paying for,
that I would see cherished. Believe me, I do not urge this principle on my own account. To me its enforcement is never likely
to render any essential service; on me its enforcement has already

---

they are, almost without exception, under the control of persons who have
left the sterile, provincial theatres of Great Britain to seek their fortunes in
this country, and to enrich themselves by the despised authors, and, sometimes, we find, despised audiences of America.

brought misconstruction and discomfort. But let it be cherished.
It is of vital import to our future fame and affluence in literature
and the arts. It will stimulate minds whose works will make the
world venerate our common country when we are in our graves.
Managers of theatres ought not to make it necessary for the public to act for themselves upon such a subject; but every such act
involves a comment upon the negligence and short-sightedness of
managers not to be misunderstood, and under which it is scarcely
to be wondered that they should wince. So strongly am I persuaded that demonstrations like the one which calls forth this
letter are doing a national service, in awakening national attention to a most important subject, that it is my purpose, at the first
fitting opportunity, to petition Congress to compel that justice
from managers towards authors, by a public law, which is now
only to be looked for in the public feeling.

"But, I have said I was invited, on my return to my native
land, from various parts of the United States to receive similar
testimonials. I was. To New Orleans, among other places, I
was expressly invited, and by Mr. Caldwell, when he was in the
management. I did not, however, think it delicate to visit any
place expressly for such an object, although I felt no hesitation in
acquiescing whenever such an object might be presented. I did
not visit New Orleans for the purpose. I did not visit it till I
had matured a plan for rendering to my country the greatest
service which I supposed that the chances and experience of my
life had qualified me for rendering. I had projected a periodical
which should supply to the mind of Europe opportunities for
appreciating that of America, by showing the energies of both
combined in one great work,—a periodical which, out of the joint
patronage of America and Europe, should create for me the means
of paying American talent with a liberality which no support yet
obtained for any work in our own country has thus far been
able to afford, and a periodical which should stand ready, in the
very centre of those by whom we have so often been misrepre-
sented, to uphold, by the power of the press, my native land against
all Europe, should she, in Europe, be defamed. In the pursuit of
support for this periodical I visited New Orleans,—not for any theatrical benefit. But I found that Mr. Caldwell had not forgotten
his invitation, although the managers, to whom in the interim he
had let his theatre, had forgotten the promise they made him, to
give effect to the invitation by coming forward unsolicited when-

ever I might appear; and I found, too, from yourselves, gentlemen, and the gentlemen associated with you in various committees, the same spirit which I had already found elsewhere, and for
the results of which I have now to give you thanks. Various arts
were put in action by the envious and disaffected to disgust me
from accepting the attention you proffered, and to disgust others
with me for not having repelled it; but what you could think fit
to offer it would have been presumption in me to have refused;
and what I had ever felt justified in receiving from other places
I could not have had the bad taste to have declined from a city
like New Orleans.

"The nature of this subject has led me into a much longer letter
than I could have desired to trouble you with. But I am a stranger
in this city, and would make myself distinctly understood upon a
subject which has in some degree engaged public attention, and
which involves my own character as a citizen and a gentleman.
And, on such an occasion, I consider it especially incumbent on
me to press upon my countrymen the propriety of following up
the feeling for the rights of the literary department of the drama,
which benefits, like the one which elicits this letter, proves to be
in some degree awakened. The public voice has been uttered;
let it still be eloquent, and it will ultimately arouse the legislature
of the land.

"Having offered this explanation, once more allow me to thank
you and the other committees for the attention with which I have
been honored, and to beg that you will convey to the citizens generally, with whom I have been acquainted in New Orleans, my
sincerest acknowledgments for their hospitalities.

I have the honor to be,
Gentlemen,
Your most obedient servant
John Howard Payne./

CHAPTER V.

PAYNE AMONG THE INDIANS.

" They waste us; ay, like April snow
In the warm noon, we shrink away;
And fast they follow, as we go
Towards the setting day,
Till they shall fill the land, and we
Are driven into the western sea."

THE benefit at New Orleans was the last of Mr. Payne's associations with the drama, and we now take him up in an entirely new character.

As we have once before stated, Mr. Payne travelled through many of the States to obtain subscribers to his new periodical. It was on this occasion that, being attracted by the difficulties then existing between the United States government and the Cherokee Indians, he went among them, and the wild scenery of Alabama and Georgia, for the purpose of obtaining material for his journal.

Payne was one of those men who was never satisfied by being a mere "looker-on in Denmark." The battle in the distance was nothing to him: he must be in the thick of the fight; and, therefore, the first thing he did when he got into the wild lands of the Cherokees was to seek out the great chief himself. We soon find Mr. Payne not only talking with the red man in the depths of the forest, but eating at his table, sleeping in his hut, and advising the chief Ross what to do, and how to act with the United States government in obtaining a treaty that would protect them from the rascalities of the border agents and secure a proper remuneration for their lands.

When Mr. Payne first approached Ross, the chief of the Cherokees, he was about to meet in council the agents of the government, which council Payne attended. Here he at once became a sympathizer with the Indians, and deeply interested in their affairs; so much so, that he became a sort of adviser to Ross, and for several years was mixed up with the transactions of Ross and the United States government, which resulted in the treaty that finally led to the removal of the tribe to the far West. All of Ross's petitions and statements to the government were drawn up by Payne. There is no doubt but that Mr. Payne upset the treaty that was on the eve of being ratified at the time he arrived among the Cherokees, and was the means of procrastinating a final settlement. In this matter Mr. Payne did not stop to think that by his advice to Ross he was in opposition to his own government. It was a matter only of philanthropy.

The government agents, after Mr. Payne's connection with Ross and his chiefs, found it far more difficult to carry out their plans with the red men, and, observing Payne constantly with Ross, they complained of him to the government at Washington. Payne in the mean time became more bold, openly advocating their cause, and finally wrote an address in behalf of the Cherokees, dedicated to the American people, which he caused to be published in the "Knoxville Register" of December 2, 1835. This was copied extensively throughout the United States, especially so by the papers of the opposition party to the one in power.

The military that had been placed along the borders of Georgia to keep peace between the Georgia State whites and the Indians, during the negotiations, took it into their heads one night to rush upon the hut of Ross, made the chief and Payne prisoners, and marched them off over twenty miles to their headquarters. This adventure appears to have been done without orders. Both Colonel Benjamin F. Curren and Mr. Schermerhorn, the principal agent for the government, denied to Lewis Cass, Secretary of War, that they had anything to do with it. Payne and Ross were held as prisoners for several days. The adventure caused considerable excitement among the Cherokees. The press teemed with many exaggerated stories of their arrest. Mr. Schermerhorn, in one of his communications on the subject to the Secretary of War, stated that at the time Mr. Payne was arrested he was at Tuscaloosa, Alabama, and that he at once hastened to the headquarters of the agency to investigate the matter, but when he reached the spot, he found that Mr. Payne and Ross had been set at liberty several days before. Mr. Payne's brother, as soon as he heard of the affair, wrote the annexed letter to the Secretary of War:

"New York, November 27, 1835.

" To Hon. Lewis Cass.

" Sir,—I have just received information that my brother, John Howard Payne, on the night of the 10th of November instant, while in company with John Ross, the Cherokee chief, at his dwelling in the Cherokee nation, was seized by a party of about twenty-five of the Georgia guard, and conducted by them to the headquarters, about twenty miles distant from the place of seizure, where, as I am informed, he is now imprisoned. Mr. Payne's general object, in a tour through the Western and Southern sections of the United States, has been partly to obtain subscribers to a periodical work in which English and American writers may meet upon equal grounds, and partly to collect such materials for his own contributions to the work as a personal acquaintance with the various peculiarities of our extensive and diversified country may supply.

" To one acquainted with his pacific disposition and exclusively literary habits, the supposition of his entertaining any views politically dangerous, either in reference to the State of Georgia or the United States, in their respective relations to the Cherokees, if it were not accompanied with results painful, and perhaps perilous to himself, would seem ludicrous. My informant, a stranger, states that ' it is there reported that he is considered by the officers of the government to be a spy ;' whether by 'officers of government' is meant those of Georgia, or of the United States, I am not informed.

" He likewise states that ' Mr. Payne is supposed to have some influence in producing the *failure of the late treaty with the Cherokees.*'

" In the present excited state of feelings in that section of the country on subjects connected with the Indian removal, these may, perhaps, be serious charges to the personal safety of one coming under suspicions of the character above alluded to, however groundless.

" I take the liberty (I hope not unwarrantable) to request and urge a speedy inquiry into the circumstances of the case, and the use of the means within the power of your department of the government to procure his release if, as will undoubtedly appear, upon investigation, he shall be found to have been wrongfully detained.

" I am, with respect,

" Your most obedient servant,

" Thatcher M. Payne."

By looking over the "State Documents, 2d Session of the 25th
Congress," in which there is a full report of the whole matter, we
do not find that the government of the United States ever held
Mr. Payne particularly responsible for any of his actions towards
the government while connected with John Ross. We also find,
by letters in our possession from Mr. Payne to parties in New
York, that he was still concerned in the Cherokee affairs up to a
date as late as 1840.

To a man of Payne's peculiar disposition, his stay among the
Indians must have been highly interesting. Always eager for
adventure, and fond of the marvellous, he must have enjoyed
greatly these strange people, and the wild, beautiful scenery that
surrounded them. It was all new to him; he had been absent
from his own country for over twenty years, and had left it at a
time of life when his young mind as yet had not been impressed
with the character of the red men of the forest, and the vastness
of his own country. Payne possessed all the feelings of a true
artist, and, when he travelled, nothing in the way of scenery
or the habits of the people escaped his notice and comments.
If he did not give object form and color by using the pencil
or the brush, he did so by the constant use of the pen in letter-
writing.

His large and familiar acquaintance with English and French
celebrities, all apparently his personal friends, and with whom we
have every evidence he had a voluminous correspondence, sus-
tains us in this opinion.

Among his most intimate friends we may enumerate such as
Charles Lamb, Washington Irving, with whom he roomed while
in Paris, Thomas Moore, O'Connell, Counsellor Phillips, Talma,
John Philip Kemble, Kean, the elder Charles Mathews, Shiel, the
Irish orator, Washington Allston, Haydon, to whom Payne introduced Charles R. Leslie, R.A., who painted Payne in the characters of *Douglas* and *Hamlet*, Robert Owen, who was in the habit
of taking breakfast with Payne when in London, Kenney, Bishop,
Elliston, Dr. Crowly, Scott, and the editor of the "Champion,"
who fell in a duel in consequence of an attack upon Lockhart,
Pool, and many others whom we could readily name,—all of
which names are taken from many of Mr. Payne's own letters
now before us, but unfortunately too disconnected to form a complete whole.

While in the country of the Cherokees, he frequently wrote to his brother or some one of his sisters letters of ten and fifteen pages, descriptive of all things of interest that met his observation. His handwriting is remarkably clear and neat, each letter is well formed; hence his pages are as legible as a book. Not a blot, not an erasure, is to be found even in letters containing a dozen pages, such as the one we now copy, descriptive of the Creek Indian festival, which, from its graphic clearness and minute details, possesses historical value in connection with a race of people who, ere long, will be numbered among the things of the past, and to whose peculiarities and history stories of the wildest fiction cling to fascinate the more civilized.

"MACON, GEORGIA, Aug. 9, 1835.

"MY DEAR SISTER,—You find me much in arrears with you for letters; that is, I have only written you several to your none, and therefore, of course, you have reason to complain. But it is not too late to make atonement for my sins of omission. Here I am, all alone in a strange place,—Macon, in Georgia,—a good-sized, handsomely-built town nearly twelve years old, and with 4000 inhabitants. I arrived about eleven last night. I have no acquaintances here yet, so, for the sake of company, I will brush up my recollection of some of my adventures. I have been among the Indians for a few days lately. Shall I tell you about them? You make no answer, and silence gives consent, so I will tell you about the Indians.

"The State of Alabama, you will remember, has been famous as the abode of the Creek Indians,—always regarded as the most warlike of the Southern tribes. If you will look upon the map of Alabama, you will find on the west side of it, nearly parallel with the State of Mississippi, two rivers,—one the Coosa, and the other the Tallapoosa,—which, descending, unite in the Alabama. Nearly opposite to these, about one hundred miles across, you will find another river, the Chattahoochee, which also descends, to form, with certain tributaries, the Apalachicola. It is within the space bounded by these rivers, and especially at the upper part of it, that the Creeks now retain a sort of sovereignty. The United States have in vain attempted to force the Creeks to volunteer a surrender of their soil for compensation. A famous chief among them made a treaty a few years ago to that effect; but the nation arose against him, surrounded his house, ordered his family out, and bade him appear at the door after all but he had departed.

He did so. He was shot dead, and the house burned. The treaty only took effect in part, if at all. Perpetual discontents have ensued. The United States have assumed a sort of jurisdiction over the territory, leaving the Creeks unmolested in their national habits, and their property,—with this exception in their favor, beyond all other tribes but the Cherokees,—they have the right, if they wish to sell, to sell to individuals at their own prices, but are bound to treat with the republic at a settled rate, which last mode of doing business they rather properly looked upon as giving them the appearance of a vanquished race, and subject to the dictation of conquerors. So, what the diplomatists could not achieve was forthwith attempted by speculators, and among these the everlasting Yankee began to appear, and the Indian independence straightway began to disappear. Certain forms were required by government to give Americans a claim to these Creek lands. The purchaser was to bring the Indians before a government agent; in the agent's presence the Indian was to declare what his possessions were, and for how much he would sell them. The money was paid in presence of the agent, who gave a certificate, which, when countersigned by the President, authorized the purchaser to demand protection from the national arms, if molested. All this was well enough; but it was soon discovered that the speculators would hire drunken and miscreant Indians to personate the real possessor of the lands, and, having paid them the money, they would take it back as soon as the purchase was completed, give the Indian a jug of whiskey or a small bag of silver for the fraud, and so become lords of the soil. Great dissatisfaction arose, and lives were lost. An anonymous letter opened the eyes of government. The white speculators were so desperate and dangerous that any other mode of information was unsafe. Investigators were appointed to examine into the validity of Creek sales, and the examiners met at the time I went to see the Indian festival. It was necessary for me to be thus prolix to make you understand the nature of the society and the sort of danger by which we were surrounded; on the one side white rogues—border cutthroats—contending, through corrupted Indians, for the possessions of those among them who are honest and unwary. The cheated Indian, wheedled by some other white cheat into a promise to sell, payable in over-charged goods, at a higher price, to the one who should expose the fraud; and, when the decision was reversed in favor of the pretended friend, the foiled thief flying at the over-reaching one with fist and knife, and both in good luck if either could live to see what both had stolen. I beheld a fine, gentle, innocent-looking girl—a widow, I believe—come up to the investigator to assert that she had never sold her land. She had been counterfeited by some knave. The investigator's court was a low tavern bar-room. He saw me eying him, and some one had told him I was travelling to take notes. He did not know but government had employed me as a secret supervisor. He seemed to shrink, and postponed the decision. I have since heard that he is as great a rascal as the rest. This ill-starred race is entirely at the mercy of interpreters, who, if not negro slaves of their own, are half-breeds, who are generally worse than the worst of either slaves or knaves.

" In the jargon of the border they call them *linkisters ;* some say because they, by interpreting, form the *link* between the nations; but I should think the word a mere corruption of *linguist.* The Indians become more easily deluded by the borderers than others, because the borderers know that they have no idea of any one being substantial who does not keep a shop; your rascal of the frontier sets up a shop, and is pronounced a *sneezer ;* if his shop be large, he is a *sneezer-chubco ;* if larger than any other, he is a *sneezer-chubco-mico ;* but in any of his qualities, a *sneezer* is always considered as a personage by no means to be sneezed at. The sneezer will pay for land in goods, and thinks himself very honest if he charges his goods at five hundred times their worth, and can make it appear, by his account against the Indian's claim, that he has paid him thousands of dollars when, in fact, he may scarcely have paid him hundreds of cents.

" Well, now for the festival.

" When the green corn ripens the Creeks seem to begin their year. Until after certain religious rites it is considered an infamy to touch the corn. The season approaching, there is a meeting of the chiefs of all the towns forming any particular clan. First, an order is given out for the manufacture of certain articles of pottery for a part of their festival. A second meeting gives out a second order. New matting is to be prepared for the seats of the assembly. There is a third meeting. A vast number of sticks are broken into as many parts as there are days intervening previous to the one appointed for the gathering of the clan. Runners are sent with these, made into bundles for each clansman. One is flung aside each day, and every one is punctually on the last day at the appointed rendezvous. I must now mention the place where they assemble.

"It is a large square, with four large, long houses, one forming each side of the square, and at each angle a broad entrance to the area. These houses are of clay and a sort of wicker-work, with sharp-topped sloping roofs like those of our log houses, but more thoroughly finished. A space is left open all around at the back and sides of each house to afford a free circulation of air; this opening came about up to my chin, and enables one to peep in on all sides. The part of the house fronting the square is entirely open. It consists of one broad raised platform, a little more than knee-high, and curved and inclined so as to make a most comfortable place for either sitting or reclining. Over this is wrought the cane matting, which extends from the back to the ground in front. At each angle of the square there is a broad entrance. Back of one angle is a high, cone-roofed building, circular and dark, with a sloping entrance through a low door. It was so dark that I could not make out the interior, but some one said it was a council-house. It occupied one corner of an outer square next to the one I have described, two sides of which outer square were formed by thick and tall corn-fields, and a third by a raised embankment, apparently for spectators, and a fourth by the back of one of the buildings before described. In the centre was a considerably high circular mound. This, it seems, was formed from the earth accumulated yearly by removing the surface of the sacred square to this centre of the outer one. At every Green-corn festival the sacred square is strewn with soil yet untrodden; the soil of the year preceding being taken away, but preserved, as I explain. No stranger's foot is allowed to press the new earth of the sacred square until its consecration is complete. A gentleman told me that he and a friend had chanced once to walk through, along the edge, just after the new soil was laid. A friendly chief saw him and remonstrated, and seemed greatly incensed. He explained that it was done in ignorance. The chief was pacified, but ordered every trace of the unhallowed steps to be uptorn and a fresh covering in the place.

"The sacred square being ready, every fire in the towns dependent on the chief of the clan is at the same moment extinguished. Every house must at that moment have been newly swept and washed. Enmities are forgotten. If a person under a sentence for a crime can steal in unobserved and appear among the worshippers, his crime is no more remembered. The first ceremony is to light the new fire of the year. A square board is brought with a small circular hollow in the centre. It receives the dust of a forest tree or of dry leaves. Five chiefs take turns to whirl the stick until the friction produces a flame. From this sticks are lighted and conveyed to every house of the clan. The original flame is taken to the centre of the sacred square. Wood is heaped there and a strong fire lighted. Over this fire the holy urns of new-made pottery are placed ; drinking-gourds, with long handles, are set around on a bench, officers are over the whole in attendance, and here what they call the black drink is brewed with many forms and with intense solemnity.

"I cannot describe to you my feelings as I first found myself in the Indian country. We rode miles after miles in the native forest, neither habitation nor inhabitant to disturb the solitude and majesty of the wilderness. At length we met a native in his native land. He was galloping on horseback. His air was Oriental ; he had a turban, a robe of fringed and gaudily-figured calico, scarlet leggings, and beaded belts and garters and pouch. We asked how far it was to the square. He held up a finger, and we understood him to mean one mile. Next we met two Indian women on horseback, loaded with watermelons. We bought some. In answer to our question of the road they half covered a finger, to say it was half a mile further, and, smiling, added ' *Sneezer-much,*'—meaning that we should find lots of our brethren the sneezers to keep us company. We passed groups of Indian horses tied in the shade, with cords long enough to let them graze freely ; we then saw the American flag (a gift from the government) floating over one of the hut-tops in the square; we next passed groups of Indian horses and carriages and servants, and, under the heels of one horse, a drunken vagabond Indian asleep, or half asleep; and at length we got to the corner of the square, where they were in the midst of their devotions. I stood upon a mound at the corner angle to look in. I was told that this mound was composed of ashes from such fires as were now blazing in the centre during many preceding years; and that these ashes are never permitted to be scattered, but must thus be gathered up, and carefully and religiously preserved.

"Before the solemnities begin, and, I believe, ere the new earth is placed, the women dance in the sacred square. The preliminary dance of theirs is by themselves; I missed this. They then sepa-

rate from the men, and remain apart from them until after the
fasting and other religious forms are gone through.

"On my arrival, the sacred square, as I gazed from the corner-
mound, presented a most striking sight. Upon each of the notched
posts, of which I have already spoken as attached to the houses of
the sacred square, was a stack of tall cones, hung all over with
feathers, black and white. There were rude paint-daubs about
the posts and roof-beams of the houses fronting on the square, and
here and there they were festooned with ground-vines. Chiefs
were standing around the sides and corners alone, and opposite
to each other, their eyes riveted on the earth and motionless as
statues. Every building within was filled with crowds of silent
Indians, those on the back rows seated in the Turkish fashion,
but those in front with their feet to the ground. All were turbaned, all fantastically painted; all in dresses varying in ornament
but alike in wildness. One chief wore a tall black hat, with a
broad, massy silver band around it, and a peacock's feather; another had a silver skull-cap, with a deep silver bullion fringe down
to his eyebrows, and plates of silver from his knee, descending his
tunic. Most of them had the eagle-plume, which only those may
wear who have slain a foe. A number wore military plumes in
various positions about their turbans, and one had a tremendous
tuft of black feathers declining from the back of his head, over his
back, while another's head was all shaven smooth, excepting a tuft
across the centre from the back to the front, like the crest of a
helmet. I never saw an assembly more absorbed with what they
regarded as the solemnities of the occasion.

"The first sounds I heard were a strange, low, deep wail,—a
sound of many voices, drawn out in perfect unison, and only
dying away with the breath itself, which, indeed, was longer sustained than could be done by any singer whom I ever yet heard.
This was followed by a second wail in the same style, but shrill,
like the sound of musical glasses, and giving the same shiver to
the nerves. And, after a third wail, in another key, the statue-
like figures moved, and formed two diagonal lines opposite to each
other, their backs to opposite angles of the square. One by one
they then approached the huge bowls in which the black drink
was boiling, and in rotation dipped a gourd, and took with a most
reverential expression a long, deep draught each. The next part
of the ceremony with each was somewhat curious, but the rapt
expression of the worshippers, and the utter absence of anything

to give a disagreeable air to the act took away the effect it may produce even in description. By some knack, without moving a muscle of the face nor joint, they moved about like strange spectres more than human beings. But soon the character of the entertainment changed, and I more particularly observed two circular plates of brass and steel, which appeared to be the remains of very antique shields. They were borne with great reverence by two chiefs. The nation do not pretend to explain whence they came; they keep them apart, as something sacred; they are only produced on great occasions. I was told, too, that ears of green corn were brought in at a part of the ceremony to-day which I did not see and presented to a chief. He took them, handed them back with an invocation that corn might continue plenty through the year among them. This seemed to be the termination of the peace-offerings, and the religious part of the affair was now to wind up with emblems of war. These were expressed in what they call a *Gun-Dance.* When dispositions were making for it, some persons in carriages were desired by a white *linkister* to draw back and to remove their horses to a distance. Some ladies especially were warned. ' Keep out of their way, ma'rm,' said the *linkister* to a lady, 'for when they come racing about here with their guns they gits powerful sarcy.' I saw them dressing for the ceremony, if it may be called dressing to throw off nearly every part of a scanty covering; but the Indians are especially devoted to dress in their way. Some of them went aside to vary their costume with nearly every dance.

"Now appeared a procession of some forty or fifty women. They entered the square and took their seats together, in one of the open houses. Two men sat in front of them, with gourds filled with pebbles. The gourds were shaken so as to keep time, and the women began a long chant, with which, at regular intervals, was given a sharp, short whoop from male voices. The women's song was said to be intended for the wail of mothers, wives, and daughters at the departure of the warriors for the fight; the response conveyed the resolution of the warriors not to be withheld, but to fight and conquer. And now appeared two hideous-looking old warriors, with tomahawks and scalping-knives, painted most ferociously. Each went half round the circle, exchanged exclamations, kept up a sort of growl all the while, and at length stopped with a war-whoop. We were now told to hurry to the outer square. The females and their male leaders left their places inside and went to the mound in the centre of the

12

outer square. This mound their forms entirely covered, and the effect was very imposing. Here they resumed their chant. The spectators mounted on the embankment. I got on a pile of wood, holy wood, I believe, and heaped there to keep up the sacred fires. There were numbers of Indian women in the crowd. Four stuffed figures were placed erect in the four corners of the square.

"We now heard firing and whooping on all sides. At length in the high corn on one side we saw crouching savages, some with guns of every sort, some, especially the boys, with corn-stalks to represent guns. A naked chief with a long sabre, the blade painted blood-color, came before them, flourishing his weapon and haranguing vehemently. In another cornfield appeared another party. The two savages already mentioned as having given the war-dance in the sacred square now hove in sight, on a third side, cowering. One of these, I understood, was the person who had shot the chief I mentioned in the first part of this letter, the chief who made an objectionable treaty, and whose house was burned. Both these warriors crept slyly towards the outer square; one darted upon one of the puppets, caught him from behind, and stole him off. Another grasped another puppet by the waist, flung him in the air, as he fell tumbled on him, ripped him with his knife, tore off the scalp, and broke away in triumph. A third puppet was tomahawked, and a fourth shot. These were the emblems of the various forms of warfare. After the first shot, the two parties whooped, and began to fire indiscriminately, and every shot was answered by a whoop. One shot his arrow into the square, but, falling short of the enemy, he covered himself with corn, crept thither to regain it, and bore it back in safety, honored with a triumphant yell as he returned. After much of this brush-skirmishing, both parties burst into the square. There was constant firing and war-whooping, the music of chanting and of the pebbled gourd going all the time. At length, the fighters joined in procession, dancing a triumphal dance around the mound, plunging thence headlong into the sacred square and all around it, and then scampering around the outside and pouring back to the battle-square; and the closing whoop being given, all then from the battle-square rushed helter-skelter, yelping, some firing as they went, and others pelting the spectators from their high places with the corn-stalks which had served for guns, and which gave blows so powerful that those who laughed at their impotence before rubbed their shoulders and walked away ashamed. We resumed our conveyances homeward.

and as we departed, heard the splashing and shouting of the warriors in the water. Leave was now given to taste the corn, and
all ate their fill, and, I suppose, did not much refrain from drinking, for I heard that every pathway and field around was strewed
in the morning with sleeping Indians.

"We passed the next day in visiting the picturesque scenery
of the neighborhood. We saw the fine falls of the Tallapoosa,
where the water tumbles over wild and fantastic precipices, varying from forty to eighty or a hundred feet; and, when wandering
over the rocks, passed an old Indian with his wife and child, and
bow and arrows. They had been shooting fishes in the stream,
from a point against which the fishes were brought to them by
the current. The scenery and the natives would have made a
fine picture. An artist in the neighborhood made me a present
of a picture of these falls, which I can show you when we meet.

"The next part of the festival consisted, as I was told, in the
wives urging out their husbands to hunt deer. We went down
to the square towards night. We met Indians with deer slung
over their horses. The skin is given to a priest, who flings it
back to the young man who gave it the first shot, to retain as a
trophy; and, at the same time, asks from the great Spirit that
this may be only the harbinger of deer in abundance, whenever
wanted. There was some slight dancing in the evening; but all
were reserving themselves for the winding-up assembly of the
ladies on Sunday morning. Some of our party remained after I
left. They found a miscellaneous dance at a house in the vicinity,
negroes, borderers, and reprobate Indians, all assembled in one
incongruous mass. A vagabond frontier man asked a girl to
dance. She refused, and was going to dance with another. He
drew his pistol and swore, if she would not dance with him, she
should not dance at all. Twenty pistols were clicked in an instant,
but the borderer swore there was not a soul who dared against
him to draw a trigger. He was right; for the pistols were dropped
and the room cleared in an instant, whereupon the borderer clapped
his wings and crowed and disappeared.

"The assemblage of the females I was rather anxious to see,
and so I was at my post very early. I had long to wait. I heard
the gathering-cry from the men on all sides in the cornfields and
bushes; it was like the neighing to each other of wild horses.
After a while the ladies began to arrive. The spectators crowded
in. The Indian men went to their places; and among them a

party to sing while the women danced; two of the men rattling
the gourds. The caldrons had disappeared from the centre of
the sacred square.

"And now entered a long train of females, all dressed in long
gowns, like our ladies, but all with gay colors and bright shawls
of various hues, beads innumerable upon their necks, and tortoise-
shell combs in their hair; ears bored all around the rim, from top
to bottom, and from every bore a massy eardrop, very long, and
generally of silver. A selected number of the dancers wore under
their robes, and girded upon their calves, large squares of thick
leather, covered all over with terrapin-shells, closed together and
perforated, and filled with pebbles, which rattled like so many
sleigh-bells. These they have the knack of keeping silent until
their accompaniment is required for the music of the dance. The
dresses of all the women were so long as nearly to conceal the
feet, but I saw that some had no shoes nor stockings, while others
were sandalled. The shawls were principally worn like mantles.
Broad ribbons, in great profusion and of every variety of hue,
hung from the back of each head to the ground, and, as they
moved, these, and the innumerable sparkling beads of glass and
coral and gold, gave the wearers an air of graceful and gorgeous
and at the same time unique wildness.

"The procession entered slowly, and wound around the central
fire, which, although the caldrons were removed, burned gently,
and the train continued to stretch itself out until it extended to
three circles and a half; the shorter side then became stationary
and kept facing the men seated in that building which contained
the chanters, and in this line of dancers seemed the principal
wearers of the terrapin-shell leg-bands. These make their rattles
keep time with the chant. Two leaders at each end of the line
(one of them an old woman and the other not young) had each a
little notched stick with two feathers floating from them. At a
particular turn of the dance they broke off and went the outside
round alone and more rapidly than the rest. The body of the
dancers slowly proceeded round and round, only turning at a
given signal to face the men, as the men had turned to face the
emblem of the Deity, the central fire. Every eye among the
women was planted on the ground. I never beheld such an air
of universal modesty. It seemed a part of the old men's privilege to make comments aloud, in order to surprise the women
into a laugh. These must often have been very droll and always

personal, I understand, and not always the most delicate. I saw
a few instances among the young girls where they were obliged to
smother a smile by putting up their handkerchiefs. But it was
conquered on the instant. The young men said nothing, but the
Indian men all seemed to take as much interest in the show as
we. The chief, Apotheola, had two daughters there. Both were
very elegant girls, but the eldest delighted me exceedingly. She
seemed about seventeen or eighteen; she is tall and of a fine
figure. Her carriage is graceful and elegant and quite European.
She had a white muslin gown, a small black scarf embroidered
with flowers in brilliant colors, an embroidered white collarette
(I believe you call it), gold chains, coral beads, gold and jewelled
ear-rings (single ones, not in the usual Indian superabundance),
her hair beautifully dressed in the Parisian style, and a splendid
tortoise-shell comb, gemmed, and from one large tuft of hair upon
one temple to that upon the other there passed a beautiful gold
ornament. Her sister's head-dress was nearly the same. The
elder princess Apotheola, I am happy to say, looked only at me.
Some one must have told her that I meant to run away with her,
for I had said so before I saw her to many of her friends. There
was a very frolicsome, quizzical expression in her eyes, and now
and then it seemed to say, 'No doubt you think all these things
very droll; it diverts me to see you so puzzled by them.' But,
excepting the look at me (which only proved her taste), her eye
dwelt on the ground, and nothing could be more interestingly reserved than her whole deportment. The dance was over, all the
ladies went from the square in the same order that they entered it.
In about an hour it was repeated, and after that signal was made
for what they call the dance of the olden time, the breaking up of
the ceremonial, when the men and women are again allowed to
intermingle. This was done in a quick dance around and round
again, all the men yelping wildly and merrily, as struck their
fancy, and generally in tones intended to set the women laughing,
which they did and heartily. The sounds most resembled the
yelpings of delighted dogs. Finally came the concluding *whoop*,
and all the parties separated.

"Between these two last dances I sent for a chief, and desired
him to take charge of some slight gifts of tobacco and beads which
I had brought for them. The chief took them. I saw the others
cut the tobacco and share it. Ere long my ambassador returned,
saying, 'The chiefs are mighty glad, and count it from you very

great friendship.' I had been too bashful about my present. If I had sent it before, I might have seen the show to more advantage. As it was, I was now invited to sit inside of the square, and witnessed the last dance from one of the places of honor. But I was obliged to depart at once, and give up all hopes of ever again seeing my beautiful princess Apotheola. My only chance of a guide through the wilderness would have been lost had I delayed. I reluctantly mounted my pony, and left the Indians of Tuckabatchie, and their Green-corn festival, and their beautiful princess Apotheola.

"It was a great gratification to me to have seen this festival; with my own eyes to have witnessed the Indians in their own nation; with my own ears to have heard them in their own language; nor was it any diminution of the interest of the spectacle to reflect that this ceremony, so precious to them, was now probably performing in the land of their forefathers for the last, last time. I never beheld more intense devotion; the spirit of the forms was a sight, and a religious one: it was beginning the year with fasting, with humility, with purification, with prayer, with gratitude; it was burying animosities, while it was strengthening courage; it was pausing to give thanks to Heaven before daring to partake its beneficence. It was strange to see this, too, in the midst of my own land; to travel, in the course of a regular journey, in the new world, among the living evidences of one, it may be, older than what we call the old world; the religion, and the people, and the associations of the untraceable part in the very heart of the most recent portion of the most recent people upon earth. And it was a melancholy reflection to know that these strange people were rapidly becoming extinct, and that, too, without a proper investigation into their hidden past, which would perhaps unfold to man the most remarkable of all human histories."

CHAPTER VI.

PAYNE AS CONSUL AND EDITOR.

"My Lord he has been sent upon an embassy,
And will, I know, perform his duties well."

IN 1838 we find Mr. Payne spending considerable of his time in the city of Washington, and frequently furnishing the " Democratic Review" with articles from his graceful pen. At this time the efforts of William Cullen Bryant, J. G. Whittier, Nathaniel Hawthorne, Ralph Waldo Emerson, and Miss Sedgwick and Miss Du Ponte adorned its pages. In the February and March numbers of the "Review," 1838, he contributed an article entitled "Our Neglected Poets" (the one included in this work). In this essay he has done a good service, he has preserved for us a few poems that give additional value to the pages of American poetry. There is a graceful simplicity, a warmth, and a touch of pleasantry in this contribution that remind us of Charles Lamb's style. Payne never overrates, he is always truthful, and irresistibly carries you to the end, and you are satisfied. The story of William Martin Johnson, the subject of "Our Neglected Poets," is admirably told, and attracts all our sympathy, while it presents to us, for the first time, some verses of great sweetness. In this paper he alludes to East Hampton, the scene of his earliest childhood. He describes it with the affection and with the feelings of a true poet.

One who has studied the character of John Howard Payne cannot fail to discover in his picture of the old homestead a deep, unsubsiding love for the place, as if the spirit of his boyhood had come back to awaken memories of a delightful past. Indeed, it was here where his earliest inspirations were winged, where his eyes were first opened to the beauties of the world, where he first took breath of the broad, green fields, where the waves of the seashore, as they broke their white crests at his young feet, whispered to him strange stories of the deep, where he first tried to count the stars, and where, each early morn as he awoke, hope painted new pictures for his imagined future. Indeed, if he was thinking of any one place on earth when he wrote his song of "Home, Sweet Home!" it was of "the lowly cottage" at East Hampton.

In 1840 a change of administration took place at Washington. Payne at once became acquainted with all of the most prominent members of the new cabinet, and was one of the most welcome and frequent *habitués* of the presidential mansion. Many of his friends suggested that he should receive an appointment as consul abroad. At first Payne doubted that such an end could be brought about, but several prominent members of the party in power spoke in his behalf, and on the 23d of August, 1842, he was appointed, by President Tyler, consul at Tunis. The position was procured for him principally through the efforts of Mr. Webster and Mr. Marcy. These facts of his appointment, and the names of those who interested themselves in his behalf, are taken from Mr. Payne's own letters to his brother, Thatcher Payne, who resided in Brooklyn. Mr. Marcy's name was particularly mentioned as being his best friend in the procuring of his consulship. A school-mate of Payne's, who wrote a sketch of him after his death, states that, on the evening of the day when Mr. Payne received his appointment, he sat with him at his table, and that Mr. Payne pointed to his full-length picture hanging upon the wall, representing him in the character of *Zaphna*, remarking that he still had the dress, and desired to know how it would do for him to be presented in such a costume to the Grand Bey. But Mr. Payne's friend continues to say, that Mr. Payne never made a joke of his official business.

I have looked over his letter-books, and I do not believe the government has often had agents who have better filled their places. I remember the book, too, as a feast to the eye. His handwriting was beautiful in the extreme; indeed, in whatever belonged to him, from verses to furniture, from the choice expression of a letter to the folding of the sheet that bore it, there was a rare, governing elegance and taste.

Mr. Payne's appointment was not secured as a partisan one; the prominent men of both parties endorsed him. At the same time he was also made colonel in the staff of Major-General Aaron Ward, of the Fourth Division of Infantry of the Militia of the State of New York.

In February, 1843, Mr. Payne left for Tunis, and arrived there on the 13th of May. On his way to the Court of the Bey he stopped at Havre, Paris, Marseilles, and London, and met in these several places many of his old friends, who congratulated him on his official appointment.

A few days after he reached Tunis he sent home the following letter, which is full in its description of the place and the characteristics of the people. The story is told in such a manner as almost to persuade the reader that he is an eye-witness to the events:

"UNITED STATES CONSULATE,
"TUNIS, Feb. 14, 1844.

"MY DEAR SISTER ELIZABETH.—Why your most kind letter of August 27th, 1843, has not been answered before I have already explained to Thatcher; therefore I will not dwell upon an omission the memory of which is to me so disagreeable, but proceed to carry on my account of my way hither and of my ways here, as if I had never sinned by silence.

"Where did I leave off? I told you of my trip across to London. It all seems a strange dream. London looked odd and changed. I had been so long disaccustomed to the odor of coal in the air and the dinginess of coal-smoke everywhere, that both gave me a sort of uneasiness; especially as change on all sides, and a multitude of recollections and apprehensions, concurred to depress my spirits, all buoyant with hope and novelty when, from America, so many years before, I first entered the vast metropolis. A busy look in all the people, throngs of strangers where I used to meet familiar faces, altered streets and buildings, met me in every direction; and yet the old landmarks were unremoved, old play-bills stood exactly in the same type of old at the same shops, and old book-stalls retained the same old books. In one lone street a blind beggar was playing 'Sweet Home' on a flageolet before a barber's shop, into which I went for a shave. At night, when I strolled like an unseen spectre into Drury Lane Theatre, I found the vestibule adorned with a full-length statue of Kean, whom, on quitting England, I had left alive. There was a skull in its hand, which pointed to an inscription: 'To this complexion must we come at last.' The dead, marble eye of my old acquaintance seemed to rest upon me, and his stony lips to direct on me their melancholy smile.

"Presently came the railroad again, all new, all since I went from England, the whirl back to Southampton, the steamer, the going to bed in one country and waking up in another, the jolting in the old-fashioned diligences to Rouen, and from Rouen to Paris, and then the retracing my old haunts at Paris, and the rush of changes there, as well in the looks of the people as in their rulers. Embellishments which were in progress when I departed were now complete. Napoleon was no longer named, but mighty works set on foot by Napoleon had at length found their accomplishment, rendering Paris, ever praised for its beauty and grandeur, still grander and more beautiful. But the dainty and curled Frenchman of my first acquaintance with Paris had given place to the Frenchman not only with his lips overshadowed by moustache, but with beard descending to the bosom; a fashion of looking venerable devised in honor of the New France in old Algiers. Then, ere long, appeared diligences once more, and I was launched upon my way to regions entirely new.

"What absolute fraud and folly it is for any one to pretend that a country can be described from thus travelling over it anyhow, especially by diligences, or even steamer! My route to Marseilles was first by land, then by water, then by land again; but I will be honest, and only tell you what I really remember. This is scarcely more than that there were queer passengers shut up together with me in the lumbering conveyances, and that they caused and expressed sundry little vexations during joltings, day and night, and most especially when, the moment we had sat down to a meagre meal anywhere, came the cry, 'En vitesse, messieurs! Dépêchez! En vitesse!' Then followed the hurry to pay, the pretended difficulty to make full change, the greater difficulty to get settled again all in our right places. I had my guide-book, and looked out of the window (whenever I was awake) as we rattled through a town, but I could only gather the names of the places, and sometimes not even the names; their aspect I had no time to fix in my mind, even if I caught it. Occasionally, however, it seemed, while I went on thus, now by land and now by water, as if I were passing through the appendix to a vast bill of fare, a gigantic amplification of that at Delmonico's, after the dinner items, down among the wines; for at one time I came to Beaune, and at another to Macon, and so forth, and, on hearing these names called out, could almost fancy myself in New York again, at the big stone house where Thatcher and I had a bachelor repast together not long before my embarkation.

. . . "But if the entire way from Paris to Marseilles leaves only a confused recollection, it is not so of main features and particular places where I made a brief pause to take breath. You must bear in mind, first, that the diligence took me to Chalons-sur-Saone; there I entered a steamer, which conveyed me to Lyons; from Lyons another steamer bore me to Avignon, and at Avignon I resumed the diligence to Marseilles. Now I had thought the nearer I got to Marseilles the more luxuriant would everything appear. I expected to find Lyons a matter-of-fact manufacturing place, with large shops in long, wide streets, and full of fine silks, but no attractions of scenery. In Marseilles I expected a laughing, gay city, like Paris before its age of tragedies. But nearly the reverse occurred. The loveliest and the most luxuriant appearances are on the river-banks between Chalons and Lyons, long before you draw near Marseilles. The Saone presents a succession of most fascinating landscapes; picturesque little towns, and a vast number of beautifully-finished stone bridges, mostly new, crossing from side to side. The immediate approaches to Lyons are full of life and variety: high hills, with lofty structures above and below; an antique, castle-crowned island in the middle of the river, near the town; large quays, fronted and parapeted with stone; wide bridges; near the water, tall, ancient houses, and facing it lines of shops in lower stories; more remote from it, at many points, eminences towering almost into mountains, and most of them surmounted by chapels. From one of these I had a fine view of both the Saone and the Rhone at once, so different in color and in swiftness. On the Rhone side of Lyons are bridges and edifices newer and more splendid than on the Saone side. But the streets in the older and most populous part of the city disappointed me. They are narrow, so much so in places that huge beams stretch across to prop the lofty walls from toppling upon one another. The shops are small, and make no show to be compared with ours in Broadway.

"The Rhone, where I expected to find the banks one garden, offers to the eye only stoniness and aridity, though in some instances its rocks and cliffs assume a fantastic and striking variety, approaching to the sublime, and antique-looking towns carry one back to the olden time. Perhaps the coming on of the *mistral* (the northwester) of the country during our passage made the Rhone look to me, especially when some showers fell, altogether more unsmiling than it might have seemed in brighter weather. Still, I experienced one sensation while rolling in the steamer there, of which language cannot give an adequate idea. What huge, white-topped masses are those, like clouds, in the horizon?'

asked I, just as if I were looking at any of our familiar scenes, not thinking where I was. 'The Alps,' was the quiet reply. My start of astonishment and sudden change of manner made my informant stare as if he thought me crazy. It was some time before I could speak.

"In times gone by, it happened that I voyaged in what I then thought the first steamboat, when the old Albany sloops were put out of countenance by Robert Fulton. I have since been a passenger in many a Robert Fulton, a name which bore undisputed super-eminence among our steamboats, till a second came up to push it from its throne, and on the Ohio appeared a John Fitch, in compliment to the true originator, so called, of travelling by steam. But, during the excursion now in question, I found another true and genuine name immortalized like the former two, and the rivers of France bearing upon their bosoms multitudes of Jean Papins, with guide-books all eloquent in praise of the genius of Jean Papin, to which they declare that mankind is indebted for the introduction of steam navigation, never even deigning to mention Robert Fulton, and still less John Fitch! 'There's honor for you!' as Falstaff says. But, after all, what signifies that which we call fame? What matters it even during life to any one but the inventor whether his invention bear his name? And when he is dead, who cares a jot, or knows a difference, whether it be ascribed to Jean Papin, or to John Fitch, or Robert Fulton? The main point is gained when an obtuse world is persuaded to permit a great improvement, either mechanical or moral, to make it happier or better.

" Well, leaving the Papin, after a late dinner at Avignon, whereby I was prevented from seeing either the town or any memorial of Petrarch and Laura, once more behold me shut up in a diligence, whence, after a very cold night, in the morning I caught a first glimpse of the Mediterranean, and entered Marseilles, passing, as I went in, a procession of priests who bore a crucifix and other emblems, and were hastening along with some occasional chant. But did I find Marseilles what I expected? A light and laughing place, more French than all preceding France? Not I. To be sure, I saw of Marseilles scarcely more than the newer part; but what I did see was staid and business-like and neat, more like parts of Philadelphia than like any town abroad. It has, however, what Philadelphia has not,—picturesque eminences, with fine sea-views.

" And now I come again to shipboard. I pass out of the crowded artificial harbor, sail by the forts and the rocky points and islands, and toss about and roll about till near dinner-time on the following day, when, lo! Minorca! It appears like a long line in the horizon, swelling to a sugar-loaf shape in the centre. What is that eminence? There is a story about it, so we will stop a moment while I tell it.

"That eminence is called Mount Toro. It was famous for a chapel to the Virgin of more than ordinary unction. In earlier times that chapel was in a small village at the mountain's foot. But one day its silver image of the Virgin had disappeared. Consternation shook the neighborhood. Men, women, and children gathered from every side to seek for the lost image. In the midst of the search, a strange and awful bull appeared. It was not an Irish bull, nor any relation to John Bull of England, nor of his stock-exchange; it must have been a bull of the pope! Its singular movements created a curiosity in the crowd that overpowered their terror. They followed it to the mountain-top, where, suddenly pausing, it turned, struck its horns into a rock, which fell asunder, and then the bull vanished. The throng flew to the mysterious rock. They found the lost image where the rock had been cloven asunder. The hint was not lost on them. They transferred the Virgin's chapel to that spot, immortalizing both the event and the bull by naming their new structure *The Chapel of our Lady of Mount Toro.* The best of its influences which yet survives is that by Mount Toro vessels direct their course to any point of Minorca Island for which they steer, and by so doing are sure to get in safe.

"Of Port Mahon, in Minorca, I believe I have told you already. It is a long, well-sheltered harbor, of deep water. The ruins of a fortress once deemed impregnable stand on the left hand of the entrance as you go in, and one of the largest and best of lazarettos on the right hand. Near the inner end, on a left-hand eminence, stands the town, high and dry. It is the neatest town I ever saw; has narrow streets paved with round stones, and houses of white, green, yellow, and red, always kept in good color within and without. The ceilings wear an awkward aspect to eyes accustomed to all white and smooth overhead. They look like some of our garret-roofs: huge beams run fore and aft. and rows of joists cross between them from beam to beam. These are all whitewashed or painted. There are excellent gardens in the neighborhood of Mahon, but the island is stony and bare, as far as I strolled, excepting of olives and the prickly pear, neither of which grow tall, though the latter spreads wide and is bulky. They say, however, that forests of oak and pine clothe the mountains, and that other trees prosper in other parts. The roads cut one's feet with their flintiness, and the sea views are often shut out from them by tall walls of round stones,—an amplification of such stone walls as may be seen in our country,—and over the top of them bristles the prickly pear. Few horses appear, and seldom a cart or carriage. I saw but one carriage, and that one a sort of minor omnibus, used as a post-coach once a week between the two extremities of the island. The people are gentle, civil, and superstitious. Priests are evermore seen parading the streets in religious processions of various sorts; and the Minorcan's pride might be taken for the human voice. They say that the Carthaginians possessed the island for a long time, and that old Hannibal was born at Port Mahon.

"I remained long enough here to feel perfectly at home; got acquainted with everybody, and was amused by being carried about the harbor from ship to ship. One day when I was going on board the Fairfield to dine, a sailor who had been sent up the hill to me to announce the boat, stopped short as we got to a turn near the bottom, which shut him out from the view of the men, and, after considerable stammering, and much bowing and scraping, commenced the following dialogue:

"'Will you excuse me, sir? I am going to take a great liberty, but I hope, sir, you'll excuse me.'

"'Certainly. Speak.'

"'Well, sir, I don't want to be rude, but I hope you'll excuse me.'

"'Speak, I say, my good fellow.'

"'Well, sir, I want to take the liberty of asking if your name is *John* Howard Payne?'

"'It is; what of that?'

"'By ——! I said so! I saw your trunk coming over the side, and I said to the men, "If those trunks belong to the man I think, d—d if I don't stand up for him, and so shall you." But the men said your name wasn't John, but James; so, "If it is *James* Howard Payne," said I, "that alters the case——"'

"'And being John Howard Payne——'

"'Being John Howard Payne,—pardon me, sir, but give me your hand; and all I have to say is, I'm satisfied with you.'

"'Thank you.'

"'I'm satisfied with you, because I've made more money out of you than ever I made out of any man, or ever shall again. Why, sir, I've been an actor, and have acted your "Brutus" over and over again, and with great applause, too; and I've been a manager likewise, and had others of your plays performed, and made my profit out of them, and, by ——, give me your hand again, for, John Howard Payne, I'm satisfied with you!'

"An officer heaving in sight our conversation was broken off, and I went on board, where I told the story in the captain's cabin. The man was inquired about. The captain said, 'Yes. Our men look upon you as their property. They'll be greatly disappointed if they don't take you to Tunis.' But on the unexpected change of commodores it was differently ordered, and I left the Fairfield for the Preble.

"The next change was the *sortie* of the squadron. 'Twas really a noble sight. Boats followed the different vessels with salutations and benedictions. Numbers of both sexes stood on the shores and in the balconies waving farewells.

"Out we sailed, and then commenced sea-manœuvres, which lasted a couple of days, such as forming by signal in a line and in single file, and in double file, and so on. At last, while we were at dinner, a midshipman announced that the commodore had made signal, 'Part company you may.' The various vessels then went alongside of the commodore's ship. Their shrouds were lined with men. Three cheers were given by each. Finally, all were answered by an equal number of cheers to each from the commodore's ship, then each turned off in a different direction, and, forthwith, I was on my way to Tunis.

"We sailed, and sailed, and sailed. In the Mediterranean we met scarcely anything, excepting at two different times, sleeping on the waves, a turtle, one of which we put out a boat for and took, but the other waked and got off.

"'There, sir,' said a lieutenant to me at last, as he lowered his glass,—'there, sir, is your new home; there is the coast of Africa.'

"Taking the glass, I discerned a long line of hills in the horizon, seemingly treeless, and, midway through their entire length, a wide yellowish streak, lighted by the sunshine, and apparently of sand. But to a landsman coasts from shipboard look pretty much alike, so we will pass over certain intermediate islands, and here we are just entering the harbor of Tunis.

"I must give you an idea of the form of this harbor. Do you

remember the shape of what they call the Saracenic arch ? You
will then remember that it is two parts of a wide arch, whence
springs an entire, but narrower, one; or, if this won't do, suppose
we turn it upside down, and so compare it to a fine, full-cheeked
half-moon, with a noble pair of regular, branching horns, as thus:
. . . such (making due allowance for the drawing) is the form of
Tunis harbor. Here we are, as I said before, just entering it at
the wider part. Away off to the left appears a large island, and
nearer the cape a small one. Don't forget these islands, for I
have something to say about them.

"Now we sail onward. At last we get to the inner arch.
Within its right side as we enter tower the hills of ancient Carthage. From the outermost point of land on the side opposite
are wildly picturesque mountains, jagged and steep. Far ahead
of us, on the edge of the innermost arch-top, stands the Goletta
castle; behind it, inclining to the left, is the large lake of Tunis,
and behind the lake, on a rising ground, but dimly perceptible
from the sea, and overlooked at the left by greater elevations
crowned with ports, stand Tunis-wall and Tunis. Between the
two sides of the shore facing us the land is flat. From the harbor,
trees are only seen in one or two spots, and those only dwarfish
olives.

"Come. It is time for us to try to be classical. You wish to
know why I desired you to bear in mind the two islands at the
left? It is because the smaller one, nearest the coast, is the scene
of the wreck of part of Æneas' fleet. At the shore adjacent the
remainder of the fleet landed. To the heights overhanging this
part of the shore Æneas went up for the purpose of seeing into
what sort of a region he had been cast, and thereabout met his
mother Venus, disguised as a huntress, who gave him a deal of
valuable information. Farther in towards Tunis, near one of the
mountain-tops, is the cave where he and Dido sought refuge, later
in their history, from the tempest that arose, while young Ascanius
was galloping after the stags on the plain below. And farther in
yet, towards Tunis, are the other eminences whence Æneas caught
his first glance at Carthage, on the opposite elevations across the
water. Of Carthage, on our right-hand side, nothing appears but
one of the finest of positions for a noble city. About one hundred
and eighty feet, as they say, from the water's surface, rises, by very
long gradations, the site of the Temple of Esculapius and the Cit-
adel of Byrsa. The famous spot where the Carthaginian leader

Asdrubal deserted his country's cause, and his heroic wife Sophonisba, rather than imitate his baseness, fired the temple, plunging
with her children into its flames, is now marked by a meagre little
red chapel, recently built by the French, in memory of St. Louis,
who is said also to have died there. Thence runs a second long
slope, mounting to a still loftier eminence, from the summit of
which springs a tall watch-tower, and under it descends a white
Moorish village, consecrated to Sidi-Bon-Saed (literally, Our Lord
Father of Felicity), a Mahometan saint, whose tomb there is a
sanctuary for Mahometan criminals of every sort. From the
latter height Dido might have gazed her last at Æneas escaping, and it is only on the former that we can place the palace
wherein the Trojan told her his adventures with such fatal
eloquence and subsequently was built her funeral pyre. In
short, from the vessel's deck in the harbor nearly all the points,
either in poetry or history, which give Tunis its fame, are discernible. One takes as much interest in verifying the truth of
fiction here as the truth of history, and we realize the events
connected with Æneas and Dido as we do those of Hannibal or
Regulus, Scipio, or Asdrubal, or Sophonisba, or St. Louis, or
Charles V., or any of the rest, and the poetical ones, perhaps,
even more intensely than the other, because Virgil has laid
the hearts of those whom he describes open before us, making
us their confidants.

"Mighty, however, as may have been the sensations produced
at various times by the arrival in these regions of Æneas, and
Regulus, and Scipio, and Louis of France, and Charles V., and
others, I will venture to assert that, on the 12th of May, 1843, the
arrival of John Howard Payne, consul from America, occupied
the attention of numbers, while not a soul, far or near, gave a
thought or ever knew of the existence of any of the rest, and
among the numbers in question were those grim warriors here
who are specially charged with the important duty of firing
salutes. At eight in the morning, subsequent upon the anchoring
of our vessel about sunset, up went the flag, and bang! went the
cannons at the Goletta fort, one-and-twenty times. 'Count their
guns,' cried the officer on duty. When they ceased, 'Twenty-one,
sir,' was the reply. Meanwhile, our men had been placed at their
posts. 'Larboard, fire!' called our officer on duty. Bang! went
a Preble gun on one side. 'Starboard, fire!' Bang! went a
Preble gun on the other side, and so on, to the twenty-first.

13

This ceremony over, I was formally invited to name a day when I would dine with the gentlemen in the wardroom, and the captain was asked to be of the party. It was then announced that the boat was manned, and the captain and I in full costume descended, some one guiding my honorable heels as I let myself down by a rope to the edge of the capering boat. Just as we were clearing the vessel, Bang! went a gun once more from the Preble. 'That is for you, sir,' said the captain, whereupon I stood up, as instructed, the captain steadying me on one side and a midshipman on the other, retaining that position till nine guns were fired, when I reposed for a while upon my glories. Dance, dance, dance, went the boat for about two miles. Along the low, bare, empty shore appeared only the Goletta fort, and between it and Carthage heights on one side but a single building, a large, new one, much resembling those ingenious structures which young people form of playing-cards. On the other side of the Goletta, and at some distance from it, there was a range of little crooked trees with dark, bushy tops, which proved to be an olive-grove. In the corner of the harbor, fronting this grove, were many ships at anchor. The Goletta fort looked just as it does in the engraved view of it annexed to Noah's book on Tunis, Mordecai Manasseh, and matters and things in general. As we passed, the fort fired another salute of nine guns. We went round the point of a pier, terminating in a line of heaped rocks and stones, entering within the Goletta by a straight passage, on either side of which were queer-looking barges, full of queerer-looking sailors, black and brown, some turbaned, some with red skull-caps. Sentries saluted us at posts along the shore. Then we passed a steamer at the wharf-side, then other vessels, and then we stepped on classic ground, rendered most prosaically commonplace by ragged sailors and work-people and double lines of galley-slaves, marching by in chains from one task to another. At the house of a native, of French parentage, a very gentlemanly man, who is our agent at the Goletta, I found two large, four-wheeled cabriolets in waiting. A little man standing at the door eyed me intently. He had a long, grisly beard and vast mustachios, tall, red cap, from behind which hung a profusion of blue silk thread, a short Mameluke jacket, a broad red sash, immense, large blue breeches, gathered below the knee, naked calves, Turkish slippers, and a large sabre. This person I afterwards found to be one of my dragomans. He had been in his boyhood an Italian captive, turned Mussulman as he grew up, and in his prime became

eminent as a pirate. He mounted his charger and galloped on
ahead. Captain Wilson and I entered one cabriolet and the chev-
alier, my agent at the Goletta, another, and off we rolled through
the conglomeration of misshapen buildings, large and little, under
the gates of a wall, into the plain leading around the lake's side
to Tunis, turning our backs on Carthage.

"We rode, and we rode, and we rode,—two hours in the hot
sun. So flat was the way, so silent, so lonely, so treeless, I might
have fancied myself on an American prairie, had there been more
vegetation. The lake by our left-hand side was streaked across,
here and there, with hues of a pea-green. Birds flew about its
borders, that made our captain long for his gun. Now and then
we met a rider on a mule, another on a horse, and wrapped in
what seemed a white sheet, with an immense nondescript straw-
covering over his head, a little like the caricature of a coarse Leg-
horn bonnet, and a good deal more like a huge, unstrung umbrella,
open, lofty, crowned, and most amazingly wide in the brim, which
went flapping up and down as either rode. To an aged horseman,
in passing, our *avant-courier*, the dragoman, galloped up, when,
each kissing the other on the shoulder, both darted onward their
respective ways. Then came by some two or three loaded camels ;
then a crazy Maltese cab, with a half-starved horse, the cabman
now running along by its side, and now springing in to drive as
he sat on the cab-bottom, with his legs dangling out over the side.
Once or twice we passed flocks of sheep with tails resembling old-
fashioned, full-bottomed wigs. Startling the Bedouin shepherd,
as he was stretched full length along some small slope, wrapped
in his burnouse to watch them, he would lift up his head, gaze a
moment, and then lay it down again. Here and there we saw at
a distance from the road groups of coarse, Bedouin, black tents of
hair-cloth, the unchanged *mapalia* of the ancient Numidians, to
the form of which Sallust compares a ship-keel inverted, and concerning which the Song of Solomon says, verse fifth of chapter
first, 'I am black, but comely, as the tents of Kedar;' comely,
or pleasant to the eye, I presume, in allusion to the delight derived from the indication of social life afforded by one of these
movable villages in the desert. A black, hair-tent village of this
sort is supposed to have crowned the upper height of Carthage
(now the Sidi-Bon-Saed already mentioned), and to have formed
the ancient town that Dido found there, and which retained the
title of Niagara, that the learned are said to regard as identical

with *mapalia*, and with *magar*, the still more antique, and, probably, the parent term.

"But what else did we meet on the road to Tunis? Moorish
ladies out for an airing, but we did not see them. They were curtained up in a little, close carriage on two large wheels, and which
was enveloped in a sort of brown Holland carriage-cover, bearing
on each side a black caricature of five outstretched fingers, signi-
fying 'five in your eye!' the severest curse of the Arabs, and
meant as a spell against the evil eye, and to express, 'Fie, and bad .
luck to you, if you dare peep at our fat ladies!' More than midway between us and the lake we passed a little, square, white,
stone building of one story, where horses and mules were drinking
at the door,—a Moorish coffee-house and baiting-place for man and
beast. Farther on we passed through a grove of olives that looked
exceedingly like a superannuated, old, Yankee apple-orchard; and
at last appeared the white walls, and round domes, and minarets
of Tunis; pleasant eminences covered with olives, a mile or two
off, facing and overlooking it; and above, and on a line with it,
a windmill (the only remembrancer of familiar scenes); and,
crossing the way ahead, in the distance, beyond the city, a tall
line of narrow arches, sustaining an aqueduct, but not of that part
of the olden time which is classical.

"A little more riding, and a little more riding, and lo! the
American flag waving over a tall house, just behind the inner wall
of Tunis; and over other houses equally tall, flags of European
nations; and on the walls the flag of Tunis, with its crescent and
its single star. (These flags, I would have you to know, by way
of parenthesis, were raised in compliment to the new consul.)
The outer gate is before us. A square, ragged old structure, open
on all sides, and disclosing a saint's tomb within; an unfenced
burial-ground by its side, with raised, flat stones, lengthwise,
wider at one end than the other, and surmounted often with a
straight stem, occasionally bearing a turban on its top. A drove
of camels on the other side of the road, some with their legs
doubled under them, reposing; others standing and staring. We
have passed by these, and now we are under the outer gate-way.
Dirt! Dirt! Queer, grim-looking creatures stretched on wide
stone benches that are built against the wall beneath the canopy.
Boys and men half naked, standing and walking about, with
earthen pots of antique form, crying, 'Water! Who'll buy water?'
Blind beggars shouting, 'Charity, for the love of Mahomet!'

'Bahlick!' (Take care!) 'Hempshee!' (Clear out!) bawls the driver, meaning that the way must be freed from that drove of donkeys, puzzling to and fro, and running under the wheels. 'Bablick!' The dragoman gives that camel a cut with his whip, and he stalks aside indifferently. 'Bablick!' The Maltese cart must stop against the wall and make room for the consul!

. . . "We have passed under the passage. We are within the limits of Tunis city.

"A short, unpaved street of moderate width; low, one-story, dirty, white houses, with little ragged sheds projecting over them, eyelet holes for windows; dirty-looking squatters of every color and age, with turbans of every color, in the door-ways and on heaps of dirt at each side of the street. Donkeys loaded with panniers of greens, of charcoal, of almost everything. Camels with huge skins of water slung across them like giant saddle-bags, flocks of sheep, herds of black goats; but all must push aside to make way for the carriage. 'Bablick! Bahlick! Hempshee!' From the short street we enter a wide, open space, in its middle two rising grounds on either side, of the largest of which runs to one point, a road. We take that at the left. What does this open space look like? It most resembles the burnt district of New York after the great fire of 1835. Right and left hand of our road arise burial-grounds unfenced. What are those waddling masses of draperies, gowns, one would say, and shawls, of every hue and texture hung around the sides of a huge barrel, with a black masked head thrust through its top, and a pair of thick legs through its bottom? · Foregad!' as the old nurse says in 'Romeo and Juliet,' 'how every part about it quivers!' Behold! Another, and yet another of these monsters! Some unmasked! Hush, man! These are Moorish women! The one or two with their broad faces bare are Jews. That fourth one so carefully muzzled with a black silk scarf, as if nature had mixed her Indian ink inadequately, is a she-nigger! 'Bablick! Bahlick!' women though you are, you must cling up close to the side, or you'll be run over. We have got to a narrow turn over a short bridge. Now we have crossed—up we go—down again along a pinched-up way between dead walls and low houses, with only a grated slit here and there for windows. The other carriage coming from the opposite direction must back and let the consul pass! 'Bahlick!' We are through another gate. There's another wall and gate over the bridge, sole tribute to past glories; the gate is called 'the Carthaginian.'

'Bablick! Bablick!' Every one gets out of the way but that yellow chap with bushy black hair, shirtless, shoeless, and bare-legged, and only girt with a dark cloth descending from his waist. He is a SAINT, *anglice*, a crazy man. He does not fear, and we must take care not to hurt him. None are truly respected among the Moors but those who have lost their senses. 'Bablick!' How that gray-bearded Jew, who has picked up a superannuated three-cornered hat like an old Continental colonel's, somewhere, and mounted it over his Moorish garb, pins himself against the wall to keep secure from being run over! We jolt under and across the gate-way, a short, very short turn. 'Bablick! Hempshee! Bablick!' Why don't those men, women, children, donkeys, goats, and camels mind what they are about? We are through the gate, into a winding street, each side of which can be touched from the carriage if we outstretch our hands. No danger of upsetting here,—ruinous-looking houses, dead-walls. Now the walls grow higher and more regular on one side, and the houses taller on the other. We are among the ministerial and the consular mansions. A short turn. A small, open space. We shoot under a long arch-way. Halt! We stop, descend, turn short again. We are con-ducted under another archway. In a high, quiet, vaulted place like a huge cave stands a band of musicians. Is not that an attempt at 'Hail Columbia'? It is. When I appear all of the musicians bow and play, and play and bow. These are my premises. I am at the foot of my own staircase; up we pass, to deafening music, groping our way over a long ascent of clumsy stone steps. We come to sunshine again in a square hall lighted by rickety win-dows from above. Rooms open into it. A young man advances and holds out his hand. 'Mr. Gale, I presume?' 'Yes, sir.' He shows me into a drawing-room. His power as consul *ad interim* is at an end, and mine begins. Oh, the uncouth place! Great iron bars everywhere! I look out of the window. The city wall is on the opposite side of the unpaved street, its top cut by way of ornament into the shape of a long range of gravestones. 'Con-genial horrors, hail!'

"'Have you anything for me?' 'Oh, yes, letters and papers.' I open a very agreeable epistle from Mrs. Thatcher Payne, for-warded by Mr. Ballard from Gibraltar, wherewith I also receive one of my old night-caps.

"Dreary, indeed, seemed everything. A YAHOO of a HOUSE meagrely furnished, and none of the furniture mine. Not a comfortable bed in it. Some hard wool-mattresses, and harder wool-pillows were laid on boards raised about two feet from the ground. On one of these at night I sought repose in a recess. I looked up at the rafter-ceilings, all in the Mahon fashion, and just at the wall-top was a black, irregular blot.. My imagination was full of scorpions. I thought of Miss Phœbe Filer's customary malediction at East Hampton. After long watching the spot till it seemed to move and crawl downward, at last I got asleep, while thinking how the bite of a scorpion could be cured.

"The official visits to the Bey, and from the consuls, next ensued. For the former, I was glad to find the modes grown more European. I need not take off my shoes nor attempt to smoke.

"Accompanied by the consul *ad interim*, and Captain Wilson, I went to the fortified palace of the Bey, about two miles out of Tunis, on a plain. We passed through the arches of the aqueduct I spoke of entering the city, and which is about midway from Tunis to Bardo, for so they call the palace. An irregular mass of edifices combined, and a number of others standing apart, are enclosed within an extensive oblong square by lofty walls, with cannon and watch-towers, and surrounded by a wide, deep moat. The crescent-and-star banner of the Bey waved over the main building.

"We enter the gate-way. Sentries and guards salute. Grim throngs, some standing and some reclining, fill long dark passages, on either side of which are low rooms. An open space with many carts and carriages, a turn to the left, another passage into an unpaved court with a fountain in the middle, an ascent up several wide marble stairs to apartments seemingly important. Under this colonnade we stop. Persons with anxious and busy faces pass to and fro, some in humble garb, some richly clad, and wearing diamond orders. One of the apartments forms the hall of justice, where a move of the Bey's hand may be to his subjects either All the world can give or Death.

"After broiling for some time in the hot sun, we were asked up into a little room set apart for a consular antechamber. Thence we were at length summoned to the royal presence.

"Down-stairs under the colonnade, a turn through a central door into a passage lined at each side with guards, who presented arms. Before me, my dragoman; at my left, one of the Bey's ministers; behind me, the vice-consul and Captain Wilson.

"We enter a long drawing-room.—carpeted, a range of numerous windows on one side. Wide Moorish sofas against the wall, facing each other, from end to end.

"At the corner of the left-hand extremity, fronting me as I entered, sat a person in a tall red cap. At his left stood, with similar caps, two others, young and plump. All had long, double-breasted blue frock-coats, closed from the top, descending to the heels, the yellow buttons stamped with the crescent and the star, and converging from each shoulder to the waist, till they formed there nearly the point of an angle. All had diamond orders, but the diamonds of the one who was seated were the richest and most numerous. The minister who accompanied me wore a costume similar to the others.

"We are at our destination, my dragoman has kissed the royal hand, for it was the Bey who sat before us.

"'Peace between us,' said his highness in Arabic. 'Be pleased to take a seat,' continued he, pointing to the sofa at his right, 'and to receive my welcome of you and of your friends.'

"Chairs being placed, Mr. Gale and Captain Wilson sat in front of the Bey, and the minister, standing at their right, interpreted Mr. Gale's Italian in Arabic, after my English to Mr. Gale.

"Presently I asked Mr. Gale for my letter of credence, and having received it, I rose, and said,—

"'In presenting these, my credentials, I am instructed to assure your highness of the cordial friendship of the President of the United States, and of his earnest desire that the amicable relations now subsisting between Tunis and our republic may long continue unimpaired.'

"His highness interrupted me by declaring, with emphasis, that no one could cherish more strongly such a desire than he himself did.

"'Permit me, at the same time, to avail myself of this occasion, on my own part, to express the gratification I feel in being honored by my country with a mission of which the duties promise to be rendered not only easy but agreeable, by their bringing me into communication with a prince universally characterized as wise, and good, and just.'

"While the minister was translating what I had said, his highness frequently put his hand to his heart and said, 'Meleeah!' which means 'good!'

"I then handed my letter of credence to the minister, who handed it to the Bey.

"His highness hoped I should find my new residence comfortable and happy, and assured me that nothing should be wanting, within his power, to make it so.

"Some general chat ensued. in which Captain Wilson took part. The captain expressed the pleasure it would give him to receive his highness on board the Preble, and his highness said he should be gratified, some day when he went to the Goletta, at any rate, to take a look at the corvette from his windows there. I observed that I hoped our vessels would visit Tunis more frequently hereafter, as we had a large squadron in the Mediterranean. The Bey replied that he was always happy to welcome the ships of *friends*, dwelling on the word *friends*. A question whether our squadron was actually in the Mediterranean, or only expected, was answered that it was at that moment cruising there. A black now entered with little coffee-cups on a silver tray. We all partook, made our bows, and departed. I felt considerably annoyed, that from the combined effects of so long standing in the sun, and of the unsettledness arising from my recent voyage and novel situation, my hand trembled so in taking the coffee that the cup went tap, tap, tap ! against the saucer, when I set it down, as though I were under a fit of ague. You may guess from that how glad I was when, my bow being made, I found myself once more through the guards. out of the palace, and on my way back to Tunis.

"Visits from all the consuls and all their respective suites, glittering in gold and silver. immediately ensued. They were consumed in hollow, diplomatic civilities, and in hints that I should find Tunis a most unendearing residence, all social relations being broken up by a miserable spirit of village prying and scandal, which has destroyed even the unreserved and agreeable intercourse once subsisting among the consular families. There was more truth in this than always comes from ministerial agents.

"So, the Preble went. and I was left alone, all alone ; but soon I got used to the looks and ways of the folks around me. There is a minaret of a mosque close by my mansion, and even the five-times-a-day call to prayer, repeated at each of the four corners of the square top. has lost its strangeness, and is now uttered without my being aware of it. One of the oddest things at first seemed to me when I asked, ' Where is Mr. (such a one) ?'—the reply, ' Oh, he's gone to breakfast at Carthage ; he'll be back to dinner.' And it was long before I could really feel and believe that *real* Carthage was meant, and not some Carthage in our far West. But I must defer any further mention of Carthage, or the neighborhood, or Tunis itself, for future letters, and proceed to the next great court-ceremonials which it came within my course of duty to attend.

"Probably you are aware that there is a Mohammedan Lent, during the ninth month of their year, and which they call Ramadhán. At the next new moon following, Ramadbán ceases, and the lesser Beiram, or feasting, begins, and lasts four days. The greater Beiram, or feasting, begins on the 10th day of the twelfth moon, and also lasts four days.

"The Ramadbán this year fell on the 24th of September, the first day of the lesser Beiram on the 24th of October, and the first day of the greater Beiram on the 24th of December.

"For the week preceding the Ramadhán all sorts of preparations were made for it. All the Moorish servants wanted presents for the purpose of enabling them to lay in their stock of extra provisions for the thirty nights to come, no buying being permitted during the thirty days.

"Cannons, drums, and guns at midnight announced the commencement of this fast. All the day after, every Moor looked most forlorn, and daily, till it ended, worse and worse. On the first night, great illuminations had been talked of, but they consisted merely, I believe, of lighted lanes, and extra-lighted coffeehouses, with the novelty of a row of lamps all round the minaret's balustrade on each mosque. The moment the sun sets, eating and drinking begins, and is only suspended when the drum goes about beating for the fast to be vigorously resumed.

"I took a turn in the town, well attended, on one of those nights during this fast, when the Moors are permitted, after sunset, to indulge a little more than usual. I stopped at a coffee-house which was greatly crowded, but very orderly. Groups were sitting all about on Moorish divans, drinking coffee, smoking, playing at draughts. Curiously-cut tin lanterns hung in every direction as did cages with canary-birds. In the centre was a long table, and Moorish sofas on each side and at one end. Various adornments stood on the table, among them, for instance, a large glass vase of gold-fish. Some famous singers, one of them blind, very old, very celebrated, and with a most venerable white beard, sat on the end bench, bearing in his hand a musical instrument. Six or seven others were squatted, tailor-like, on each side of this one. They had a something like pipes and tabors; and little instruments with a couple of strings each. played on like a violoncello. and others like mandolines, and accompanied them with the earthquake fury of stentorian lungs in Arabic songs—as I was told, but never should have suspected—of most melting tenderness. As it was known that I intended to visit the café that evening, I and my suite (among whom was Mr. Ballard) received the honor of the most conspicuous place there, and chairs were placed for us so near the musicians that we were almost deafened. To mend the matter, every now and then, when the voices were most outrageous, the keeper of the coffee-house would go round with a staff, and violently slapping cage after cage, startle up the wearied out and slumbering birds. who would begin also to sing most vociferously, by way of chorus. Yet the whole scene was most amusingly Oriental. Both a gallery overhead, and an open apartment over-looking it. were crowded with Moors, as were the steps leading up to them.

"During this fast a native Tunisian, who called upon me, mentioned a strange scene and a stranger history which had just come under his notice. His curiosity was excited by the view of a tall, haggard, turbaned person, with long white beard, and skin-pails filled with water girt all around him, and bearing in his hand a cup. He made seven steps and paused, knelt, bowed his face to the ground, licked the dust. rose up, and then went on again, but repeated the same at every seventh step. All looked on him with respectful silence and a sort of awe. My informant learned that he was a Turk from Egypt. During the French invasion he fled thence, leaving behind him a wife and child. He obtained employment on board a vessel that brought him to Tunis. Meanwhile, unknown to him, the troubles of his country drove his wife and child away from it, and chance also led them to Tunis. The wife died. The motherless child found a protecting friend, who brought her up as her own daughter. The Egyptian Turk bearing a description of this young girl's attractions. demanded her in marriage; courtship in these countries always going on through others, and without personal acquaintance. After some months of marriage, the husband and wife happening to disclose each their history to the other, the Egyptian, horror-struck. discovered his wife to be his daughter. He flew distracted to the cadi and told him all. The cadi forthwith decreed a divorce, and condemned the man

through life to give water, without pay, to all who should desire
it, and at every seventh step to lick the dust. This he has done
for years, and is often seen performing his penance, especially at
Moorish funerals.

"The Ramadhán is over when the new moon of the Beiram is
discovered. Great, indeed, is the noise and the rejoicing. On the
morning following, the national banner is raised everywhere, and
the cannons, wherever planted, fire a national salute. The Bey
goes through various ceremonies at Bardo Palace, and, among the
rest, receives the bow of felicitation, while seated in state upon
his throne, from all the consuls.

"My honorable self, of course, with my vice-consul, went, on
the 24th of October, to grace this ceremony with my presence.
The road was alive with even a more motley group than used to
animate that from Boston to Cambridge on the commencement-
days of Harvard University. And what crowds of white-mantled,
and red-mantled, and green-mantled Moors in the passages and
first open space of the approaches to the palace! and how carriages and carts and splendidly caparisoned horses were, in the
latter, wedged together! The first court-yard, the unpaved one,
with a fountain in the centre, was entirely covered with a thick
bed of sand, for what purpose you shall know anon. We ascend
the high, wide range of steps, jostled there and in the short passage above by multitudes of persons in various rich costumes, and
by dense masses of epauletted officers, white, yellow, and black,
returning from paying their devoirs to the Bey. We enter the
inner and paved court-yard that I spoke of as surrounded by a
colonnade. Opposite the entrance, in the door-way to the apartment where I was first received by his highness, sat the king of
Tunis, on either hand his officers of state, the superior ones generally in the uniforms of the frock-coat form, which I have noticed
before, but glittering with rich embroideries and a greater number
of diamond decorations. A child of some seven or eight years old,
decked out in the same style, the orders, and the sabre, and the
epaulettes, all in little, stood at the right hand of his highness.
Of course, finely-dressed persons hemmed in every side, but the
area was unencumbered.

"Ahmed Pacha Bey was seated in a white chair, of some peculiar fishbone, put together with silver rivets. No doubt the chair
has intrinsic claims to admiration of which its exterior gives no
sign, nor could I learn what they were supposed to be. His

highness was magnificently decorated with embroidery and diamonds, and had a splendid scimitar before him. His right hand
rested on a yellow cushion. Facing him stood a Herculean figure,
wrapped in a dark burnouse.

"The Bey's countenance was unmoved as marble while he received the various obeisances, but, when he desired to give a mark
of signal favor, he would turn the palm of his hand upwards, after
the back had been kissed, and he who obtained that honor would
again kiss the hand on the palm; and throughout this ceremony
I observed that none were content with a mere kiss, but after it
the forehead was bent down and pressed upon the open palm, and
then the lips again, all of which pressures probably meant something particular, but I could not find out what beyond entire devotedness of body and soul. But there was a more significant
manœuvre than the rest, and which proved how much these
potentates confide in the aforesaid public testimonials of entire
soul-and-body devotedness. It was this, the Herculean figure that
I mentioned as standing in front of the Bey grasped firmly each
bending devotee's shoulder, never relaxing his hold till the faithful slave was too far from his royal master to stab him while he
kissed. The manual exercise of courtesy is not expected, even on
these occasions, from the consuls. All their kissing of the barba-
rous high and mighties is done, like the courtship of kings, by proxy
all by their dragomans. Each, preceded by his own dragoman,
after the royal hand is duly saluted, makes the best bow he can,
and goes away in silence. The presentation of the Divan is more
imposing. This is the nominal council of the ruler, whom formerly
it could crown or decapitate at pleasure. It consists of long-
bearded and gravely but elegantly attired old men, who advance
in a row, single file. As they appeared seats were brought, and
placed on a line from the Bey to the entrance-door, and at his
right, but considerably distant from him; to which seats, after the
kissing of hands, these dignitaries went, and coffee was handed to
them and to his highness, which being disposed of, they rose and
uttered a prayer from the Koran, that was every now and then
interrupted by a loud cry, Ahmeen! synonymous, as I was informed, with our Amen! This over, and the Bey having withdrawn for a while, the next move was another presentation of all
the principal personages to the Bey of the Camp, as he is called,
the lieutenant-general of the army, and heir presumptive, at
present, of the throne, but who, in a direct line, would now have

been reigning. He sat in a dark room, and the same forms to him as to his royal cousin were observed.

"His highness Ahmed Pacha Bey, with all the great folks, followed by multitudes of the ordinary ones, reappearing, crossed this main court-yard to the top of the staircase overlooking the ante-court-yard, unpaved, which has the fountain in the centre, and was, as I told you, entirely covered with a thick bed of sand, you will now perceive for what purpose.

"Near the fountain stood a number of swarthy, tall, athletic Bedouins, with bodies and limbs bare, and entirely shaven pates unturbaned, all shining from head to foot with oil. At their left, as they faced us great personages on the stair-top, squatted queer-looking musicians before queer-looking instruments. On each side of the wide, open space before the fountain was a throng of turbaned and mantled Moors, and Turks, and Arabs, and Bedouins, and Negroes.

"All this array was for a Barbaric wrestling, practised from time immemorial, on such occasions, in presence of the king and court. Directors and judges stood near. The ladies of the harem have a place allotted to them overlooking the court-yard, where they may see the sport, themselves unseen.

"Drums and other music; a signal; two of the wrestlers start forward. They curvet around, flinging their arms and legs about and striking their palms together, like capering sailors half drunk about to jump Jim Crow. Coming in front of the Bey, they suddenly cast themselves each upon his knee, up again, and jump Jim Crow back to their starting-place, where each, with neck and knee bent, stands like a statue, while a priest (I suppose it was) advances, and, placing a finger on the back of the right-hand one, loudly utters some words, which I understood to be a prayer to excite them to do their best, and to invoke Mahomet to carry them through the trial uninjured; for, sometimes, it is said, they do not quit the struggle alive. The invocation over, they start up, watch their chance awhile, then close.

"If they become exasperated and make any move contrary to rule, or if they display such equal prowess and dexterity as to render it clear that neither is likely to conquer, the judges stop the struggle. In the latter case, or in the case of a victory, the band plays, and then another pair contend. After each encounter there is a small caper, and a kneeling obeisance to the court. I understand that they were ushered before the Bey after the trial, for the honor of kissing his hand, and to receive gifts or prizes. This, however, I did not witness, but, when the sports were past, pushed through the crowd as soon as possible to my carriage.

"It would have diverted you to have seen what odd-looking military officers passed us on the road. We saw, mounted on a little donkey, two of them, one astride, the other sideways, each with fine epaulettes; and though they had clumsy shoes on their feet, their pantaloons, being without straps, had worked, in riding, up to their knees. Others, however, were on noble steeds, and both horse and rider were gorgeously caparisoned.

"The same forms in every respect were repeated on the 24th of December, the beginning of the greater Beiram; but all upon a grander scale. I saw the account the Bey paid to the French merchant who got the new coat and sword-belt embroidered that his highness first wore on this occasion. Its amount was six thousand seven hundred and seventy francs.

"Here, then, my 'full, true, and particular story' draws to a close; and high time it did, say you. But Anna asked me to relate everything about my life here, public and private, and I do not hold myself responsible for the consequences of complying for once with such a request, though I think you will find it more agreeable that I should in future be regulated by the rule given to dyspeptics about food, 'less at a time and oftener.' For the present occasion, however, I will suppose I may take with me, even into Africa, the license which has always been allowed wherever else I have lived ere now, of spoiling as much paper as one chooses on Valentine's Day in honor of the ladies.

. . . "Ah, Eloise! Did you get a valentine this year? Though Uncle Howard's words do come to you now, with black faces, from the country where the negroes grow, what a pretty valentine you should have if I were in France, where they make paper with such beautiful pictures on it, and ink all bright with silver and gold! There! That's a kiss for you, my dear, and take that for Uncle Howard's valentine. I would send one valentine to *my* Miss Van Rensselaer, and another to Miss Julia Sands, were I not afraid my little Eloise would be jealous. You may, nevertheless, thank Miss Sands for giving me the pleasure of her appearance, and of the flashes of her wit, in a dream last night; and say to her that her literary glory has even extended to Barbary, for I myself saw it here recorded in Picket's 'Academician,' side by

side with that of Miss Miller and others, whom it delighted me to
find thus honored in the land of Dido.

"But here I am talking of love and ladies, when everything
around me threatens war. I had almost forgotten to mention
that, for the last three months, forts have been building, monitors
arriving, troops collecting, and hostile fleets looked for, by some
from Sardinia, by some from Austria, by some from Constanti-
nople; but I can scarcely think the difficulties (for there are real
ones with all these powers) will have any results so serious.
Therefore you may assure Mrs. Barnes and the ladies that I hope
at some future day to see them all again in spite of cannons and
scimitars, and to tell them how much their little Turkish slippers
have been admired even by genuine Turkies.

"I would add a list of those to whom I desire to be particularly
remembered, Miss Sedgwick and her connections, the Bryants, Mrs.
Bradish, your father, and many others, but you will be glad to be
spared the inconvenience of reading any more from me just now,
on condition of yourself calling them all to mind without my
naming them. To Mrs. Osborn and Aunty I mean to write when
the next scribbling fit comes on, so you are set free from the effects
of the present one, with assurances how sincerely I remain

"Ever yours faithfully,

"JOHN HOWARD PAYNE."

After his presentations to the Bey, Mr. Payne immediately devoted himself to the duties of his office. Mr. Hodgson was the
preceding consul, but this gentleman spent the most of his time
in Italy, and left the affairs of state in the hands of his clerk, a
young man by the name of Gale, whom he appointed to act as
consul *ad interim*. The business of the office was found to be in a
state of neglect, which caused Mr. Payne much hard work to put
into proper condition; besides this, he found the consular residence in frightful disorder and dilapidation, entirely unfit for persons of the most ordinary circumstances to live in, far more the
representative of a great nation, and, had the prior consuls to
Mr. Payne properly respected their office, they would have demanded other apartments of the Tunis government. It did not
take Mr. Payne long to discover the place far beneath the dignity
of his position, for he at once made a representation to his government at Washington of the vile condition of the consulate mansion,
and asked for the necessary authority to repair the dungeon-like

place, with iron-barred holes for windows and rafted ceilings. But
the government at the time did not think it expedient to take any
steps in the matter, as there was a disposition on the part of Congress to suppress its Tunisian consulate altogether. Meantime,
Mr. Payne had discovered that the Bey himself was his landlord,
and sometimes put such of his houses as were occupied by consuls in order, and that he was at that time actually spending quite
a sum of money on the building assigned to Queen Victoria's representative. "On this hint he spake." He forthwith wrote to
the secretary of the Bey in the spirit of complaint, declaring that
it was almost offering an indignity to his government to remain
in the building. This was done in such a manner, and so impressive was the style of the communication compared with those
hitherto sent by earlier American consuls, that it received an immediate answer, with the promise of repairs. After some two or
three days had passed and no workmen appeared, he appealed to
his royal highness again. Then workmen were sent, who fooled
about the place, and who only took something away and left no
substitute. Then came another pause: this was too much for
Payne. He made up his mind to press the matter until his residence was put in handsome order. He made out a list of the
alterations that he desired, got it translated and written down in
Arabic, put on his full uniform, and, with his interpreter and
vice-consuls, posted off in battle array to Bardo. One of the
ministers, whom, according to usage, he first had to meet, asked
the object of his visit, and when he told the gentleman of state his
object, he declared that he was extremely grieved to hear of our
consul's inconvenience, but that there was no necessity of his
seeing the Bey, who was at this moment much occupied with an
important case in the Hall of Justice, and that his highness had
already issued orders that all should be done that he desired.
Payne was not to be put off any longer; he insisted on seeing the
Bey. The minister retired for a moment, and then returned with
the message from the Bey that if Mr. Payne would have patience
for a few seconds he would be happy to receive him. In a few
moments more his highness adjourned a cause that was then
before him, and Payne, with his attendants, was escorted to the
Hall of Justice. Payne entered in the true court-style. His highness was reclining on a long sofa; at his right stood his minister,
and on his left the interpreter. A dense crowd of white burnouses
were on each side of the room, leaving a large open space between

14

them and the Bey. Payne's dragoman walked up and kissed the
hand of his highness as his (Payne's) proxy, observing court etiquette, and then his interpreter, who did his own politeness, also
kissed his royal hand, whereupon his majesty fixed his eyes upon
Payne's majesty, and exclaimed in Arabic,—

"I bid you welcome. What can I do that will afford you
pleasure?"

Payne answered, "I am sorry that I am forced to distress or
inconvenience your highness, but ever since my arrival I have
been much annoyed about my residence, which now has been rendered so vexatious that unless something is immediately done I
shall be forced to find apartments elsewhere, and make a complaint to my government."

"But I have given orders to have the patio newly roofed, as
you requested," replied the Bey.

"This is the least of the things needed. I have informed one
of your ministers that there are other things infinitely more required than the roof your highness specifies." Handing the list,
Payne in addition remarked, "This will prevent further misunderstanding."

His highness appeared to be struck on finding the communication written in Arabic, and half opening and then closing it, and
then looking at his minister, and again half opening it, he acted
as if he desired to read the communication before the proper time.
He then said to Mr. Payne,—

"I myself will read your list, and see that all your wants herein
expressed shall be with promptitude attended to."

Mr. Payne evidently had made an impression, and, perfectly
satisfied with his own august display, left the apartment of his
majesty, once more to inhabit his tottering palace.

A few days more passed and nothing done; he sent another
message to the Bey by his vice-consul, stating that he would at
once take the trouble off his highness's hands, make the required
improvements, and deduct the expenses from the rent until he
should be reimbursed. He directed his messenger, Vice-Consul
Mr. Gale, and his interpreter to insist on a reply, either oral or
written.

On this occasion, as before, the approaches to his highness were
already crowded with consuls and others waiting on special business, in such numbers when Payne's ambassadors arrived that
there was a general titter, as if to say, "Gentlemen, you come

too late; your case is hopeless, for we must be served before you."
But Payne's officers had learned a lesson but two days before, assumed a dignity that did not belong to them, and pressed through
the crowd to the immediate door of the grand court, where the
minister who previously presented Mr. Payne to his highness at
once recognized the messengers, treated them with the most
marked civility, and attended to them forthwith. The expression
upon the faces of the crowd that stood about at once changed to
wonder and astonishment, and Mr. Payne's ambassadors had the
satisfaction of hearing a muttering complaint from the bystanders
thus set aside, and who were unable to understand why the
United States should be so promptly attended to. A badge signi-
fied the consulates to which they belonged. In a quarter of an
hour or so the following written answer was placed in the hands
of Mr. Payne's plenipo, when he and his coadjutor departed,
highly delighted with their success and importance.

"Glory to the one only God! From the slave of All-powerful
  God, the Mouchir AHMED PACHA, Bey, Emir of the Tunisian
  armies,
"To our Ally, Sidi JOHN HOWARD PAYNE, Consul-General of the
  American Government at Tunis.
  "We acquaint you that we have received your letter regarding the affair of the consul's mansion. We had even previously
ordered our L'oukie (architects) in relation to the subject; we
now come from despatching the Bache Bouck (chief of the guards)
to compel that everything might be done which you have desired.
                "May God be your holy guardian!

"Written this ninth day of the month of El Hadja, in the year
1259." (Corresponding with the month of January, the 8th,
1844.)

Scarcely had the answer been read by Mr. Payne when a giant
of a guard, covered with tunics, and jackets, and cloaks, all brilliant here and there with gold (the same man stands before the
Bey on presentation-day), who assured Mr. Payne that the work
would go on in the morning. The work did go on as promised,
and Mr. Payne ordered just whatever he desired. Walls were
cut through; iron gates disappeared; eyelet-holes were turned

into magnificent windows; all the terraces were newly covered
and painted; all the floors newly paved with the most expensive
painted tiles, and an arched dome towered above the roof, giving
a grandeur to the building almost equal to that of the Bey's own
palace, and, over this again, our consul caused to be erected a

CONSULATE AT TUNIS.

flag-staff of a size that had never before been witnessed in Tunis,
and a new American flag was flung out to the winds, of such
magnificent proportions that it became the subject of public comment. These improvements cost the Bey over thirty thousand
piastres (almost four thousand dollars). When all was complete,

Mr. Payne congratulated himself on having the finest consulate building in Tunis.

Mr. Payne became a great favorite with the Bey. He induced Mr. Horace H. Day, of New York, the manufacturer of rubber goods, to present the Bey with some specimens of his best work, among which there was a large India-rubber boat, for which his highness expressed himself much pleased, and in return presented Mr. Day with a gold snuff-box, set with brilliants, valued at one thousand dollars.

Mr. Payne had not much more than got his consulate affairs in good working order, and felt comfortable in many respects, when by a change of government at Washington and the intriguing of a person who had formerly been the consul at Tunis (and who desired a reappointment) he was recalled. This was a great disappointment to Mr. Payne in several respects. The most important one was that he had been engaged for over a year on the history of Tunis, and, to accomplish the work properly, it was absolutely necessary to be there, where he could come in contact with the materials required for the work.

He received the official notice of his recall on the 20th of November, 1845. On his way home he stopped for some twelve months or more in Italy, Paris, and London, and reached New York in July, 1847. He then went to Washington, where he was received with great warmth and respect by every one who knew him, and especially so by Governor Marcy. Many of his old friends were astonished to see him back at home, as they had not previously heard of his recall, and protested that he should be returned to a post he had filled with so much dignity and patriotism.

Mr. Payne had not been in Washington for a great while before Mr. Marcy and Mr. Clayton made a strong move for his reappointment. This was done on the ground of the dissatisfaction given to the Bey and the people of Tunis by the consul who took Mr. Payne's place. The matter, however, dragged along for some time, and he was not reappointed until a change of administration took place, and in 1851, Mr. Webster stood by his "old friend," and caused Mr. Payne to be reinstated. Payne, now once more "an exile from home," left his country and his friends, for the last time, in the latter part of April, 1851. When he bade his friends good-by, in Brooklyn, where he had been residing with his brother, Thatcher Payne, he did so in broken health. On his way to Tunis he stopped at Paris for a little over a month, and then taking ship (the Mississippi) July 25th, at Marseilles, under the command of Commodore Morgan, of the United States navy, he was directly *en route* for Tunis, and in sixty hours afterwards he once more lay in the harbor opposite to the classic grounds of Carthage. Salutes were fired, he was visited from the shore, and was every way received with all the signs of marked respect. When the Bey heard of his arrival, he exclaimed, "Let him be welcome." All the flags were displayed, and all the foreign consuls, in full uniform, immediately called on him; his old personal friends hastened to give him a cordial reception. Once more Mr. Payne sat down to his work, with his characteristic determination to do it faithfully and well.

In the early part of the winter of 1852 his health commenced to fail rapidly. Rheumatism and great prostration followed. He was confined to the house the whole of the winter. In March, feeling somewhat better, he ventured out, to entertain and show the interesting features of the place to three American gentlemen who were travelling for pleasure, and had crossed over from Italy to see Tunis and Carthage. The Hon. D. S. Pickett, of Frankfort, Kentucky, was one of this party, which were the last Americans for whom Payne signed a passport. The undertaking was too much for him, and on his return home he was prostrated to his bed again, from which he never arose. He died on the 9th of April, 1852, in the sixty-second year of his age.

The following is a translation of the official letter announcing his death to the government of the United States:

"Tunis, the 9th of April, 1852.

"To the President and Government of the United States.

"Monsieur,—I hasten to have the honor to bring to your knowledge the decease of Colonel John Howard Payne, our consul, who died this morning at six o'clock.

"Gaspary."

At the moment that Mr. Payne died, his Moorish domestics and two Sisters of Charity were at his bedside. During the whole of his last confinement to his sick-room he received the kindest consideration and nursing at the hands of these good women. Not a day passed without some one of them standing at his side, administering the consolation that so lifts the drooping spirit of the sick, and those delicacies that moisten the parched taste, and for a moment, at least, revive the lost appetite. The Sisters of Mercy who attended him were Rosalie, Josephine, Marie Xavier, and Celeste. A priest of the Greek Church said prayers over

ROOM IN WHICH PAYNE DIED.

his remains at the grave. His remains were laid in the old time-honored burial-place that overlooks the bay and the ruins of Carthage. The United States government caused to be placed over his grave a marble slab, with the following inscription on it:

IN MEMORY OF

COL. JOHN HOWARD PAYNE,

Twice Consul of the United States of America for the
Kingdom of Tunis,

This stone is here placed by a grateful country.

He died at the American Consulate in this city after a painful illness, April 1st, 1852. He was born in the city of Boston, State of
Massachusetts, June 8, 1792.

His fame as a poet and dramatist is well known wherever the
English language is spoken, through his celebrated ballad of " Home,
Sweet Home," and the popular tragedy of " Brutus," and other
similar productions.

The stone that bears this inscription is an oblong slab of white
Italian marble, raised a few inches above the grave. On each of
the four margins of the slab are the following lines of poetry :

"Sure when thy gentle spirit fled
 To realms beyond the azure dome,
With arms outstretched, God's angels said,
 Welcome to Heaven's ' Home, Sweet Home' !"[1]

PAYNE'S GRAVE AT TUNIS.

---

[1] These beautiful lines were composed by Mr. R. S. Chilton, who at the
time held the position of clerk in the Consular Bureau at Washington. As
Mr. Payne's personal friend, he took great interest, on behalf of the government, in having the monument erected over him at Tunis.

So ended the singular and constantly varying life of John Howard Payne, unquestionably a man of genius, but who failed to accomplish a very high position in any of the several professions of poet, dramatist, or actor from the want of exclusive devotion to some one of them.

A life-long friend of Mr. Payne, a gentleman of the finest literary attainments, and of whom we have already spoken as having published a sketch of our subject in the " Boston Gazette," thus comments upon the close of Mr. Payne's life:

"Many mourn him: the fascination of his early brilliancy has left its record on many minds. The tidings of his departure touch many hearts with very tender memories. Always buoyant, full of resource, rich in the stores of a varied and peculiar experience, his society always had a singular attraction. Always busy about something, he always kept his mind cheerful and wide-awake. His abilities did not fulfil their early promise. His faculties were never sufficiently disciplined by the healthy toil of exact study, nor was his knowledge enlarged by methodical and various acquisitions from books. But, if he did not assimilate or amass in the way necessary for a higher eminence than he attained, so quick a mind with such opportunities could not fail to collect a great deal of what was profitable and pleasant for immediate use; his grace of expression, from boyhood to age, combining remarkably the exactness of art with the ease of nature, had a singular charm; and, I presume, a collection of his letters might be made, which would take a high rank in that department of composition. But what I like most to think of is, that a life, begun in some respects so unpropitiously, should have passed to its end so blamelessly, and so happily. To be the spoiled child of public enthusiasm and not to be a ruined man; to lose the huzzas that have cheered one on at the threshold of life and not become *blasé* or a misanthrope; to be made drunk with admiration in the feebleness of one's teens and not wake to a chronic imbecility or spleen, bespeaks the presence of elements of a noble nature."

When we were preparing a paper on Mr. Payne to read before the Faust Club of Brooklyn, for the purpose of inciting the members to assist in erecting a memorial to the author of " Home, Sweet Home," we wrote to Mr. Amos Perry, who, some few years after Mr. Payne's death, filled the consulship at Tunis, and who, on arriving there in 1862, took a great interest in all matters concerning Mr. Payne's consulship, and the literary effects which he left behind him, which perhaps are now lost forever. Indeed, had it not been for the appreciation and manly sympathy of Mr. Perry, hardly an autographic letter of Mr. Payne's would have been saved for his admiring friends to look at. In answer to the communication we sent to Mr. Perry on the close of Mr. Payne's life, we received the following:

" GABRIEL HARRISON, ESQ.,
  "380 Wyckoff St., Brooklyn, N. Y.

"DEAR SIR,—Your esteemed favor of the 3d instant is before me. I am gratified to learn that you have made a movement for the erection of a monument in Prospect Park to the author of 'Sweet Home,' and I desire to make my grateful acknowledgment to you and the high-spirited Faust Club of Brooklyn for the effort to do simple justice to the memory of one who deserves the respect and admiration of every American citizen. I am also gratified to learn that you are engaged in preparing for publication a biography of Mr. Payne, which I doubt not will be a graceful and a fitting tribute to his genius and industry, and will supply a manifest demand in the republic of letters.

"I had no knowledge of Mr. Payne on my arrival in Tunis, —— 1862, except that he was the author of 'Sweet Home,' and had held the consular office in that city. Paying an early visit to his grave in the Protestant cemetery, I plucked and pressed flowers that I found growing luxuriantly around it. In writing to friends across the ocean, I frequently enclosed these flowers with a copy of the inscriptions upon the gravestone, and I subsequently learned from the various sources that the memorials were greatly prized.

"I soon became interested to learn about Mr. Payne's life, and especially about the sad, closing scenes in his consular career and his earthly existence. But here my inquiries were not, in general, cheerfully or satisfactorily answered. A shadow seemed to rest upon his name. Estimable and worthy persons spoke of him with ominous reserve. In searching the archives of the consulate, I found comparatively little to gratify my curiosity. I saw convincing proof of method and order in his transactions. His letters and accounts were duly filed. His despatches to the Department of State, and his communications addressed to the Tunisian government, were neatly copied in his own clear hand. There was abundant proof that he did not pass his time in ignoble ease.

He had animated controversies with the Tunisian government, and with one of his colleagues, on some matters that have long since ceased to interest the public. It was through his official interference and untiring exertions that a superior consular mansion or government-house was secured for the use of the American representative at the Tunisian court. The old consular building, whose foundations date as far back as the days of Venetian greatness and glory, was, through his official service, thoroughly remodelled or rebuilt in a style of grandeur bordering on extravagance. On the top of this great structure was erected a towering mast, from whose heights was suspended a liberal supply of bunting, with the stars and stripes in such ample proportions as to be seen and distinguished at a distance.

" Mr. Payne labored indefatigably for the honor of the American government. Believing that, without a stately official mansion, and a tall mast from which to suspend the national standard, the representative of his country could not secure becoming respect, he applied himself to what seemed at the time a hopeless task. At a formal audience given to him by the Bey, he pronounced the dilapidated old building, with its diminutive flag-staff (that had once served the republic of Venice). beneath the dignity and honor of America, and demanded in unequivocal terms a suitable mansion. The Bey, roused to indignation by his bold manner and utterances. caught up the word America, and with the severest irony and derision replied, ' America! America! where is it? I do not know of any such country.'

" One of my informants. an intelligent and outspoken republican, born at Venice, and long a resident at Susa (ancient Hadrumetum), said that Mr. Payne, on receiving this reply, determined that the Bey should learn something about the country of whose situation and existence he professed to have no knowledge. To this end he besieged the Bey and his ministers, persistently pressing his claims for a new consulate, till ' His Highness' acquired a practical lesson in geography and history. In fine, the Bey came to the conclusion that America actually existed somewhere on the globe, and that its representative was entitled to courteous and respectful treatment. His coffers were speedily opened, and America thus secured the finest consulate and the tallest mast in the city. It was a trial of wits, in which Mr. Payne proved victorious. The completion of the consulate was observed in a marked manner. The consul procured a national standard, of quality and dimensions in harmony with the occasion. The stars and stripes were unfolded to the breezes in the presence of a multitudinous throng. A brass band, stationed on a platform fastened with iron bands to the flag-staff, twenty-five feet above the roof of the consulate, made the welkin ring with their shrill and boisterous blast, while the spacious and the tasteful apartments in the second story were the scenes of feasting and gayety. One of Mr. Payne's Moorish friends, in speaking of this celebration, called it 'An American jubilee.'

"While Mr. Payne was successfully carrying out his project of securing for the use of the American representative at Tunis a stately and commodious mansion, he took a step which, in connection with official rivalry, envy, or malice, and in the absence of needed aid from personal friends and relatives, seriously impaired his reputation in that city. Not content with the great outlay made by the Bey, he expended on his private account for his darling project some borrowed money, thus involving himself in a debt, which subsequently increased, in Mussulman phrase, by the hand of God.

"A proud-spirited man, Mr. Payne found himself, despite his success in getting a new consulate, weighed down and chagrined. In this state of affairs his health gave way. His plans for literary labor, on which he depended for funds, were broken up. He drooped, sickened, and, after a lingering and painful illness, passed on to

> " ' That undiscovered country, from whose bourn
> No traveller returns.'

" It was a sad issue, and a cruel lot. He was in a foreign land, deprived of the pleasures of the sweet home about which he had sung, and of the presence of long-cherished friends. Yet he was cared for. Sweet charity from Christians, Mussulmans, and Jews failed him not. He was tenderly and lovingly nursed, till his spirit departed from the clayey tabernacle.

" The saddest part of the case was his disappointed hopes and unfulfilled obligations. His plans were all frustrated, and his account was closed. For the want of a strong, friendly hand to gather up his effects, and protect the interests of his creditors and of his heirs-at-law, irreparable losses, confusion, and dissatisfaction resulted. Some to whom he was indebted, regarding themselves as the victims of misplaced confidence, became sour and uncharitable.

Smothered malice and animosity broke out. Many-tongued scandal started up, and ranged through that city and over that coast, as in the days of Æneas and Dido. The consul, silent in death, became a veritable victim. Could he have looked on he would have witnessed haggling and contention. The love of money was at the root of the evil. Mr. Ambrose Allegro, who was one of the appraisers of Mr. Payne's effects, and who had unusual means of understanding the condition of his affairs, thought that six or seven hundred dollars would have paid all the demands upon Mr. Payne's estate. For the want of this amount of money, after due notice had been given to Mr. Payne's relatives in America, his library, household furniture, pictures, sword of office, and numerous manuscripts and works of art were appraised and sold at auction. His personal apparel, an extensive collection of manuscripts, mostly in bound volumes, an autograph-album of distinguished contemporary authors, and numerous choice keepsakes, were not appraised or sold.[1] What became of them is rather a matter of conjecture than of proof. They were unquestionably taken away by unauthorized persons, and were effectually scattered and lost. The autograph-album referred to has, I am assured, been offered for sale in New York at a price sufficient to have paid all Mr. Payne's debts. One of his keepsakes, of which I have seen no mention, was brought to me with a mysterious air just before my departure from Tunis. It was a compact box, made to resemble a well-bound volume, entitled 'Code of Texas.' On opening it were found two well-finished and finely-polished Colt's revolvers, together with some implements needful to keep them in order, and an inscription on a brass or copper plate, showing this to have been presented to Mr. Payne by the inventor as a token of affection and respect. Having no taste for implements of war, or for this kind of keepsake, I declined to accede to the terms of the appreciative possessor.

"At the request of the venerable poet, scholar, and journalist, Wm. C. Bryant, and under instructions of the Department of State, I instituted, while at Tunis, careful inquiries with the view

---

[1] Many of these manuscripts of plays, and bound volumes of autographic letters, were at last discovered in 1883 by the author of this book to be in the possession of William Penn Chandler, of Philadelphia, ex-consul of Tunis. Mr. Chandler kindly presented the writer with several manuscript plays and Mr. Payne's journal, which he kept on his way from New York to Tunis.

of restoring these things, if possible, to Mrs. Rev. Lea Luquer (*née* Eloise E. Payne), the niece and nearest living relative of Mr. Payne. But my efforts proved of little avail. A few manuscripts, some of them diaries, and numerous packages of letters were found mixed up with mouldy newspapers and decaying rubbish, in a dozen or more bags and boxes that were stored in a damp cellar at the Goletta. The most valuable volumes of manuscript, and choice mementos of friends, including photographs and miniature portraits, a quaint old seal-ring with a Hebrew inscription (a family treasure that used to belong to his grandfather), a cane given him by Washington Irving, and other keepsakes of more or less value, known to have been in the consulate at the time of his death, were sought in vain.

"The Catholic bishop of Tunis, who was on terms of intimacy with Mr. Payne, recognized in him superior refinement, cultivation, and nobility of sentiment. The Greek priest who officiated at his funeral spoke of him in terms of unqualified praise. Of the four Sisters of Charity who, two at a time, ministered by turns to his wants during his protracted illness, I saw only Sister Rosalie. She complimented Mr. Payne's patience and gentleness, adding that he exhibited throughout his sickness the instincts and refinement of a gentleman. His Mussulman servant Mohammed, who stood by his bedside when he breathed his last, and who was in my service nearly five years, never wearied in speaking his praise. He esteemed it a privilege to go into the room where Mr. Payne died, show how the bed and chairs were arranged, and describe scenes and conversations that had occurred. Mr. Ambrose Allegro, the veteran Italian secretary, who began the service in the American Consulate near the close of the last century, under General William Eaton, expressed the opinion that Mr. Payne was engaged up to the time of his sickness in the preparation of a work on the regency of Tunis, containing sketches of Barbary corsairs and slavery. In confirmation of this view, Mohammed said he kept constantly on this table two large volumes of manuscript, in which he was writing much of his time.

"The grave of Mr. Payne, in St. George's Cemetery, is an object of interest to most American tourists, and is also sought out by some Englishmen. One intelligent and gentlemanly British tourist learned there, for the first time, that John Howard Payne was the author of 'Sweet Home.' He gave it as his opinion that this song was more sung at British firesides than

'God Save the Queen,' and having seen it stated in print that Barry Cornwall was the author of it, he was slow to credit the American. This incident led me to seek authentic information in regard to this matter. Accordingly, I addressed my inquiries to the late John Miller, who was at that time United States despatch agent in London. The following is the reply I received:

LETTER OF JOHN MILLER.

"'To Amos Perry. Esq., U. S. Consul at Tunis.

"'Sir,—I first published "Sweet Home" as an interlude in a play entitled " Clari," the title-page of which is as follows:

"' "Clari," an opera in three acts, as first performed at the Theatre Royal. Covent Garden, on Thursday, May 8, 1823, by John Howard Payne, Esq. The overture and music (with the exception of the national airs) by Henry R. Bishop, Esq. London, John Miller, 69 Fleet Street, 1826. (Price two shillings and sixpence.)

"'I gave Mr. Payne, who was introduced to me by Washington Irving, £50 for the copyright, and he was to revise the proof.

(Signed) "'John Miller.

"'London, Office U. S. Despatch Agency,
"'Sept. 19, 1865.'

"During my residence at Tunis the removal of Mr. Payne's remains to his native land came up for consideration among his friends in America, and I was consulted by letter in regard to the best means of accomplishing this object. The removal was not regarded with favor in that city, fear being expressed lest, if it were effected, Americans might take less interest in keeping St. George's Cemetery in order. Evidently, no hostility exists against Mr. Payne's ashes. It was conceded that their presence was a pledge of interest on the part of Americans, exerting an influence in securing for the cemetery an annual contribution from our government.

"The only direct charges I ever heard uttered against Mr. Payne at Tunis were, that he was stern, ruling the Bey, as it were, with a rod of iron, and that he was extravagant at the expense of the Bey and of his creditors.

"I regard the first of these criticisms, made to subserve rival interest, as a virtual compliment.

' Cæsar wept ;
Ambition should be made of sterner stuff.'

"Mr. Payne was at a post of duty in the service of his government. It was his part to sustain the honor and dignity of his country. Others might cringe and succumb before an imperious prince, seeking personal comfort and pleasure at the expense of the government. That was not in accordance with his nature or line of action.

"I am here reminded of Capulet and Montague (without their Romeo and Juliet), and am cautioned against stirring up smouldering embers. But from my stand-point no embers—only pale ashes—are visible. I would fain believe, for charity's sake, the fire gone out and the days of strife gone by. No smoke now obscures the vision of the great American public. We can all, throwing a mantle of charity over weaknesses and foibles, look calmly and dispassionately on the rivals, sleeping the sleep of death. They can no longer harm and supplant each other. Each lives, though dead, in the light of his own deeds. Leaving the benevolent physician and the successful courtier, some of whose descendants are among our dearest friends, with naught but kindly expressions and sentiments of respect, we turn to the dramatist, the man of letters, the poet of our homes, the energetic consul and the efficient champion of our country's dignity and honor. No defence or apology is required at our hands. A people who hold Bainbridge, Decatur, and their compeers in grateful remembrance for humiliating, at the cannon's mouth, the defiant despots of Tripoli and Algiers, cannot fail to appreciate the man who, by dint of diplomatic skill and energy, gained a controlling influence, if not a signal victory, over the proud and insolent ruler of Tunis. In the light of his literary and official services, no right-minded American citizen can stoop to indulge in harsh and ungenerous criticism. Sternness, when it subserves a worthy cause, is rightfully accounted a virtue, and thus the charge we are considering does actual credit to the man it was intended to disparage.

"In like manner, the other charge or criticism is divested of its power of evil the moment it is examined in the light of truth. To begin with, Mr. Payne never had in his hands any of the Bey's money to squander or use in that way. He simply furnished the plans which the Bey adopted for the rebuilding of the

American consulate. The plans were indeed on a generous scale, requiring a large outlay; but it was the Bey, not the consul, who incurred the expense, and assumed the responsibility of the enterprise.

"Mr. Payne's sickness and death, brought on, no doubt, by labor and anxiety, were, in my opinion (which is based on varied testimony taken at Tunis), the main cause of his insolvency. Misfortune—not prodigality—produced the derangement in his affairs. True, his was not the type of character that belongs to successful financiers and bankers. The philosophy of exorbitant interest was not his favorite study. He failed to invest in real estate and bonds. He left for his heirs no bank-stock or well-endorsed notes. He failed, sometimes, to avert from his humble abode the trials of pinching want.

" He did not, however, fail to produce during his life such fruits of genius, industry, and perseverance as will make fragrant his memory, and prove a better legacy than bank-notes and real estate. He did not fail, while in the severest straits, to record his name on the rolls of fame, in connection with his song of ' Home.'

" I am, then, of the opinion that the proposed memorial is appropriate and deserved. Your action in Brooklyn will, I am confident, awaken a responsive chord at thousands of firesides that have been enlivened and blessed by the author's life and labors.

" Truly yours,

" AMOS PERRY.

" PROVIDENCE, R. I., May 26, 1873."

Some months after the first edition of this volume had been published, the writer received a letter from Mrs. Eloise E. Luquer, the niece of John Howard Payne, bitterly complaining that great injustice had been done her father, Thatcher Payne, in my book by certain portions of the above letter from the Hon. Amos Perry. The above-named lady is the only important and nearest relative of Mr. Payne living, and to her the writer has been indebted for many autograph letters and manuscripts, which have tended largely to the fulness and value of this book. She is a lady of refinement and delicate sensibility, and, no doubt, felt keenly anything that would in the least reflect upon her honored father. But as Mr. Perry, a gentleman of equal refinement, did not intend to do any one injustice, and merely stated what facts he came across while acting as United States consul at Tunis, it is right

15

that he should be exonerated from any culpable intention. As for the author of this book, how could the lady for one moment think that he, of all men, should desire to tarnish the memory of her father, after the evidence of his twenty years' devotion to gather, arrange, and perpetuate the honors due to her neglected uncle, John Howard Payne?

However, we here introduce one of the lady's own letters, which throws additional light on the subject of the much regretted manuscripts of Mr. Payne, which were with other valuables sold and disposed by auction after his death. The letter is a noble tribute from a child to her honored father, and should here have a place in justice to her father and herself and the writer:

"Bedford, N. Y., Jan 20th, 1877.

" Mr. Gabriel Harrison.

" Dear Sir,—While it was impossible for me to avoid alluding to my painful disappointment in the matter of the one page of the memoir, I can most truly and sincerely say I did not intend to wound you. Your promise was made to me (the day you visited us in Bedford) to add to Mr. Perry's letter a note explanatory of the passage in Mr. Perry's letter to be found on the 8th and 9th lines of the 219th page, which reads as though we had neglected or refused to do what we should have wished to do to preserve my uncle's effects, while in truth my father was making every effort in his power to arrange the business satisfactorily. He repeatedly offered to pay the debts at once on the receipt of the proper vouchers. Each mail brought a statement of increased indebtedness; each returning mail carried a promise to cancel these enlarging debts upon the production of the proper papers, which were never sent.

" Finally, my dear father, convinced that the affair was managed with the intention of imposing upon him, and also knowing that the furniture of the consulate ought to bring more than any amount that had been named, ordered the furniture to be sold for the purpose of paying the debts, and also ordered that everything else should be carefully packed and sent home at *his own expense.* No orders or requests of his were at any time attended to, but the same dishonest and grasping spirit, which afterwards mutilated and scattered things of real value, prevented their reaching the hands of those to whom they rightfully belonged. There were family heirlooms in my uncle's possession, as oldest son, which no one with any proper feeling would have thought of retaining. Had my father been a man of robust health he might have saved the effects by a personal presence, but no other means could prevail where there was any object in preventing his accomplishing his wish. You must also remember that this was not the first time that my father had been called on to pay debts of my uncle's contracting, but he had been doing it at intervals since his boyhood, always willingly and cheerfully, no matter at what sacrifice to himself. Had the vouchers been sent from Tunis, my father would have paid the money. When such evil designs were abroad, I do not think you can blame my father for not stopping openeyed into the trap set for him. Had he paid $700, the next mail (it is my firm belief) would have brought a demand for $1000. Neither would we have received any of the treasures we desired. Now, I think, if you will take the trouble to read my letter over again, you will find that you have somewhat misjudged my words. I never, at any time or in any way, even intimated that you had failed in justice to my uncle. You have certainly done, and *well done, everything possible for a friend of his to do to honor his memory and to keep it green, and you deserve the thanks and grateful remembrance of all who love John Howard Payne.* Your injustice (and it was not yours in the first place, but Mr. Perry's, and he spoke only as was natural for one who had been in the Tunisian atmosphere, which would of course be adverse to us),—your injustice, I say again, was not to Uncle Howard, but to my father. You cannot blame a daughter for honoring her father's memory above *all others*, and desiring to shield him from every aspersion. It would certainly give me pleasure if, in your second edition, you would append a little note to Mr. Perry's letter, throwing the blame where it should be, and stating the fact that no vouchers were ever sent to my father for the money demanded of him. This fact would, I think, clear my father's memory from any blame of carelessness or indifference in a matter on which he only acted as any man of business would.

" Yours with respect,
" ELOISE E. LUQUER."

Mr. Amos Perry justly alluded with regret to the loss of Mr. Payne's literary effects, and mementos of great value. Even from the comparatively scanty number of letters, memoranda, and journals now extant, and over which we have carefully looked, we feel certain that manuscripts of value have been lost. In one letter to a dear relative, he particularly mentions that he "had been devoting much of his time in preparing a history of the Barbary States, and that the work would contain a large amount of highly interesting matter." In addition to this, Mr. Payne had in his possession several manuscript plays, which had never been performed, or published.[1]

The writer, while spending two or three days with Mr. Edwin Forrest, at his residence in Philadelphia, alluded to Payne's tragedy of "Romulus," inquiring why he never performed it. Mr. Forrest answered that he never could understand why Payne did not make the alterations he requested; that it was a fine play, and would have been, in his opinion, as great a success as "Brutus."

Mr. Payne was never a married man: a heavy shadow was cast over his eventful life by the unhappy termination of a romance of his early manhood when he became devotedly attached to a lady of Boston, whose rare beauty and mental accomplishments made her the idol of the social circle in which she moved. The affection of the gifted lover was warmly reciprocated, and a marriage would have completed the happiness of both but for parental interference. One of the largest characteristics of Mr. Payne's nature was its gentleness,—a disposition that bespoke more of the mother's than the father's nature within him. His love for children throughout his life amounted to a passion. Some of his letters to little Eloise, written but a few years previously to his death, are perfect models of child-letters, and show him to have understood their simple natures as comprehensively as he did the manly and womanly characters which grace his many dramatic efforts. Although throughout his life he seemed to have met with considerable harsh treatment from those for whom he worked the hardest, still he was ever confident and trusting. Hence, with all his industry and talents, his life was not as great a material success as it would have been with narrower and lower aims.

---

[1] Many of these valuable manuscript letters, plays, etc., have recently been discovered, and are alluded to in the preface.

CHAPTER VII.

THE BEGINNING OF THE END.

THE PAYNE MEMORIAL AND THE FAUST CLUB.

THE Faust Club of Brooklyn, Long Island, was organized in the early part of 1872. The object of the club was to provide a place for the social gatherings of gentlemen belonging to the several professions,—authors, artists, actors, journalists, and musicians. The constitution provided that one-half of the whole number of members should be of the above professions, while it left in the residue of its membership ample room for non-professional men who might desire to become members of the club. One of the most delightful features of the association was "the Saturday-night entertainments," which consisted of exhibitions of works of art, music, recitations. and the reading of original papers by the members. It was on one of these occasions, the 20th of October, 1872, that Mr. Gabriel Harrison read a paper on the life and writings of John Howard Payne, for the purpose of enlisting the sympathy and co-operation of the club in the erection of a suitable memorial to Mr. Payne.

Mr. Harrison said,—

"GENTLEMEN OF THE FAUST,—We meet here to-night for the purpose of listening to a paper which I have prepared on a topic that may be known to some of you; but. as the subject of my paper has been resting in his grave. in a far-distant, half-civilized country, for over twenty years, and we seldom hear of his name, I have no right to credit more than two or three of the gentlemen present with much. if any, knowledge of the man whose name I deem worthy to honor; and, little as he is known to you, his name should stand among the first of those Americans whose works have helped to make famous no less than four distinct and separate departments of art,—the Press, the Stage, Dramatic Literature, and Song. The fact cannot be erased that this man of whom I have chosen to speak was the youngest editor that a public journal

ever had. He was the first and only young 'American Roscius.'
He was the first American actor that trod the boards of a foreign
stage with prominence. He stands to-day at the head of all American dramatists, for he was the author of the only successful classic
tragedy written by an American, and which, after the test of
half a century, still holds its place in the standard English drama.
Above all else that he did, he was the man who wrote the one
song that alone has struck the key-note of every heart, that is felt
and sung in every land, and makes all humanity akin in acknowledging its sweetness and truth. I allude to the immortal song
of 'Home, Sweet Home!' and to John Howard Payne, who was
born within a few thousand feet of this very club-house, only a
few steps from the South Ferry landing on the New York side
of the East River. John Howard Payne, who, in his boyhood,
frolicked among the waves that rose and broke with crests of
snowy foam upon the beautiful beach of East Hampton, Long
Island, the lovely sea-girt retreat, where he watched the birds that
'came at his call,' where he learned to love the humblest of 'homes'
better than any palace he ever saw abroad. John Howard Payne,
among the best of American consuls, who, when he left his country
for the last time, to go and discharge his patriotic duty as consul
to Tunis, North Africa, embarked from this city, where he had
made his home for several years previous. This city, for which,
as my own ears heard him say, he had 'much love,' just ere he
departed to die in other lands.

"Come, gentlemen of the Faust, let us stop for one moment to
think of something more than ourselves and our club pleasures,
necessary as they may be to social brotherhood of men,—men who
meet for the interchange of wholesome thought to make lighter
the burdens of business life; men who meet to learn of each
other, that they may go back into the outer world to cheer and
to make it brighter and better. But, while happy in this club-
world of ours, let us stop for a few moments and listen to the
tinkling of a little bell, so faint that it is only like the echo of a
distant sound,—the bell that warns the curtain to draw aside to
let us look into the past, and see a shadowy spectre beckoning to
us for recognition, for justice, and acknowledgment. That spectre
is John Howard Payne. Let this club erect a monument to his
memory in our beautiful Prospect Park. Let it be in bronze and
granite. Let its graceful and artistic proportions tell the world,
'This monument honors not only the author of "Home, Sweet

Home!" but also honors the Faust Club,' linking its name with his. And, after the club has passed away forever, new generations will read the record upon its tablet, and say, 'Well done, Payne and the Faust.'

" Now, gentlemen, the first thing that will claim your attention is, where will the money come from to pay for this tribute to the memory of Mr. Payne ? In answer to that, I here promise you that I will devise the means. We will take the Academy of Music. We will get the members of the dramatic and musical professions of New York and Brooklyn to volunteer their aid, give one or more performances, and thereby obtain the amount required for the object. All I ask is your endorsement and interest, and in one year from this, on some beautiful mound, amid the drapery of gracefully falling foliage, in Prospect Park, will stand complete a monument to Payne and the Faust. This monument shall be unveiled in the midst of ten thousand people, saluted, as the mystic gauze falls and reveals the manly features of actor, poet, dramatist, with the sweet strains and words of 'Home, Sweet Home!' as sung by one thousand lovely children."

At the conclusion of Mr. Harrison's paper, a committee of twenty-five, with Mr. Gabriel Harrison as chairman, was appointed to carry out the object.

Mr. Henry Baerer was proposed, by Mr. Harrison, as the artist to make the design for the memorial.

The material furnished and used by the artist to produce the likeness was a very fine, large-sized daguerreotype taken of Mr. Payne in 1849, a short time previous to his leaving this country to fill, for the second time, the position as consul at Tunis, and less than three years prior to his death. In a few months the large model from which the bronze bust was finally cast was exhibited before the members of the Faust Club. To make perfectly sure of the fidelity of the likeness, the only two surviving relatives of Mr. Payne, his brother Thatcher Payne's widow and daughter, with whom for the last twenty years of his life he spent all of his leisure moments, and resided with them in Brooklyn, were called in to pass their judgment on the likeness. Their verdict was favorable in the extreme, and, after passing under the opinion of several other old associates of Mr. Payne, who pronounced the likeness faultless, it was finally placed in the hands of the artist to be cast in bronze. Among those who attested to the fidelity of the likeness is Mr. James Rees, of Philadelphia, who was contemporaneous with Mr. Payne, and had been perfectly familiar with him. Mr. Rees's opinion on this point is contained in the following letter:

" PHILADELPHIA, July 10, 1878.

"To GABRIEL HARRISON, ESQ.

" DEAR SIR,—I have just received the beautiful little bust of my old and much lamented friend, John Howard Payne, as a copy of the large, bronze bust proposed to be placed on Prospect Park, Brooklyn, N. Y. I can only say, a more striking likeness of the author of 'Home, Sweet Home!' I have never seen, not excepting several other likenesses of him I have in my possession. The artist seems to have caught that mild expression, with a 'shade more of sorrow than anger' around it, an expression which I have so often seen upon his face when speaking of the past.

" The artist, we repeat, deserves much credit for the piece of work, a view of which satisfies me that it more than realizes in faithfulness of features all that his most ardent admirers ever anticipated. In the years that are to come, when we have passed away, the words of ' Home, Sweet Home!' will have an additional charm to those, while gazing upon this striking likeness of their gifted author.

" Yours truly,
" JAMES REES."

The casting of the bronze was made at the National Fine Art Foundry of Mr. Powers, New York, and was in every respect a great success.

The work, when completed, cost over three thousand dollars.

The club, to assist them in obtaining means to pay for the memorial, gave two performances, afternoon and evening, at the Brooklyn Academy of Music. To accomplish this, a circular was sent by the club to the members of the dramatic and musical professions, soliciting their volunteer aid, to which an immediate and generous response was made, resulting in the following programme:

BROOKLYN ACADEMY OF MUSIC.

MANAGER..MR. GABRIEL HARRISON
STAGE DIRECTOR...MR. JAS. SCHONBERG
MUSICAL DIRECTORS............Messrs. M. PAPST, JOHN M. LORETZ, JR., & H. TISSINGTON
PROMPTER..MR. ALFRED BECKS

THE JOHN HOWARD PAYNE MEMORIAL.

TWO PERFORMANCES UNDER THE AUSPICES OF THE
"FAUST CLUB,"

AFTERNOON & NIGHT, RENDERED BY A LARGE NUMBER OF VOLUNTEER ARTISTS.
  The dramatic portion is presented mainly through the cordial co-operation of LESTER WALLACK. Esq.,
of Wallack's; EDWIN BOOTH, Esq., of Booth's; A. M. PALMER, Esq., of the Union Square Theatre;
Messrs. JARRETT and PALMER, of Niblo's, who have freely granted permission for members of their
companies to appear.
The **AFTERNOON PERFORMANCE** will commence at 2 P.M. with John Howard
Payne's drama,

CLARI!
THE MAID OF MILAN.

Rolamo.. Mr. John Gilbert
The Duke Vivaldi..Mr. E. M. Holland
Jocoso...Mr. Robert Pateman
Nimpedo...Mr. C. E. Edwin
Nicolo...Mr. W. H. Jones
Geronio..Mr. Geo. W. Browne
Pelgrino...Mr. J. W. Leonard
Nobleman...Mr. H. M. Brennan
Page..Mr. Frank Lamb
Clari, (with the song of "Home, Sweet Home," in the same situation in which it
    was originally used)...Miss Phillis Glover
Vespina..Miss Fanny Hayward
Leoda...Miss Imogene Fowler
Fidalma..Mme. Ponisi
Ninetta...Miss Kate Holland
Pelgrino's Wife...Miss Blaisdell

To be followed by a
GRAND MUSICAL OLIO.
OVERTURE—"Maritana"   Musical Conductor, Mr. H. Tissington
                          Orchestra.
SONG   .   .   .   .   - Mr. Mark Smith
BALLAD—"The Last Rose of Summer"   .   .   .   .   .   - Madame Anna Bishop
                      Accompanist, Mr. Wagner.
SONG—"La Donna e Mobile"   .   .   .   .   - Verdi
                      Mr. H. R. Humphries.

After which the celebrated TELEGRAPH SCENE from
THE LONG STRIKE.
Mr. Moneypenny   -   -   -   -   -   -   -   -   - Mr. J. H. Stoddart
Jane Learoyd   -   -   -   -   -   -   -   -   - Miss Julia Gaylord
Telegraph Clerk   -   -   -   -   -   -   -   -   - Mr. E. M. Holland
Betsy   -   -   -   -   -   -   -   -   -   -   - Miss Kate Holland
                To conclude with a
RECITATION—"The Bells"—(by Edgar A. Poe)..............................Mr. Steele Mackaye

OVERTURE..ORCHESTRA

THE **EVENING PERFORMANCE** will commence at 8 P.M. with John Howard
Payne's comedy,

CHARLES II!
Charles II.   .   .   .   .   Mr. J. W. Carroll
Rochester   .   .   .   .   - Mr. James Dunn
Captain Copp   .   .   .   .   - Mr. Thomas Morris
Edward   .   .   .   .   - Mr. Maurice Pike
Lady Clara, with Sontag's "Echo Song"   .   .   .   .   - Miss Ellen Morant
Mary Copp, with Song, "The Bird on the Tree"   .   .   .   - Miss Jennie Lee

To be followed by a
GRAND MUSICAL OLIO.
1. OVERTURE—"Pearl of Bagdad"   -   -   -   Musical Conductor, Mr. J. M. Loretz, Jr.
2. BOLERO—"Sicilian Vespers"   -   -   -   -   -   -   -   - Verdi
            Mrs. Jennie Van Zandt, accompanied by Mr. Geo. W. Colby.
3. ADELAIDE   -   -   -   -   -   -   -   -   -   - Beethoven
            Sung by H. R. Humphries, accompanied by Geo. W. Colby.
4. HOFFNUNG—(Hope)   -   -   -   -   -   -   -   -   - Mohr
            Brooklyn Saengerbund—Mr. Groeschel, Conductor.
5. BALLAD—"Home, Sweet Home," (words by J. H. Payne)   -   -   - Bishop
            Mrs. Jennie Van Zandt, accompanied by Mr. Colby.
6. "MEIN SCHIFFLEIN" (my little bark)   -   -   -   -   -   - Beschnitt
            Brooklyn Saengerbund.

The performance will conclude with John Howard Payne's Comedietta,

LOVE IN HUMBLE LIFE.
Ronsalus, a soldier   .   .   .   .   Mr. Hy. C. Rynar
Barlitz, a peasant   .   .   .   .   - Mr. Edward Lamb
Christine   .   .   .   .   - Miss Fannie Hayward
Crandt   .   .   .   .   - Mr. H. Brennan

The receipts of the two performances amounted to about two thousand dollars; this result not reaching the amount required, another plan was immediately put into operation in the form of an art-drawing among the members of the club. The artists in and out of the club donated some of their best works. Their liberality was remarkable. Among the gentlemen who contributed were Mr. James Hart, Rufus Wright, Gabriel Harrison, Ferdinand T. Boyle, John Williamson, J. A. Parker, W. M. Brown, J. B. Whitaker, Mr. Lanthier, Mr. Wiggins, George Hall, Mr. Henry Baerer, Mr. Groos, J. A. Faulkener, Mrs. Nagle, and others. Among the members of the Faust Club who took a liberal and very active interest in the art-drawing and the erection of the memorial were D. M. Tredwell, J. Y. Culyer, and F. T. Hoyte. Not to have made especial mention of their names here would have been an act of injustice and ingratitude. The drawing was a success; whereon a committee of five was appointed to confer with the Commissioners of the Prospect Park, for the purpose of selecting a site for the monument. This done, the committee determined on the day for the unveiling, and the following programme was observed:

UNVEILING

OF THE

COLOSSAL BRONZE BUST

OF

John Howard Payne,

AT PROSPECT PARK,

Saturday, September 27th, 1873.

PROGRAMME:

OVERTURE—"Semiramis," - - - - - - - Rossini

TWENTY-THIRD REGIMENT BAND.

1. CHORUS—"America," - - - - - -

BY THE CHILDREN OF THE PUBLIC SCHOOLS OF BROOKLYN.

2. PRESENTATION of the Bust of John Howard Payne to the Commissioners of Prospect Park by the President of Faust Club, Thomas Kinsella.

3. THE UNVEILING BY THE SCULPTOR,

Mr. Henry Baerer.

4. HOME, SWEET HOME! sang by one thousand public-school children, in which the assemblage are requested to join the chorus.

5. ACCEPTANCE of the Bust by Hon. J. S. T. Stranahan, President of Commission.

6. ODE—(Written for the occasion), by Jno. G. Saxe, LL.D.

READ BY THE POET.

7. GALOP—"Clear the Track," - - - - - - - STRAUSS.

TWENTY-THIRD REGIMENT BAND.

8. ORATION, - - - - - - - By William C. DeWitt.

9. CHORUS—"Flag of the Free," - - - - - MILLARD.

BY THE CHILDREN OF THE PUBLIC SCHOOLS.

10. GRAND MARCH—"Coronation," - - - MEYERBEER.

TWENTY-THIRD REGIMENT BAND.

COMMITTEE OF ARRANGEMENTS.

GABRIEL HARRISON, CHAIRMAN.

THOS. KINSELLA,	W. H. CLARK,	G. G. BARNARD,
FRANCIS S. SMITH,	E. P. ACKERMAN,	J. M. LORETZ, JR.,
S. D. MORRIS,	W. N. GRIFFITH,	D. M. TREDWELL,
HENRY MINTON, M.D.,	J. Y. CUYLER,	D. B. THOMPSON,
E. LAMB,	F. T. L. BOYLE,	W. C. HUDSON,
J. J. McCLOSKEY,	A. G. TORREY,	C. H. PARSONS,
ANDREW McLEAN,	JAS. TERRY,	M. PAPST,
W. H. WOODWARD,	J. W. CARROLL,	T. B. SIDEBOTHAM, JR.
H. T. CHAPMAN, JR.,	A. W. PETERS,	

Union Print.

THE PRESENTATION BY THOMAS KINSELLA.

"Mr. President, and Gentlemen of the Park Commission,—
On behalf of the Faust Club of the city of Brooklyn I have
the honor to present to you to-day, in trust for the citizens of
Brooklyn and for their descendants, a colossal bust of John Howard Payne. The present is from a club made up for the most
part of journalists, artists, dramatists, musicians, and actors. This
present is made because the Faust Club desired to contribute something to the attractions of this popular domain; to add something
to the means of cultivating and gratifying public taste; to perpetuate the fame of one who may be said to have labored and
succeeded in a majority of the callings I have enumerated; to
show that in their opinion it is not all of life to make a living; to
incite, it may be, citizens of greater affluence to follow their example, so that in time the counterfeit presentments of the representative men of all nations may be found in Prospect Park, and,
side by side with them, the statues and busts of the men whose
names light up our country's history, and whose deeds give weight
and character and dignity to the word American. From the bead-
roll of the great names of native-born men we selected John
Howard Payne,—because he was connected with so many professions represented in the Faust Club; because he was among the
first of Americans who established a reputation in Europe as an
actor and an author; because in his life he was not fortunate;
because his memory seems to have been neglected; because he is
connected by residence and by ancestry with Long Island; because his remains have been allowed to mingle with the dust of a
foreign land; because—and I confess it, sir—there was, running
through his life, a streak of Bohemianism, which is not without
its attraction to men who follow those professions which contribute less to the necessities than to the grace, the culture, and
the refinements of life. It is for my friend to speak of John
Howard Payne to-day as a journalist, an actor, a dramatist, a
representative of his country abroad, and as a man. To the
masses he will never need any other introduction than this,—he is
the author of 'Home, Sweet Home.'

"The bust which is about to be presented is the work of Mr.
Henry Baerer, a retiring, unobtrusive, and most meritorious
sculptor. It is regarded as a work of art of exceptional excellence, and the members of the Faust Club believe they have per-

formed a service for art in the wide introduction they have secured to-day for Mr. Baerer. Would that the dust of Payne could be deposited to-day in his native soil, and in some such delightful spot as this, and that, placing this monument to his fame above it, we might say, in the language of one of our living poets,—

'Oh, Mother Earth! upon thy lap
Thy weary ones receiving,
And o'er them silent as a dream
Thy grassy mantle weaving,
Fold softly in thy long embrace
That heart so worn and broken,
And cool its pulse of fire beneath
Thy shadows old and oaken.'

"Let me say, in closing, that it affords me peculiar pleasure to make this presentation directly through you, Mr. President, to whom, of all men in Brooklyn, we are indebted for this beautiful domain set apart for the use, enjoyment, pleasure, and education of the people of Brooklyn."

At the conclusion of Mr. Kinsella's remarks, Henry Baerer quickly cut the cord that held the covering over the bust, and as the star-spangled veil fell to the earth, loud and prolonged applause greeted the artist's work. Simultaneous with this the voices of over one thousand children filled the air with the song of "Home, Sweet Home!" while the great multitude of twenty-five thousand people joined in the chorus. The effect was electrical, and, before the song was completed, many eyes in the vast crowd were overflowing with tears.

This done, the Hon. J. S. T. Stranahan, President of the Prospect Park Commission, arose and addressed the people and the members of the Faust Club as follows:

"MR. PRESIDENT AND GENTLEMEN OF THE FAUST CLUB OF BROOKLYN,—The Park Commission, representing this city and speaking for all the people, gratefully accept the monumental gift which your generosity has furnished, and which by the ceremonies of this hour is transferred to its possession and future keeping. The splendid bust just unveiled, so complete as a work of art and so true to life, will hereafter be one of the attractions of Prospect Park, while paying a becoming tribute to one so well deserving, but hitherto so little known to, fame.

"The duty imposed on me is mainly accomplished in receiving at your hands this bust, so fitly located, surrounded by and associated with the scenes of pastoral life, and by its very situation suggesting the quiet repose to which, though vainly sought by him, he gave expression in the tenderest strains of song. You have, gentlemen of the Faust Club, evinced a delicate and appreciating discrimination in selecting John Howard Payne as the man who deserves this commemorative honor. His name will hereafter be more familiar to the people."

Immediately on the conclusion of Mr. Stranahan's remarks, John G. Saxe, LL.D., read the ode which he had written for the occasion.

ODE.

I.

"To him who sang of ' Home, sweet home,'
In strains so sweet the simple lay
Has thrilled a million hearts, we come,
A nation's graceful debt to pay.
Yet, not for him the bust we raise;
Ah, no! can lifeless lips prolong
Fame's trumpet-voice? The poet's praise
Lives in the music of his song!

II.

"The noble dead we fondly seek
To honor with applauding breath;
Unheeded fall the words we speak
Upon ' the dull, cold ear of death.'
Yet, not in vain the spoken word;
Nor vain the monument we raise;
With quicker throbs our hearts are stirred
To catch the nobleness we praise!

III.

"Columbia's sons—we share his fame;
'Tis for ourselves the bust we rear,
That they who mark the graven name
May know that name to us is dear;
Dear as the home the exile sees,—
The fairest spot beneath the sky,—
Where, first—upon a mother's knees—
He slept, and where he yearns to die.

IV.

" But not alone the lyric fire
    Was his; the Drama's muse can tell
His genius could a Kean inspire;
    A Kemble owned his magic spell;
    A Kean to ' Brutus' self so true,
    (As true to Art and Nature's laws,)
He seemed the man the poet drew,
    And shared with him the town's applause !

V.

" Kind hearts and brave, with truth severe
    He drew, unconscious, from his own;
O nature rare ! But pilgrims here
    Will oft'nest say, in pensive tone,
With reverent face and lifted hand,
    'Twas he—by Fortune forced to roam—
Who, homeless, in a foreign land,
    So sweetly sang the joys of home !"

After the applause upon the reading of the ode had subsided,
Mr. Kinsella then introduced the orator of the day, William C.
De Witt, who spoke as follows :

ORATION.

" We meet among grand and familiar scenes. Only a short distance from the southern slope of this park the waves of the
Atlantic, breaking on our coast, present one of the ocean-bounda-
ries of the great republic which is our nation's home. Nearer
still, beneath the declining sun, gleam the more peaceful waters
of the Bay, which is the imperial gateway and harbor of our
Empire State; and down the northern and the eastern vista rise
the compact walls and steeples many of our own Brooklyn,—the
city of homes and home of cities yet to be; while all about us, in
this vast assemblage beneath the autumnal foliage, are the faces
which around our hearth-stones kindle with joy when we are
prosperous and happy, and darken with anguish when we are
stricken with sadness or affliction.

" Among scenes thus beautiful and familiar, brothers of the
Faust Club, we come to consecrate one of the cardinal virtues,
and to erect a monument to the memory of the author of ' Home,
Sweet Home !' It is not merely the individual that we wish to
commemorate, but it is, besides, the love of home with which his

name is inseparably interwoven for all time. Like Virgil, in his
Æneid, we take a double subject. We celebrate the sentiment
and the man, home and the author, the fireside and the stage—
his life.

"John Howard Payne, whose living presence long since resolved
to dust, in some measure reappears in the imperishable bronze of
this bust, was born in the city of New York on the 9th of June,
1791, and died at Tunis on the 9th of April, 1852. His life was
remarkable for personal beauty and intellectual precocity in its
youth, for great usefulness and excellence in acting and authorship in its maturity, and for versatility in literature and faithfulness in public office during its closing years.

"Some of his sweetest verses were written when he was only
fifteen years old, and at that age he had attracted public attention
by his contributions to the newspaper press. He was well educated, mainly by his parents and partly by a studentship at Union
College, broken off after two years. He went upon the stage
when only seventeen years old, and in characters peculiarly suited
to his years, won the title of the 'American Roscius,' and was
regarded, apparently with justice, as the best actor of his age in
Europe or America. He was physically so handsome that he pro-
voked criticism as being 'too beautiful for a man,' and it is evident
that he possessed those talents and graces without which beauty
is a cheat. When he went to England, in 1813, he was twenty-
one years old, and from that period he challenges attention to his
life.

"Up to this time we had produced great statesmen, good law-
yers, and generals, but letters and the arts had been neglected. Indeed, an English journal of professed friendship to America, in
descanting upon the appearance of Mr. Payne at Drury Lane,
deemed it just to speak of us in this wise:

"'A youth from a remote country—a country nearly two centuries behind us in the improvement of every art—must come
before a London audience under every possible disadvantage.
There must necessarily be a difference of manner, of deportment,
of enunciation, and even of accent, all tending to make rather an
unfavorable impression. We may form some idea of the impression
an actor from Ephesus would have made two thousand years ago
on one of the theatres of Athens, where the Greek language had
arrived at such a degree of polish that the common fruit-women
could criticise all the niceties of its pronunciation.'

"It was in the morning twilight of American art and literature that Payne prepared himself for the pen and the stage. He is first to be regarded as a pioneer in the uncultivated fields of intellectual labor in America, with no other training than that which his primitive home could afford. When it is remembered that it was with this discipline, and no more, with an education acquired in the midst of such obstacles, and no greater help, that he transferred himself to London, and there, in the presence of the wealth and genius of the old world, gave our country an honored name and fame in the history of the dramatic art in England,—the first American who thus honored his country abroad,—what praise of him can be fulsome here, what gratitude can be too magnanimous?

"In examining his life's work, his dual capacity is constantly before you, and you cannot divide it without marring his fame. It will not do to consider him either as an actor or as an author alone. It was his governing ambition to merge the two pursuits together in such measure as to produce the greatest possible usefulness.

"When he entered upon the English stage it was blazing with the glories of Kemble and of Kean, and lighted occasionally by the still greater brilliancy of Talma, who, at Paris, divided the hearts of the French people with the first Napoleon. It is not likely that Payne was the equal of these masters. yet he competed with them in all their greatest characters, and through all his star engagements in England and Ireland gained the applause of the people and the laudations of the press.

"As a dramatist, Payne wrote in all about fifty plays. It is true most of these were reproductions from the French, and during his stay at Paris, under contract with English managers. London may be said to have been largely dependent upon his pen for its dramatic novelties and entertainments. Yet his reproductions from the French stage were in no sense literal translations, for Payne's taste and experience enabled him to alter a plot whenever it displeased him, and so many were his inroads upon the speeches that the originals would scarcely be recognized in the copy. Utility marked all he did. His adaptations were practical and popular, and although surrounded by competition in this pursuit, he eclipsed all his rivals.

"The greatest of the dramatic works which he called his own was his tragedy, entitled 'Brutus; or, The Fall of Tarquin.' While he had the assistance of seven plays previously devised

16

upon the main incident of 'Brutus,' yet the feebleness of their help may be judged from the fact that five of these plays were absolute failures, and two occupied the stage for only a few unprofitable nights. Payne's 'Brutus' is one of the most popular and enduring tragedies in the English language. The intensity of its arrangement, its strong, brusque, startling characterization, and the fiery eloquence of its speeches justly entitle its author to fame. His comedy of 'Charles II.' is more wholly original than 'Brutus,' and is popular and meritorious, while his adaptation of 'Thérèse' to the English stage was regarded at the time of its production as a master-stroke of art.

"Of the purely poetical works of Payne, there is a large number of beautiful, small poems, all remarkable for their richness of sentiment, and the opera of 'Clari' in which the immortal ballad had its birth. He wrote also a biographical work, entitled 'Our Neglected Poets,' and was a contributor of essays to many of the political controversies in this country after his return from abroad.

"Such were the literary and dramatic labors of John Howard Payne. They are not, however, to be separated from each other. They did not occur at different or distinct stages in his career. All through his life the two pursuits of acting and authorship ran together, and his highest claim to renown is in his excellence, not in one, but in both, and in his unparalleled usefulness to this double calling. The debt due him from posterity is one purely of gratitude. He does not extort admiration by the dazzling splendors of extraordinary genius, but he has earned an honest fame by the utility of his talents, and the abundant fruits of his patient and laborious life.

"But, my friends, just and kind and becoming as it would have been for you to have selected John Howard Payne for this monumental compliment, because of these great services to dramatic and poetic literature and art, it was, after all, the immortal ballad that peculiarly endeared him to your hearts.

"'Home, Sweet Home!' What memories these simple words recall! What ties of kindredship flash through their Promethean heat! How burdened with sacred thoughts of rest and peace they are! And here in Brooklyn—our home, and peculiarly fitted to be called the city of homes—it was touchingly appropriate that this song should have a shrine.

"This little poem, like its author, is largely indebted to providential aid for its celebrity. It was not the coinage of many years of meditation, like Gray's 'Elegy,' nor was it written, like our national anthem, amid the scenes it sought to consecrate. Payne never knew what it was to have a home after he was thirteen years old. About this period of his life his mother, whose love and virtue probably planted within him those sentiments which burst from his soul years after she was gone, and his father, who stood behind the scenes in tears when his boy first trusted himself to the temptations of the stage, went to their long home beyond the grave.

"From this moment Payne was a wanderer, and despite the tenderness of his heart, and the fascinations of the fair sex, with which he must have been constantly assailed, he maintained his celibacy and hopelessness until he consummated it by death upon the remote and hoary shores of the Mediterranean. Strange that a wanderer should have sung this song of home. Nevertheless, it was while in Paris, engaged in writing 'Clari,' which he subsequently converted from a pantomime into an opera, and when his mind was doubtless dwelling upon his delightful boyhood at East Hampton, that he wrote 'Home, Sweet Home!'

"The song is short and simple. It is remarkable neither for elegance of diction nor harmony of numbers. But it has crowded into a few lines every thought and sentiment and scene of its blessed subject: 'the lowly thatched cottage,' 'the singing birds,' the 'hallowing charm from above,' and 'the peace of mind better than all.' It is full of the fruit and essence of its theme. It wanted the tune which was to hum it wherever the English language was or should be spoken. Music was needed, and music came. As when some parent bird, on lofty pinions, circling above his eyrie, seeing its young prepared to fly, yet fearful of the elements, descends, and bearing the fledgling forth to mid-heaven, puts him on his experimental voyage through the air, so music came to this rich germ of poetic thought, and upbearing it upon the cloud of melody, in which it has ever since lived and moved and had its being, sent it chanting and singing, forever and forever, through the world.

"I said a while ago that after his thirteenth year Payne never knew what home was. Yet this I know not. For where is our home? Is it that first one in which we were born? Is it the household that rang with the laughter of later boyhood? Is it the scene of our first nuptials or the last, or is it the more solemn tenement in which old age lies down to die? These fade and merge with the march of time, and the organic thing keeps shift-ing into the infinite. Where is our home? Shall we seek for it in the realms of fancy? Is it upon the Elysian fields where Homer pictured heart's ease and glory, or is it in the fabled Atlantis be-yond the Herculean pillars of the sky? Is it in that new world in quest of which the venerable Ulysses sighed to sail 'beyond the sunset and the baths of all the western stars until he died?' or is it among the many mansions and upon the eternal hills? This is the wondrous mystery. All I know is, that where the soul dwells, that is our country, and where the heart is, there is our home.

"And now to the sentiment of the song and the memory of the man let this monument be dedicated, and to the honor of its founders may it endure forever."

Mr. Henry Baerer, the sculptor, was then introduced to the assemblage. After which "Home, Sweet Home!" was again sung by the children and the multitude, at the termination of which all departed for their homes.

Gloom and disappointment may have hung over the life of the man whom twenty-five thousand people had met this day to com-memorate in bronze and granite, but, if this world was ever blessed with a perfect day, it was the day the bronze bust of John Howard Payne was unveiled. The whole summer had been a beautiful one; the frequent falls of rainbowed storms had refreshed the growth of trees, and fields, and flowers, and nature all around was in a per-fection seldom seen. The broad plazas of bright green fields were relieved here and there by the long, outreaching, darker green in shadows from the massive groups of tall trees. Flowers of every kind were out in their bright colors, and the birds busy among the park trees made the mild air of a September afternoon bewitchingly sweet with their melody, while aqua fontana dashed upwards from their subterranean beds in grand crystal columns, cresting over and sparkling in the sunbeams like showers of diamonds, until, fading into a mist of transcendent splendor, they disappeared in their marble basins below, and, as you stood upon the gentle sloping mound, on which the memorial lifted its graceful propor-tions, with the eye sweeping over the great space that led to the main entrance of the park, watching the scattering throngs of people departing for their homes, it awakened the reflective mind to the importance of the occasion. In this event the Faust Club accomplished a thing that will ever reflect to their glory and memory, and have set an example to other organizations that will in the future be imitated, and thereby many an art-work will not only adorn our public parks, but will restore to memory the deeds and accomplishments of others, who, perhaps, had too long rested in the gloom of forgetfulness.

The bust is a masterly production. "The modelling is really fine. It gives the intellect of the poet in the most pronounced manner; the lines express thoughts touched with care. In this dual expression the sculptor has achieved his greatest triumph; the nose, too, is beautifully modelled; and the mouth expresses the firmness of the inflexible resolution of the man. All these facial characteristics are brought together by the sculptor into a harmonious whole. The pose of the head is downward, the reflective, inward look of the deep-set eyes seems to express a sad sentiment of inner life, and as you look on the colossal head, the mind of the beholder at once suggests, so must he have looked when he wrote the song of 'Home, Sweet Home!'"

Mr. Henry Baerer, the sculptor, was born at Kirchhain, in Hessen-Kassel, Prussia, in 1837. Here he was educated in one of the public schools until his fourteenth year, after which he became a student for three years at the Polytechnic Industrial School. In his early youth he was infatuated with everything relating to the fine arts. He gave evidence of his talent by his sketches, but received no encouragement from his parents to become an artist. He had some relations residing in New York City, and determined to go to America, where he intended to devote his life to art. He arrived in New York in 1854. He soon made the acquaintance of Robert E. Launetz, the sculptor, and the pupil of the celebrated Thorwaldsen. With Launetz Mr. Baerer studied for six years, at the end of which time he returned to Europe to finish his studies, and remained at the Academy in Munich for four years, after which time he assisted Professor Widemann to model several colossal statues,—one of *Victory*, which was placed on the top of the king's palace, and one of *Thalia*, for the opera-house at Munich. While here he also modelled his beautiful statue of *Pandora*. Having received liberal pay for his assistance to Widemann, he was enabled to still persevere with his studies at Berlin, Dresden, and Paris.

In 1866 he returned to New York, and obtained several handsome commissions. Among them were the busts of Roebling, the constructor of the Niagara and East River Bridges; the colossal bust of the philanthropist, Conrad Poppenhusen, of College Point, Long Island; the Beethoven Monument in Central Park, New York City; the bust of George Ehret; a life-size medallion of Gabriel Harrison; the *Fisher* group (after the poem of Goethe); the group of *Ossian with his Daughter Minona;* a group of *Theseus wrestling with Scirron,* and others, all of great merit, and placing Mr. Baerer among the best sculptors of the day.

CHAPTER VIII.

PAYNE'S CHARACTERISTICS.

WE may be modelled too much when children, and as the modelling is done by others, we are too apt to partake too much of the characteristics of the nature or notions of the modeller, and thereby our own natural form of manners and ideas may become somewhat distorted. "Just as the twig is bent the tree is inclined." From all that we have learned about the subject of our biography, we are satisfied that he commenced his early life too much obeying the notions of others. The boy, naturally brilliant, attracted the attention of everybody, and everybody had some notion of his own as how the twig should be bent. This may have been all very well in some things for our precocious youth, but there were some things which were neglected in the forming of the boy's character that made the tree grow a little out of symmetry. The boy was flattered beyond judicious limits. No one bade him beware of vanity, and vanity became one of the elements of his character throughout his life. Therefore it made no matter how well Mr. Payne may have been treated, or how highly his talents were appreciated, he always seemed to think and act as if he was not receiving his full deserts. This was strongly evidenced when a boy, in his conduct with Mr. Price, of the Park Theatre, concerning the dresses of Mr. Cooper, which had been loaned to set him off at the time of his *début*. His arrogance toward that venerable manager upset all prospects of success in this country, and was really the cause of Master Payne's leaving his own country to try his fortune abroad. No youth nor man ever had a larger number of friends take a deeper interest in him than Mr. Payne had. This arose from the fact of his talents, and his possessing other qualities that drew others towards him, as the pole attracts the needle.

Mr. James Rees, of Philadelphia, was on the most intimate terms with Mr. Payne. They were frequently together, and he had the opportunity of minutely observing Mr. Payne's peculiar disposition. Mr. Rees kindly sent us his journal, from which we

make the following extracts, which picture Payne in strong
"lights and shades."

Mr. Rees says in his letter:

"My dear Mr. Harrison,—My first introduction to John Howard Payne laid the foundation of a friendship which lasted until
the day of his death, and it affords me great pleasure to furnish
you with some details of our many frequent meetings. These
will be given in the plain, familiar style in which we conversed.
I would observe here that Mr. Payne was not what we term a
sociable man. Like many other literary characters, his mind became occasionally so absorbed in thought that, unless he was
awakened, as from a dream, to realize life in its social sense, you
never would have been enabled to arrive at the true character of
John Howard Payne. Once aroused and awake to the realities
of life, I never met a more brilliant man. Not that brilliancy
which great conversational powers elicit, but that of the mind,
which dazzles while it charms.

"To the stage was he indebted for the dramatic effects his conversation produced, to study and application for the beauty of his
imagery and the sweetness of his poetry.

"The following notes which I send you are leaves from my
daily journal, which I kept at the time:

"New Orleans, February 20, 1835.

"I called upon John Howard Payne. He had taken rooms in
the house of a Mrs. Dunn. These rooms were on the ground-
floor; one was used as a sitting-room, the other for a sleeping.
Payne was seated at a table, literally covered with books and
manuscripts. Everything was methodically arranged, denoting a
man of order. He was dressed in a loose gown, drawn tight around
his somewhat rotund form. On his feet he had ornamented slippers, evidently the embroidery-work of a female artist in that line,
and, taking him altogether, he looked a very respectable middle-
aged gentleman. His age at that time was forty-four.

"After exchanging the civilities of the day, and having talked
over some matters of a local character, he said, 'I like a man who
writes and speaks as he thinks. I have read your criticisms with
much pleasure, for your *nom de plume*, "Colley Cibber," is familiar
to me; but there are times and occasions, my dear sir, when our
national prejudices should lean a little on the side of a native

author. Understand me, I allude to your criticism on the new drama of " Charlotte Temple," said to be written by a gentleman of this city. I witnessed the drama, and I think you were not only too severe but positively unjust.'

" · Perhaps so. But, as I am the author of the drama, I can assure you I wrote it, I mean the criticism, fully impressed with the justice of every word I wrote. I did not see its many faults until it was played.'

" ' Well, this is something new to me. Is it the custom for authors to condemn their own plays here ? I always found *good friends* enough to do it for me. But I admire your *sang-froid*, and only wish I had a little of your philosophy. I could tell you many things in connection with my plays, but, as they are not very pleasant to recall, we will dispense with their recital, but——— Now, only look there, sir. Did you ever see anything so provoking ?'

" ' What is it ?'

" ' That vile woman, Mrs. Dunn, has left that side door open. Here have I been sitting all the evening exposed to a northeast wind. Mrs. Dunn! Mrs. Dunn, I say!'

" Mrs. Dunn made her appearance. She was a light mulatto, rather good-looking.

" ' Well, Mr. Payne, what is the matter?'

" ' Matter? Do you see that door? I pay you forty dollars a month for these two rooms and my breakfast included. A very high price, Mrs. Dunn ; double what I paid in London. Now, Mrs. Dunn, if that door is to be left open on every occasion to suit your convenience, I will leave the house. Mrs. Dunn, will you keep that door closed ?'

·" ' Certainly, Mr. Payne.'

" Exit Mrs. Dunn.

" ' Excuse this little interruption. You are aware of my purpose in coming South. Your name was given me while in New York by Mr. John Jay Adams and Mr. Samuel Jenks Smith, of the " Sunday Morning News." You can aid me materially in the proposed benefit offered to me in this city.'

" At this moment he gave a sudden start, and exclaimed, ' Get down, Tom !' I turned round to see who he was speaking to, when, to my surprise, I saw a huge black cat very deliberately climbing up the back of the chair and making preparation to take up its quarters on his shoulders, no doubt its usual resting-place in the absence of strangers. 'Somehow,' said he, 'cats take a fancy to me.' He took the cat gently down and placed it on the table, where it lay, and I really do not believe it moved during the continuance of our conversation. 'There, sir,' taking up a letter, and handing it to me; 'it is from the managers, Messrs. Rowe & Russell. You see the terms are high, very high, and the house is not large. No matter, we must take things as they are.' We then talked on the matter of the benefit, and arranged certain matters preparatory to the event.

"'By the way, Mr. Payne, I notice here a play of yours which I do not remember ever having seen in print.'

"No. sir, nor perhaps you never will. The 'Guilty Mother' was a failure, I regret to say. There are times, my dear sir, when it seems to me that actors and managers conspire against an author. This piece, had it been properly brought out, would have been a success. It is not, however, the only one of my pieces that failed. Those that were a success and still retain possession of the stage have been published. The managers in this country say they can buy a printed copy of any of my plays for a shilling, and actually laugh at me when I propose to sell them an original MS. copy of a play for one hundred dollars!"

"March 12, 1835.

"I took tea with John Howard Payne; he drinks it very strong and uses very large cups, or rather bowls. No one present but ourselves. I spent a delightful evening. For a while his mind was withdrawn from his personal affairs, and then he was positively brilliant. His scrap-book, one in particular, was the finest I ever saw. It contains the autographs of nearly all the great artists at that time in Europe, besides original scraps of poetry, sketches, etc. It had views of the principal cities in Europe, public buildings, etc. I copied the following lines from his album, written by himself:

"'Cheer the mourner! let not woe
Bow your noble heart so low.
Sky was ne'er so overcast
But the bright came at last.
They who sorrow only see,
Part of what the gods decree,
When the whole design you know,
You will bless them for your woe,
Love, where you despair'd before,
Where you doubted, will adore.'

"These lines are not given for their excellence in verse. They were evidently written in haste, more, I should say, to retain the thought contained in them rather than a specimen of his style. Among the autographs I noticed one of the celebrated French tragedian Talma. It was attached to a letter directed to Mr. Payne. I made the following extract:

"'Impregnated with the character and the situation of your personage, let your imagination be exalted, your nerves be agitated. The rest will follow; your arms and legs will properly do their work. The graces of a dancer are not requisite to tragedy. Choose rather to have a noble elegance in your gait, and something historical in your demeanor. Believe me, my dear Payne, your truly affectionate friend,   Talma.'

"After tea we visited the theatre to witness the first representation of my drama, entitled 'The Mistletoe Bough; or, The Old Oak Chest.' The piece was well played. Tom Williamson, a Bostonian, enacted the part of *Lord Lover*, and sang the music in fine style. Miss Petric, *Adda*, and Mrs. Entwistle, *Alice*. Between the first and second acts there occurs a lapse of forty years, during which time Payne and myself went out to take some refreshments, the latter remarking, in his quiet way, 'We have plenty of time.' Next day I called upon him at his rooms. Tea of course, strong as usual, awaited me. Almost the first words he spoke were,—

"'I am a miserable man.'

"'Miserable? Nonsense! sitting there the very picture of robust health, the whole country teeming with your praise?'

"'Even so, my friend; yet am I miserable. Do you see that fawn?' pointing to a young deer sporting in the yard.

"'Yes; what of it?'

"'It was a present. I value it because it was presented to me by a friend. I have reason to value it, for it costs me more than it is worth. It eats and drinks enough to support a family. You remember the story of a subject receiving from the hands of his monarch the present of an elephant,—it ruined him. That little deer, not to perpetrate a bad pun, is a *dear* present to me.'

"'Why, my dear sir, it cannot take much to keep it?'

"'Three dollars per week, sir, besides fifty cents to a negress to wash its *dear* little legs.'

"I would observe here that Mr. Payne was very fond of pun-ning. which he often indulged, in his quaint way. Having given another look at the animal, I observed, turning to my host,—

"'Well, Mr. Payne, I will relieve you of that expense,—let me take charge of it.'

"'Will you? Kind, considerate friend, I bless you. There, that is settled. Let me thank you for those books you sent me. You have no idea how acceptable they are to me in my loneliness.'

"'I see you are progressing with your story,' I remarked, taking up a portion of the manuscript of his 'Uses of Adversity.'

"'Yes; but rather slowly. My friend Jenks is urging me by every mail for more copy. The fact is I started wrong with it; it is getting dry, and I am afraid too dull for the generality of readers.'

"'The fault, Mr. Payne,' I observed, 'does not lie in the incidents of your story, but occupying too much of it with your own personal feelings, and a desire, too (excuse me), of being deeply versed in the legendary lore of the aboriginals of our country.'

"'Eh, sir!' he exclaimed, as he turned his little eyes sparkling with excitement. 'Do you accuse me of *vanity?*'

"'No, sir; I do accuse you of introducing matter entirely irrelevant to the story.'

"'Explain?'

"'What I mean to say is this, the story is well enough, written in your usual style of elegance, taste, and judgment, but in the last chapter published you go into a long detail of the Indian race, and quote from all sorts of people passages to sustain your theory.'

"'Do you call that uninteresting which treats of the Indian race?'

"'Yes, when it is thrust in like a wedge between the heroine and the reader.'

"'Point out what you consider the dry part, if you please.'

"'I did not say it was dry, that remark was yours, but——' taking up the paper I pointed out the following from his story, which he read very carefully, putting on occasionally a sort of quizzical expression as he proceeded:

"'The prophecy of Obadiah, whether we trace the Edomites to Central America or leave them in their own land, has been distinctly and literally fulfilled by the house of Jacob, which house, Obadiah says (v. 18), "shall be for the house of Esau for stubble, and they shall kindle in them, and devour them; and *there shall not be any remaining of the house of Esau;*" and (v. 10) "*they shall be cut off forever.*" Previously to this, by the incorporation of the Idumeans with the Jews (Josephus, Ant. 1, xiii. c. 9, and 1 or c. 17), the Jews were actually *possessors* of the *kingdom of Edom*, and *judged* and *governed* the *mount* of *Esau*, as predicted in Obadiah (v. 19 and 21): they shall *"possess the mount of Esau,"* and shall *"come up on Mount Zion to judge the mount of Esau."* The words "house of Esau" when here applied to its extinction, should perhaps be understood as referring to those descendants of Esau who had no share in the Ishmaelite blood.' 'Well,' he observed, as he laid the paper down, 'I must admit it has very little to do with the story. I have wandered away from the subject, and yet you are partly the cause.'

" 'How so?'

" 'Look there,' pointing to some books on the table.

" 'Why, they are the books I presented you.'

" 'True, and the title of one is "Ross Cox's Tour through the Indian Nations"!'

" I laughed, and the subject was changed.

" It is a mistaken notion many persons have that Mr. Payne was a lonely wanderer on the earth. The only reference he ever made to his loneliness was when speaking of his 'Home, Sweet Home!' he said, ' Few persons indeed have known less the comforts of a domestic home than your humble servant. But what of that? I always try to make my lodgings comfortable; for instance, look around you. As to where I shall die, that is in the disposition of a power which we cannot control, and when dead I desire to be let alone. The Bard of Avon expressed this thought unequivocally to my mind in his own epitaph.'

" Payne had this peculiar tact. I will call it, added to his great love of order, that wherever he went he made his rooms so neat and agreeable that, although *alone*, and a cosmopolite from inclination, they always appeared like— Home.' The man who associated with the most eminent men in England and France, and whose name was a passport to loyalty itself, was no houseless, penniless wanderer!"

When the author of this work began (over thirty years ago) to collect matter concerning the history of John Howard Payne, he did so through the tenderness of friendship excited by the sad stories told by Mr. Payne of his many hardships and disappointments through life. His expressive face, sad voice, and graceful manners grasped your attention and sympathy just as some beautiful child or flower would. His conversation, highly interesting from its variety of subjects, would always incline you to listen, rather than to talk. His memory was remarkable. His language was picturesque, and always, in talking of others, he had the faculty of gracefully introducing himself as a part of his story or anecdote, and gaining for himself your sympathy to such an extent that you soon felt like an old acquaintance, disposed to offer him any assistance in your power. But in writing the biography of any man, however much he may claim our kindly feelings towards him, the biographer has no right to speak of his merits only and to hide his faults. If his life is worthy of a pen-painting at all, it should be truthful, as a photograph of the sun reveals alike its spots and its glory. This alone would be doing justice to the world, for it might serve as a caution to men who strive for fame not to lose sight of the moral traits of the personal characters which should always be a vital part of the sustenance of his deeds. The fruit may not only be beautiful in form, color, and flavor, but must also have no worm at its heart. For instance, Washington's is complete, for the reason that his moral character was fully as faultless as his deeds, so that when investigated and contemplated both, we find a perfect whole. But who can read Byron or Poe without regretting that even the slightest spot should mar the disks of their genius? Men who write the noblest sentiments of the human heart and do not practise them must appear like gilded lies. During their lives deceitful men may find a way to cover up their faults and to ward off investigations, but when death strikes, their sword and shield fall with them, serving no longer in their own defence; and when the biographer follows, searching for truth, he often finds things covered that should never have been tolerated, and which must, of their own force, see the light, even though it be at the eleventh hour.

It has been so in Mr. Payne's case, as there has very recently come under our observation no less than eight volumes of his private letters and answers to them, carefully transcribed in his own hand, and elegantly bound at his own expense, as if they would be of the most vital importance to his own history, while in fact one-half of these very letters should have fed the flames as soon as they were perused. We would not have introduced these remarks about Mr. Payne's private character did we not feel perfectly assured that others would in time make known much more than we record.

Mr. Payne took just as much pains to record the least of things as he did to write his plays. His memorandum-book, which lies before us, and which he carried with him on his way from Paris to Tunis, when he went to fill for the first time his position as United States consul at Tunis, is a marvel in penmanship and detail of little things. The writing is so small that the naked eye can hardly read it, yet with the magnifier each letter is perfectly formed. The record is in French and English on opposite pages. As he went from place to place he changed the value of the currency with perfect accuracy. If he gave a beggar a penny, he would note the fact and describe his costume. If he purchased a candle or a cent's worth of milk, they were recorded with equal care.

Among the recently discovered manuscripts and letters of Mr. Payne, we possessed ourselves of a large bound volume entitled "Egotisms, Play-Bills, and Correspondence." The play-bills represented every night he performed while abroad. Also a correspondence between Payne and the honorable Douglass Kinnard, chairman of the Drury Lane management. The same book contained the engraved portraits of Payne in the characters of *Hamlet* and *Douglas*. The correspondence commenced in 1815, when Payne was twenty-four years of age, and for one so young it shows smartness and egotism combined. Payne had the faculty of ingratiating himself with all managers, but by a singular fatality he always ended with a misunderstanding, as he did on this occasion. Mr. Payne was always full of ideas, and never hesitated to express his opinions at every opportunity. His correspondence with Douglass Kinnard is highly interesting, and had Kinnard have been David Garrick, Payne, but twenty-four years of age, would not have hesitated to give his opinion of his management, whether solicited to do so or not. What was Kinnard to Payne? The history of great old Drury Lane Theatre, made imposing by the dramatic genius of nearly two centuries, could not deter Mr. Payne from finding fault with its present management if he saw errors to be corrected, and there still lingered in this time-honored temple of Melpomene and Thalia some faults, both before and behind the curtain, that had existed in the days of Charles II.,—the permitting people of station and wealth behind the scenes during rehearsals to stare at the actors as if they were a set of tamed animals. He called Kinnard's attention to these facts, and to a large extent the error was corrected. He also suggested the propriety of the management of the Drury Lane committee—then consisting of Kinnard, Lamb, and Lord Byron—of inviting the celebrated Talma to London, and even drafted the letter of invitation, which was adopted, and Payne was commissioned to deliver it to the great French tragedian. This was done with great success. Talma became Payne's personal friend, and wrote several letters to Kinnard commending in high terms Payne's ability as a translator of French plays.

A more precise man than John Howard Payne perhaps never lived. Facts, order, and detail in dramatic writing were his strongest points. In reconstructing the Rev. Mr. Miller's translation of Voltaire's tragedy of "Mahomet" for the Drury Lane stage he researched all Mahometan history, and enumerates in his description of the play to Mr. Kinnard how many swords and shields this impostor had, for the purpose of having the properties of the piece correct. In looking over several of his manuscript plays which he had prepared for the London theatres, we could not help admiring the careful handwriting, the underscoring with rule and colored inks, sketches of the different scenes in water-colors, with stage-sets, etc. All this labor was spent on plays of moderate merit, and never could be made successful on the stage.

When he was bothering himself with Captain Ross and the Cherokee Indians, as his manuscript of the matter shows, he took the same pains to detail a statement of the least thing that occurred, even transcribing Indian girls' love-letters, which were the merest twaddle imaginable. His descriptions of their war-dances and their habits are highly interesting, and may be of use to writers in the future who may desire to give in detail the habits of our Indian tribes.

We have also seen a considerable amount of manuscript relating to the history of Tunis; but it appeared to be more of a translation from the French than an original work by Mr. Payne.

The following letter from an old Tunisian friend of Payne's will present his last hours in sad and affectionate words:

"TUNIS, 28th of Apl., 1883.

"MY DEAR MR. WORTHINGTON,— . . . My recollections of poor Payne's last years here are still fresh in my memory. He was a small man, with a fine, intelligent face, but of a very serious and melancholy expression. He spoke slowly, with great dignity of manner. He was highly educated, and very well informed. His conversation was extremely pleasant and interesting. Though rather cold and reserved in his manners, he had a strong temper and will. The many ups and downs he had had in his life had made him rather sceptical and given him a strong touch of misanthropy, which increased in his latter years. He never spoke of his theatrical life before me. Politics were the ordinary topics of his conversation, as it is generally with U. S. Americans. He liked to talk about poetry, too, although I do not think he cultivated it any more at that time; at least I have not heard he left any composition after him.

" He had a good collection of books, which has been in a great way dispersed here. He used to show us a certain quantity of Indian weapons, and was very fond of natural history. He used to collect numerous specimens of our African birds and wild animals, which he got from the Arab sportsmen, and sent home. He professed a great friendship for the English consul at Tunis, Sir Thomas Reade, who used to invite him for whole weeks at his beautiful country-house at Mawsa. It is there that he met Mr. Moses Santillana, the English interpreter, who became a great friend of his, and to whom I am indebted for some of the present details. He (Payne) spent nearly all his time in writing and studying. Mr. Santillana told me he thought he was preparing a work on Tunis. I know he went two or three times in the interior of the Regency, but I never heard him say anything about this work. I do not think he left anything on the subject. All his papers were, after his death, thrown just as they were found, that is, in the greatest disorder, in several baskets (at least twelve), and stored in damp magazines, where they remained for years, and from whence many must have been lost or stolen. It was very long after his demise that they were claimed by his sister.

" Payne's official occupations were altogether nominal. It was rare to see any American ships in our bay, and there were no American traders in Tunis. His task was altogether political, and gave him no trouble. He had, therefore, all his time free, and spent it in reading and writing. I remember the negotiations he had with the Tunisian government for the repairings of the consular house. They were, I am sure, the most important fact of his official career here. He succeeded, though, in getting what he wanted, and the house was completely remade according to the plans of a German architect, Mr. Honnegar, who was a great friend of Payne's. The Bey had to pay a famous sum for it.

17

Poor Payne did not enjoy it very long, though. He died some time after, and Dr. Heap, his obstinate competitor for the Tunisian consulate, succeeded him at last.

"Payne had in the last year of his life become of very sedentary habits, and very gloomy in his ideas. I remember to have seen him many times sitting in his arm-chair, by a red-hot stove, drinking brandy and water, and looking very sad. He seemed to have no ties left in this world. He saw very few persons here, and did not seem to like new acquaintances. He was at last taken with a slow fever, which, neglected, took a bad turn and became dangerous. We saw, to our great consternation, that his constitution was giving way before it without the least resistance, and we soon found out that our poor friend's days were numbered. Every care was taken of him with no effectual result, except showing him that he was cared for and surrounded by friends. He died after ten or twelve days' illness without suffering, and like a lamp whose oil is exhausted. We had him taken to our cemetery, and I took care of his tomb ever since. The slab was put upon it by the care of my excellent friend, W. P. Chandler, of Philadelphia, once American consul here, who wrote the epitaph which is upon it.

"These are the few details I can give you upon our regretted friend. I have been in a position to ascertain fully the precious qualities with which he was endowed, the loyalty of his character, the frankness and dignity of his manners, and the depth of his intelligence and information. Other voices more able and more authorized than mine have made his biography and spoken of his qualities, but few have been in the position to appreciate them as I did. I saw his remains going home with a real grief, although it was time that his fellow-citizens should honor his memory. It is sad to think that those honors are always posthumous. You and Mrs. Worthington have had the good fortune to give him a last farewell. I was deprived of this consolation, for the exhumation and expedition of his remains, through the indifference of those who were intrusted *here* with it, were made in a too much *business-like way*, and we should have been happy to see a great deal more respect paid to the last remains of such a man.

"Believe me,

"Always truly yours,

"A. CHAPOLIE."

CHAPTER IX.

"Time works wonders."

A LAPSE OF TEN YEARS.

IMMEDIATELY after the uncovering of the monument to Mr. Payne in Prospect Park, there was a revival of interest in almost everything relating to him. The newspapers published short notices of his career as they could best glean them from the scanty materials that then existed in print. The song of "Home, Sweet Home!" that for many years had been almost totally withdrawn from the public, once more was heard everywhere. It was sung at concerts; at the theatres, orchestras discharged the audiences with the sweet melody as the curtain dropped upon the last scene of the play. Bands of music performed it as the closing piece at their Saturday concerts in all our public parks, and even the street organ once more made the air resonant with its domestic fervor. Edwin Booth revived the tragedy of "Brutus," and added new glory to his name by his excellent performance of the stoic father. Other celebrated actors did the same; once more the villain advocate *Carwin* prowled about the stage wrapped in his dark mantle, and *Thérèse* stood amidst the flames of the burning chateau holding the bloody knife on high. *Charles II.* in licentious luxury again appeared upon the scene of his recklessness, arm-in-arm with his audacious companions. *Captain Copp* captured his audience with his blunt and unctuous and noble nature.

In a few months after the uncovering of the monument the writer issued his octavo volume of four hundred pages on the life of the author of "Home, Sweet Home!" It was the first complete biography of Mr. Payne ever published. It was the first time that the real circumstances in which he wrote the song of "Home, Sweet Home!" had ever been given to the public in authentic form. The newspapers were liberal in their notice of the book, and made large quotations from its contents, thereby giving a still wider publicity to the character and works of the man who had slept forgotten in a foreign clime for over twenty years. The

writer then had two large quarto volumes of the work elegantly
bound, and presented one to the library of Congress and one to
the library of the consulate at Tunis. The latter copy was in the
handsomest manner forwarded to Tunis, free of all expenses, by
the Secretary of State.

Soon after its arrival there the writer received a warm letter of
thanks from the Hon. George W. Fish, the American consul, who
said that the work had awakened a new interest in John Howard
Payne, and that steps were about being taken to place a memorial window in his honor in the new English chapel, and that the
British consul, and English people especially, were taking the
greatest interest in the matter. This was soon accomplished.
We here introduce the Hon. Mr. Fish's letter in evidence of the
devotion shown by the parties concerned, as well as a part of the
history of a singular man. Mr. Fish also took a great interest in
the memory of the dead consul, and wrote to the Hon. William M.
Evarts, Secretary of State, informing him that the grave of John
Howard Payne was in decay and required restoring.

Mr. Evarts ordered the consul to have the tomb restored as perfectly and as permanently as was suitable. This was promptly attended to by Mr. Fish, and at an expense of two hundred and fifty
dollars. An American gentleman, Mr. Whitehouse, there at the
time, added twenty-five dollars to the amount to pay for the plant-
ing of flowers about the grave. The burial-place of the poet was
thus made beautiful to the eyes of all its visitors.

"UNITED STATES CONSULATE,
"TUNIS, Oct. 22, 1881.

"GABRIEL HARRISON, ESQ., Brooklyn, New York.

"MY DEAR SIR,--I write to thank you for the copy of 'The Life
and Writings of J. Howard Payne,' presented by you to the library
of this consulate, and sent through the State Department, which
I have just received in good order. As a beautiful specimen of the
art of book-making in our country I cannot see how this volume
could be improved, and the work itself seems to me both timely
and appropriate to perpetuate the literary fame of a versatile and
gifted poet and writer. The friends and admirers of Mr. Payne
are under great obligations to you for the manner in which you
have accomplished the difficult task. I again thank you for myself, and in behalf of the government, for your beautiful present.
I write this in the room where Mr. Payne spent the last years of

his life, and in which he died; and in this room stands the library where the book will be kept. Governmental affairs in this country are just now in a most unsatisfactory condition. A widespread and formidable insurrection among the interior tribes threatens to overthrow the authority of the Bey, and we look to the French to restore order, which they have not yet succeeded in doing. We hope tranquillity will soon be restored.

"I remain, dear sir, with great respect,

"Very truly yours,

"Geo. W. Fish."

In another letter Mr. Fish writes:

"You probably know about the tomb of Mr. Payne. Three of the former consuls of the United States are buried here,—James Dodge, D. Heap, and Col. Payne. I found the tombs of Dodge and Payne in a deplorable state of dilapidation, and wrote to the Secretary of State, the Hon. Wm. M. Evarts, and asked permission to have them repaired. The permission was promptly granted, and the tombs have been thoroughly restored. Some friendly hand many years since planted a tree of the species eucalyptus, which has grown into such large proportions that it quite overshadows the grave of Payne. The roots of this tree had ruined the foundation of the tomb. It was necessary to remove the old and build a new foundation. I am greatly pleased with the work, and am of the opinion that the present foundation will remain for half a century.

"After the restoration had been finished, the British consul, the English Church's acting chaplain, myself, and a few friends expressed ourselves well pleased with what had been done. The British chaplain proposed a memorial window in the English Church, and a subscription was immediately started. I headed the list with thirty dollars, and we soon had enough subscribed to warrant the enterprise. Mr. Shepherd, the acting chaplain, wrote to a London firm concerning the window, and the firm answered very promptly, proposing to place the window as desired, and without further cost. On consultation, it was decided to send the money we had on hand, and accept the company's donation for the balance to the amount of £9, and so the window has been ordered, and is expected in a few weeks. . . . I will send you a full description of the window when in its place. All this must prove of great satisfaction to you, who have so beautifully celebrated John Howard Payne and his ballad by biography and monument. I shall be most happy to answer any questions, and give you any information in my power, that will add to the interest of your revised edition of the poet's life. It is to be deeply regretted that the papers of Mr. Payne were not promptly secured by some relative or friends. I am informed, by parties who know, that they were neglected, and finally scattered and wasted.

"I am, sir, with great respect,

"Yours,

"George W. Fish."

"United States Consulate,

"Tunis, April 26th, 1882.

"Gabriel Harrison, Esq.

"Dear Sir,—Your letter, dated and postmarked Brooklyn, N. Y., Sept. 7th, 1881, reached me by the regular Italian mail just two days ago,—the 24th inst.,—having been seven and a half months *en route*. Such accidents do not often happen. My New York mail usually reaches me in about eighteen or twenty days. Perhaps you may have wondered why I have not replied to your letter, as I had, why I had received no answer to mine. Both mysteries are explained by the unusual delay of your letter in transit. The beautiful book, 'Life and Writings of John Howard Payne,' forwarded from the State Department at Washington, was duly received in good order, and I immediately acknowledged the receipt of it to the author and to the Department. I hope you received my note. In your letter you mention your intention to send twenty dollars for photographs. Nothing of the kind has been received, and, as yet, no pictures have been taken. There was considerable delay in receiving the window from England and placing it in the church. It is now in place, looks well, and we are pleased with it. The window is in the end of the church, in rear of the chancel, so that the congregation, when seated, face it. Across the bottom of the lights, in plain letters, is printed, 'In memory of J. Howard Payne, author of Home, Sweet Home.' About the centre of the middle light, on a scroll, is painted, 'The Lord hath brought me home.' It is very plain, simple, and in good taste. The British consul Mr. Thomas Reade, and the chaplain, Rev. Mr. Shepherd, have taken special interest in this work. Mr. Reade is anxious to get a copy of the book, having seen and greatly admired the copy you sent me. I told him I would mention it to you, and presumed, when another edition was printed, he would be able to procure one. I intend, when I can afford it from the savings of my modest salary, if that time ever comes, to have a series of pictures, either photo's or sketches, taken of the exterior of the consulate, and perhaps, also, of the room in which Mr. Payne died, of his tomb, and of the memorial window, and a few other points of Tunisian scenery of the period when Mr. Payne was consul. It seems to me such a series of pictures would add to the interest of the illustrated work, and would be a natural and most fitting addendum to the book. I have had two white-rose bushes planted at the tomb, and a few other pretty flowers, and when I was there last there were two exquisitely beautiful white roses in full bloom. I mention these things to you, knowing that you are interested in everything that relates to our talented countryman.

"Just now Tunisian affairs are tranquil. All important towns are occupied by French troops. The insurgent chief, Ali ben Ammava, with a few thousand followers, have taken refuge in Tripoli, while most of the remaining tribes have submitted to the Bey. We hope the peace may be permanent, but have not much confidence in it.

"I shall be glad to hear from you, and to know that you have received this.

"With best wishes for your health and happiness, I am, dear sir,
"Very respectfully and sincerely yours,
"Geo. W. Fish."

Hardly had the sod settled again around the new foundation of Mr. Payne's grave when the public were informed that W. W. Corcoran, Esq., a wealthy and philanthropic gentleman of Washington, District of Columbia, had made application to the Hon. Frederick T. Frelinghuysen, Secretary of State, to have the privilege of removing the remains of Mr. Payne to his native country and placing them in Oak Hill Cemetery, West Washington.

We here give place to that part of the correspondence between the Department of State and Mr. Corcoran necessary to show how the remains were procured for reinterment in this country.

"WASHINGTON, D. C.,

"Oct. 14th, 1882.

"THE HON. FREDERICK T. FRELINGHUYSEN,

"Secretary of State.

"DEAR SIR,—I respectfully ask permission of the State Department to disinter the remains of our countryman, John Howard Payne, which now rest in a grave near Tunis, in Africa, that they may receive more appropriate sepulture in the bosom of his native land.

"Mr. Payne died. as is well known, in the service of the State Department, on the 9th of April, 1852, while acting as consul of the United States at Tunis, and I understand that a marble slab, erected by order of the Department, still marks the spot where his body was laid.

"It has seemed to me that the precious dust of an American citizen who sang so sweetly in praise of 'Home, Sweet Home!' should not be left to mingle with any soil less dear to him than that of the land which gave him birth, and which, by the beauty of its home-life, gave to him his best poetical inspiration.

"If you concur with me in this sentiment, I beg leave to say that I will, when favored with your official permission, charge myself with the duty of providing for the removal of his remains to this country, and, on their arrival here, will give to them a new and suitable resting-place in Oak Hill Cemetery, taking care, of course, to mark the spot with a monument, which shall perpetuate in the eyes of his countrymen the name of the poet already embalmed in their hearts by his immortal lyric.

"I ought to add, that I make this application to you because, as the honored head of the State Department. you seem to be the natural custodian of Mr. Payne's grave in Tunis. I am further induced to make this appeal to you because, after careful inquiry, I am led to believe that Mr. Payne has now no descendant or collateral kindred to whom I could address a communication on the subject. In evidence of this fact, I beg to invite your attention to the accompanying letters.

"I have the honor to be, sir,

"Your most obedient servant,

"W. W. CORCORAN."

" DEPARTMENT OF STATE,
" WASHINGTON, Oct. 21, 1882.
" W. W. CORCORAN, ESQ., Washington.

" DEAR SIR,—I have had the pleasure to receive your letter of the 14th instant, in which you ask the sanction and aid of this Department for your project of bringing to this country the remains of John Howard Payne, now interred at Tunis, in Africa, and giving them appropriate sepulture in his native land. Your proposal meets with my warm approbation, and I hasten to assure you of my readiness to do what I can in rendering fitting tribute to the memory of one whose touching verses have so endeared him to his countrymen.

" In the absence of any present consular representation at Tunis, I have instructed Mr. Lowell to request the kindly assistance of the British Government in obtaining from the government of the Regency of Tunis permission to exhume the remains of Mr. Payne, and in making the necessary arrangements to transport them to this country. I doubt not that this assistance will be cheerfully and effectively rendered.

" As soon as I receive Mr. Lowell's response I will hasten to communicate it to you.

   " I am, my dear sir.
    " Very truly yours,
      " FREDK. T. FRELINGHUYSEN."

     " DEPARTMENT OF STATE,
     " WASHINGTON, December 2, 1882.
" W. W. CORCORAN, ESQ., Washington, D. C.

" SIR,—Referring to the reply of this Department of the 21st of October last to your letter of the 14th of that month, in relation to the removal of the remains of the American poet, John Howard Payne, from Tunis to this capital, I now have the pleasure of informing you that Mr. Lowell, having brought the subject to the attention of the British Government, received, on the 16th ultimo, a note from Earl Granville, in which his Lordship says that he has caused instructions to be addressed to Her Majesty's Consul-General at Tunis in the sense indicated by Mr. Lowell, and that the result of the action taken by the consul will be duly communicated to the Legation at London.

   " I am, sir,
    " Your obedient servant,
      " FREDK. T. FRELINGHUYSEN."

"Department of State,

"Washington, January 4, 1883.

" W. W. Corcoran, Esq., 1611 H Street, Washington.

"Sir,—Referring to previous correspondence in relation to the removal of the remains of Mr. John Howard Payne, I have now the honor to inform you that this Department is advised by a telegram received this day from Mr. Lowell, that the Consul-General of Great Britain at Tunis has telegraphed Lord Granville that the remains will be shipped to-day, consigned to the United States consul at Marseilles.

"I am, sir,

"Your ob't servant,

"John Davis."

"Department of State,

"Washington, January 6, 1883.

" W. W. Corcoran, 1611 H Street, Washington.

" Sir,—Referring to my letter to you of the 4th instant, in relation to the bringing to the United States of the body of Mr. John Howard Payne, and to the telegram of Mr. Lowell of the same date, relating to the same subject, the substance of which was communicated to you, I have the honor to further inform you that the consul at Marseilles was yesterday instructed by telegraph to receive the remains.

"No mention was made in Mr. Lowell's telegram of the shipment of the marble slab which marked the grave at Tunis, which you desired forwarded with the remains, and the consul at Marseilles was consequently instructed, in case the slab was not shipped with the remains from Tunis, to hold the latter until the former should be received, when they were both at the same time to be shipped to New York, consigned to your care, and permission was given the consul to proceed to Tunis if it was thought his presence there would facilitate the shipment of the slab.

"I am, sir, your obedient servant,

"John Davis."

"Department of State,

" Washington, January 10, 1883.

" W. W. Corcoran, Esq., Washington, D. C.

"Sir,—Referring to previous correspondence concerning the removal of the remains of John Howard Payne to this country, I take pleasure in transmitting herewith for your information a copy of a despatch on the subject, which has just been received by this Department from Mr. Lowell, the American Minister at London.

"I am, sir,

"Your obedient servant,

"JOHN DAVIS,

"*Acting Secretary.*"

"LEGATION OF THE UNITED STATES,

"LONDON, January 2nd, 1883.

"SIR,—I have the honor to acknowledge the reception of your Number 506, of the 8th ult., in relation to the removal to the United States of the remains of John Howard Payne, and to say that immediately after its arrival I addressed Lord Granville, communicating the additional requests of the Department of State. I have to-day received a reply from the Foreign Office, by which it will appear that your wishes in the matter will be attended to.

"I enclose a copy of the correspondence.

"I have the honor to be

"With great respect,

"Your obedient servant,

"J. R. LOWELL.

"THE HON. F. T. FRELINGHUYSEN, Secretary of State, Washington, D. C."

Enclosures :

1. Mr. Lowell to Lord Granville, December 23, 1882.

2. Lord Granville to Mr. Lowell.

(COPY.)

"LEGATION OF THE UNITED STATES,

"LONDON, December 23d, 1883.

"My LORD,—I have to apologize for not replying sooner to the note which Mr. Lister was kind enough to address to me on your Lordship's behalf on the 16th ultimo, informing me that instructions had been sent to Her Majesty's Consul-General at Tunis to promote the wishes of Mr. Corcoran, communicated through the Department of State, in relation to the removal of the remains of the late John Howard Payne to the United States.

"Your Lordship was so good as to say that, upon learning the result of Mr. Reade's application to the Tunisian authorities, you would write me again upon the subject.

"I have now to say that the gentlemen who have assumed charge of this matter desire, if possible, that the body, when exhumed, should be sent by water from Tunis to Marseilles, where the United States consul, acting under instructions of the Department, will receive it and forward it to the United States.

"Mr. Frelinghuysen requests me to ask your Lordship if, in furtherance of the purpose you have so promptly aided, you will be so kind as to instruct Her Majesty's Consul-General at Tunis to endeavor to have Mr. Payne's remains shipped from Tunis to Marseilles, consigned to Mr. Horace A. Taylor, consul of the United States at that port. I beg to repeat that all expenses incurred will be borne by the Department of State in behalf of Mr. W. W. Corcoran, and I am directed to say to your Lordship that any drafts and accounts for expenses of disinterment, casing, and shipping, which the British consul at Tunis may send to Washington, either directly or through Her Majesty's Foreign Office, will be met at once. If that officer desires to draw at once for reimbursement, his draft should be upon 'The Secretary of State of the United States at five days' sight.'

"I am also directed to renew the thanks of my Government to your Lordship for the courtesy which you have already shown in this matter.

"I have the honor to be, etc.,
"J. R. LOWELL.

"THE RIGHT HONORABLE
"THE EARL GRANVILLE,
"Etc., etc., etc."

(COPY.)   "FOREIGN OFFICE,
"December 30th, 1882.

"SIR,—I have had the honor to receive your note of the 23d instant relating to the exhumation and transmission to Marseilles of the body of the late Mr. John Howard Payne, and I beg leave to inform you that I have this day telegraphed the purport of your communication to Her Majesty's Consul-General at Tunis, with instructions to comply with the wishes of your Government in this matter.

"I have the honor to be,
"Etc., etc., etc.,
"GRANVILLE.

"J. R. LOWELL, ESQ.,
"Etc., etc., etc."

"WASHINGTON, January 22d, 1883.

"THE HONORABLE

"JOHN DAVIS, Acting Secretary Department of State.

"SIR,—I have to acknowledge the receipt of your favor of the 19th instant, enclosing copies of the correspondence between the Department, the Earl Granville, and Mr. Lowell in reference to the removal of the remains of John Howard Payne to the United States, and beg to express my appreciation of the prompt and satisfactory action of the Department in furthering my wishes in the premises.

"On the receipt of the draft for the expenses incurred, as referred to by Minister Lowell, the Department will please allow me the pleasure of reimbursing the amount.

"I have the honor to be

"Very respectfully yours,

"W. W. CORCORAN."

"DEPARTMENT OF STATE,

"WASHINGTON, February 8, 1883.

"W. W. CORCORAN, ESQUIRE, Washington, D. C.

"SIR,—With reference to previous correspondence in regard to the removal of the remains of John Howard Payne from Tunis to this capital, I take pleasure in enclosing herewith for your information a copy of a recent despatch from Mr. Lowell, the American Minister at London, on the subject.

"I am, sir,

"Your obedient servant,

"FREDK. T. FRELINGHUYSEN."

Enclosure:

Mr. Lowell to Mr. Frelinghuysen, No. 479, January 12, 1883. Copy.

"No. 479.

"LEGATION OF THE UNITED STATES,

"LONDON, January 13th, 1883.

"SIR,—Referring to my Number 471 of the 2nd instant, in relation to the removal of the remains of the late John Howard Payne to the United States, I have the honor to acquaint you that late in the evening of that day I received the following telegram from Mr. Davis, Assistant Secretary:

"'Have you received news from Tunis relative to Payne's remains?'

"I answered this by cable the next day, as follows:

"'No direct news from Tunis. Lord Granville informed me yesterday he had telegraphed December Thirtieth to Consul-General instructions to comply with wishes transmitted in your Five Hundred Six. See my Four Seventy-One.'

"I sent you a copy of Lord Granville's letter in my Number 471.

"On the 4th instant I received a further note from Lord Granville, dated on the 1st, stating that the Consul-General at Tunis had telegraphed on the 31st December that the remains would be shipped to Marseilles on 4th of January.

"I immediately telegraphed this information to you, as follows:

"'Lord Granville informs me Consul-General of Tunis has telegraphed remains will be shipped Fourth January, consigned to United States consul, Marseilles.'

"I have received this morning another letter from his Lordship, with enclosures giving an account of the exhumation of the remains and their shipment on board of the Charles Quint, to the care of Mr. Taylor, the consul at Marseilles.

"I enclose copies of such of this correspondence as has not already been transmitted.

"I have written to Lord Granville an expression of my thanks for his courtesy, and that of the British officials at Tunis in this matter.

"I have the honor to be
   "With great respect,   •
      "Your obedient servant,
         "J. R. LOWELL."

"FOREIGN OFFICE,
"January 1st, 1883.

"SIR,—With reference to my communication of the 30th ultimo, I have the honor to inform you that a telegram was yesterday received from Her Majesty's Consul-General at Tunis, stating that the late Mr. J. H. Payne's remains will be shipped for Marseilles

•

on Thursday, the 4th inst., consigned to the care of the United
States consul at that port.

"I have the honor to be, etc.,

"GRANVILLE.
"J. R. LOWELL, ESQ.,
"Etc., etc., etc."

"FOREIGN OFFICE,
"January 11, 1883.

"SIR.—With reference to my communication of 1st instant, I
have now the honor to transmit to you, for the information of the
United States Government, a copy of a despatch and its enclosures
received from Her Majesty's Consul-General at Tunis, giving further particulars relating to the exhumation and shipment of the
remains of the late John Howard Payne.

"I have the honor to be, etc.,

"(For Earl Granville,)
"PHILLIP W. CURRIE.
"J. R. LOWELL, ESQ.,
"Etc., etc., etc."

"No. 1.

"TUNIS, 6th January, 1883.

"MY LORD,—I have the honor to report that pursuant to the
instructions in your Lordship's telegram of the 30th ultimo, the
remains of John Howard Payne were this day shipped on board
the French steam-vessel Charles Quint, to the consignment of
Mr. Taylor, the U. S. consul at Marseilles.

"Owing to the impossibility of complying with some of the
formalities, which under ordinary circumstances would have been
strictly enforced in connection with the exhumation of the body,
and to my communications with the U. S. Consulate at Malta, in
the hope that some ship-of-war of that nation might be charged
with its conveyance across the Atlantic, some delay occurred in
the execution of the instructions with which I was, in the first
instance, honored by Yr Ldp.

"As stated in my telegram of the 30th ultimo, I had arranged
to ship the remains two days ago, but in order to allow of the arrival of the U. S. consul at Malta, who had expressed a wish
to be present at their disinterment, the shipment did not take
place until this morning.

"I beg, in conclusion, to enclose a copy of the act executed on the occasion of the exhumation of those remains, and of my despatch to the U. S. consul at Marseilles announcing their shipment to his address.

"I have, etc.,
"THOS. F. READE.

"THE EARL GRANVILLE, K. G.,
"Etc., etc., etc."

"No. 2.
"TUNIS, January 6th, 1883.

"SIR,—I have the honor to inform you that, conformably with the instructions of H. M.'s Principal Sec. of State for Foreign Affairs, I this day shipped on board the French steam-vessel *Charles Quint*, and to your consignment at Marseilles, a case covering three coffins, two being of wood and one of lead, the innermost of which contains the remains of John Howard Payne, the distinguished poet and dramatist of your nation, who died in this city on the 1st of April, 1852, while serving his country in the capacity of consul.

"The exhumation of those remains took place yesterday with all the required formalities, Mr. Worthington, the U. S. consul at Malta, being among those who were present on the occasion.

"Two keys of the outer coffin are enclosed, which I beg you will have the goodness to forward to that coffin's destination in the States.

"I have, etc.,
"THOS. F. READE."

"No. 3.
"In pursuance of instructions which, at the request of the Government of the United States of America, have been communicated to the English Representative in this country by H. M.'s Principal Sec. of State for Foreign Affairs, the exhumation, prior to removal to the U. S. of the remains of J. H. Payne, the distinguished citizen and poet, who died at Tunis on the 1st of April, 1852, while serving his country as consul, took place this day in the presence of Thomas Fellows Reade, Esq., H. B. M.'s Agent and Consul-General, and the following officers and gentlemen: Dr. F. Arpa, H. M.'s Consul and Judge; John Worthington, Esqr., U. S. Consul at Malta; Mr. M. Pisani, British Pro-Consul; Dr. G. E.

Pratz, M.D.; Dr. Achille Perini, M.D.; Comm'r W. M. Bridger, R.N.; Mr. G. Carbinaro; and Mr. Alf. M. Camilleri, LL.D., and with all the formalities required by law.

"In testimony of which the undersigned have hereto subscribed their names in the Protestant Cemetery of St. George, at Tunis, this 5th day of January, 1883.

"Thos. F. Reade,

"H. M.'s Agent and Consul-General.

"F. Arpa,

"H. M.'s Consul and Judge.

"John Worthington,

"U. S. Consul at Malta.

"M. Pisani,

"British Pro-Consul.

"Dr. G. E. Pratz,

"Médecin de S. A. le Bey de Tunis.

"Dr. Achille Perini,

"Médecin de Police de S. A. le Bey et Médecin honoraire du Consulat-Général d'Angleterre.

"W. M. Bridger, R.N.

"G. Carbinaro.

"*Arote* Alf. M. Camilleri."

"Department of State,

"Washington, Feb. 9, 1883.

"W. W. Corcoran, Esq.,

"Washington, D. C.

"Sir,—With reference to previous correspondence concerning the removal of the remains of John Howard Payne from Tunis to this capital, I now take pleasure in enclosing herewith for your information a copy of a letter to this Department from Mr. Reade, Her Britannic Majesty's Consul at Tunis, transmitting a statement of the expenses incurred by him in carrying out your wishes in regard to the matter, and expressing the hope that a suitable memento may be placed on the spot where the remains of Payne rested for so many years in Tunis.

"I am, sir,

"Your obedient servant,

"Fredk. T. Frelinghuysen."

18

"Tunis, January 18th, 1883.

" The Honorable
" Secretary of State for Foreign Affairs,
" Washington.

" Sir,—In accordance with the instructions of Her Majesty's Principal Secretary of State for Foreign Affairs, I have the honor to transmit to you a statement of the expenses incurred by me in the exhumation and subsequent shipment to Marseilles of Mr. John Howard Payne's remains, for the amount of which expenses I have drawn on you at five days' sight, as proposed.

" Subsequently to the removal of the body, Mr. W. A. Taylor, son of the United States consul at Marseilles, arrived here, bringing a letter requesting delivery of the inscribed stone slab which covered the vault in which Mr. Payne was buried. Although I had no instructions on the subject from my Government, and notwithstanding the regret which, in common with the whole Protestant community here, I could not help feeling at the removal from this country of the last memento of your distinguished citizen, I did not hesitate, on my own responsibility, to comply with the request made; and Mr. Taylor leaves Tunis, this day, taking with him the slab in question. I venture to express a hope that, through your good offices, some memorial of Mr. Payne may be erected on the site of the grave in this country in which he had for so many years lain. The slab now removed was always sought for with eagerness by travellers, and formed one of the most cherished objects of this almost historic cemetery. If this suggestion commends itself to you, as I trust it will, I shall be happy at all times to further your views in the matter; and I venture to add that, if necessary, some suitable memento may be procured on the spot.

" I have, etc.,

(Signed)   " Thos. F. Reade."

" Department of State,
" Washington, February 12, 1883.

" W. W. Corcoran, Esq.,
" Washington. D. C.

" My dear Sir,—The Department is just in receipt of a telegraphic despatch from the consul of the United States at Marseilles, stating that the remains of Colonel John Howard Payne have been forwarded by the French steamer Burgundia, which is expected to arrive at the port of New York about the 15th proximo.

"Very truly yours,

" FREDK. T. FRELINGHUYSEN."

" HER BRITANNIC MAJESTY'S MISSION,

" TUNIS, 3 March, 1883.

" DEAR SIR,—In compliance with the request contained in your letter of the 28th of January last, I have much pleasure in enclosing copies of five official documents, which will tell the story of the disinterment of the remains of John Howard Payne in all its details.

" I knew Mr. Payne personally in my youth, and remember the generous and warm-hearted support he gave to my father, the late Colonel Sir Thomas Reade, who then occupied the post I now hold, when, on the occasion of the execution of a Maltese assassin, the other foreign representatives entered into an unworthy cabal against him.

" You will find an interesting account of the cemetery in which Payne's remains had lain for thirty years in a work called 'Tunis, Past and Present,' by A. M. Broadly, which was published last year by Messrs. Blackwood & Sons, of Edinburgh.

" If any other particulars are required by you, I shall have much pleasure in furnishing them. I trust you will support my proposal for a permanent memorial of the poet in Tunis.

" I had already commenced this letter when I received the fifth enclosure from the Secretary of State at Washington, and I am happy to learn that my idea of some suitable substitute for the engraved slab, which has been removed from this cemetery, with the poet's remains, is approved by your government.

" I remain, dear sir,

" Faithfully yours,

" THOS. F. READE.

" GABRIEL HARRISON, ESQUIRE,

" Brooklyn, New York."

CHAPTER X.

THE EXHUMATION.

"Did these bones cost no more the breeding, but to play at loggats with them? Mine ache to think on't."—*Hamlet.*

OF the several descriptions of the exhumation of the dead poet's remains sent to the writer by those who beheld the sad scene, the one written by the Hon. John Worthington, United States consul at Malta, and despatched to Mr. Brown, chief clerk of the Department of State, seems to cover the matter with the most feeling and satisfaction.

"TUNIS, January 5th, 1883.

"MY DEAR MR. BROWN,—Learning that the body of John Howard Payne, author of 'Home, Sweet Home!' was to be exhumed from its grave in Tunis and sent to America, at the expense of W. W. Corcoran, Esq., of Washington, and learning, too, that probably not any American would be present, I resolved to take a run over to Tunis, and, if possible, get there in time to witness the disinterment.

"I had written and telegraphed Mr. Thomas Reade, the British Consul-General at Tunis, asking him to inform me on what day the exhumation would occur, he replying, 'On Wednesday, the 3d instant.' As no steamer would leave Malta for Tunis (after the receipt of Mr. Reade's telegram) until noon of the 3d inst., I had doubts whether I would be able to reach Tunis in time, particularly as my steamer would not arrive at Tunis till Thursday, the 4th inst.; but, fortunately, upon reaching this place, and calling upon Mr. Reade, I found the exhumation had not taken place, but would occur to-day at 10 A.M. You can imagine how glad I was, then, that I had chanced coming, and that Mrs. Worthington had accompanied me. Of course I did not come in an official capacity, but simply as an American citizen, who could not bear the idea that the body of the author of 'Home, Sweet Home!' (once a distinguished United States consul at Tunis, who died and was buried there in 1852) should be taken from its grave and sent to its native land and not one of his countrymen be present. Hence I came.

"This morning at 12 M. the exhumation took place, in the presence of about twenty persons, a few being Tunisians attracted to the spot through curiosity, the others being laborers employed, and a few gentlemen acting as witnesses at the request of Mr. Reade. I also signed the paper as a witness that the exhumation took place as stated. There were two persons present who were also at the funeral and interment of Payne,—*i.e.*, Mons. Pisani and a dragoman.

"The coffin was badly decayed, and was kept from falling apart, when raised, with difficulty, but everything relating to the remains was scrupulously and reverently preserved and handled. There was little else than the blackened skeleton left. Traces of the colonel's uniform, in which Payne was buried, were distinguishable,—some gold lace and a few buttons. I asked for a button, which was given me, and which I enclose to you. Mr. Reade also retains a button. I likewise enclose a twig from the large 'pepper-tree' that is growing at the head of the now empty grave, this twig having fallen on the coffin from which I took it.

"At three o'clock, after the body had been put in its lead coffin and soldered, and then into its hard wood, and then its outer box, it was brought to the little Protestant church, where it will rest to-night under guard, and to-morrow morning be taken to a vessel leaving for Marseilles in the afternoon.

"I will add that I tried, unsuccessfully, to procure a band to play Payne's immortal song as his remains should leave the marina of Tunis, but not any could play 'Home, Sweet Home!' although I had the words and notes with me. However, as the body was brought into the chapel an English captain, Bridger, played a dirge on the little American organ there, after which Mrs. Worthington sang 'Home, Sweet Home!' very sweetly, and then we all came away, leaving the poor body lying under the memorial window in the chancel, which a few large-hearted Englishmen had put in there in tender and gracious memory of one they loved and honored, not alone for his authorship of the most touching of all songs, but for the half-melancholy and wholly beautiful character of the man himself.

"Faithfully yours,
"JOHN WORTHINGTON.

"SEVELLON A. BROWN, ESQ.,
    "Chief Clerk Department of State."

And thus the above is the description of the exhumed, rotted remains of the poet and dramatist, the author of "Home, Sweet Home!" The pen-picture is a sad one: "The coffin was so decayed that it fell apart, and all there was to be seen was the blackened skeleton, the traces of a uniform, some gold lace, and a few buttons,"—the latter distributed to those who attended the desecrated grave and uncovered the secrets of the dead-house: a spot that should ever be held sacred in the estimation of all who respect the Christian religion. Never should the tomb be thus disturbed but for the most urgent reasons, including their more sacred seclusion and rest. What a sad and gloomy picture for the human mind and the sensitive heart to dwell upon! How sombre the coloring of the blackened bones and coffin! How grotesque the outlines and mouldering fragments of the dissolving body! What graphic and startling effects the master-hand of a Gustave Doré could give in black and white to such a composition! Nothing in his illustrations of the "Inferno" could excel the chilling sensation that would vibrate throughout all properly constituted human muscles and nerves when beholding so ghastly a picture! Who will ever again sing the song of "Home, Sweet Home!" without seeing the spectral phantasm of a blackened skeleton, a decayed coffin, and a few corroded buttons?

It makes no difference *now* as to where the remains of John Howard Payne are placed, whether in the State of New York, his birthplace (where they rightfully belong), or at the capital of his country. Still, the mind will wander back to his first burial-place at Tunis, in the soil of Carthage,—the soil that was permeated with the effluvia of his decaying flesh, where the flowers and grasses that grew around his grave took a nourishment that gave form, color, and perfume to the eye and to the atmosphere. There, too, he was surrounded by the dead consuls of other nations, who, like himself, had died at their post in the discharge of duty. Like a group of leaders, there they rested with their chieftain and head, the centre of the sacred circle, as in a soft, low converse, heard by Fancy's ear, to tell us of their life-battles lost and won. Alas! the hallowed spot now mourns the eternal loss. Its moan is blended with the melody of the song that once lent rather a sweet than a saddening charm to the sacred ground. As instinctively will the human mind go down into the poet's empty grave at Tunis as the human mind looks upward in the recognition of its God. As instinctively as the human mind feels these thoughts, it will see the spirit of the author of "Home, Sweet Home!" fleeting from his little curtained death-chamber of the consulate at Tunis, as it must see his birthplace in the old-fashioned brick mansion in the city of New York. We are but human, and in that humanity these are the things from which we cannot flee any more than we can fail to recognize the essential facts of life and death. It is astonishing how many letters the writer received urging him to do something to prevent the removal of the remains of John Howard Payne, and, if removed, to have them placed in his native State, New York. As soon as I found that the Department of State had given Mr. Corcoran permission to bring home the remains of John Howard Payne, I wrote to the honorable gentleman, and said that "if he desired to make his act toward the memory of Mr. Payne one of perfect philanthropy, he should give his remains to their birthplace, the State of New York. But Mr. Corcoran "deemed the capital of his country the most befitting place for the poet's re-entombment." Longfellow, Bryant, Emerson, and Poe are the memorial shafts of light and fame that shoot upward to that part of the heavens that hangs immediately over the States that gave them birth; who ever thought of placing their honored remains in the District of Columbia? Who ever thought of placing the martyred Lincoln in Washington, or the assassinated Garfield there? Some madman lately proposed to remove the remains of Thomas Jefferson to Washington, breaking the long repose of the grave where he requested to be laid at rest forever. Mr. Corcoran is a noble gentleman, a gentleman graced with a grandeur of munificence that rivals the grandest things in the capital of his country. His gifts to that city rank in value to the people as the next best thing to the mighty shaft whose granite peak writes upon the clouds, as they float over it, the name of the immortal Washington. His art gifts to the city of Washington are the cynosure that will guide onward young aspirants to art accomplishments.

Mr. Corcoran's emotion in regard to bringing home the remains of John Howard Payne was right as an emotion to feel, but wrong as a passion or a purpose to execute. A little deeper thinking on the subject would have caused him to believe it far better that the poet should still have laid in his original grave. We can feel the tears that swept like a flood over his honored manly cheeks when the air of "Home, Sweet Home!" greeted the return of the half-frozen explorers of the ice-ribbed Arctic as they entered the streets of the summer-clad capital of their country. We can see, and feel, and honor all the noble deeds Mr. Corcoran has done, and ascribe them all to desires of noble and grand purposes. But what motives should be ascribed to the Department of State when it consented to an act of ingratitude to be rudely committed against a friendly nation who had cherished and honored the memory of our dead son? The Department of State, which in all its boasted wisdom and republican liberality allowed a private citizen the honor of bringing home to the nation the remains of that poet who sung the only song on "Home" that the whole world claims as its own! Why, if the State Department acting for the nation at large, endorsed by proper enactment of Congress, had brought home the remains of the author of "Home, Sweet Home!" the act of disturbing the dead would have been palliated somewhat by the thought that a nation desired to honor one whom it had too much neglected, and thereby would have been upon the nation's brow a crown of glory, glittering as clustered stars. Such acts would have given the nation a name for philanthropy that would have burned its way down through ages of time. It would have acknowledged that Poetry and Art are the graces of civilization, and that they do as much toward making a nation's renown as her soldiers and her statesmen.

That the reader may see that the writer is not the only one that expresses regret on the subject of the removal of Mr. Payne's remains, some testimony is subjoined. We quote the following from the "Boston Transcript," a paper proverbially careful in forming its opinions and in selecting the subjects on which it treats:

"John Howard Payne's remains have been taken from their resting-place in Tunis, and are awaiting shipment to New York, if, indeed, they are not already on the way. It is a matter of sincere regret that the question of removing these honored ashes was not more fully considered before any steps were taken. The English residents in Tunis, and other Englishmen at home, have shown their regard for the American poet by accomplishing a perfect restoration of his tomb, and by placing a memorial window in the chapel at Tunis. These evidences may not be too strongly urged as reasons why the poet's remains should not be brought away from the soil of Africa; but, inasmuch as they were proffered in a foreign land by citizens of another nation, they serve as proof that Payne's fame was not so closely confined to the land of his birth that only in America, so far as sentiment is concerned, should his bones find rest; and, if sentiment is to rule, somewhere near his birthplace, in New York, would be the only fitting place for them to lie. In Prospect Park, Brooklyn, stands a monument erected in memory of Payne; beneath that his mortal remains might properly be newly buried. It has been said of this country, and with too much reason, that influence can procure anything here. Let it never be said that, though successful in Payne's case, wealth has the power to disturb the resting-places of those who have reflected honor on the country in her councils, on fields of war, or in song."   •

The following highly interesting letter from our late consul, Hon. George W. Fish, should not be omitted. It is not only a part of the consular history of Tunis, but also an expression of disapprobation on the removal of the remains of Mr. Payne by one whose opinion must be respected, from the fact of his intimate acquaintance with the consulate and the grave of Mr. Payne at Tunis:

> " FLINT, MICHIGAN,
> " 29 Dec., 1882.
>
> " GABRIEL HARRISON, Esq.
>
> " MY DEAR SIR,—Yours of the 11th inst. came to hand by due course of mail. The last session of Congress made no appropriation for paying consuls at Tunis and Tripoli, and, of course, the consulates were discontinued. The Senate made an effort to restore the appropriation, but the House of Representatives persisted, and the consular and diplomatic appropriation bill passed as it came from the House committee, without any provision for the consulates named, and, as a matter of necessity, the Secretary of State must recall the consuls, as he had no provision for paying the consular expenses. Our country now has no representative, and our flag is not shown from the Straits of Gibraltar to the mouth of the Nile. Two of our oldest and most responsible consulates were discontinued, on the pretence of economy, by the same Congress that passed the monstrous river and harbor appropriation bill, the navy appropriation, and other equally questionable bills. I think it very mortifying to Americans that two of our oldest and most important consulates should be given up for want of funds (?), while many millions are appropriated for such very doubtful purposes. The Tunisian consulate had existed from a very early period in the history of our government. Now the North African people, from the Nile to the ancient ' Pillars of Hercules,'

will know nothing of our government. This is a great mistake. To me the project of removing the remains of John Howard Payne from Tunis to Oak Hill (Washington) Cemetery seems unreasonable. Mr. Payne died at his post, representing his government at the court of an old Oriental sovereign. He was buried in a beautiful cemetery, set apart for such purposes by the government to which he was accredited. Near his grave lie the remains of several distinguished British, German, and Swedish consuls who died at their post, and two other of our own consuls, one of whom died A.D. 1806, lie under the shadow of the same tree. Our government caused a plain but every way appropriate monument to be placed over his tomb. The inscription on the slab of white Italian marble that covers the grave is, I doubt not, as appropriate and every way as satisfactory as anything that will be likely to take its place in the new arrangement. Scores, and I might safely say hundreds, of English-speaking people every year visit the tomb of Payne at Tunis. Only about two years ago our government caused the tomb to be thoroughly repaired, and it is now in good condition and of respectable appearance. It is more than thirty years since he died, and all that will be found to remove will be a few cylindrical and other scattered bones, and a skull covered with a dirty-looking mould. My choice would be to let the remains of the author of 'Home, Sweet Home!' remain under the monument erected over them by his government, where he died, at the post to which his country had called him. If there were near kinsmen who asked that the remains might be placed with those of his family, it might be an argument in favor of removal, or something might be said in favor of placing them under the monument erected by his friends in his native State. Nevertheless, my voice would be in favor of letting J. Howard Payne sleep on where he has been resting these thirty years, and where the English-speaking world has long thought of him as a representative of our country. Thanking you for your expression of good feeling, and wishing you success in the new issue of the revised edition of your book,

"I remain respectfully yours,

"Geo. W. Fish."

The effort to remove the remains of Mr. Payne is not of recent origin. As we have shown elsewhere in this volume, the Hon. W. P. Chandler, of Philadelphia, when he arrived at Tunis to assume the duties of the consul two years after Mr. Payne's death,

found his grave without a sign to mark the spot. He immediately
wrote home to his government the facts, and suggested the removal of his remains to his native country. But the government
neglected the proffered opportunity to do a graceful act. The
Hon. Amos Perry, of Providence, Rhode Island, took charge of
the consulate in 1862, and remained at the post till 1867. This
gentleman, while there, not only made himself busy in writing
one of the finest histories of "Carthage and Tunis, Past and Present," but industriously investigated everything relating to Mr.
Payne's conduct and history while holding the position of United
States consul. It seems that the more he learned about Mr.
Payne the more he felt that a larger tribute of memory should be
paid to him by his government than a simple slab of stone. This
fact induced him to write the following letter, which was published in the "Evening Post," of New York. Not to give it a
place in the history of the life of John Howard Payne would be
doing a great injustice to the man who was the first to make a
strong effort, though unsuccessful, to bring home the remains of
the spirited consul. If removed at all, this was the time to do it,
yet little or no notice was taken of the matter:

"TUNIS, November 5th, 1863.

"REV. SAMUEL OSGOOD, D.D.

"DEAR SIR,—During my residence here of more than one year,
I have often thought of addressing you a line as an expression of
personal respect and friendship. But now I have an object in
view aside from personal considerations. It is to secure some
kind of a monument in America to commemorate the author of
'Home, Sweet Home.' John Howard Payne, to whom belongs
the honor of producing this poem, was one of my predecessors in
this office, and died in this consulate ten years before my arrival.
As you probably know as much as I do of Mr. Payne's career as
an author, an actor, and an officer of our government, no effort
of mine is required to throw light on his life, except so far as relates to closing scenes enacted in this city, where his remains repose under a plain marble slab placed there by the direction and
at the expense of our government. The inscription on his gravestone, in the Protestant Cemetery, speaks to the point.

"At the head of the horizontal marble slab is the United States
seal, with thirty-two stars, and then follows the inscription.

"Mr. Payne was an able and efficient representative of his

country, whose honor and prosperity he sought to promote. Through his persistent efforts the dilapidated old edifice that had served as the residence of United States consuls since the close of the last century, and had been previously occupied for a long period by consular agents of the famous Venetian Republic, was remodelled and converted into a neat, commodious, and substantial residence, the benefits of which, owing to his sudden death, have been enjoyed by his successors rather than by himself. Upon the top of this consulate was erected the tallest mast in the city, and at the top of this mast was exhibited, on state occasions, the largest flag in the Regency.

"Shortly before his death, Mr. Payne stated to Dr. Nathan Davis, the author of 'Carthage and her Ruins' (see London edition, page 408), that he wrote 'Sweet Home' in Paris under circumstances that gave him a realizing sense of the sentiments of that poem. Alone in a foreign city, his yearnings for home found versified utterance suited to the needs of fellow-mortals the world over. The story of Mr. Payne's long and painful illness need not be rehearsed here. His Mussulman servant, Mohammed, who is now in my service, and two Sisters of Charity, with one of whom I have often conversed, attended him day and night for successive weeks and months, and finally closed his eyes in death, and a priest of the Greek Church said prayers over his remains at the grave. Soon after his death his effects, including many keepsakes, were sold to liquidate his debts. Not even the cane which Washington Irving gave him was spared, though that was subsequently purchased and sent to America. Mr. Payne received his appointment at Tunis as a citizen of New York, where he had some relations and numerous friends and acquaintances, and it seems to me that a plan for a monument in his honor might better originate there than elsewhere, and perhaps with the New York Historical Society than with any other body. Only let the subject be agitated, and I am satisfied the work will not be long delayed.

"To help the business forward I take the liberty to suggest that a marble bust of Mr. Payne be procured at the cost of one hundred pounds sterling.

"When recently in Florence, I learned from J. A. Jackson, an American sculptor of much promise, that a casting of Mr. Payne's head was made some years since, and is now in the possession of Mr. Charles H. Brainard, of Boston. This casting was made by Mr. Jackson, who offers to furnish a good marble bust for the sum

named above. I introduce Mr. Jackson's name alike from the
force of circumstances and because I have confidence in him as
an artist and as a man. Cannot the required sum be raised in
pound subscriptions? I am ready with my pound, and let him
refuse to give a pound whose home has not been benefited to that
amount by the song of 'Home, Sweet Home!'

"I venture another suggestion in this connection, viz.: that an
elegant monument edition of Mr. Payne's works be published
with a notice of his life, and with 'Sweet Home' set to music, and
that the net proceeds of this edition go towards a monument.
I believe the book would sell on both sides of the ocean. Mr.
Payne's song of 'Home' has touched the hearts of all English-
speaking people, and is, I am informed, as well known in Great
Britain as in the United States. This publication enterprise
could not fail, it seems to me, to bring funds that would enable us
to have a monument to our Home Poet in Central Park, or at
least within a brief circle of the spot that gave him birth. Please
give this whole matter attention, exercising your better judgment
thereon. In a hasty line addressed to my friend, Mr. Henry T.
Drowne, I have introduced this subject, and have requested him
to converse upon it with some of the leading citizens of the metropolis where Mr. Payne was cradled,—the metropolis which he
honored, and which may in turn honor itself by paying a graceful
tribute to his memory."

CHAPTER XI.

HOME AT LAST. THE ARRIVAL AND RECEPTION OF PAYNE'S REMAINS.

On Thursday, at three o'clock P.M., March 22d, 1883, the steamer Burgundia, from Marseilles, bearing the remains of John Howard Payne, was moored to her dock in Brooklyn, at "Martin's Stores," opposite New York. It was the steamer's first trip across the Atlantic. After a lapse of thirty years thus were brought back the remains of Mr. Payne to the city of Brooklyn, that had done so much toward honoring his memory, the city in which he had last lived for several years prior to his departure from his native country for the last time. For some unexplained reason, or from mere oversight, the party that controlled the possession of the remains of the dead poet did not notify any one in Brooklyn that the Burgundia would land the remains of John Howard Payne as above mentioned, thereby preventing many warm admirers of Payne's memory from showing their respect to the remains of the man they had so highly honored. Had it not been for the enterprise of one of the editors of the "New York Telegram" in forcing attention to the fact that some mark of respect should be paid to Mr. Payne's relics on their arrival in New York City, where he was born, it is more than likely that his remains would have passed through his native city to Washington without the slightest notice beyond the fact of their arrival. On the dock at Brooklyn were waiting to receive the remains Mr. Corcoran's committee of two —Mr. Charles M. Mathews and Lieutenant R. F. Nicholson, United States Navy—and the committee of five appointed by the New York Board of Aldermen, consisting of Messrs. Duffy, Kirk, Fitzpatrick, De Lacey, and McLoughlin, and all of them escorted the remains to New York. The box containing the remains was covered by the American flag, and carried down the gang-plank by six sailors of the steamer, then placed in a hearse and conveyed to the Governor's Room, City Hall, New York. There the coffin was placed upon a stand in the centre of the room for public view. Not a single prominent citizen of New York, representing any of the several departments of literature and art in which Mr. Payne had filled a place creditable to himself at home and abroad. was present to do honor to the occasion; nor a prominent member of the press, to which he had been a bright ornament in boyhood and manhood; nor poet, though it was in this capacity that his remains were brought back to his native country to be honored; nor a dramatist, although in the drama he, as an American citizen, was and is, after the lapse of half a century, still deemed the best; not a single actor, although in this profession he, when a mere boy, was the first as an American who trod the boards of a foreign stage as a star, and was received with marked approbation.

The writer, who had entertained a life-long interest in the memory of Mr. Payne, felt that of all men he should at least be one to see the remains in state. On entering the Governor's Room, he found but a single flower on the coffin. Deeply impressed that something better should be done by some citizen of Payne's birthplace, he at once procured a wreath of immortelles, and placed it upon the box containing the poet's remains. This simple act of friendship he strove to do *incognito*, but was discovered. What a tidal wave of thoughts rushed over my brain as at one bound I leaped the gulf of three-quarters of a century in my thoughts of Payne, as I stood within a stone's throw of the site where once stood the old Park Theatre, in which he, when a boy of seventeen years, full of bright fancies and glowing hopes, began his career as an actor and his public life, and in that city where as a child-editor he had become the wonder of men of letters, was courted. adored, and handed about as a marvel of boyhood! As I stood there, I saw him struggling for eminence as an actor and a dramatist in Europe; I heard anew his song of " Home, Sweet Home!" whisper its sad strain in my ear; I saw him standing once more upon the stage of the " Old Drury" of America. thanking a packed house for their greeting on his return to his country after twenty years' absence; I saw him among the Indian tribes of his own country pleading in their behalf; I saw him as consul at Tunis; I saw him drawing his last breath among strangers; I saw him resting for over thirty years in his grave in the land of Carthage; now I beheld his exhumed bones returned to the city where he first saw the light of heaven, honored in state, with flags at half-mast upon the City Hall, and thousands of people filing past his coffined bones. Could he in his wildest thoughts have ever fancied such results?

The following is from the "New York Tribune" of March 23d :

" The coffin containing the remains of John Howard Payne lay in state yesterday in the Governor's Room of the City Hall, which was visited by many persons. A wreath of immortelles, inscribed in purple flowers with the words ' From a Friend,' lay on the coffin-lid. It was presented by Gabriel Harrison, a friend of Payne in his younger days, and his biographer. Soon after three o'clock, Gilmore's Band appeared on the balcony of the City Hall and played several pieces of music, among them ' Home, Sweet Home!' ' The Lost Chord,' ' Nearer, my God, to Thee,' ' The Star-Spangled Banner,' and ' Rest, Spirit, Rest.' At four P.M. a hearse, drawn by four white horses and followed by half a dozen carriages, drew up in front of the City Hall. The coffin was borne to the hearse in the presence of the Mayor, most of the members of the Board of Aldermen, several of the heads of departments, and a large throng, who uncovered their heads as the coffin came in view. The committee and others who were to accompany the remains to Washington entered the carriages, and the cortege took its way down Broadway to the railway ferry. The special car containing the party in charge of the remains was furnished by the Pennsylvania Railroad Company free of charge."

The remains arrived in Washington early on the morning of Saturday, March 24th. Although Mr. Corcoran desired that their arrival should be with as little publicity as possible, yet a large crowd was in attendance at the depot and witnessed the transfer of the body to the hearse, and it was immediately conveyed to the chapel of the cemetery, which Mr. Corcoran visited, to do honor to John Howard Payne's remains. The noble old philanthropist, as he stood there, must have felt that he had interwoven forever the letters of his own name with those that formed the words of " Payne" and " Home, Sweet Home!" The next day the writer received the following letter from Mr. Corcoran, showing his appreciation of the offering of the wreath :

" WASHINGTON, March 24th, 1883.

" MR. GABRIEL HARRISON.

" DEAR SIR,—Your beautiful wreath of immortelles now rests on the bosom of Payne as fresh as when you placed it there, and . there shall it rest till the 9th of June.

" Yours very truly,

" W. W. CORCORAN."

THE REINTERMENT OF MR. PAYNE'S REMAINS IN OAK
HILL CEMETERY, WASHINGTON, D. C., JUNE 9TH, 1883.

The writer having been invited by Mr. Corcoran to act as one
of the pall-bearers, left Brooklyn on Friday, June 8th, and arrived
there the same day, ten P.M.

Mr. Corcoran had carefully provided rooms at the Arlington
Hotel for all who had been invited from a distance to take a
prominent part in the ceremony.

On Saturday morning, June 9th, a clear hot Southern day, with
the temperature at ninety degrees. at ten A.M., we called on Mr.
Corcoran at his residence, where we had the pleasure of meeting
the philanthropist for the first time. We found him in his library
surrounded with all the luxuries of well-selected books, statuary,
and paintings. He gave us a kindly welcome, and said, "I am
very glad to meet you, Mr. Harrison, and especially so for the
reason that we have both taken a great interest in Mr. Payne, a
gentleman whom we knew and admired."

We found Mr. Corcoran a hale and handsome-looking gentleman, in a remarkable state of preservation for a man at the age
of eighty-seven.

After talking for a few moments, he invited me to visit with him
his art-gallery, where the remains of Mr. Payne lay waiting the
hour of removal, which was to take place at five P.M. We
went there, and I was much impressed with the character of
the scene that presented itself to my view. The large hall with
its walls covered with pictures of some of the best foreign and
native artists, with a soft light falling from the high windows
down upon a coffin resting in the centre of the hall upon an elevated black velvet pall. The coffin was covered with pure white
cloth and adorned with rich silver mountings. The wreath of
immortelles, inscribed " From a Friend," rested upon the lid. All
these presented a scene novel in its character and full of inspiration of thought. On the walls back of the coffin hung Church's
fine picture of "Niagara Falls," with its rainbow of prismatic
colors spanning the troubled waters below. To the right, opposite
the foot of the coffin, hung the great picture by Jean Gérôme of
"Cæsar Dead,"—slaughtered by his patrician foes, outstretched
and bleeding at the base of Pompey's statue. To the left. at the
head of the coffin, was Huntington's large picture of "Mercy's
19

Dream,"—"Methought I looked up and saw one coming with wings towards me, and he said, 'Peace be to Thee.'"

In front, the impressive picture of "Charlotte Corday" in prison, by Müller. Her pensive face with thoughtful eyes, large and beautiful, looked through the prison-window bars as if to see what the white-clothed coffin contained. Around this picture hung a cluster of portraits, painted by Stuart, Elliott, Durand, Healy, Sully, and others, representing the heads of John Randolph, Guizot, Clay, Lincoln, Grant, Jefferson, and Washington, all looking down upon the sad scene as similitudes of those who had paid the last debt of nature and had passed beyond earth's toils and disappointments. As we stood there alone in the sombre stillness of the place, we both felt that whatever we had done in honor of John Howard Payne was but a graceful tribute towards one who had given at least one leaf to the wreath of fame that adorns the brow of the nation.

After asking me several questions concerning the history of Mr. Payne, we parted, Mr. Corcoran to his palatial home and the writer to the Arlington, there to wait till the hour for the moving of the funeral cortege, which was to start at five P.M. At half-past four o'clock all who were to take part in the ceremonies had assembled at the Corcoran Gallery with the exception of the President and his Cabinet. Promptly by five P.M. the President arrived This notified the bringing of the body by eight men down the broad stairway leading from the gallery. In the vestibule to the street doors it was rested for a few minutes. The pall-bearers then formed in line on each side of the coffin, and as the navy-yard band struck up "Home, Sweet Home!" they moved down the steps into the street bearing the body to the hearse, and then took their places in the carriages immediately behind the hearse.

The pall-bearers were General J. G. Parke, of the United States army; Commodore W. G. Temple, of the United States navy; Gabriel Harrison, Esq., of Brooklyn, New York; W. T. Dunlop, Esq., of Washington, D. C.; Colonel T. L. Casey; Hon. N. A. Maury; Professor Baird, president of the Smithsonian Institution; and Major A. S. Nicholson, of the United States army, each wearing a broad white silk scarf mounted with purple rosettes and deep fringe.

The troops were in line along the avenue in front of the Corcoran Gallery, and saluted the remains as they were carried to the hearse. The line of march was begun, the artillery firing one gun at the moment of starting.

First rode General R. B. Ayres, of the United States army, with his aides, Lieutenants George Mitchell, Sibree Smith, Lotus Niles, H. H. Dodge, and Robert S. Chew. The band preceded a regiment of rifles under the command of Colonel J. O. P. Burnside. Then followed the Marine Band, leading the light battery of the Second Artillery, Captain John A. Rogers, of the United States army; the Washington Light Infantry, Colonel W. A. Moore; the High-School Cadets, Captain A. A. Smith; and an artillery battalion under Captain L. L. Langdon, of the United States army, brought up the rear of the military.

The Right Rev. Dr. Pinkney and Rev. W. A. Leonard came next in closed carriages. The hearse, drawn by four horses, followed next, escorted by the pall-bearers. Then a carriage containing the Rev. Dr. and Mrs. Laquer, of Bedford Station, New York, and Mrs. Baker, of East Hampton. Other carriages followed containing old acquaintances of Mr. Payne. Among them was the Hon. D. S. Pickett, of Frankfort, Kentucky, the last American to whom Mr. Payne granted a passport just previous to his death, while visiting Tunis.

The third section of the funeral was headed by President Arthur and Rev. J. C. Welling. D.D., chairman of the Committee of Arrangements, and with whom rode Colonel Cutts, Mrs. Botts, and her little daughter. Then came Mr. Leigh Robinson, the orator of the day, and the poet, Mr. R. S. Chilton. The diplomatic corps was represented by M. Roustan, escorted by Mr. Brown, chief clerk of the Department of State.

In the carriages that followed were Secretary Frelinghuysen, Secretary Lincoln, Secretary Teller, Secretary Folger, General Sherman, General Hancock. Justice Matthews, Justice Strong, Marshals Nicolay and Fassett; several clerks of Departments, Judge Edmunds, General West, Major Lydecker, and Dr. Tyndall preceded the last carriage, containing W. W. Corcoran, Esq., and his friend, Mr. Campbell, of South Carolina.

The broad avenues along the line were crowded with lookers-on, who, with suitable respect, uncovered their heads while the hearse passed by.

THE SCENE AT THE CEMETERY.

This was beautiful in the extreme. Almost immediately on the inside of the entrance was a great platform of seats filled by invited guests. This was covered overhead by the rich, green foliage of drooping oaks, while in the centre of this amphitheatre of people and trees stood the white marble monument, surmounted with the bust of Payne. At its base was an exquisite elevation, four feet in height, constructed of every kind of flowers that the luxuriant month of June affords. The coffin was removed from the hearse, followed by the pall-bearers and the only relatives,—Mrs. Laquer and her husband. Then came the President of the United States, side by side with Mr. Corcoran ; next came his Cabinet, followed by the rest of the funeral cortege. The coffin was placed upon the bed of flowers, and all took their seats upon the platform in the rear of the monument and of the passage at the base, which led into the brick-built chamber for the reception of the dead.

On the front of the platform were draped flags, held up by a crescent and a star, as emblems of Payne's consulship at Tunis. In the centre of the device was a portrait of Payne when a boy, painted by the celebrated Jarvis, surrounded by a wreath of flowers.

On the left was another platform, upon which were seated the singers of the Philharmonic Society.

As the wreath of immortelles "From a Friend" was being placed upon the coffin, over one hundred voices sang "Home, Sweet Home!" Near the head of the bier was a floral design of a harvest-field, with the last sheaf standing, with a sickle resting against it, and the words, "At Rest." At the head of the coffin was a crown of flowers. At the foot lay an anchor of white flowers. On the coffin-plate was the inscription :

"John Howard Payne.
Born June 9th, 1791.
Died April 9th, 1852."

The whole audience rose in respect for the dead, while the Marine Band rendered a mosaic from "Lohengrin."

Dr. J. C. Welling, president of the Columbian University, rose and announced that the time had come for the ceremonies to begin. The Rev. W. A. Leonard, D.D., then read selections from Genesis, chapter xxiii. At the conclusion of his reading the following music was rendered: Quartette and chorus, "Blessed are the Departed" (Requiem), (Last Judgment), Spohr, Philharmonic Society and organ, R. C. Bernays, conductor; R. W. Middleton, organist. Following this, Mr. Robert S. Chilton, the poet of the day, read a poem, a graceful and touching tribute to the dead poet.

POEM.

"The exile hath returned, and now at last
    In kindred earth his ashes shall repose.
Fit recompense for all his weary past,
    That here the scene should end,—the drama close.

"Here, where his own loved skies o'erarch the spot,
    And where familiar trees their branches wave;
Where the dear home-born flowers he ne'er forgot
    Shall bloom, and shed their dews upon his grave.

"Will not the wood-thrush, pausing in her flight,
    Carol more sweetly o'er this place of rest?
Here linger longest in the fading light,
    Before she seeks her solitary nest?

"Not his the lofty lyre, but one whose strings
    Were gently touched to soothe our human kind,—
Like the mysterious harp that softly sings,
    Swept by the unseen fingers of the wind.

"The home-sick wanderer in the distant land,
    Listening his song hath known a double bliss:
Felt the warm pressure of a father's hand,
    And, seal of seals! a mother's sacred kiss.

"In humble cottage, as in hall of state,
    His truant fancy never ceased to roam
O'er backward years, and—irony of fate!—
    He of home sang who never found a home!

"Not even in death, poor wanderer, till now;
    For long his ashes slept in alien soil.
Will they not thrill to-day, as round his brow
    A fitting wreath is twined with loving toil?

"Honor and praise be his whose generous hand
Brought the sad exile back, no more to roam;
Back to the bosom of his own loved land,—
Back to his kindred, friends, his own *Sweet Home.*"

The monument was then unveiled, and Payne's "Home, Sweet Home!" was sung by a full chorus with organ accompaniment; R. C. Bernays. conductor; R. W. Middleton, organist.

ORATION BY LEIGH ROBINSON.

"Payne's career was the unhappy one of disappointment, a history of baffled aims, a life nowise proportioned to boyish promise and precocity, but rather the melancholy non-fulfilment thereof. Nor can it be said that his way was more beset with difficulty than that of many a man who, in the hard encounter with the obduracy of his lot, has known how to throw into the doubtful scale against the odds of fate the sword of a persistent will. Payne had all that was needful to start him fairly,—first and foremost, a boy's best blessing, parents entitled to his love; a sweet lap of virtuous manners; a home, we may well believe, imbued with the 'plain living and high thinking' of that early day. Outside of his home he was a praised and petted boy, *protégé* of editors and authors, popular and precocious, and precociously fond of the stage. Partly, it may be, to repress this longing, a desk in a counting-house was the portion first assigned him. But friends of the bright boy, won by his charms, resolve that he shall have the advantage of a college training. In the heyday of youth, as in the corruption of the grave, philanthropy has loved him. And now we have the old, old story of natural parts and aptitude for shining. irksomeness of college rules, impatience of restraint and admonition, even that of his benefactors. Then follow in swift succession a mother's death, a father's bankruptcy. The ill wind which smote the four corners of his father's house blew him the questionable good of a reluctant permission to pursue his bent. The alternative lay between, on one side, the busy and the beaten track, a life of labor, possibly obscure, at all events monotonous; and on the other a life of pleasing activity and variety, before which spread itself the applause of multitudes, perchance the smile of fortune on her favorite. The muse of his fancy was the muse of his adoption. That which had been his stolen satisfaction was to become his serious life. He entered what was for him a garden of enchantment. The plaudit of friends from the gallery to the ground was there to welcome him.

"Perhaps it had been well for Payne if, at this time, adversity had been stirred more freely in his cup, and from its dregs, the primer of greatness in every school, he had drawn its desperate force. It happened otherwise. Life betrayed him with its kiss.

"Let us not underrate, then, as possibly Payne did, the career which he now set before himself, and for which he seems to have had a fair endowment. As it was said of Leibnitz, that he drove all the sciences abreast, so it may be said of the stage, that all the arts are tributary to it. To create before the footlights a little world, which shall be the successful mimicry of the great and universal theatre; to picture there in miniature the perplexities and passions of man's life, his laughter and his tears; to unfold there the various wealth of tone and color, by the illusions of sense and sound, the poet's, the painter's, the musician's art, by the expressiveness of countenance and gesture, to throw upon the stage a form which shall be the glass of life, a voice which shall be its echo; by the very body to figure thought, is a field of labor wide enough for the widest, and the widest has labored in it. The greatest word ever spoken in English literature floated swan-like from the boards of the Globe Theatre. To be the poet of representation is not a small art, but a great one. It is the art by which the word of genius is made flesh. With every fascination and prepossession of youth upon his side, the charm of the social circle, the prodigy of the intellectual, with an engaging manner and person, a bell-like voice, a good ear, and, above all, the quick sense of beauty, Payne sallied forth to sway the sceptre of the stage. Fondled by the fond, many from Boston to Charleston, in his native land, his native land grew insufficient for him. Ambition whispered that on the ampler theatre of the English stage he might snatch a nobler laurel. He arrived in time to witness there the advent of the elder Booth, who, as it seems to me, with a wiser discrimination, saw in America, rather than in Europe, the field for rising genius. He was present the first night of the return of Mrs. Siddons to the stage, and beheld the majesty of those powers which, even in the dry tree, were challenged solely by the glorious blossom of their earlier stem. The friend of Washington Irving obtained swift access to the first literary and dramatic circles. With no undue diffidence, he flung himself against Kean and Kemble, in the arena of those triumphs which had made each 'a stately hieroglyphic of humanity.' He achieved laudation, the promise of distinction, not distinction itself, and not success. Other things in this unyielding world go to the make-up of success besides the most sweet voices and the most applauding psalms. Payne never did command, but had always to conciliate his theatre. All credit should be given him, however, for the celerity and cheery heart with which he now bent himself to that series of translations, adaptations, compositions, dramatic, operatic, tragedy, comedy, and farce, numbering some forty-nine in all, which consumed the best years of his life.

"It is always a pathetic spectacle, the conflict of taste, talent, and sensibility; the striving and pursuing of the beating heart and proud honor of ingenuous youth with the iron world of business; the encounter of the porcelain with the earthen vase in that flood of destinies which we call human life. It is so hard for the endowed and admired one to realize that over against him is the jealous eye, which is ever turned on insecure and unestablished strength; that his house, like the temple at Jerusalem, must be builded with the trowel in one hand and the sword in the other; that his various gifts and graces are scanned as coldly as ever slave upon the block by the spirit of trade, which stands there not for sentiment but bargain. Payne's versatile struggle through all these years of disappointment, deception, and undeception is to me the flutter of the bird against its bars, trying them all in turn, and all in vain.

"Thus it came to pass that middle life stole upon him, and found him not unfriended, indeed, but undemanded and unavailing. In all that made life beautiful and noble to him failure was his familiar voice. He was one who had crossed swords with the world and had not overcome. The fight of life which had been woven for him, which, in so great a measure, he had woven for himself, had left him among the slain. In that flood of destiny into which he plunged so ambitiously, the hammer of destiny shivered his ambition. His life was in ashes before he was forty. The enchanted garden he had hied him to so swiftly and so gladly shut its gates in his face, and when he turned to the future, it was to that future of the defeated, whose very veil is of stone. And now, when his heart was even more bankrupt than his purse, and when his purse was empty, he felt that many of the best years of his life had been a waste in pursuit of the dramatic laurel that nature never intended should grace his brow. And then, in his vision, rose his far-off home, to which the heart was as the snail torn from its shell.

"If sweet is health to the sick, sight to the blind, liberty to the captive, rest to the heavy-laden, what should be the hunger and thirst after home by the homeless? In the irreverence of the times, whatever other faith hath famished, the temple of the hearth is sacred. As St. Columba says in his farewell to Aman, so we say of home, 'Paradise is with thee; the garden of God within sound of thy bells.' In the sinking fate of the man this, too, came to him like the memory of spring in winter, of the ripple of the waters in the desert of his life,—the bells of a paradise lost. This is the forlorn pathos of that which makes him famous; that is the song of home by him who had not where to lay his head. It is like bright light on deep shadow. The sweet rose of life had faded from him. Only its thorn was pressed against his breast. A wandering bird cast out of the nest startles the midnight with the song of his earliest morning; a flood of sweetness, all the more exquisite that it is poured from the throat of sadness; beauty from ashes, the bird-song of home from the mouth of the homeless. It is the sorrow in the throat which makes the song so sweet. This song, born of suffering and sadness, like all immortal things made perfect by suffering, is to-day his song of triumph.

"In 1832, after an absence of twenty years, Payne came back to his native land. Why he should have remained away so long when so warm a welcome awaited him in it is a mystery. Complimentary benefits in Boston, New Orleans, and New York awaited him, public receptions and dinners, for all which he returned his acknowledgments in the graceful terms which never failed him. But the projects which thenceforth engaged his attention were the desperate after-game of life: international reviews, sacred history, Cherokee Indians, and what not,—projects of a fertile rather than a practical brain, the double-flowering tree, fruitful of promise, void of fruit. Finally came the consulship to Tunis in 1842, recalled in 1845, renewed in 1851. There, amid the dusky aspects and the fallen columns of that ancient land, hard by the spot where Caius Marius was seen sitting on the ruins of Carthage, Payne laid him down,—there, in the shadow of the broken and dejected column of his own life, lay down to die. In Tunis, on the 9th of April, 1852, in the sixty-second year of his life, he passed away. Two Sisters of Charity and his Moorish domestics were with him when he died. A priest of the Greek

Church said prayers over his grave. The breath was hardly out
of his body when his furniture, library, works of art, and sword
of office were seized and sold at auction for his debts. His personal apparel even disappeared in the general wreck. Sad exit of
one whose entrance was so blithe! And yet as his life sank behind
a cloud his face was turned toward the morning. As the breath
of life left his body his life in the breath of others began. As his
earthly abode became the spoil of his creditors, every home in
Christendom became his spoil. The light of his life went down
like that Norway sun, which sets into sunrise. The world is the
debtor to-day of him whose whole substance the world sold in
execution. Every home is the sweeter for him, as it is also admonished by him. He might be termed the Apostle of Home. In
some sense we might say, without irreverence, I trust, 'the chas-
tisement of our peace was upon him, and with his stripes we are
healed.' Therefore it is that the grave cannot confine him in the
land of the stranger, nor the ocean divide him from his own. The
ship of a mighty people has spread its sail, and brought him up
from the under world and over the deep water to rest at last under
the oaks and beneath the violets of his country. The magistrates
and the masses of his country are here to-day, equally his
mourners,—the music and the verse, the chivalry and the beauty
of his own land and the ambassadors of all others. Here in the
consecrated stillness of the wood and by the holy murmur of the
stream, which in life he haunted with his love, his restless ghost
will fold its wing. A charm from the sky will seem to hallow him
here. As I see awaiting him the sepulchre prepared by one the
venerable snow of whose winter has dropped no flake upon his
open hand, it is to me as though the figure of that charity which
never faileth were bowed in benediction over this grave. It is as
though we were witnessing the ineffable voyage of Payne's soul
from the earth, which was his tavern, to the heaven, which is his
home; as though this, the translation of his mortal part from the
land of old bondage to the land of new promise, from the dark
continent to the bright one, were the likeness of his far greater
resurrection, not from hemisphere to hemisphere, but from death
to immortality."

The exercises were then continued as follows :
Interment ceremonies, the Rt. Rev. William Pinkney, D.D.,
LL.D., officiating.

After the impressive prayer was delivered by the bishop, the pall-bearers, with Mr. W. W. Corcoran, Esq., and Mr. and Mrs. Laquer, took their positions on each side of the grave. The coffin was lowered and shoved under the base of the monument. While this was being done the "Grand Hallelujah Chorus" (Messiah) of Handel was performed by the Philharmonic Society of a hundred voices, and accompanied by the full Marine Band, Professor Frederick Widdows conductor. The benediction was pronounced, and thus ended the reinterment of John Howard Payne.

Whatever may have been Mr. Payne's life, his successes, his disappointments, or his character, no poet, actor, editor, or consul was ever laid to rest with higher honors than occurred at Oak Hill Cemetery. The display, both military and civic, was of the highest character; the Head of a great nation, with its Cabinet, many high officials, and men of acknowledged genius in science and war, with a funeral cortege over a mile long, and with at least ten thousand people to witness it, with decorations of art and flowers, all combining to do the occasion honor.

If Mr. Payne had such an ambition, his wildest dreams never could have pictured so splendid a demonstration. Such an extreme as this funeral, however, must be attributed to the princely philanthropy of one man, more than to the deserts of the person whom they were meant to honor. This fact must be admitted by every reasonable mind who may have any considerable knowledge of Mr. Payne's character and works. The many absurd and romantic stories told about the circumstances under which he wrote the words of "Home, Sweet Home!" were the cause of a great sympathy towards the man more than any genius in the song. But, while this is the fact, yet his bones now rest in the soil of his country through the generosity of one man, W. W. Corcoran, Esq., of Washington, District of Columbia.

> " The play is done, the curtain drops,
>   Slow falling to the prompter's bell ;
> A moment yet the actor stops,
>   And looks around, to say farewell.
> It is an irksome word and task ;
>   And, when he's laughed, and said his say,
> He shows, as he removes the mask,
>   A face that's anything but gay."

JUVENILE POEMS,

CHIEFLY WRITTEN AT AND BEFORE THE AGE OF SIXTEEN,

BY

JOHN HOWARD PAYNE.

"He lisp'd in numbers, for the numbers came."

COMPILED BY

GABRIEL HARRISON.

PREFACE.

THIS little selection has been prepared as a shelter from the
trouble of transcription, an office which the author has been solicited much oftener than he could spare the time to accomplish
it, by the kind desire of friends to receive copies of the juvenile
efforts of which it is composed. With regard to the work itself,
the author is so conscious of the feebleness of its claims that he
desires not to trust it beyond the indulgence and partiality of
personal friends. It gives him no pleasure but from the associations it recalls. His ambition for verse-making never soared beyond the wish to amuse his friends; and repeated experiments
have convinced him that his talents for the business will never
exceed the domestic quality of his ambition. In some instances,
the last production which has been the subject of his admiration,
before sitting down to write, will have insensibly diffused the
influence of its impression around what he has written.

This is always so much the case with young writers, that it
would have been named here only from an apprehension that the
age at which these trifles were framed might not be always remembered; and cases of imitation might suggest themselves to
others, which, had they been committed knowingly, would have
been specified by himself; but as, after this long interval, the
course of his reading and reflection at the moment is so entirely
forgotten that he cannot retrace the paths from which he might
have plucked flowers to deck his own wild wreath, he must refer
the discovery to readers, with whom he could not have risked
these infants of a mind never much given to poetry, unless fortified
by the consciousness of having put them in the way of being
judged with that good-humored prejudice which people seldom
bring to a new book, the determination that nothing shall prevent
them from being pleased.

JOHN HOWARD PAYNE.

LONDON, February, 1815.

LISPINGS OF THE MUSE.

VALEDICTORY.

This poem was written at Boston, in 1805, when the author first quitted his home, and the academy in which he had been educated, for New York. The author's father, Mr. William Payne, was the founder and director of the seminary alluded to, which was known by the title of "Berry-Street Academy."

O TIME! forgive the infant muse
Who dares to sing thy speedy flight,
And waft a sigh in silent views
To realms of permanent delight!
In vain I glance a wistful thought
O'er joys too precious to be bought,
Where no sad change
Can e'er estrange
From scenes which erst engaged my feeling heart.

With fond remembrance I retrace
The years, the months, the weeks, the days,
Which "creeping in this petty space,"
I've spent in childhood's blithesome maze:
Now fled, like Ganges' sacred stream,
Or, like a visionary dream;
Now here—now gone—
Still passing on,
Or, like myself—*appears* but to *depart!*

Friends of my life, and dearest held,
My filial vows to you I pay,
By love and duty both impell'd
While, from your guidance call'd, I stray,
With lively gratitude inspired;—
May all the bliss to be desired
On you descend
Till time shall end,
And crown the wish convey'd in my *adieu!*

20   299

Still, fond rememb'rance, ling'ring, dwells
O'er my lov'd ALMA'S nurt'ring shade,
And painful recollection swells:
 The clust'ring branches there display'd,
 While nursed in Science' lib'ral store,
 And fed with literary lore—
  Oh, may they still
  Thy vot'ries fill,
 And they, like *me*, shall own their debt to *you.*

[At the age of thirteen.]

EPILOGUE TO THE WANDERER,

AN AMERICAN PLAY, ACTED AT THE NEW YORK THEATRE.

Written at the age of fourteen, spoken by Mrs. Jones, who performed the part of *Julia,*
the Wanderer.

So, then methinks we'll leave, without repining,
This sobbing, monkish, methodistic whining:
One serious part (at least, if they will tease one)
Is *quantum sufficit* for half the season.
Oh, dear! I scarce can force a smile to ask
How you approve our author's infant task?
If to his "Wanderer" a home you'll give
And bid the hope of trembling genius live?—
"Pshaw!" cries old *ten-per-cent,* "don't talk to me
Of trembling genius, hope, and—
 (Hesitating, then with a mimicking flourish,)
                        ti-tum-tee!
All stuff and nonsense! If the *cash* be rare—
What, genius, is thy boasted lot?—despair!
Though his bold flight reached worlds at every bound,
Its end—what is it? *two-pence* in the *pound!*
The silly wight is left at last to curse
His learned noddle, with an empty purse!
Give me your plodding man of common sense,
Whose wiser study is to soar at *pence;*
Who thinks no style like *invoice* half so terse is,
And *contra credit* worth a ton of verses!
If wits will write, why, let them write, and starve;
For me, thank Heav'n! I have my *goose* to carve,
And cellar furnish'd to my heart's desire:—

Prithee what more can man or beast require?"
This said, he takes his quid, looks wise, and stirs the fire.
From judges such as these we gladly turn
To eyes that sparkle, and to hearts that burn,
That conscious, kindle at *Columbia's* name,
Proud of their country's letters, as her fame!
That rear th' exotic, if the flowers be fair,
But guard the native plant with tenfold care;
Nourish its tendrils like the dew of dawn,
And bid it bloom to cheer its parent lawn!
Warmed by such favor, Genius learns to rise,
Like our own Eagle, a career to run,
Free as the air, and brilliant as the sun!
A devious "Wanderer" fondly turns to you,
To ask indulgence, not to claim a due;
And oh, believe her! she would rather roam
O'er any wilds, however far from home,
Than fail to court, in modest merit's cause,
The sanction of your smile—the fame of your applause!

FRAGMENT OF POETRY.

FOUND AT THE FALLS OF MOUNT IDA, TROY, IN THE STATE OF NEW
YORK.

Several passages were obliterated, by having been frequently trodden on; and those
which remained were traced out with much difficulty.

SHUNNING the noisy haunts of men,
He loved to wander here. His friends were few:
He cared not for the crowd. He heard, unhurt,
The scornful jest of cruel ignorance.
The poison'd arrows, which misfortune aim'd,
Pierc'd not his heart, in such bold armor clad,
That every point was blunted at the blow,
And dropp'd unheeded down!
  *   *   *   *   *   *   *
Oh! he would gaze,
With rapture gaze upon this fairy scene,
And he would moralize the opening leaf,
And in each little, curious fibre find
The noblest tribute to its *Maker's* praise.
  *   *   *   *   *   *   *

He joy'd to mark
The silver stream swift gliding twixt the banks,
Which seem'd to smile in ecstasy to see
Their lovely foliage in the polish'd wave!
In silent rapture would he sit and view
These distant waters, torn up by the crags,
Rippling and sparkling as they sprang in air:
Then traced with hasty steps the forest path,
Where stream impetuous plunges the abyss;
Then rolls along exulting to be free,
With roar at which earth trembles.   Here he paus'd:
For inspiration lived in every wave,
And the aw'd soul was mute.   ·

*   *   *   *   *   *   *   *

Within the cataract where th' embodied stream
Leaps the high cliff, with dash of fury foaming,
Sleeps the wild spirit of the storm.   A cave,
Formed by the jutting of that cliff, her cell;
The water-sheets, its wall, through which the sun
Darts tempered hues of strange and various light;
And as the tumult stills,—the waves subside,—
And distant echoes die upon the ear,—
With printless tread, along its flowery banks,
The Muses love to wander, hand in hand—
There, as it gently winds among the vales,
To trace, through fairy lands, its silver course.

NOTE.—The scenery of the foregoing is described from nature.   It is peculiarly picturesque.   The jutting out of the top of the precipice throws the wave forward with a
magnificent sweep, leaving an immense chasm between the sheet of water and the side
of the cliff, to which the Poet cannot help assigning some inhabitant from among the
numberless spirits who are always in waiting for appointments of that nature.   The
author, therefore, put the storm-spirit into it, and hopes she will be pleased with her
residence, which certainly possesses great attractions from the rainbow effect of the
sunbeams, as they come subdued into moonlight mildness by their passage through the
stream.

ODE

FOR THE THIRTY-FIRST ANNIVERSARY OF AMERICAN INDEPENDENCE.

Written as a College Exercise.

WHEN erst our Sires their sails unfurl'd,
  To brave the trackless sea,
They boldly sought an unknown world,
  Determin'd to be free!
They saw their homes recede afar,
  The pale blue hills diverge,
And, Liberty their guiding star,
  They plough'd the swelling surge!

No splendid hope their wand'rings cheer'd;
  No lust of wealth beguiled;—
They left the towers that Plenty rear'd
  To seek the desert wild;
The climes where proud luxuriance shone
  Exchang'd for forests drear;
The splendor of a Tyrant's throne
  For honest Freedom here!

Though hungry wolves the nightly prowl
  Around their log-hut took;
Though savages with hideous howl
  Their wild-wood shelter shook;
Though tomahawks around them glared,—
  To Fear could such hearts yield?
No! GOD, for whom they danger dared,
  In danger was their shield!

When giant Power, with blood-stain'd crest,
  Here grasp'd his gory lance,
And dared the warriors of the West
  Embattled to advance,—
Our young COLUMBIA sprang, alone
  (In God her only trust),
And humbled, with a sling and stone,
  This monster to the dust!

Thus nobly rose our greater Rome,
  Bright daughter of the skies—
Of Liberty the hallow'd home,
  Whose turrets proudly rise,—
Whose sails now whiten every sea,
  On every wave unfurl'd ;
Form'd to be happy, great, and free,
  The Eden of the world !

Shall we, the sons of valiant Sires,
  Such glories tamely stain ?
Shall these rich vales, these splendid spires,
  E'er brook a Monarch's reign ?
No ! If the Despot's iron hand
  Must here a sceptre wave,
Raz'd be those glories from the land,
  And be the land our grave !

TO A LADY,

WHOSE INFANT DAUGHTER DELPHINE WAS REMARKABLE FOR THE
BEAUTY, FIRE, AND INTELLIGENCE OF HER EYES.

THE Rose, which boasts so rich a dye,
  And wantonly with Zephyr plays,
Woos the delighted traveller's eye,
  Yet blushes at the traveller's gaze.

That Rose, in but a little while,
  Shall bloom and blush no longer there,
Shall pass away, like beauty's smile,—
  Be pale and cheerless, like Despair.

But when another Spring shall rise,
  Another Rose shall there be found ;
Another Rose of richer dyes
  Shall shed a sweeter fragrance round.

Thou art that earlier Rose. O ! long
  Be friendship with thy virtues blest !
The theme of many a Poet's song ;
  The idol of affection's breast !

And, if thy little one confirm
  The promise of her sparkling eyes,
In DELPHINE we behold the germ
  Of the next Rose, of richer dyes.

O! may this child surpass in worth
  The bright example thou hast given,
Charm the enraptured sons of Earth,
  Then flourish in the fields of Heaven!

MARY.

"Ah me! how sweet is Love itself possest,
When but Love's shadows are so rich in joy!"
                                    SHAKSPEARE.

IF Reason could the heart control,
  If Memory from itself could fly,
I'd quench the fire that burns my soul,
  Nor drink the poison from her eye!

How often have I vainly sought
  To guard against Love's madd'ning sway,—
But flashing deep into my heart,
  One glance has swept resolves away!

Since Reason, then, can ne'er assuage
  Presumptuous reveries like mine,
Rage on, my soul! still madly rage,
  And be a fancied Mary thine!

Long may the fairy vision spread
  Its soothing spell around my mind,
That joy, itself forever fled,
  May leave the phantom still behind!

And when, at length, this life shall fade,
  And earthly scenes recede in gloom,
My Mary's fondly cherished shade
  Shall light my passage to the tomb!

A very accomplished lady, by the name of A IR, residing at Providence, in the State of Rhode Island, was on the eve of departure from Boston, where she had been some months on a visit. A gentleman, celebrated for the frequency and felicity of his puns, was solicited by a friend of this lady to express his admiration in a farewell poem, which was, of course, expected to have been a poem of puns; but the parties were surprised to receive, in place of the expected *jeu d'esprit*, a grave series of compliments, conveyed in delightful poetry, but not one pun in the whole collection. This incident called forth the following

LINES,

ADDRESSED TO MRS. AIR, ON HER DEPARTURE FOR PROVIDENCE;

WHICH OUGHT TO HAVE BEEN WRITTEN BY SOMEBODY ELSE.

YES! I am lost! By those bright eyes
Entrapp'd before I was aware!
Ev'n Hope deserts me! for my sighs
Are given to *unconscious* AIR.

Like the *mild* AIR which sweetly swells
The notes of an Æolian lyre,
Whose magic every woe dispels,
And fills us with seraphic fire,—

This soothing, *lovely* AIR can make
The passions bend to her control,
And, with ethereal mildness, wake
The softest music of the soul!

Thy smile (like the *pure* AIR which blows
Where spirits of the blest unite),
Exhilarating AIR![1] bestows
A dear delirium of delight!

I live—I move—by means of AIR;
Yet gentle AIR resolves to fly!
Oh, stay! protect me from despair;
By AIR *deserted*, I must DIE!

---

[1] *Exhilarating air* is Sir Humphry Davy's term for what is called, in the technical phrase of chemistry, *gaseous oxyd of nitrogen*. When inhaled, it produces the wildest ecstasy. A late writer on the subject poetically imagines that the atmosphere of *Heaven* is composed of that kind of air.

DERMODY.

"Whether by accident or design, I know not, but never were the remains of a Bard deposited in a spot more calculated to inspire a contemplative mind with congenial and interesting feelings."—*Monthly Mirror*, London, 1802.

IF, pensive stranger ! in thy breast
   The flowers of Fancy ever bloom,
Come hither, stranger ! come and rest
   Upon this rose-encircled tomb !

This tomb, to which at eve retires
   Neglected Genius :—here, alone,
He weeps, despises and admires
   The wretch whose wrongs describe his own !

The aged Minstrel, pausing here,
   Of many a plaintive lay beguil'd,
Laments, with many a tribute tear,
   The Poet " wonderful and wild."

Could but that Poet swell the song,
   And *now* with phrensied touch inspire
The harp whose notes he'd *once* prolong
   Till his whole soul would be on fire,—

Ah ! could he touch—the thrilling strain
   Would wake a kindred ecstasy,
And thou wouldst sigh to hear again
   The lyre of luckless DERMODY !

And o'er his lov'd remains, which sleep
   Cold in this dark, sepulchral bed,
Then wouldst thou sit, like me, and weep
   The wild-ey'd Bard of Erin dead !

And thou wouldst bathe the flowers that wave,
   Till ev'ry flow'r that bloom'd before
Should, bending, kiss the sacred grave,
   And bow, and weep, and bloom no more !

The following was dedicated to an English lady who had been twice married. The happiness of the earlier part of her life was blasted by the ill-treatment of a very profligate husband; but her felicity was restored by the second marriage, which was remarkably prosperous. These circumstances will explain some allusions in the poem.

MAY AND HER PROTÉGÉ.

RESPECTFULLY INSCRIBED TO MRS. A. V. H. ON THE ANNIVERSARY
OF HER BIRTH IN MAY.

BY THE POET-LAUREATE TO HER ROSY-CHEEKED MAJESTY THE RIGHT
WORSHIPFUL QUEEN FLORA.

MY DEAR MADAM,—The inspiration of your birthday sets even *me* into a humor for rhyming. What a magical day, to inspire *me*, of all the stupid people in the world! I hope you will not, true woman-like, be vexed at my making May *your* Queen, instead of making you the Queen of May, as is usual on such occasions. I could not consign you to a better protector than this blooming nymph; and I think it is fully proved in the enumeration of her past bounties, with which I have the honor to accompany my congratulations on the return of this anniversary.

> SWEET MAY! thy magic charms inspire
>   Poets, as well as birds, to sing;
> Each hopes to utter from his lyre
>   The best turn'd compliment to Spring.
>
> The flowers which start beneath thy tread,
>   The graces which around thee throng,
> Have madden'd every Poet's head,
>   Since the first Poet lisp'd in song.
>
> But, lovely May! although thy smile
>   Turns deserts into rosy bow'rs;
> Beams forth such raptures as beguile
>   The wretched of their gloomiest hours;
>
> Yet higher joys thy happy dawn,
>   Enchanting month! to me unfurl'd,
> When, on AMELIA'S natal morn,
>   Thou, smiling, gav'st her to the world!
>
> Yes! at that hour didst thou impart
>   Thy softness to her eye and face,
> With thine own warmth inspire her heart,
>   And o'er her form diffuse thy grace!

When tyranny, neglect, and woe
  Low'r'd awful o'er thy lovely trust,
NOVEMBER would have bid her go,
  And skulk into a grave accurst:—

But taught by *thee*, Heav'n's darling MAY,
  When the black tempest hid the skies,
She bow'd to its o'erwhelming sway,
  Then saw a *cloudless sun* arise!

Yes, lovely May! to thee she owes
  That conscious purity of soul,
Which, though it cannot *shield* from woes,
  Spurns their *unlimited* control!

Drear was the past detested hour!
  Her present bliss by contrast charms—
That past, forgotten, through thy pow'r,
  In a *deserving* husband's arms!

Still o'er her destiny preside.
  And grant that every future day,
Which, gentle month, shall o'er her glide,
  Be soothing and serene as MAY!

THE TOMB OF GENIUS.

WHERE the chilling north wind howls,
  Where the weeds so widely wave,
    Mourn'd by the weeping willow,
    Wash'd by the beating billow,
  Lies the youthful Poet's grave.

Beneath yon little eminence,
  Mark'd by the grass-green turf,
    The winding-sheet his form encloses,
    On the cold rock his head reposes—
  Near him foams the troubled surf!

"Roars around" his tomb "the ocean,"
  Pensive sleeps the moonbeam there!
    Naiads love to wreath his urn—
    Dryads thither hie to mourn—
  Fairy music melts in air!

O'er his tomb the village virgins
Love to drop the tribute-tear;
Stealing from the groves around,
Soft they tread the hallow'd ground,
And scatter wild flow'rs o'er his bier.

By the cold earth mantled—
All alone—
Pale and lifeless lies his form:
Batters on his grave the storm:
Silent now his tuneful numbers:
Here the son of Genius slumbers:
Stranger! mark his burial stone!

The following *jeu d'esprit* was written in the honor of a celebrated lady in Virginia by the name of MAYO, whose virtues, beauty, and accomplishments deserve a higher eulogium from an abler pen. The effort was more immediately prompted by a remark that the name of MAYO was no way susceptible of a pun. The poem was intended to be complete as an independent allegory, and, at the same time, appropriate in every reference to its subject.

PUZZLE.

FATIGU'D and restless, on my bed
I languish'd for the dawn of morrow,
Till slumber sooth'd my aching head,
And lull'd, in fairy dreams, my sorrow.

I seem'd in that serene retreat,[1]
Which smiles in spite of stormy weather;
Where flowers and virtues, clustering, meet,
And cheeks and roses blush together:

When soon twelve sylph-like forms, I dream'd,
Successive on my vision darted,
And still the latest comer seem'd
Fairer than she who just departed.

Yet *one* there was, whose azure eye
A melting, holy, lustre lighted,
Which censur'd, while it wak'd, the sigh,
And chid the feelings it excited.

---

[1] *The Hermitage,*—a delightful country residence of the lady, afterwards the wife of General Scott.

" Mortal!" a mystic speaker said,
" In these the sister months discover :—
Select from these the brightest maid,—
Prove to the brightest maid a lover."

I heard, and felt no longer free!
The dream dissolves, the sisters sever,
While raptur'd, I exclaim, " With thee,
Dear May! O, let me dwell forever!"

EPILOGUE.

An original play called " Pulaski" was acted at college, and Master Howard Payne,
at that time only fourteen years of age, and who sustained the only *female* character in
the play, was appointed to write and pronounce the epilogue. He spoke it in the dress
of *Lodoiska*, who entered hastily as the curtain fell.

I HASTE, kind guests, as you perhaps will say
A wretched pleader for a wretched play.
Oh, had you seen, repentant for his errors,
Our trembling author's frown-subduing terrors,
Even if you disapprov'd you would not show it,
But spare the work in pity of the poet!

But soft a while—let me a moment pause—
Speak for myself—and then assert his cause;
Tell me, *ye beaux*, are your affections free?
You need not answer, for I plainly see
That you're all dying, *luckless* beaux, for me!

Ladies! do you no indignation feel
That *Lodoiska* should your lovers steal?

Be calm, dear ladies! set your hearts at rest,
You shall retain your beaux, and make them blest!

For, lest a late discovery prove inhuman,
In time I'll tell them that their *fair's*—no woman.
" No woman!" say you?—gentle folks, don't stare!
The transformation is no more than fair!
So many women now *our breeches* wear
That *we must sport their dresses*, or go bare!

Says that young lady in the gunboat bonnet,
Or seems to say,—" WE, sir,—WE *wear the breeches,* sir !　Fie on it !"
Sweet Miss, I ask your pardon, but if you
The fact deny, I'll try to prove it true.

Are you not *soldiers ?*　Fight ye not with—eyes ?
And many a stout heart carry by surprise ?
Who can withstand " th' artillery of charms" ?
The harvest heroes yield—to woman's arms !

Are ye not *merchants ?* and to lose vexation
Do you not marry upon speculation,
And with the highest bidder make a trade
On which embargoes can be laid ?

But, woman-like, my tongue once under weigh
From the main point, has gone so far astray
That, self-absorb'd, I've quite forgot " Our play."

" Our play !" the critics sneeringly exclaim,—
" *Our farce*" were surely a much fitter name.

Remember, *critics,* what you've seen this night
Is but an unfledg'd poet's infant flight ;
'Tis yours to tempt him with bright plumes to rise,
Spring from the plain, and glitter in the skies ;
Like our own Eagle, a career to run,
Free as the air, and brilliant as the sun.

Ye lovely fair ! beneath whose guardian eyes
The humblest bud of genius never dies,
And with *your* cheering smiles this honest claim,—
" The *smiles of beauty* are the wreaths of fame."

FLATTERY.

Lines addressed to a lady who told the author she feared that the attention of the
world would spoil him, and unfit him for anything serious.　Written in 1806.

Oh, Lady ! hadst thou ever seen
The tear unbidden fill my eye,
Or mark'd me in the sportive scene,
To half suppress the rising sigh,—

Thou wouldst not think that Pleasure's glare
  Had blinded, and subdu'd my heart,
Or planted deep was, rankling there
  The poison of her glittering dart!—

True, fortune on my boyhood smil'd,
  And much of flatt'ry I have known,
Yet Sorrow claims me as her child,
  And early mark'd me for her own.

Tho' *joy has* burst its prison chains,
  And rapture started from its sleep,
They left me with severer pains,
  They taught me better how to weep!—

Few are the hours which beam like those
  That I have sweetly spent with you,
Which, brilliant 'mid a cloud of woes,
  In memory still their charms renew!

ON THE DEATH OF A LADY FRIEND.

DEATH with reluctant steps, half lingering, hies,
  And, arm'd with terror, pitying, shakes his spear!
He strikes, and as the lovely victim dies,
  Relenting, mourns her with a silent tear!

THE COQUETTE.

OH, tell me, sweet girl, ere we part,
  If your recent reproofs were sincere,
If that anger arose from the heart,
  Which glowed in those glances severe.

Did you mean, love, when lately we met,
  In earnest to frown thus and fly me?
Or, acting for once the *coquette,*
  Did you counterfeit rage but to try me?

Come! kiss and make up ere we part,
    And, dearest, I'll strive to amend!
For, depriv'd of my home in your heart,
    Where again shall I find such a friend?

ODE TO CLARA.

The following was written when Master Payne was twelve years of age, on reading some publications in a New York paper signed "Clara."

How oft have I essay'd in vain
    To swell the wond'rous wizard song,
Yet still the rude and rustic strain
    Groans on the lyre's unwilling tongue,
And hoarsely breathes, as if to chide
My erring and presumptuous pride!

Oh, Clara! since the muse denies
My wild, untutor'd strain to rise
With some bewitching melodies,
Deign thou, her darling, to inspire
My humble harp with hallow'd fire;
Teach it the magic of thy lyre,
That I may boldly forth and claim
Like thee, the choicest gift of fame,—
A deathless, great, and glorious name!

POEMS OF LATER DAYS.

COLLECTED FROM MR. PAYNE'S MANUSCRIPTS AND OTHER SOURCES

BY

GABRIEL HARRISON.

21

POEMS OF LATER DAYS.

CANZONET.

THOU,—oh, thou hast lov'd me,—dearest!
When none other cared for me,
When my fortune seem'd severest,
Kindest was the smile from thee!

Yes,—Ah, Yes!   The lorn and lonely
Hollow hearts of worldlings shun :
Theirs are flowers of day, which only
Open when they see the sun!

But while theirs were all reposing
In the absence of the light,
Like the cereus, thine, unclosing,
Gave its sweetness to the night.

THE LOSS OF THOSE; WE LOVE.

THE pang, of all severest,
Is the deep, withering one, that's borne
In being torn
From those we love the dearest.

Some griefs bear consolation!
There's none for this, no, none!   It breaks
The heart, and makes
The world a desolation!

A BIRTHDAY SONG.

WRITTEN FOR DR. DRAKE FOR A BIRTHDAY PARTY.

OH! speed the light hours!
With fancy's gay flowers
Life's dearest socialities gracefully wreathe!
Let the shadows of care
Meet like mists in the air,
While the warmth of thy sweetest kisses we breathe.

Oh! fill not the bowl!
'Tis the *wine of the soul*
That must gladden the spirits that mingle to-night:
Let it sparkle and dance
Like the dazzling expanse
Of the wave when the sunbeam has clothed it in light.

Oh! spread not the board
From luxury's hoard:
'Tis the pure *feast of feeling* we gather to share,—
Ambrosia of Heaven
Free, bounteously given,—
The East cannot furnish a banquet so fair.

Oh! cold is the heart
That would scorn to impart
Its brightness and glow to the hours as they glide:
Then hasten to weave
Sweet garlands; they'll leave
A beam, as we float, on Time's cold, ebbless tide.

STAR-GAZING:

AN EXCHANGE OF "IDLE THOUGHTS."

LIKE thee, I love the stars. In distant climes
I've stood alone and watch'd them; and have thought
I saw the spirits of departed friends
Smile in their loveliness; and then would dream

That some, not yet departed but far off,
Gazed with me on them ; and that I could feel
Their glance of kindness in the gentle light
Which cast its sweet spell round me. Then there seem'd
A music in the sphere, to charm away
The serpent sorrows gnawing at my heart,
Till, one by one, they dropp'd their demon hold,
And left me, all alone with contemplation,
Like thee, to love the stars.

Like thee, I love the stars. And thou hast made
Their radiance dearer yet. The poetry
Of thy imaginings, like sunbeams flung
Upon the waterfall, has wrapp'd those stars
In colors new and beautiful ; and now
O'er me bring visions of deeper power :
They call the mighty from their monuments ;
They fill the sky with old historic wonders ;
And, all commingling with the thoughts of her
Whose wand has wak'd this witchery, my soul
Swells with the blended glories, and I thrill
Like thee, to love the stars.

Like thee, I love the stars, and yet my fortunes
Have often seem'd to tell me, " Do not love them,
But give them hate for hate !" They never bless me ;
They hurl'd me forth on thwarted hopes, false friends,
And left me to those triumphs from the little
Which make the spirit wither up in scorn,—
But I can have no quarrel with them now,
Since one has risen o'er me in the west
Whose gentle beauty speaks for all the rest.
Shine on, sweet star ! still let me feel thy light.
For, though I know that light is not for me,
I would not have thy pity cloud the spell,
Whate'er its peril, which has taught me here.
In thee, to love the stars.

THE WATER-WITCH AND THE PILGRIM.

There is a tradition of Correggio, which some Italian poet has wrought into a play, that contains the following singular fancy for its plot. Penniless, he had hurried from his home to the mansion of a rich man with a picture which had been ordered, urging him for immediate compensation. The rich man pompously paid the amount all in *coppers*, but Correggio, exulting in the good fortune of getting all his pay, accepted the indignity without particular notice, and hastened away with the relief so anxiously sought for. When near his destination, overpowered with fatigue and thirst from the weight of his treasure and the terrible heat of the day, he came to a beautiful pond of water with a natural fountain springing from the side of a brook. The cool, clear, bright waters invited him to partake of the refreshing treasure. He eagerly drank from it, and while he drank, mysterious music came over his ear as from a fairy spirit in the water. For a moment he was fluttered and thought it a warning or a prophecy, but with a light heart he passed on to his home, and the song of the fountain was soon forgotten in his rapture at the bright face and the warm welcome his charming little wife gave on his return. Yet scarcely had he caught her sweet smile when the poison of the icy draught darted through him, and in an instant he remembered the mystic song of the waters, and, as he flung the sack of money before his adored wife, he expired. The following is the substance of the song of which the Italian poet has given the idea.

A WATER-NYMPH lurks in the cliff's hollow side,
And a pilgrim lies faint by the wild, whirling tide ;
Where, 'midst rainbow and cloud, the lone waterfall springs,
And its curtain of foam o'er the haunted cave flings.
     . Hark ! the lay
     Of the Fay !
"Come hither, come hither, poor pilgrim to me ;
From sorrow and sighing thy bosom I'll free ;
And thou shalt a fairy's blest paramour be !

" Plunge, world-weary pilgrim ! plunge deep in the wave !
Once mine, thou wilt smile as it storms o'er our cave ;
For never false friend or sad heart-ache may come
Through the rush of white waters that curtain our home.
     And away
     Shall the spray
Wash mortality's clay from the care-canker'd soul ;
Long dreams of delight o'er thy senses shall roll,
And new life wilt thou quaff from the fairy's charm'd bowl."

He struggles to rise as he hears the fond strain,
But sinks on the flood's giddy margin again ;
From her wave-curtained cavern the water-nymph trips,
And fatal the goblet she holds to his lips.
     Quick the thrill
     Of death's chill
Has run through his marrow and curdled his blood ;
His faint shriek is echoed by cavern and wood,
And wildly he plunges beneath the dark flood.

His winding-sheet was a whirlpool's white spray,
And a bubble bore his last life-breath away ;
Deep, deep lies the pilgrim beneath the cold stream,
And dimly his bones through the clear water gleam.

But at night
The false sprite
In pale moonshine oft glides from her damp-dropping hall,
The ghost of the wave-buried pilgrim to call;
And they dance, and they shriek o'er the wild waterfall!

— .

THE THRONE AND THE COTTAGE.

I.

THERE once was a king on his throne of gold seated ;
His courtiers in smiles were all standing around ;
They heard him with news of fresh victories greeted ;
The skies with the joy of his people resound ;
And all thought this king was most thoroughly blest,
Till sadly he sigh'd forth his secret unrest:

" How much more delight to my bosom 'twould bring
To feel myself happy, than know myself king!"

II.

" Ah, what, while such power and such treasure possessing,"
(A courtier, astonish'd, stept forward and cried,)
" Could fortune bestow in exchange for the blessing?"
And thus to the courtier the king straight replied :
" Health, a cottage, few friends and a heart all my own
Were Heav'n, in exchange for the cares of a throne !"

" Then, sire, if no longer to empire you cling,
Seek these, and be happy, and let *me* be king !"

III.

The king gave the courtier his throne and descended;
He long'd for delights of retirement to prove,
And now for the first time around him there blended
The smiles of contentment, and friendship, and love
But the courtier soon came to the king in his cot ;.
" Oh, no !" said the king, " I'll no more change my lot !
Think not, that, once freed from the diadem's sting,
I'll give up my cottage and stoop to be king !"

VALENTINE.

TO A BEAUTIFUL YOUNG ACTRESS.

THERE is a heart, (I dare not say
　　Where that heart dwells,) whose fondest dream
(Though wild and hopeless,) many a day
　　Has been the angel which you seem :
And though the world has taught that heart,—
　　(Oh, may such lessons ne'er to thee
The world—stern monitor!—impart!)
　　Taught it to seem is not to be;

Yet who would not such doubt discard,
　　That see thy loveliness and youth
Enshrine the visions of the bard,
　　And turn his poetry to truth?
Would that I knew thee! and yet still
　　So strongly do I feel its dangers,
The very wish to know thee will
　　Perhaps forever keep us strangers!
When once we met, of all who live
　　I thought that there was none but thee
Who could a charm to bondage give,
　　Or take the charm from liberty,—
And therefore 'tis on such a theme
　　My truant feelings dread to dare,
And rather choose of hope to dream
　　Than rashly to ensure despair;
For I'm not vain enough to think
　　It were not madness to aspire
To charms like thine,—and so I shrink
　　From that which I the most desire—
The most desire, though love which seeks
　　By selfishness its truth to prove,
Is undeserving thee—and speaks
　　The voice of passion, not of love!
Then never shalt thou know whose hand
　　'Tis now declares the secret feeling
Which at once dreads disclosure, and
　　Still finds relief in the revealing!

And while, at times, I hope once more
That we may meet as once we met,—
Grow more acquainted than before,
With chances more propitious, yet
If ne'er by me to be possess'd,
Elsewhere thy love turns,—let it go—
Enough for me to know thee blest,
And feel thee worthy to be so.

HOME, SWEET HOME!

AS ORIGINALLY WRITTEN. THE ACCEPTED VERSION AS ARRANGED FOR
THE MUSIC IS INTRODUCED IN THE FORE PART OF THIS BOOK.

'MID pleasures and palaces though we may roam,
Be it ever so humble, there's no place like Home!
A charm from the skies seems to hallow us there,
(Like the love of a mother,
Surpassing all other,)
Which, seek through the world, is ne'er met with elsewhere.
There's a spell in the shade
Where our infancy play'd,
Even stronger than Time, and more deep than despair!

An exile from Home, splendor dazzles in vain!
Oh, give me my lowly, thatch'd cottage again!
The birds and the lambkins that came at my call,—
Those who nam'd me with pride,—
Those who play'd by my side,—
Give me them! with the innocence dearer than all!
The joys of the palaces through which I roam
Only swell my heart's anguish—There's no place like Home!

The following additional verses to the song of "Home, Sweet Home!" Mr. Payne
affixed to the sheet-music, and presented them to Mrs. Bates, in London, a relative of
his, and the wife of a rich banker:

To *us*, in despite of the absence of years,
How sweet the remembrance of *home* still appears;
From allurements abroad, which but flatter the eye,
The unsatisfied heart turns, and says, with a sigh,
"Home, home, sweet, sweet home!
There's no place like home!
There's no place like home!"

Your exile is blest with all fate can bestow;
But *mine* has been checkered with many a woe!
Yet, tho' different our fortunes, our thoughts are the same,
And both, as we think of Columbia, exclaim,
"Home, home, sweet, sweet home!
There's no place like home!
There's no place like home!"

THE LAND OF MY BIRTH.

A SONG.

I.

I'VE rov'd 'mid the wonders of many a clime,
Fair cities, sweet valleys, and mountains sublime,
But ne'er saw a clime half so lovely on earth
As the land of my first love, the land of my birth!
Land of my first love! Oh, land of my birth!
Thou, thou art the loveliest land upon earth.

II.

Far away have I hung on the love of the wise,
And bask'd in the sunshine of soul-thrilling eyes,
But the land of true wisdom, and beauty, and worth,
Is the land of my first love, the land of my birth!
Land of my first love! Oh, land of my birth,
Thou, thou art the loveliest land upon earth;
Land of my first love! sweet land of my birth!

III.

Still dear and more dear, the more distant thou art,
My footsteps have left thee, but never my heart!
That magnet still turns from all over the earth
To the land of my first love, the land of my birth!
The land of my first love, the land of my birth,
Thou, thou art the loveliest land upon earth;
Land of my first love! blest land of my birth!

INCLEDON'S DÉBUT IN AMERICA.

The following was written to be sung by Incledon himself. Shield made admirable music for it: whether it was sung or not, I could never learn—J. H. P.

HAIL Columbia! patriot nation!
Star of hope to the opprest!
In battle, darting desolation!
But in peace, sole ark of rest!

Parted far from friends that lov'd him,
Torn from children he adores,—
Driv'n from those who first approv'd him
To the shelter of thy shores—

Shores which shar'd his youth's affection!—
Hither forc'd in age to roam—
Here, the stranger seeks protection!
The "Wandering Melodist"[1] a home!

Free as the wave your coast thus dashes,
To glory your young eagle springs!
But tho' her eye with terror flashes,
Comfort dwells beneath her wings!

THE WANDERER.

THE mother of a young lamb died,
And left it helpless on the wild.
A shepherd found it, 'twas his pride,—
He lov'd it almost like a child,—
It never left him—'till one day
He looked and 'twas no longer there!
"My precious lamb is gone astray!
In vain I seek her everywhere!

[1] "Wandering Melodist" was the title given by Incledon to an entertainment with which he travelled, and in which he was the sole performer.

She's gone! my lov'd one's gone!" he cried,
" My hope is gone, my joy, my pride!"
And only Echo's voice replied,
           "She's gone! she's gone!"

But soon the thoughtless truant yearn'd
  For him she left so desolate,
And when the shepherd home return'd,
  He found her at his cottage gate!
The shepherd did not then disdain
  The lamb he had so loved before,
But took it to his heart again,
  Forgave it, and it stray'd no more!
" She's here!" the exulting shepherd cried,
" She never more will quit my side!"
And both with Echo now replied,
           " She's here, she's here!"

LEARNING, LOVE, AND VICTORY.

I.

WHEN the Parson woo'd me, then
I could never say " Amen!"
When the doctor,—what a pill!
His addresses made me ill!
When the Lawyer,—what a pest!
I was—" non inventus est!"
But oh! now the soldier comes,
With " presented arms" to me,
He may—" Hurrah"—" Victory!"

II.

What girl in the Parson's whine
E'er discover'd aught divine?
When did the Physician's art
Cure the ague of the heart?
Or the Lawyer's *habeas* move
Suitors to the court of Love?
But when martial steeds are bounding,
And the war-like clarion sounding,
Who would not " ground arms" like me?
To the " Hurrah," " Victory!"

THE LOSS OF THOSE WE LOVE.

THE pang, of all severest,
  Is the deep, withering one, that's borne
    In being torn
From those we love the dearest.

Some griefs bear consolation!
  There's none for this,—no, none! It breaks
    The heart, and makes
The world a desolation! .

A GIRL'S MESSAGE TO HER LOVER.

I.

TELL him, though fortune dooms that we must part,
I cannot make his image leave my heart;
Tell him that they may keep me from him,—yet
He's with me still, as though we hourly met.

II.

Wealth and Glories, tell him, all are dim
To the sweet sunshine of one thought of him,—
And feelings, deeper than the tongue can tell,
Have grown even deeper since I sigh'd Farewell!

FIRST LOVE.

How refin'd the feeling
O'er the bosom stealing,
A new sense revealing,
    In the heart's first love!

Its soft spell extending,
Smiles to all things lending,
The whole world seems blending
      With the heart's first love!

If to new themes turning,
Soon, such lightness spurning,
Stronger grows our yearning
      For the heart's first love.

THE MEETINGS OF LOVERS.

Oh, how sweet, how sweet,
  The rapture felt at last,
  Wearisome exile past,
When lovers meet, when lovers meet!

Then love's sorrow fleet!
  Hours so hard to bear between
  Are as though they ne'er had been,
When lovers meet, when lovers meet!

BEAUTY'S GLANCE.

WRITTEN FOR AN INTERLUDE.

Woe to the heart! when Beauty's eye
  O'er its unwaken'd pulse first rushes,
Kindling wild visions,—like the sky
  New lighted up by morning's blushes.

For storm-clouds may convulse the air,
  As the uncertain day advances ;
And Beauty's eye may flash despair
  On the adorer of its glances.

Ne'er did a sigh this bosom swell
  Till thy enchantments smil'd around it ;
And, oh! it trembles now to tell
  Its throb to her whose spell has bound it.

But do not, dearest! do not blame
This falt'ring utt'rance of a feeling,
My tongue has not the strength to name
Nor my heart courage for concealing.

Cast one—one rapturing glance, to end
The doubt I tremble to discover;
I must—I must be—more than *friend*,—
And may I not be—more than lover?

THE FORSAKEN.

A SONG.

SCENES of my childhood, the roseate hours,
Passed in your shelter, are faded!
Gone are the spirits which gladden'd your bowers,
Gone with the pleasures they shaded!
Farewell!

Dove of the ark! to thee Providence gave
Rest, once thy pilgrimage ended!
Fate, which flings me on the world-troubled wave
Dooms me to toss there unfriended!
Ah me!

Eyes of affection! Life's pathway no more
Beams, with your radiance lighted!
Hope, Love, and Friendship, which shone there before
Leave me to wander benighted!
All's dark!

SUNRISE.

HAIL to thee, orb of morning!
O'er the darkness breaking,
Earth with thy smile adorning,
Man to his God awaking;
Hail! Hail! may our devotion be
Warm as the light we hail in thee!

THE CONSOLATION.

COMFORT, mourner! why despair?
Storm like sunshine 's from on high—
Tempest only clears the sky—
    Man is heaven's peculiar care—
Heaven brings joy from misery!

Comfort, mourner! why despair?
Woe a part is of a plan
Ending in the bliss of man—
    Whereof but a little share
Our imperfect sight may scan!

Comfort, mourner! why despair?
All that is disclos'd we find
Proveth an All-bounteous mind—
    Impious is it then to dare
Deem what's undisclos'd unkind!

Arouse thee! comfort! Learn to bear!
No *ill* is cureless *but* despair!

UNHALLOWED AND VIRTUOUS LOVE.

UNHALLOW'D love's a withering flame
Which kills the heart and blasts the name,
    By its wild flashes risen;
While virtuous love, like sunlight showers,
But wakes the heart's most lovely flowers
    And opens them to heaven.

THE WORLD.

I.

Oh ! no ! I have no wish to try
   Those heartless mockeries of joy
Whose charm is like the serpent's eye,
   Which only dazzles to destroy !
Ne'er let me be among the mad—
   Nay, worse,—the guilty million hurl'd,—
I never yet have known the bad—
   I never yet have known the world !

II.

Can the world aught, for what is this
   Seclusion I should lose, bestow?
Our little home is full of bliss,
   But the great world is full of woe !
My humble heart, like yonder vines
   Around our lowly cottage curl'd,
With all I here have known, entwines,—
   And here, oh, here shall be my world.

BEAUTY SLEEPING.

   Sweet is her sleep !
As moonlight that sleeps on the river
Where evening's soft sighs scarcely quiver.
   Sweet is her sleep !

The charm of that beautiful face
O'er the image of death beams a grace !
   Sweet is her sleep !

The angel of slumber she seems,
Reclined in her heaven of dreams !
   Sweet is her sleep.

22

THE FRIENDLESS ORPHAN GIRL.

WORDS TO AN OLD IRISH MELODY.

FROM slumbers that cheer not, with dawn's blush upspringing
Woe-worn, I wander o'er mountain and plain,
And hear parent birds to their little ones singing
    Songs of affection in that touching strain,
            From others
            Than mothers
        We seek for in vain!
        There's many a tie
        The world may supply,
        But oh! there's no other
        The loss of a mother,—
            Oh, none!
            Not one!

But scenes of endearment which round me are thronging,
    Bitterly teach me how much I'm alone!
A parent's fond care to all beings belonging—
    Tenderness ever in infancy shown
            To others
            By mothers
        I never have known!
        There's many a tie
        The world might supply,
        But oh! there's no other
        The loss of a mother,—
            Oh, none!
            Not one!

———— ·· ——

THE HARP.

On, lady! take the harp,
    And let the silent string,
Exulting at thy touch,
    Around its magic fling!

Enshrin'd there, as in thee
  Enchantments, slumb'ring deep,
A wait a master-hand
  To break their bonds of sleep!

Thanks, lady! how the harp,
  By thee awaken'd, beams
The light upon despair
  Of soft Elysian dreams:
Could I but thus awake
  The slumbering thrill in you,
The dreams your harp inspires
  Your smile would render true.

—

PASSION AND PRAYER.

THE holy prisoner doom'd to bear
  Demoniac persecution's chain,
Hop'd humbly a protection where
  Sincerity ne'er hopes in vain!

Lo! on the darkness of his cell
  The glory of an angel flash'd!
The jailers slept! the fetters fell!
  The bolted portals open dash'd.

Prisoner of passion! if sincere
  Your trust in Heaven's protection be,
An angel will to you appear,
  And when least look'd for, set you free!

— — — —

THE HOPES OF YOUTH.

To youth, exulting, soon delighted,
    The coming hours,
Seen by Hope's April sunshine, lighted,
    Blooming with flow'rs
Ne'er to be blighted!

                    Proudly the barque
        Sails, when blue skies and blue seas flatter :
                    The storm comes.   Hark—
        A shriek I her sides the wild waves shatter !
                    She's gone !—all's dark.

        Such are youth's fairy dreams of gladness ;—
                    And thus they end
        In tempests of unlook'd for sadness,—
                    Tortures,—that send
        The soul to madness !

                        —

SLANDER DIES IN LIGHT.

                        I.

        FROM the coward who stabs in the dark
            What valor can give us protection ?
                    But once let me know
                    Where to fix on my foe,
        And see how he'll shrink from detection !

                        II.

        The pride of the forest, whose strength
            Bends not to the hurricane's fury,
                    May fall by the sting
                    Of the venomous thing
        Which the least of its small leaves would bring.

                        III.

        But, drag forth the reptile, he'll writhe,
            He'll die when the day-beam is brightening,
                    As the mischievous lie
                    Of the imposture shall die
        In the blaze of Truth's glorious lightning !

TO MISS O'NEIL, THE ACTRESS.

Written after sleeping in the room she had occupied the night before. Waterford,
Ireland, July, 1814.

OH, deep was the gloom which my spirits deprest,
  Till each object around breath'd the joy of the past;
And the charm of that room lull'd my sorrows to rest,
  As pure as the bosom which beat in it last!

Then my proud love exulted. It felt that the hour
  Which succeeds common pleasure, is shrouded in woe,
But gloried in owning the sway of a power
  Whose remembrance alone can such comfort bestow!

'Twas a feeling extatic, I blest its control ;
  And your image, still beaming on memory's gaze,
Sheds a twilight of joy on my desolate soul,
  More soft, though less dear, than the noon of its blaze !

- - - -

A SONG IN THE OPERA OF CLARI.

IN the promise of pleasure, the silly believer,
      Home forsaking, to brave
      The betraying world's wave,
Is soon taught by woe the truth friendship had spoken,
And virtue a wreck,—pleasure's promises broken,—
Lost at last, the world's scorn by the wily deceiver,
Finds out but too late, that where ever we roam,—
There's no pleasure abroad, like the pleasure of Home !

But droop not, poor castaway ! be not dejected !
      From the tempest-wave spring !
      To your wreck'd virtue cling !
And be certain the angel of mercy takes care
Of the virtue, though erring, that will not despair !
Yes ! though from the world's heartless bosom rejected,
From your home upon earth tho' cast houseless to roam,
Throw your glance up to Heaven, and be sure of a Home !

THE EXILE.

A song written at the request of, and set to music composed by, the celebrated Mr. Heinrich.

FAR from the land which gave him birth,
  The lonely exile wandering weary,
Feels that the loveliest land on earth,
  When look'd upon thro' tears, looks dreary.
For, oh! when Fortune grew unkind,
  And in the spell of sorrow bound him,
There came a shadow o'er his mind,
  To darken every object round him.

But, as often the sunbeam breaks brilliant and warm
On the day whose beginning was coldness and storm,
Even thus unexpectedly, fortunes more bright,
Now light back the exile to home and delight!
And though since his escape, he'll oft gaze from the shore
On the billows he saw with such terror before,
Yet to think of a peril that's happily past,
Only heightens the rapture which follows at last.

THE GIRL OF MY HEART.

THERE's nothing, there's nothing so lovely that lives
      As thou art, dear!
There's nothing, there's nothing that pleasure gives,
      And thou art near!

When thou art away the world's brightest charms
      Look—oh, how drear!
But a magic spell its form disarms
      When thou art near!

When thou art away, even summer's beams
      All cold appear!
But the coldest winter a summer seems
      Beside thee, dear!

VALENTINE.

ADDRESSED TO MISS FOOT, THE CELEBRATED ACTRESS.

THOUGH other eyes have warn'd me,
Though other lips have charm'd me,
Yet transient was their pow'r,
Forgotten in an hour !

Those brows of thine which darkle
O'er eyes which sweetly sparkle
With beams from mind of brightness,
And heart of jocund lightness ;—
Have wing'd, like Cupid's bow,
With secret shaft a blow
Which binds one, thine forever
In chains which cannot sever,
Ere this, a captive never.

Perhaps, in untold anguish
That captive long will languish :—
Perhaps, a hidden stranger,
He'll guard thy youth from danger :—
Perhaps, an unseen spirit,
He'll climb thy couch at night,
And rock himself to rest
Upon thy heaving breast,
Or drink the sighs which creep
Unconscious through thy sleep.

And then, like memory's gleams,
Glide softly through thy dreams,
And catch without control
The breathings of a soul
So unstain'd in whiteness,
Malice hates its brightness !

Nymph, by whom all are charmed,
Long may'st thou live unharm'd !
—Be world and Fortune kind !
Be Argus Envy blind,—
And every wish enjoy'd,
Save that which would discover
Thy Valentine and Lover !

PRINCE ·YPSILANTI'S ADDRESS TO THE GREEKS.

YE Greeks, for deeds of glory fam'd,
The gods for freedom have proclaim'd
    The password's Liberty!
Convince the foes of human kind   .
Not adamantine chains can bind
    The men who dare be free!

Leonidas, your sire of old,
In deeds of arms proud Xerxes told
    At fam'd Thermopylæ,
That he and his brave patriot band
Could die to save their native land,
    Or perish to be free!

Immortal honors crown your deeds,
To victory Ypsilanti leads—
    Now strike for Liberty!
Teach the oppressors of mankind
No manacles on earth can bind
    The men who dare be free!

SCENE FROM AN UNPUBLISHED PLAY.

BY JOHN HOWARD PAYNE.

Argument.

Early in life Bianca of Naples returned the love of the reckless and enthusiastic Hyppolito, but his father thought a wealthier wife might be found, and sent the youth abroad; at sea he was wrecked, but saved by pirates and detained a captive. Being supposed dead by his family and Bianca, she is at length prevailed on to listen to a new suitor. She weds a Spaniard by the name of Alvar, equally a devotee to her and to the fine arts, and who met her when he visited Italy on a tour of taste. Hyppolito, escaping, returns, and hears that his betrothed is lost to him. In madness he pursues her to her dwelling in Barcelona, and, being skilled in the pencil, obtains access to her husband by spreading his fame abroad as an Italian painter of eminence, hurrying through the city. Alvar has seen his sketches, and earnestly desires from him a portrait of Bianca. On a carnival night, when she is masked for the festivities, Hyppolito consents, as a special favor to Don Alvar, to spare an hour for a sitting. His object may be guessed. It is a delirious desire to disclose himself, and carry her away with him in the confusion of the masquerade. The scene here given describes the introduction of the imagined painter.

SCENE.

An apartment in Don Alvar's palace at Barcelona. Busts—statues—an easel—swing-glass—painting apparatus.

Don Alvar enters, leading Bianca, both sumptuously habited in masquerade dresses, Bianca as a Sultana. Hyppolito follows as a painter, completely disguised. He takes his colors and pencils from an attendant. While he arranges them and reconnoitres the room, Alvar and Bianca converse apart at the front.

BIANCA. (*To Alvar aside.*) Who is this painter? Were 't not well, my
    lord,
That he should come to-morrow, not to-night?
His look is strange. You must not leave me here—
I know not why—I feel a sudden dread—
His countenance is wild—What is his name?
    ALVAR. And why so fanciful, my gentle love?
The Signor's name is Manso—known to all
As a most famous artist. He has come
To Barcelona but this morn; and flies
To-morrow—Heav'n knows where!—(*to Hyppolito.*)
    Sir, is this place
The one that suits your art?—Sit here, Bianca,
(*Aside to her.*) How your hand trembles! I'll stay with you, love!

HYP. (*Preparing to paint.*) A little from the light—a little more!
(*Aside.*) His glance is keen—those lights will show my face—
(*He tries to sketch, and stops.*) Pray you, my lord, a little farther back—
The lights fall on your robe—or, take your place—
(—Your pardon, lord)—behind me till the sketch
Is made—(*he tries, and flings down the pencil in vexation.*)
Corpo di Giovo, wrong!—This crowd of lights—
(*Pointing with a fretted gesture to the lamps on the table.*)
ALV. (*To Cariola.*) Go—carry off those lamps—their varying blaze
Will mar the pencil. Benedetto!
Order the train to hold themselves prepared
To wait upon your lady to the fête.
[*Benedetto and other servants go out, carrying the lamps, and leaving but one
light beside the easel. Hyppolito paints.*]
HYP. Please you, fair lady, cast your eyes above—
Ha! so—as if you gazed upon some star!
(*Looking at her.*) Now press your hand—deeply—upon your heart
As if you vowed that heart's fidelity
And sealed it by your hopes of love in Heaven.
ALV. A most romantic painter! But his art
Or finds men mad, or makes them so —That touch
(*Looking at the picture.*) Is life—I see the master-hand! How fine
The power to fix the hue of beauty's cheek,
The sparkling of the diamond eye,—the look
That speaks without a tongue, yet speaks the soul
Quicker than tongue e'er uttered—Glorious art!
That, with the power of miracle, defies
The truth of time, the blight of worldly woe,
All earthly trouble! On its tablet smiles
Beauty unsullied; cheeks unwash'd by tears;
Lips that will ne'er grow pale with anxious sighs;
Youth, love, and loveliness, alike immortal!
(*He looks at the picture.*) Magnificent! Divine!
The artist does you justice, my Bianca.
BIAN. My lord turn'd flatterer! Nay, I fear I'll shame
The Signor Manso's pencil.
HYP.   'Tis but honor'd
Too highly in its subject.—Now look down—
—Heavens, what a rich possession!—(*to her.*) But one smile—
(*As in soliloquy.*) The arching of that brow—that dazzling eye—
That lip to which the budding of the rose
Were colorless and chill—Thou paragon!—
BIAN. (*Aside, agitated at half overhearing him.*)
     What words are those? Some pressure on my soul
Tells me there's evil nigh! (*Aside to Alvar.*) Alvar! My lord!
Stay by me.—Will the Signor soon be done?—
ALV. Disturb him not, my love. He touches now

The finest lines of his most lovely work.
(*Looking over the sketch.*) Bravo, Signor! A Titian were outdone
With that delicious coloring. That glow
Is worthy the Venetian.

HYP.   I was his pupil—
An idle one—but worshipped at his feet
For some wild years, enamor'd of the fame,
The glory that he threw around his land!
But, when he died, I hated Venice—fled—
And wander'd, on a painter's pilgrimage,
To every shrine of loveliness.

BIAN. (*Aside.*) He gazes on me strangely. If on earth
There's magic in a glance—delusion wild,
Or dangerous spell, 'tis in that fiery eye!
Would that his work were done!—
(*To Alvar.*) How goes the hour, my lord? Your noble friend
Will think his banquet scorn'd by our delay.

HYP. (*Gazing on her.*) One look—but one look, gentle lady, one
And all is finished—Pray you, draw aside
That tress which hangs upon your brow like braids
Of silk on ivory. (*Aside.*) *There's* a living smile!
A glance that strikes the soul like sudden flame!

ALV. (*Gazing on the picture.*) It grows in light and beauty, as the sky
Before the rosy chariot the morn!—
—Signor, your task is finish'd for to-night,
And richly finish'd.
My lady well reminds me 'twill be late
Before we reach our kinsman's.—(*To Bianca.*) Come, my love!

BIAN. (*Aside.*) Thanks, all ye saints that guard the heart from ill!

HYP. One moment more. This must be done to-night,
Or may-be never. By to-morrow's dawn
I leave the walls of Barcelona.

BIAN. Nay, Alvar, come—'tis finish'd—lose no time—
(*Urging him.*) We must not fail in courtesy.

ALV. (*Looking at the picture.*) 'Tis beautiful!—(*Then turning to Bianca.*)
       Yet still, how feebly art
Contends with nature, when that nature's thine!
He that can thaw the ice with pictured flame,
Or banish darkness by a painted sun,
Or fill the summer sky with painted gold,
Or shower the spring's sweet lap with painted buds,
He may portray the living witchery
Of woman in her beauty—but none else!

HYP. Fair lady, look again—
ALV.   Yes—rest awhile—
I will but go a moment, to command
That all be ready for our cavalcade.

(*To Hyppolito.*) Signor! the moment you sought is given—
I shall return—(*to Bianca*)—as swift as thoughts of love!

[*Exit Alvar.*

HYP. (*Looking after Alvar—aside.*) He's gone!—Now, love and ven-
    geance!

(*Starts up, throws off his disguise, and exclaims,*) Bianca!

BIAN. (*Terrified and springing back.*) Hyppolito!—

*   *   *   *   *   *   *   *

OUR

NEGLECTED POETS.

BY

JOHN HOWARD PAYNE.

OUR NEGLECTED POETS.

PART I.

WILLIAM MARTIN JOHNSON.

In the State of Massachusetts there are four towns rejoicing in the quaint names of Needham, and Wareham, and Wrentham, and Mendum. Modern refinement may perhaps have seen proper to reform this expressive nomenclature, as there is no knowing what it will stop at; it is to be hoped not, however. The town of Wrentham, the one with which we have now to do, is in Norfolk County, nearly midway between Boston and Providence; and has long been famous for its manufactures, especially of cotton goods and straw bonnets. About the year 1775 a sea-captain by the name of Ebenezer Albee, though in low circumstances, had withdrawn from active life and settled down at Wrentham. He was a man of great kindness of heart, but blunt in his manners, and boisterous in his temper. He had no children. He was fond of reading, but, unfortunately, with the revolutionary sentiments of the day in politics, he had also imbibed those which, in the general agitation of ideas of the time, were too prevalent in religion.

A vagabond pair, concerning whose origin nothing can be learned, were in the habit of prowling Massachusetts and Connecticut on foot, sometimes together, sometimes apart, but in either case both of them often reeling under the influence of the Bacchus of New England,—cider. They had all the tastes and habits of wandering beggars. They had a child with them, a squalid, unhealthy, but quick-witted boy. No one knew whether they had ever been married; but they called themselves Johnson, and said the child was theirs, and that his name was William Martin Johnson. The father never took much notice of the boy. The mother always seemed to have a strong attachment for him.

These rovers frequently came to the house of Captain Albee. The good-hearted captain had ceased to hope for children of his own. Little Johnson's answers and observations delighted him He proposed to adopt the boy. The father was pleased with the chance of getting rid of a burden. The mother was reluctant to give up her child. Finally, however, with tears, she consented. For a while she occasionally visited him; but ere long was seen no more. Thus did the subject of this narrative enter within the pale of civilized and decent life.

Albee, by all accounts, among other habits of "a rude and boisterous cap-

tain of the sea," was somewhat given to the great vice of our country, intemperance. This may account for outbreaks of unreasonable passion, succeeded by fits of equally unmeasured indulgence, which rendered the situation
of his adopted favorite very uneasy, and equally unpropitious to a sound formation of character. Still, the boy was strongly attached to his protector.
Albee imparted to him all the instruction he had to communicate, and Johnson repaid his pains with an unusual precocity. He early learned to write
his signature at full length, William Martin Johnson Albee. But the affectionate captain had a sort of primitive, puritanical, as well as maritime respect
for the efficacy of the rope's end and the rod in education; and whenever he
had nothing else to do, would belabor his favorite so heartily that the boy
would run away and remain from home until there should be time for the
paroxysm of discipline to give place to one of endearment, and then, like a
beaten pet pup, he would creep back again to be caressed. It was not long
before the lad began to get ahead of his domestic teacher in accomplishment,
and to add to his stock of solid and reputable knowledge, from the spelling-
book and the five first rules of ciphering, certain acquirements of an extremely
doubtful virtue, which greatly alarmed the serious good people of Wrentham;
for it was discovered that he could draw, and even that he could rhyme; and
nobody could divine how these unhallowed arts could have been obtained by
a child, in his position, unless through some vestiges of the witchcraft, which
might have been still left, by imperfect exorcism, to disturb the but recently
achieved repose of New England from the spirits of mischief. To this suspicion, it is likely, we may attribute divers misadventures which materially
influenced the future career of young Johnson. When his protector had
taught out all he himself knew, he considered the boy entitled to the advantage of such instruction as was to be derived from certain peripatetic peda-
gogues who used periodically to visit the villages of New England, for the
purpose of qualifying young folks for college. Johnson was now about
twelve years of age. His progress in Latin was rapid, and he got a smat-
tering of Greek. But his teachers were often of the Dominie Sampson breed,
and the boy had a quick sense of the ridiculous, and an unfortunate talent
for expressing it equally with the pen and pencil. His tasks were dis-
patched with a rapidity perfectly inexplicable to the duller scholars and to
the obtuse master; and the leisure which remained to him was usually devoted to the gratification of his taste for the roguery of caricature. Though
he was so far from ever being found wanting in the fulfilment of his duties,
that the rest of the boys could never get at all near him, his instructors
thought it peculiarly unfair that his merits should deprive him of the benefits
of flagellation; and as he was too perverse to give himself a legitimate claim
to the birch, they would show their high consideration by favoring him with
it as a sort of gratuitous perquisite. After any of these frequent scenes, the
master would be greeted, either on scraps of paper scattered about the school-
room, or in a colossal effigy charcoaled upon the wall, with a view of his own
dignified person, set off by such grotesque additions as the artist's invention
could supply, and flourishing the awful wand of inspiration over some scream-
ing recipient of virtue and wisdom, most remorselessly administered. This

style of retribution was not very likely to better his condition, and he was regarded as utterly irreclaimable. He would continue to escape and to return; but was, nevertheless, every day increasing his stock of knowledge; and at sixteen had added a very considerable progress in algebra to his acquirements in the languages.

As nearly as we can conjecture, it must have been about the year 1787 that young Johnson found employment with a store-keeper in Boston. His hand-writing was very beautiful, and he was a ready accountant. I am in posses-sion of a sheet (amongst a great variety of interesting papers and relics of poor Johnson which fell into my hand by a series of strange accidents) covered with fragments in his autograph of that period; and among them the following broken lines, which I can well imagine were scribbled at the shop-counter, in the intervals of the uncongenial task of posting the account-book. They may have an interest to the reader, as affording an unconscious glimpse of his mind, and an illustration of the strange, rambling, unbalanced child of genius that he was at the time. They are all evidently the desultory, extemporaneous effusions of the varying mood of the hour.

> "So the proud bubble strikes the eye
> With hues that with the diamond vie;
> But search beyond its surface fair,
> There's nothing found but empty air.
>
>   *   *   *   *   *   *   *
>
> "Pleas'd thus, to worth the muse her tribute pays,
> To worth, that well deserves a nobler praise—
>
>   *   *   *   *   *   *   *
>
> "As northern lights dance o'er the evening sky,
> And strike with transient charms the admiring eye,
> So o'er her face the hastening blushes flew—
>
>   *   *   *   *   *   *   *
>
> "Oh, follow then where nonsense leads the way,
> Like idle flies that in the sunbeams play—
>
>   *   *   *   *   *   *   *
>
> "On some good bit I'd always wish to dine,
> And after dinner drink a glass of wine;
> That, too, I'd have of the most generous sort,
> Madeira, Sherry, or the best of Port—
>
> "——With perhaps a good heart, but the worst face in nature.
>
>   *   *   *   *   *   *   *
>
> "Where towering columns proudly rise,
> And gilded spires invade the skies,
> My humble wishes ne'er shall learn to rove,
> Nor sigh for more than competence and love.
>
>   *   *   *   *   *   *   *

"——People who have no ideas out of the common road are generally the greatest talkers, because all their thoughts are low enough for common conversation, whereas those of more elevated understandings have ideas which they cannot easily communi-cate, except to persons of equal capacity with themselves.

*   *   *   *   *   *   *
" The glowing sun, with life-infusing beam,
    Impregns the vegetable world; the flowers,
    Not coy nor shrinking from the warm embrace,
    But sweetly wanton, blushing soft desires,
    To meet his kisses, turn their nectary lips,
    Incessant sipping, with increasing heat,
    Till mutual vigor and intenser love
    Their nuptials crown. The silver rustling rills,
    With knotted rushes fringed   *   *   *
*   *   *   *   *   * and to the sun
    Far glittering o'er the meadow's fragrant breast,
    Hangs graceful, quivering to the breeze—"
*   *   *   *   *   *

The following stanza is given as an imitation, apparently from the French:

" While thou art true, my fair, where'er I roam,
    My heart shall sigh alone for thee;
    But if another's conquest you become,
    Thy capture, Delia, sets me free."

Of the following two epigrams, the first is from the Greek, upon a statue of Niobe:

"To stone the gods have chang'd her, but in vain,—
    The sculptor's art has made her breathe again."

———

" Joe hates a hypocrite. It shows
    Self-love is not a fault of Joe's."

With habits so desultory as those of young Johnson from the beginning, and with his taste for literature, it was scarcely to have been expected that he would remain, any very long time, the contented drudge of a Boston shop; and he did not. He was every now and then heard of, teaching at some little school, now here, now there, in Connecticut, at intervals returning to his first friends, the Albees, at Wrentham, sometimes in rags, sometimes in comfort and almost elegance; but, in either case, always with a welcome. On one occasion he is recollected to have appeared there in the garb of a sailor-boy, bearing, both in his dress and person, marks of ill-usage at sea. The following scrap, scribbled on a fragment of paper, in his early handwriting, seems to refer to his disastrous adventure:

" God's miracles I'll praise on shore,
    And there his blessings reap;
    But from this moment seek no more
    His wonders on the deep!"

From the next intelligence we can gather concerning him, he is, in the year 1790, at the head of a little school at Bridgehampton, on Long Island. He must then have been about nineteen. At this time he had, no one could conjecture by what means, become a very excellent player on the violin, and had attained to remarkable skill in architectural planning and drawing. His musical acquirements were, of course, a great recommendation to the society of the rural belles; and his scraps of verse exhibit more susceptibility than constancy, for he had already begun to adore each and every pretty Nancy, and Phœbe, and Keturah, of each and every village, as a Venus for whom Jupiter would have forsaken all his other infidelities. He remained at Bridgehampton during the winter, when, having gathered together a little money, he seems to have first formed a resolution to undertake the study of medicine. At this time he found his way to the village of East Hampton, also on Long Island, where he placed himself under the instruction of a very worthy and intelligent physician by the name of Sage. So much of his time was taken up here between making verses and making love, that his amiable tutor was entirely at a loss to account for the progress he actually gained in his professional studies. By the close of the summer, his small stock of money being exhausted, Dr. Sage procured a school for him at Smithtown, on another part of the Island, where he passed the following winter, returning with his savings in the spring to resume his medical course at East Hampton, which place seemed to have fastened itself more strongly around his heart than any other, before or after, to the end of his life.

This attachment I can readily account for. I have myself visited East Hampton; and, as it may assist my readers to enter into the feelings of the young poet who now took up his abode there, I will endeavor to give them such a knowledge of its characteristics as that passing glance enabled me to obtain. It was settled, history says, at a very early period, from the opposite shores of Connecticut. It is situated on a gently undulating plain, some score of miles from the extreme eastern point of Long Island, and about seven from Sag Harbor. Within twenty minutes' walk is the Atlantic Ocean, the waves of which may be always heard throughout the valley, "swinging slow with sullen roar," and the influence of which upon the trees is pointed out to the visitor, in the withered and discolored foliage of the two, among those lining the street, that stand exposed to the direct sweep of the sea-breeze. East Hampton is a beautiful oasis, so surrounded by sands and barrenness, that the inhabitants are confined to farms barely sufficient to enable them, with patient industry and rigid economy, to draw thence the means of sustaining their families. The village is built on the two sides of a very wide, grass-grown street; the most of its houses low, with one end to the street, and the roof of that old-fashioned and unintellectual form which may be compared to a face without a forehead, shooting abruptly backwards from the eyebrows to the high phrenological bump of veneration on the apex of the skull. The rooms are not lofty, and their walls are wainscoted, and their ceilings crossed with massive beams; and, as you stand up on some superannuated millstone, "fallen from its high estate" into a door-step, you occasionally open upon a three-cornered closet under the stairway, containing the venerable saddle and bridle, often not yet divorced from the social and affectionate pillion of the olden time, for the lady; the respectable seat of which aforesaid saddle has sustained divers generations to tea-parties at the neighboring towns, or to Sag Harbor to

look after the news, or to Montauk to look after the cattle. One small abode
was pointed out to me on a rising ground as having been, within the memory
of some of the towns-people, on its first erection, the wonder of its day; for
the panels of the wainscoting were not only painted, but painted sky-blue, and
the panes of glass in the windows were actually so vast that the new-born
child of the owner was once, to astonish the natives, put through a broken
one, the magnificent magnitude of which, considering it was at least half the
size of those now in common use, must have been looked upon with no little
amazement. In the open way, and leaning against the side of a house, you
will ever and anon encounter most creditable evidence of the universal honesty of the inhabitants, in long logs of fire-wood, standing on end, to be taken
down, and cut, and split as wanted, and the foot of the pile always strewn about
with a semicircle of chips, proving how steadily the healthful exercise of the
axe is kept up in the family. But it must not be inferred that there are no
modern, and even comparatively splendid, mansions in East Hampton, for
there are some of later date, which render the quiet antiquity of the rest even
yet more striking. Nor must I omit to name the public edifices. Of these,
a one-story wooden building, possibly at least eighteen feet square, is, perhaps,
the oldest, and it has from time immemorial been alternately made use of as
a school-house and town-hall. The presiding divinity of this temple of learning in ancient times was a celebrated dame, who used to threaten her male
and female little ones with the terrors of "sarpints and scorpings" in an
awful cellar underneath, if they did not mind their letters and their sewing.
There is another more towering edifice, called Clinton Hall. This is an academy, and surmounted by a cupola and bell, and has held a high rank among
establishments for education. I need scarcely add, there is a meeting-house,
too, put up more than a century since, and still retaining the very steeple,
bell, and clock unchanged which graced it on its first erection in the good
old times of the Province and King George the Second. A few years ago,
after numerous town assemblies and perplexing and prolonged debates, it was
solemnly concluded that the interior of the old meeting-house should, for the
first time, pass under the brush; and, when adorned with new colors within,
it seemed, like little Rip Van Winkle, with his antediluvian outside and his
new perceptions, as if actually exclaiming, "Is this really me?" It is asserted
that upon this occasion an ancient maiden, whose sympathies with the meeting-house were those of a coeval, and who could not bear to look upon her
mother-church as a painted Jezebel, cried out in an agony of pious chagrin,
"Ay, ay! jest like East Hampton folks; all for show!" At each end of the
village stands a windmill, and near one a pond, and near both an unfenced
graveyard, in the larger of which the first minister is buried, being laid in
such a position by his own desire, it is said, as to enable him on his uprising
to face his beloved flock. So endeared is this spot by the remembrance of the
generations of the good whose remains repose in it, that it is scarcely less coveted for a last home by the humble here than is Westminster Abbey by the
great in England. I have heard of but one exception, and that in the case
of an eccentric old man of the vicinity, who caused his remains to be deposited in his own orchard, that the rascally boys whom he had found so trouble-

some about the fruit-trees all his lifetime might be kept at a due distance by the dread of his ghost after he was gone.

The traditions of the place are few, but mysterious. I first sought them in the town records; but vast, indeed, was my perplexity on only encountering notices of various inexplicable hieroglyphics granted to Zephaniahs, and Ichabods, and Jeremiahs, through many generations, for the respective "ear-mark" of each. Eventually, however, it was relieved. I found out that these mystical "ear-marks" were merely registers of the stamps upon the ears of their cattle, under which the towns-people entered them, for a proportion of pasturage at Montauk, to which each freeholder had a right. In my further researches for less matter-of-fact antiquarianisms, I was more fortunate; and from unwritten history I learned that there is a spot, in the road through the pine woods to Sag Harbor, which is called the "Whooping Boy's Hollow," because in the olden time it was the scene of a child-murder; ever since which, after nightfall, screams are said to be heard there, to the infinite discomfiture of stage-drivers and belated urchins. There is a small excavation, also, on the same wayside, said to be the very spot touched by the head of the last Indian sachem as his corpse was set down by its bearers to the burial; and in which neither pebble, nor dust, nor raindrop, nor fallen leaf ever remains, although the most untiring watchfulness has not been able to detect any human hand approaching it. There is a Lebanon cedar-tree, also, on the wide, sandy heath, midway to Montauk, uprising amid tall, and thorny, and tangled bushes, and whose close-knit branches can sustain the ominous number of thirteen persons, as on a platform; and which is immortalized by some wild tale of Indian massacre and miraculous escape. But the recollections concerning the succession of clergymen, and especially those touching Dr. Buell, who was famous there during, and immediately after, the Revolutionary war,—and whose flowing gown and full-bottomed white wig still flourish in his portrait, and are still gazed upon with undiminished reverence—form the most prolific and acceptable theme of conversation among the aged; whose stories of him prove how richly he was entitled to the gratitude and the respect in which the honest-hearted villager ever holds the good man's memory.

This worthy pastor, and the little old meeting-house, of which he was the unforgotten ornament, and the worship there, as it is maintained even to the present day, can never find such a chronicler as they merit, unless they should meet with some new Oliver Goldsmith, like our own Washington Irving. The verse-poet of sweet Auburn, or the prose-poet of the "Sketch Book," could have brought the Sunday of this village vividly before the mind's eye; and none but they. Either could have shown the congregation assembling from far and near; either could have pictured the ancient wagons, filled with families, jolting onward in their high-backed chairs, of the fashion of the days of the Lord Protector Cromwell. The old horses stop, without a hint from the rein, at the very spot—and each pair plant themselves under the very tree—to which they have been for so many years respectively accustomed. The cross-board is drawn out of the back of the wagon, and a chair dropped to the ground, upon which the grandmothers, and mothers, and aunts are first carefully helped down; and then the younger wives and daughters spring over the seat jauntily, with a light touch on the husband's or the favored suitor's hand or shoulder, and post themselves in readiness to catch the little ones of the latest generation, as they jump into their arms, and are thence lightly launched by them upon the ground. The train move slowly to their places, and the old dogs of the establishment follow and stretch themselves in silent and reverential slumber during the whole service. Every hearer— from the laborer and the common sailor-boy, who is on his return to pass the interval between two whaling voyages in his humble cottage home, up to the solemn and consequential justice of the peace—appears neatly clad, and all join in the exercises with attention and devoutness. There is one parishioner, a respectable townsman, who could be seen driving a stage-wagon of a morning, and on the evening of the same day showing the hospitalities of the village to some of his stage-passengers at his own comfortable cottage,—and whom I have noticed shining brilliantly on these occasions in black pantaloons, of what is called "everlasting." I was told that this worthy person, when commissioned by his wife to make a purchase of the stuff for this garment at New York, being puzzled to remember its appellation, told the shop-keeper, —"Well, I think it is tarnity cloth, or some name o' the sort;" and upon this description got the material with which he dignified himself on Sundays, and at funerals, and at merry-makings. In the psalmody of the meeting-house every voice seems to join; and though the singing may sometimes seem like the motions of the down-easter, who said his dancing was "not for pretty, but for tough," nevertheless it is sincere; and sincerity, however unadorned, is always impressive. I have observed the ancient deacon of the congregation, —whose venerable locks, now grown thin and white, have been swept by a hundred winters,—during the entire exercises, stand in the pulpit, just below the preacher, with the best of his twin listening organs so upturned as to enable his dulled hearing not to lose a single syllable of the long prayer, nor of the longer sermon; and have also been amused with the struggle upon the lip, and in the eye, of some roguish little damsel, as the long, windmill arms of the excited divine, with an unconscious sweep, would force the deacon, of a sudden, to duck down his aged head, in order to evade the risk of an unintentional box-on-the-ear. The very dogs of the village know the precise length of the service by instinct, and at the regular moment for the benediction rise up and depart, never committing the irreverence of shaking themselves until they get outside of the great door.

Though on the way to and from the meeting-house, on Sundays, the wide street of East Hampton looks thronged and sparkling with cheerful faces and bright dresses, the habits of the people are too industrious to break its silence and solitude much during the week. Excepting on Sundays, you will scarcely meet any groups of promenaders throughout the daytime, unless it be large flocks of geese. The same multitudes of the tribe of saviors of the Roman capital, which are remembered as strutting over the grass a century ago, are still conspicuous there; and a visitor, after an absence of at least thirty years, fancied he could recognize among the numbers that were engrossing the area, as if theirs by prescription, some of the acquaintances from whose disdainful beaks he had often sheered away in great terror and tribulation when a child.

That quaint good feeling—that exemplary ambition to do their best in their own quiet and domestic way—which marks the manners of the East-Hamptoners at the meeting-house, also appears in their mode of showing hospitality to each other and to strangers ; to the most welcome of whom their highest compliment is that they are as happy to see him as if he were General George Washington. At the little parties made by ladies, there is a minute observance of their own notions of fashion, both in dress and etiquette : and perhaps there is no place in the world where the tea-table epicure could be gratified with equal variety in the forms of tea-table luxury. Every cake, and tartlet, and tart, and pie is made at home,—and for the most part by the fair hands of the lady hostess herself ; whose ambition to outrival her neighbors in cookery is only comparable with her anxiety to make her attentions acceptable to her guests. It is delightful to mark the triumphant gladness which glistens in the good lady's eyes as she sees her dainties devoured ; and it is curious to observe how character, and even the effects of local, and sometimes political, partisanship, may be read in the silent, but eloquent, eagerness with which some of the kind-hearted neighbors will show their friendship, by eating away most unconquerably, though they are full ; and others, their jealousy and ill will, by most invidiously and slanderously only nibbling, though they are empty. The various dishes, and the various degrees of skill shown in preparing them, are of course a subject of animated gossip the next day, especially if there be a quilting-party anywhere ; and established in her domestic glory, indeed, is the newly-settled-down young wife, after her first, tea-party, if she escape unscathed the ordeal of the prophesying, petticoat critics upon it. She may then hope for the standard epitaph, whenever she shall take her place in the graveyard by the pond, that she was "a virtuous woman, and a crown to her husband."

There is another form in which honest pride displays itself among the female villagers,—that of excelling each other in the manufacture of their own bed-quilts, and curtains, and fringes, and carpets, and rugs. At a house furnished by the handiwork of beautiful young girls—a homestead where, from the very sheet upward, every material was home-made—I could not resist the desire to seek a sight of the fair artists and their famed productions ; and, although half afraid of a repulse upon such an errand, I found the grace and the good nature of my reception quite on a par with the surpassing beauty of the work I was asked to look at. There was a manifest pride in this evidence of a reputation for industry ; and how much more in character with the republican spirit of our institutions is such a pride than that of an heiress in her diamonds, and equipage, and millions ! And with all the devotedness of these village females to domestic duties, and the love of order and of neatness, no lack appears among them of mental acquirement. A young girl, capable of adorning the best society, has been seen there scrubbing her floor with one hand, and pushing forward one of Miss Edgeworth's volumes, which she was reading, to keep it in a dry spot, with the other. And I have perused, from the pen of another native female, yet resident there, scraps of sentimental, and of satirical, and of patriotic poetry, which sweet L. E. L., in her happiest inspirations, might have been proud of producing.

The entertainments of the men at East Hampton are, of course, of a severer character. The greatest among them is that of drawing the seine on the Atlantic. A horn is sounded at daybreak, whenever the sea gives promise of abundance, and all the men, of all orders and conditions, hurry to the beach in their boat toggery; from head to foot all "suffer a sea-change," so thorough that the well-dressed yeoman of the preceding night is not to be recognized. The boats put off, and ere long all hands are pulling at the net-ropes, waist-deep in the water, and the sands are swarming with heaps of fish of every description, the greater part of which are used for the purpose of being left to decay upon the fields for manure. The hideous and poisonous sting-ray is usually among the captives, and I have seen from fifteen to twenty sharks strewn upon the shore from a single haul. Even the whale will occasionally appear in the distance, completing the majesty of the ocean prospect. These scenes are ever sources of no ordinary excitement on this part of the coast, and such is the inspiration of the sound of the horn-call to the sea, that all the male creation of the village rush forth on the instant. A Connecticut notion-monger who announced the arrival of his peddling-cart there one morning by the sound of his own horn, was astonished to find every house suddenly depopulated of all the holders of the purse-strings. The signal had been mistaken for a call to the seine-drawing. It may be that a taste for the adventures of the ocean is awakened in the younger villagers by these sights of grandeur and the stir of these minor dangers, for their first thoughts are generally turned to a ship-board life, and they early wander far, most frequently upon whaling voyages. "There lives a man," said a young East-Hamptoner to me, as we rode by a cottage a few miles from the village, "who has made a competency by whaling and retired from *public life!*" I have listened upon the sands, as the surf was dashing and sparkling at our feet, to harrowing narratives of bright hopes, broken by this irrepressible thirst to tempt fortune on the deep. I have heard a warm-hearted and intelligent sister disclose, in faltering accents, the sad story of her young brother, who would not be dissuaded from the peril, even by a lovely relation, who, when yet a mere child, remonstrated with him in a letter, of which the ready memory of the sister retained the following sweet burst of artless eloquence : "Recollect, a mariner's life is one of hardship, toil, and danger. Think of the many anxious hearts you will leave among your friends. Even I, in some cold, stormy night, when the wind whistles so mournfully about the house, and seems to bid defiance to the other elements,—even I shall then think of my poor little cousin, exposed to all the inclemencies of the weather, rocked by Boreas in his hammock, and, perhaps, thinking or dreaming of his dear native village and the cheerful fireside he has left, to learn his lesson of life, and mayhap to find his grave in its bosom, with naught but the billow to sing his death-song." And the apprehension was prophetic. The poor lad, when his ship was sweeping before a gale, through the Indian Ocean, ran aloft to furl a sail as the mast broke, and he was heard to exclaim, "God save me!" when the ship uncontrollably dashed onward, and he was seen no more! Volumes might be filled with the romances of real life, which sometimes beguile the evenings on this wild ocean border; and often have I desired the graphic power to detain on paper a scene of the sort, in which I was once a sharer. The gentle monitor of her lost cousin sat with his sisters and some others on the beach. Anecdotes of the sea had made the time glide away unperceived, and the conversation was wound up by an unaffected song from the innocent girl, in which devotion so beautifully mingled with touchingly appropriate allusion, that no taste, no science, no execution of the finest melodists in the world, could have rivalled the pathetic influence of the untaught music. To imagine its spell, it must be associated with the impressive recollections; with the soft breeze rippling over the calm ocean; with the waves mildly breaking, then falling back in diamond-sparkles, as they met the moonbeam; and with the vast wilderness of outstretched waters beyond, gradually more and more confused by distance, till at length undistinguishably blended with the black mist over the horizon, which seemed the only veil between the beholder and eternity.

It may be readily inferred that, in such a village as I have described, the aged must naturally feel extremely sensitive about any omen of innovation. The old families are devoutly attached to their old homes, and though I have known but fifteen dollars a year to be asked for the only house to be hired at one time in the place, the same cost and trouble which would secure a lot in East Hampton might obtain of one of ten times the marketable value elsewhere, so much beyond lucre do the inhabitants prize their modest independence. With such feelings, we cannot wonder at the distaste for all intruders. Hence it happened that when a steamboat from New York to Sag Harbor made the seclusion readily accessible to city rovers in quest of sea air and rurality, the irruption of the barbarians of aristocracy and fashion gave the old settlers evident concern; and when an accident abruptly stopped the new-fangled facility of approach, it was a source of exultation among some that East Hampton need no longer tremble for her purity, because the madness was over; the good old ways were returning; the old stage-coach had gone out, as formerly, with a passenger and a portmanteau; and there were no more arrivals of the unknown from vicious large cities, to stir up extravagant ideas in the well disposed, and unsettle the husbandman from his dependence on his plough by dreams of speculation. It is true there might have been grounds for uneasiness. Some alarming cases of genius had actually broken out among them. Many a head is even to this day shaken at the sad delusion under which an old inhabitant, who invented a combined flour-mill and threshing-machine, and another, who fashioned an orrery, imitating by mechanism the movements of our planetary system in their exact proportions, have both not only wasted time, but actually expended money! For such prejudices, however, the generation in which they prevail is scarcely to be held accountable; these good people have communicated but little with the wider world, so little that an aged one among them, after having been inveigled in a mischievous young friend's wagon, for the first time, to the neighboring town of Southold, is said to have exclaimed in amazement, " Who could have thought

that Amerikey had been so big !" This wonderer may have been of the same
tribe with the maiden of threescore and ten, who, after a hurricane which
succeeded a grand scholars' exhibition of dialogues in the Clinton Hall
Academy, cried out, with sanctimonious consternation, "This is that plaguy
'cademy work, I know ! A judgment is fell upon the town !" But I ap-
prehend that it would be impracticable for even much more potent jealousies
permanently to shut out the dreaded changes. The sweet solitude of East
Hampton is inevitably destined to interruption from the city, and many an
eye, wearied with the glare of foreign and domestic grandeur, will, ere long,
lull itself to repose in the quiet beauty of this village. It will revel in its
day-break ocean-sports. It will delight in its summer sunset, which, as the
gazer from the rising ground at the western extremity looks down the long
and ample street, flings giant shadows upon the grass, and gilds the tree-tops
and the nearer windmill, and the chimneys, and the academy cupola, and
the little meeting-house spire opposite, and the distant tavern-sign, swinging
between two posts in the centre of the road, and the far-off windmill ; while
the geese strut with slow and measured stateliness to their repose, and the
cottagers upon the benches, projecting from before each side of many of the
cottage-doors, talk news or scandal, or pertinaciously bicker away about
politics and religion, though they are said never to have voted but on one
side, and never to have listened to a sermon out of their own sect.

Such, then, was East Hampton, where the hapless, "neglected poet" of
this narrative became naturalized, by one of the accidents of his random kind
of life, as a member of this quiet, simple, and primitive little community.
Such, at least, it was a few years ago ; and with the exception of the slight
changes I have specifically recorded above, I may safely guarantee that such
it was at the date referred to. Another number will be necessary to complete
the narrative, of which it is the object to rescue from entire oblivion a name
well entitled to the tribute, by the double right of genius and of misfortune.

PART II.

I hope the reader will be the more ready to receive this minute picture of
East Hampton with indulgence, when he shall consider the influence the
place was calculated to exercise upon the mind of our poet, and that it was
here it began to disclose itself most vigorously. When the small stock of
money which Johnson had brought with him from his last school-speculation
was again exhausted, he made a bargain, which, after the view I have given
of the modes of thinking in East Hampton, it will be seen, must have raised
him considerably in the public estimation ; he contracted to pay his board
there with a cabinet-maker, by working for him two days in the week, leaving
the remainder of his time at his own disposal for study. When it was seen
with what readiness and finish the young poet-schoolmaster could turn out
chairs and tables, and all sorts of furniture, it was admitted that the village
had never been graced by so miraculous a genius. Every door was opened
to him, and he was the pride and the favorite of all, and especially, it would

seem, of the young ladies. To his professional studies, however, he gave but little time; and how he could have derived the slightest benefit, even from his miscellaneous reading, seems unaccountable, for though he appeared to make extraordinary proficiency in every branch of general knowledge, he was never known to give more than half an hour to any one book before he would fling it aside and take to another. Some of the time which was not engrossed by his mechanical labors was passed in acquiring a little French and Italian; but the greater part of it in visiting from house to house, in playing upon his violin, and sometimes in playing upon the hearts of the young girls of the village, which he attacked both in prose and poetry, and, it would seem, not unfrequently with success.

The siege of a heart in the olden time, I believe, was apt to begin with a rebus, and when affairs grew serious, it would come to an acrostic; for, especially in the latter case, the lady's name must be so unalterably interwoven with the declaration that there could be no mistake; the lover was nailed, and so was the compliment; even were the lady insensible, the verses could not be transferred to any new object. Of these rebuses and acrostics, I find not a few bearing the date of the period now in question, all of which are peculiarly easy and graceful; yet I shall quote but one specimen, and that not of a set of love-couplets, but an address to a worthy clergyman, the Reverend Herman Daggett:

> "Happy the soul, which, on religion's wings,
> Exalts her glorious flight to worlds above,
> Rapt from the sinful ties of earthly things,
> Melts into transports of celestial love,
> And ev'n on earth makes Heav'n her blest abode,
> Nor knows a wish that centres not in God!
> Dauntless this soul, this soaring soul, shall sing,
> As, eagle-like, it gazes on the sky,
> 'Great king of terrors, where's thy vaunted sting?
> Grave! boasting grave! where is thy victory?
> Exert your pow'rs! ye can but brush away
> The dust that soils my robes,—th' indecent clay,
> That keeps me from the realms of bliss and endless day!'"

In one of his love-poems at this time we find the following happy application of the incident at the marriage feast of Cana. The reader must bear in mind, in appreciating the merits of my quotations, the youth, the imperfect and desultory education, and circumstances of the author, as also the material fact of the different tone and style characterizing the poetry of the present day from that of half a century ago. Without here discussing the respective merits of the two, I merely allude to the fact, to designate the school with which the verses of poor Johnson, to which a public notice is now for the first time extended, must be compared:

> "Stern fate, severely cruel, fills
> Life's bitter and disgusting cup
> With drops of joy to seas of ills,
> And we must drink the potion up.

> " But love corrects the nauseous draught,
> And makes it nectar all divine,
> As he whose blood our souls has bought,
> Transformed the water into wine!' "

The following beautiful couplet, which I find among his papers of the present date, written as an epitaph on a lady, I cannot refrain from quoting:

> " Here sleep in dust, and wait the Almighty's will,
> Then rise unchang'd, and be an angel still." [1]

Among his various amatory stanzas are the following upon the falling of

---

[1] " BOSTON, 48 STATE STREET,
" January 24th, 1880.

" GABRIEL HARRISON, ESQ.

" DEAR SIR,—I read your volume concerning Mr. Payne with great satisfaction, it having come into my hands but recently.

" I enclose a notice of an error into which Mr. Payne naturally fell. It is a curious fact that about the same time Mr. Payne's book came to me the ' Memoirs of Gilbert Wakefield' arrived, and I sent to England for the name of the lady honored with the epitaph and the date of the inscription. I sent a newspaper addressed to the care of Mr. Munsell, not knowing your address, and I now send a slip. I have taken this liberty, so when a new edition is necessary the error may be corrected.

" Very respectfully,
" ARTHUR W. AUSTIN."

" In an article on 'Neglected Poets,' by John Howard Payne, there is an epitaph represented as having been written by William Martin Johnson, one of Mr. Payne's ' neglected poets.' The epitaph is rendered as follows:

> ' Here sleep in dust, and wait the Almighty's will,
> Then rise unchang'd, and be an angel still.'

" Mr. Payne says he found this beautiful couplet among Johnson's papers. It was from that circumstance erroneously attributed to Johnson. He might have seen it somewhere, and, writing from memory, wrote it incorrectly. It would not be right to call Johnson a plagiarist, as it was not published as his during his lifetime. The error of Mr. Payne has been carried into the ' Cyclopædia of American Literature,' from thence to Allen's ' American Biographical Dictionary,' and has been reiterated in the recent beautiful edition of ' Payne's Life and Writings,' by Gabriel Harrison. The same epitaph in substance is to be found in the ' Fugitive Poetry of the Chandos Classics,' London, 1878. There is a slight variation from the original in all these publications. The true reading is,—

> ' Rest, gentle shade! and wait thy Maker's will;
> Then rise unchang'd, and be an angel still.'

" These lines, which are superior in delicacy to the other readings, can be found in the ' Memoirs of Gilbert Wakefield,' published in 1792, and pronounced by him as ' exquisitely beautiful.' In 1770, about the year Johnson was born, the lines were inscribed by a fond husband to the memory of his wife, Ann Hollings, on a marble mural monument in the very ancient church of St. Mary, in Nottingham, England."

some flakes of snow into the bosom of one of the village belles, whom he was escorting through a storm:

> "To kiss my Celia's fairer breast,
>   The snow forsakes its native skies,
> But proving an unwelcome guest,
>   It grieves, dissolves in tears, and dies.
>
> "Its touch, like mine, but serves to wake
>   Through all her frame a death-like chill,—
> Its tears, like those I shed, to make
>   That icy bosom colder still.
>
> "I blame her not; from Celia's eyes
>   A common fate beholders proved—
> Each swain, each fair one, weeps and dies,—
>   With envy these, and those with love!"

But whatever Celia may have been, the poet's assiduities seem not to have been eventually wasted, for ere long we find him addressing "Celia Jealous":

> "What earthquake heaves those hills of bliss?
>   That breast, th' Elysium of my soul?
> Into that more than Paradise
>   What fiend accurst has stole?
>
> "Now, from th' accustom'd kiss away
>   That opening rose-bud quivering shrinks;—
> And now these precious fountains play;
>   The liquid pearl now sorrow drinks!
>
> "Like sapphires seen in melting snow,
>   Those eyes through tears new radiance dart,
> Each brow is Cupid's bended bow,
>   Each glance his arrow to my heart," etc.

With half a dozen more stanzas, which I refrain from quoting, as they exhibit the impudence of justifying his numerous infidelities, as the best evidences of the constant affection which always brings him back to the true home of his heart.

His love-effusions, addressed to different shrines, at about this time, are very numerous, and many of them very happy. By way of variety, however, he is occasionally found addressing the colder Goddess of Friendship, whom in several of the former he treats very unceremoniously:

> "Friendship, sweet power! whose fires divine
>   Our souls exalt, unite, and bless,
> I kneel before thy sacred shrine,
>   And with this verse thine altar dress.

" 'Tis not in thee, the crimson shame
    O'er cheeks of innocence to bring;
But sweet thy joys, and pure thy flame
    As the flow'r-scented breath of spring.

"Through boundless nature's various plan
    Thy spreading charm diffus'd we see,
From insect-atoms up to man,
    And heaven were joyless but for thee.

"Thou fair! whose fiat shapes my doom,
    What's love without this softening pow'r?
A fire, that kindles to consume!
    A savage, conquering to devour!

" First, love should fix the welcome chain,
    Then calmer friendship claim its turn,—
For rapture, long intense, is pain,
    But souls should glow that cease to burn."

Presently, however, he gets exclusively tender again, and despairingly addresses a new goddess, deploring that his poverty should make his love so hopeless :

"See! where to its maternal stem
    Yon filial flow'ret fondly clings—
The poet's sweet, unconscious theme—
    And heedless of the lay he sings:

" More fragrant far than parent bush,
    Than flowery Hybla's scented gale;
And sweeter far that flow'ret's blush
    Than May's first morning's dew-gemm'd veil.

" And shall some blest triumphant swain,
    How blest,—how more than doubly blest,—
Win this wild empress of the plain,
    And wear it on his raptur'd breast?

" Were I—but, ah! no cultur'd plains
    Nor gardens for such sweets I boast!
My locks are drench'd with driving rains,
    Nor hous'd my head from winter's frost.

" 'Tis mine, uncottag'd and unclad,
    Chill storms, with purpled breast, to brave,
And struggle onward, faint and sad,
    To sink into my home, the grave!

" But still thus humbly and remote,
    I sure may view a flower so fair,
And bless the too distinguish'd lot
    That bids me breathe the ambient air."

The two following descriptive pieces will serve to give a just idea of the development of his mind at that period:

"WINTER.

"Now grim amidst his gathering glooms,
 Lo! angry Winter rushes forth:
Destruction with the despot comes,
 And all the tempests of the north.

"What time he thunders o'er the heath,
 Each scene that charm'd, in terror flies,
Creation feels his gelid breath, ↘
 Affrighted nature shrieks and dies.

"Perplex'd and sad, these scenes among,
 The pondering soul, with fainting steps,
Quite sick of being, plods along,
 And o'er the mighty ruin weeps;

"Or lifts the longing eye, and sighs
 For milder climes and lovelier meads,
A vernal hour, that never flies,
 And flowers, that rear immortal heads;

"Where ne'er, unchain'd, the maniac blast
 Scours the bleak heavens, with hideous scream;
Where skies of sapphire, ne'er o'ercast,
 Incessant pour the golden beam."

"SPRING.

"'Tis May! no more the huntsman finds
 The lingering snow behind the hill;
Her swelling bosom pregnant earth unbinds,
 And love and joy creation fill.

"Over the glassy streamlet's brink
 Young verdures peep, themselves to view;
At noon the tipsied insects sit and drink
 From flowery cups the honeyed dew.

"Deep crimsoned in the dyes of spring,
 On every side broad orchards rise,
Soft waving to the breeze's balmy wing,
 Like dancing lights in northern skies.

"In ditties wild, devoid of thought,
 The robin through the day descants;
The pensive whip-poor-will, behind the cot
 Her dirge, at evening, sadly chants.

"Queen of the months, soft blushing May!
    Forever bright, forever dear,
Oh, let our prayers prolong thy little stay,
    And exile winter from the year!

"Life, love, and joy to thee belong,--
    Thee fly the storm and lurid cloud,
Thou givest the heavens their blue, the groves their song,
    Thou com'st, and nature laughs aloud.

"Let prouder swains forsake the cell,
    In arms or arts, to rise and shine,—
I blame them not,—alas! I wish them well,—
    But May and Solitude be mine!"

Dr. Sage, who was a person of amiability, intellect, skill, and integrity, in a letter now before me, describes the present crisis of Johnson's career. He says that at the close of the two years passed in so desultory a manner under him, at East Hampton, Johnson was "well versed in the most common theories of physic, was a most ready mathematician and natural philosopher, was master of the principles of music." He "possessed," adds the doctor, "a most accurate and grammatical knowledge of his own language, understood French, had some knowledge of Italian, and could translate with the greatest ease any Latin author, almost without having recourse to a dictionary. He appeared to have considerable taste and knowledge in architecture; could use with skill almost all kinds of tools, and even excelled in many of the mechanic arts; in short, whatever he undertook in mechanism, he executed with the neatness of a first-rate workman." Dr. Sage afterwards remarks, "It has often surprised me, that, at twenty years of age, and with such idle, unsteady habits, Johnson should possess such variety and degree of knowledge. Where and how he could acquire it all, unless by intuition, I could never imagine. He was a runaway boy, and had been most of his life travelling from one part of the country to another, without friends, and the most of the time poor, dependent, and wretched. When pinched with adversity, his feelings and temperament were such that he was wretched indeed; and if his better stars, at any time, should light up a little comfortable gleam of prosperity about him, he was such a careless, wretched economist, that he wasted it without an effort towards its continuation or enlargement. 'Tis true, he was capable of enjoying, in a high degree, the blessing as it passed, and without vexing himself with the probabilities, or even certainties, of to-morrow's reverse. He was enthusiastic in his friendships, and, I believe, sincere. He was generous; he felt for the wretched and unfortunate; in his resentment he was quick, and, from a certain impetuosity of temper, often inconsiderate and rash; but soon forgot these. He changed with rapidity from object to object, for his feelings were so acute and so easily excited, that he was generally governed by the impressions of the moment."

With such a disposition, there was little probability that Johnson, even with all the attractions he found in East Hampton, would have remained there permanently. Indeed, perhaps those very attractions may have hastened his departure. His compositions, beside the evidence of dissatisfaction at his present limited sphere of mental action and inglorious obscurity, indicate, as he proceeds, a striking change in his personal words, and it would almost seem that he had not fluttered so long around the light of love without at last burning his wings. His temper was now evidently grown morbid. As he ceased to write mere love-verses he became more and more sensitive and satirical.

The following epigram, written at this time, and which I find among the poet's manuscripts, will serve as an instance of this bitter spirit, like "moody madness laughing wild" at the idea of any possibility of happiness:

> "'Life is a jest,'—but God himself must own
> A sadder jest on earth was never known:
> The sides of heav'n must split to see such fun,
> In terrors ended, as in tears begun.
> Lo! there,—a wretch, extended on the rack;
> See his veins spout, and hear his sinews crack;
> And if a keener jest is your desire,
> Go, take his place,—and laugh till you expire!"

The views of our poet at this stage of his course seem to have been directed for some time towards a change of place, and he at length prepares to quit East Hampton, and try his fate in a larger sphere than he has yet attempted. He determines to plunge boldly into the city of New York. Even supposing him to have been hurt in his affections, he must have contemplated, with intense anxiety, his approaching departure from a spot endeared to him by so many kindnesses, and where he had a home in every cottage. The thought of exchanging so kind a village for the dreariest of all solitudes, the solitude of a crowd of strangers, must, to a mind constituted like that of Johnson, have been withering indeed.

The popular verse-makers of New York City were, at that period, Richard B. Davis, whose works have been preserved by one of the Irvings; St. John Honeywood, whose writings appeared under the patronage of the late Judge Hoffman; Richard Alsop, advantageously remembered, not only for original productions in great profusion, but for able translations from the Italian; Mrs. Faugieres, whose "Tragedy of Belisarius," and whose lines upon various occasions, especially one collection of them, illustrative of the Hudson River, are spoken of with much praise, and the memory of whose mother, Mrs. Ann Eliza Bleeker, was still cherished equally for her genius and her trials. A mind like that of Johnson must have met the works and story of Mrs. Bleeker, which appeared somewhere about the date of his arrival at New York, with no common interest. Her wilderness flight, on foot, from the inroad of Burgoyne's army, bearing her young daughters with her, one of them an infant; her garret shelter, and the loss of her babe from the exposure; her despair afterwards, at the mysterious disappearance of her husband, when carried off from his farm by the British; the almost fatal effects of her rapturous surprise at his unexpected restoration; and her final crush in death

24

from sensibility already fearfully shaken, when, returning to her native city, she found it desolated by the war, and bereaved of all her early friends, could not but excite Johnson strongly. Nevertheless, he could not avoid noticing how little the praises upon every tongue had contributed to the prosperity of the subject of them; and how utterly the genius of the mother, aided by the influence of connections and the spell of romantic associations, a genius which her surviving daughter had inherited and improved, failed, notwithstanding it was honored with surpassing homage, lamentably failed in benefiting the worldly fortunes of Mrs. Faugieres. The inference was obvious, and John-son cast sternly away the hopes which he had brought with him to the me-tropolis, of working out distinction and prosperity by means of his poetical genius, and, reduced to all the extremities of unfriended youth and genius in the solitude of a city, we see him struggling for a mere support of life, in any nameless occupation, such as a news-printer's and bookseller's drudge, an under teacher, in short, as anything which would enable him to pay his way in his studies to become a physician. The person with whom he studied was Dr. Amasa Dingley, to whose friendly kindness he appears to have cherished a warm sense of gratitude, and whom he characterizes, in a poetical epistle addressed to him, as possessed of the "heart of Howard and the head of Brown."

Nor was Dr. Dingley the only person of talent and worth with whom he became a favorite. He seems to have been upon terms of great cordiality not only with all the distinguished persons of the time, in his own destined profession, but with the most esteemed among the authors and the artists. There are, no doubt, many still living in New York who, should these pages ever meet their view, may bring to mind the subject of this sketch, and be ready to acknowledge the truth of this testimony in his favor. His most in-timate associate was young Joseph Osborn, who being a profound classical scholar, a critic of refined taste, and equally accomplished and amiable, was, undoubtedly, a very valuable friend, as well as delightful companion, to Johnson.

During the intimacy at New York between these young students, John-son's attention seems to have been directed principally to studies of the Greek and Roman models in their original languages; and his productions to have been confined to translations. Of these, there are, among his papers, several of great vigor and beauty; besides versions of passages in the Sacred Scrip-tures, and of parts of Ossian.

But, agreeable and intellectually profitable as such intimacies must have proved to Johnson, the persons with whom he found himself most at home were all of them nearly as ill off in the world as he was; and the occupation of newspaper paragraphing, and school usherships, even in our improved times generally preoccupied, and never more than an exceeding lean and pre-carious resource, were, in his, equally overstocked from the inexhaustible East, and still less productive than at present to the incumbent; and as for the propensity to rhyme, it seemed to be considered at best but an amiable weakness, only tending to empty pockets; poetry was the most unmarketable of all literary drugs. Though every one acknowledged the promise Johnson gave of splendid powers; though every one confessed how disgraceful it would be to allow such powers to "rest unused," and though the patriotic congratulated the country on the splendid hopes afforded by such early excellence, it does not appear that he was substantially fostered by those who could have turned his qualifications into useful channels, and made them a blessing to his age, and an honor to his character. It unfortunately happened, too, that the period in question was one in which the effects of the French Revolutionary effervescence were in full action among us, and when the multitudes were on the alert to make the success of novelties in government a plea for extending them to religion. The activity of error in seeking and promoting proselytes is proverbial: it has been accounted for by the feverish and self-doubting anxiety to fortify itself by the sanction of the enlightened; and it is not to be wondered at that a mind like Johnson's should have been assiduously courted by those who desired all the aids of enthusiasm and of eloquence, to help onward a bad cause. Ridicule is the favorite weapon exercised by such spirits upon the young and ambitious, and there are few minds capable of resisting its influence. It happened, moreover, unfortunately, that at a time when Johnson was exposed to the dangerous atmosphere described by the poet, when " *The world will call you fool,*" was ringing in his ears, it was the evil destiny of his destitution to cast him in the way of a New York publisher who had already given currency to many of the infidel works most in vogue abroad, and who sought fresh fuel for the spreading flame. There was a French work, by Boulanger, entitled " Christianisme Devoilé." The publisher we allude to found Johnson not only full of talent and entirely out of funds, but well versed in French, and desperate for want of employ. The rest may be easily imagined. He was lured into a translation from Boulanger, enforced by an original preface; and this is, unfortunately, the only work of his ever printed with his name, unless it be a scrap or two of verse, in obsolete magazines, since his decease. The volume excited much attention. Johnson was at first dazzled by its popularity. But his greatest gratification seems to have arisen from his certainty that its appearance would give so much delight to his first protector, Captain Albee. He sent a finely ornamented copy of it to his early domicile at Wrentham. The old captain was enraptured at the remembrance; and at such magnificent evidence, according to his mode of thinking, that the ancient flourishings of the rope's end over his pet protégé had at last " done the state some service."

In a country where native fame of every sort is so transitory as in ours, there is scarcely reason to wonder at the necessity for reminding the reader of the present day, that, some forty years ago, a few distinguished persons of Connecticut were regarded as a galaxy of the most brilliant stars of our literature and fine arts. There were young aspirants who obtained praise for great promise; but Dwight, the Trumbulls, Humphreys, Hopkins, and some others, now entirely forgotten, were looked upon as established in imperishable glory. But the greatest of these temporary immortalities was that of Joel Barlow. He who from a poor Eastern lad had been a soldier, an attorney, a Congregational minister, again a lawyer, and who having afterwards risen through the occupations of a shopkeeper, vending in Connecticut his own edition of psalms and hymns, of a land speculator, of an apostle of religious infidelity, of a political reformer in Europe, up to that of an ambassador, representing his native country abroad in diplomacy, was now also its representative in literature. The epic poem upon "Columbus," at the epoch in question, had been already published, not only in Paris, with a dedication accepted by the king, but in London,—a greater honor than any American poem had received; and its author was looked up to as possessing that universal renown and influence which gave his approval the potency of an oracle. To Joel Barlow, thus surrounded with glory and with power, the translation of which we have spoken was submitted by its publisher, who was his friend. Johnson's general talents, of course, came under the notice of the momentary Homer, and they were considered as too remarkable not to be encouraged for the darling purposes of the hour. In a letter written by Mr. Barlow, from Hamburg, on the 23d of May, 1795, he says,—

"I am glad to see a translation, and so good a one, of Boulanger's 'Christianisme Devoilé.' It is remarkably correct and elegant. I have not had time to compare the whole of the translation with the original, but so far as I have compared it, I never saw a better one. I wish Mr. Johnson would go on and give us the next volume, the history of *that famous mountebank called St. Paul.* I should think these two works would give such a currency to the author in America that the translator might be encouraged to go on and complete his whole works, especially 'L'Antiquité Devoilé' and his 'Oriental Despotism.' I do not know that these works have been translated; if they have, they are probably not done so well as this translator would do them."

Considering the immense weight of Mr. Barlow's opinion at that time, and the prevalence of more levity upon subjects of vital import than has since been found to be compatible with either common sense or the real "age of reason," it is almost to be wondered at that Johnson did not become a sacrifice to this encouragement; but he did not. The fact that "his poverty, but not his will, consented" to this prostitution of his talent, is evident from a letter written to a bosom friend, even while under the full influence of his devotedness to the task. "Far be it from me," observes he, "to suggest anything against true religious experiences! They are the most desirable, at all events; and may they increase till the millennium shall shed its heavenly influence over a regenerated earth! Would to God they might beam through my soul, with the heat of the love, and the light of the knowledge of Jesus of Nazareth!" The right aspirations, of which these words disclose a glimmering, gained strength. Johnson made no more publications of the sort recommended by Mr. Barlow. On the contrary, he lamented bitterly the error he had already committed. "*I do not believe,*" observes he, in a letter to a friend not long afterwards, "*that Boulanger's sentiments concerning the Christian religion are just. I believe the most prominent features of the monster in question are sophistry and rancour.*" The Roman Catholic notion, mentioned by Addison, that an author's soul remains in purgatory so long as his writings continue to do evil, conveys a striking image of what a sensitive spirit like that of Johnson must have endured from the consciousness which these paragraphs prove to have been dawning upon him, of the poison he had flung upon the winds, and could not now recall and smother. It is impossible for the splendid sentiment of Cowley, on the works of the poet being the last to perish in the final wreck of matter,

> " Now all the wide extended sky,
> And all th' harmonious worlds on high,
> *And Virgil's sacred works*, shall die,"

to be too often impressed upon the minds of those who can make an enchanter's wand of the pen. and yet not remember, while they are so doing, the enormous responsibility involved in the power which is the last conquerable by death in his last triumph.—the power of genius. To any one who feels, with Milton, that books are " as lively and as vigorously productive as those fabulous dragons' teeth ; and being sown up and down, may chance to spring up armed men," how awful may be the conviction that even penitence for having uttered a wrong book cannot kill its destructiveness ; but the giant to which a depraved fancy has given birth will still go on, like Frankenstein's fiend, mocking the impotent horror of its maker, when, on beholding his own creation in life and action, his awakened reason shows it to be malignant and a monster! Even thus stinging was the remorse of Johnson at his error. as is evident from another passage of the letter already quoted : "*Persuasion and Poverty induced me to translate this work of Boulanger.* I have risen the steep of education at the expense of many a struggle, and, in mid-air, I avoided a fall by seizing upon the first shrub that invited my hand. *It was a thorn, and do not imagine that I escaped without a wound.* My name was prefixed to the work contrary to my wish, and without my knowledge."

Three prominent events, not far apart, occurred after this in the history of Johnson : an attachment grew up between him and a young lady of superior character and endowments : he was near becoming the victim of a malignant fever, and a proposal was sent to him for commencing practice in partnership with an eminent physician in Georgetown, South Carolina. Of the attentions he received during the illness to which we now allude, in one of his letters he speaks thus : "The New York epidemic conducted me to the brink of the grave, and I am to thank Dingley, Osborn, and some other friends that I did not tumble in. So soon as I could support a removal I went to Long Island, where I stayed until a few days ago. Charles Goodrich came to see me while I was sick, and spoke to me so kindly, that I was too deeply affected to make him any answer, but what might be interpreted from my tears. Osborn watched with me several nights, and exhibited the most impressive proofs that his friendship for me was not to be shaken by any considerations of personal danger. The young gentlemen, also, of my medical acquaintance showed me every kindness that generosity and friendship could dictate. Dr. Dingley effected my removal, and Dr. McLean resigned to me his own furnished apartment. How wrong are those who preach the universal and total depravity of human nature ! Who in my situation could, without indignation, hear it asserted that mankind are naturally in a state of perpetual hostility, and that human nature always inclines to vice and malignity ? Unite with me, my friend, in undeceiving those who calumniate our race !"

Upon his convalescence, it was supposed that an entire change of place would do him service; and he was now more anxious than ever for an establishment, that he might entitle himself to the hand of one who had watched with equal solicitude and success over the diseases of his body and of his mind. The negotiation between him and Dr. Robert Brownfield, of Georgetown, South Carolina, for his removal to the latter place, was marked by a frank and manly style on both parts, which makes me regret being precluded by space from quoting the letters. The mutual friend who had made the character of each known to the other was Dr. Wickham. It resulted in Johnson's accepting Dr. Brownfield's invitation, which he did without any stipulation as to the terms of their professional connection ; and accordingly we find in one of his manuscript books the following entry :

"Left New York, Sunday, 7th February, 1796, in the ship Fame, my friend Captain G. Havens, master. My fellow-passengers were Mr. Russel, of New York, Mr. Powers, a printer, and his journeyman. We arrived at Savannah on Saturday, the 20th of the same month, at which place I was politely received by my old acquaintance, Mr. P. Havens, who had recently established himself there as a merchant. He insisted on my lodging with him at Mr. Dillon's, where I stayed until the next day, when I took passage with a Captain Dickinson, in a packet for Charleston, where we arrived the next morning. This day I dined with Mr. John G. Mayer, to whom I had a letter from the house of Gardiner, Thompson & Co., of New York. Lodged at the Globe Tavern while in Charleston, which place I left on Friday, and arrived at Georgetown the next morning, where I met a most cordial and endearing reception from Dr. Brownfield. On Sunday evening he generously proposed to take me into partnership on terms of equality. I hesitated not to accept his generous offer, and the bargain was immediately closed for one year."

Among his papers, we find some verses inscribed on a blank page of a volume of Godwin's "Caleb Williams," which appears to have been presented to the object of his affections on the eve of his departure to fulfil this engagement; which I quote as expressive of the rational and subdued views of life and the future which had now succeeded to the wild visions of his earlier youth :

> "Clad with the moss of gathering years,
>   The stone of fame shall moulder down,
> Long dried from soft affection's tears;
>   Its place unheeded and unknown.
> Ah! who would strive for fame that flies
>   Like forms of mist before the gale?
> Renown but breathes before it dies,—
>   A meteor's path! an idiot's tale!
> Beneath retirement's sheltering wing,
>   From mad conflicting crowds remote,
> Beside some grove-encircled spring,
>   Let wisdom build your humble cot:
> There clasp your fair one to your breast,
>   Your eyes impearl'd with transport's tear,
> By turns caressing and carest,—
>   Your infant prattler sporting near.

Content your humble board shall dress,
And poverty shall guard your door,—
Of wealth and fame, if you have less
Than monarchs, you of bliss have more."

Dr. Brownfield, in a letter written after Johnson's death, observes: "As a physician he very soon gained the confidence of his fellow-citizens in an extensive practice. His genius and erudition commanded the admiration of the learned, and his social virtues secured him the love and esteem of all those with whom he was most intimately acquainted. To know the strength and universality of his genius required a long acquaintance. The longer I knew him, the more reason I found to admire his talents. To a strong and elevated imagination were added a sound judgment and correct taste. To an elegant and refined taste for the fine arts, he was one of the few who united a profound knowledge of the more abstruse sciences of philosophy and the mathematics. As well in execution as design, his abilities were unrivalled. Indeed, there are few objects of human knowledge of which he appeared to be ignorant. Intellectual brightness is sometimes obscured by degrading vices; but Johnson's character had no stain of this sort. His expanded soul embraced the interests of all mankind. Often I have seen the tear of sympathy for the suffering bedew his cheek. Indeed, in every part of his conduct he displayed that tenderness, that generous benevolence, which, in my mind, exalts the character more than all the brilliancy of science or energy of genius."

That there is no exaggeration in this picture of the impression made by Johnson at his new residence, may be very easily believed. In our Southern regions, so accomplished a person could not remain uncourted. He was in every society, and wherever he appeared he was the brightest star. A long poem, written by him at the time, gives a humorous picture of a convivial musical party at which he was present. It is somewhat in the spirit of Goldsmith's "Retaliation." It portrays the character of each guest in a witty couplet, closed with a line from the particular song which each had sung, and which line is very humorously wrought into the story of the *jeu d'esprit.* He was, of course, applied to on all occasions when poetry was desired; and among others a Fourth-of-July address, written at this period, possesses high poetical merit, at the same time that it breathes a noble spirit of patriotism and love of liberty.

A streamlet in the neighborhood of Georgetown, which the poet's manuscript calls the *river* Sampit, but which is laid down in the maps as a creek, presently afterwards excited his muse; and his lines in its praise circulated at the time with an applause which cannot be denied to them even in our most fastidious day. The lines are these:

"Fair Goddess of the pensive wave,
That calmly tend'st thy little urn,
Than Tempe's lovelier vales to lave,
And quench the potent beams that burn

Thy tender offspring's verdant forms,—
Nor dost forsake thy rising care,
When Jove descends in awful storms,
And bolted thunders singe the air!
What though, along thy lonely banks,
Not oft the tuneful sisters rove,
Nor, tripping light in twilight ranks,
The fairies fill the neighboring grove;
Though thou on no Etruscan shore
Hast seen a thousand villas smile,
Nor e'er, like rapid Hebrus, bore
An Orpheus to the Lesbian isle:
Nor dost thou, number'd with the gods,
Like Nile, from Heaven derive thy source,
Nor visit Pluto's dark abodes,
Like Arethusa's latent course:
Yet hast thou charms my muse to fire,
And though her voice not long shall live,
Her trembling hand shall wake the lyre,
And give what fame her strains can give!
While the old bounds the Thunderer gave,
Thy boisterous brothers oft despise,
And, rising fierce, with impious wave,
O'erwhelm the earth, and threat the skies,—
To hoary Neptune's coral throne,
Thou duteous lead'st thy limpid race,
While pleas'd to meet his meekest son,
The monarch melts in thy embrace.
Diana oft withdraws her gaze
From dull Endymion's slumbering charms,
And flies to keep, with brighter blaze,
A tenderer vigil in thy arms.
Like fairy knights, in silver clad,
To sportive war advancing gay,
A shiver'd beam each radiant blade,
Thy waves, in bright confusion, play.
Along thy banks, where canes compose
The humid bower, and tiny grove,
Thy naiads through the day repose,
And consecrate the night to love,—
If, chance, no monster from the deep,
In scaly terrors grim, invade,
And, stretch'd immense in dragon sleep,
Fright the fair tremblers from the shade.
To catch the breeze and court the muse,
At jocund dawn, or evening gray,
Oft shall my sandals brush the dews
That richly gem the devious way:
But thee, staid eve, most sweet I prove,
When, gently led by insect light,
Thought wanders wild with hapless love,
And sadness sighs along the night.

Yes, sweet thy cells and rayless groves,
  Where lonely woes delight to haunt,
And wounded hearts, like dying doves,
  With pangs too big for utterance pant!
Yon gloomy pines, that stand aloof,
  With thick and darkly waving locks,
Amidst whose shades, with silent hoof,
  The trembling deer, wild gazing, stalks;
The thickening cloud, the screeching storm,
  The flashing lightning's lurid glare,
The gliding phantom's half-seen form,
  Though sad, not all unlovely are.
The nerve by pity interwove,
  Pale grief low bending o'er the bier,
The poignant sympathies of love,
  And suffering friendship's confluent tear;
All these their mingled pleasures know,—
  A little gold amidst the alloy,
And from the poisonous mass of woe
  Extract a melancholy joy.
In fate's worst cup of bitterest spite
  Some drops of comfort still are found;
In pain itself there is delight,
  If love and pity bathe the wound :
Thus some pale flowers in deserts bloom,
  Where never pierc'd the solar beams;
Thus some lone star, through midnight's gloom,
  With tremulous radiance, dimly gleams.—
Curst be the passions' stoic sleep,
  The marble heart, the nerve of steel!
Give me to suffer and to weep,
  But let, ah! ever let me feel!—
But see! what goddess yonder moves!
  Is it the silver-shafted queen,
Or Venus, with attendant loves
  And graces, gliding o'er the green?
Sweet stream! assist my fearful muse,
  O, make her mine,—and thou shalt be
To future years a new Vaucluse,
  Thy Petrarch I, my Laura she.
So still may each less sacred rill
  From thee its turbid tribute turn,
And Heaven its purest dews distil,
  To feed thy ever-flowing urn !
Soft blushing, to thy vales and bowers
  May Spring her earliest visits bend.
Deck first thy brow with new-born flowers,
  And in her bosom warm thee and defend!
Neglectful of Pierian streams,
  The muse shall drink thy richer wave,
And fir'd to fancy's sweetest dreams,
  Upon thine urn an annual verse engrave."

The seeds of the illness which has already been mentioned, and which Johnson complained to one of his friends "had produced an irritability both in body and mind which was unknown to him before," were yet lurking in his frame; and in the autumn of the same year, at Georgetown, he was again much reduced by a bilious remittent, from which he did not perfectly recover during the winter. Early in June, 1797, he was again seized by a fever. As it appeared slight at first, he resisted the urgent advice of his friend, Dr. Brownfield, to try the effects of a Northern climate, and preferred retreating to a sea-island. Here, however, his spirits forsook him: he pined for the society of those who were precious to him, and especially for the one comforting smile which had cheered him during his first disorder. Under these feelings, he dictated from his sick-bed the following version from Ovid's "Tristia," which seems to have been intended for the object of his affection, and is probably the last of his productions:

"Since trembling illness has unnerv'd my own,
I must address thee in a hand unknown.
'Midst savage strangers in a foreign land,
On life's extremest verge aghast I stand;
'Midst cruel climes and people more unkind,
What objects, think you, occupy my mind?
Here, gloomy clouds the cheerless landscape load,
And air and earth proclaim the unus'd abode.
Stretch'd, sick and unregarded, here I lie,
And wildly cast around an hopeless eye:
No friendly face, with cheering smile, appears;
No eyeballs stream with sympathetic tears;
No voice of music bids my pangs retire,
Rekindling in my breast th' accustom'd fire;
No gentle accents through the tedious day
Recite sweet tales to cheat the time away.
In all I feel or hear a foe I find,
And ev'ry object round me seems unkind;
With mingled thorns offends the bed of down,
And in the hangings angry demons frown.

"Here, as I pine, all friendless and remote,
The pleasing past o'erwhelms my laboring thought,—
By turns lost pleasures pass in sad review,
And all those pleasures yield by turns to you;
To you my feeble voice incessant cries,—
I see your phantom with deluded eyes;
And when a thousand tender things I've said,
I blame the silence of th' unanswering shade;
And then thy friendship is esteemed a cheat,—
I curse the name my lips so oft repeat!
But if the damps of death my brow bedew'd,
And to the roof my palsied tongue were glued,
And skill were pos'd and remedies were vain,
Thy soft approach would vanquish all my pain:

Thy healing voice would all my strength replace,
And I should rise in health to thy embrace.—

" While dire disease my feeble frame destroys,
Borne round the giddy world of thoughtless joys,
Dost thou forget thy lover's faithful name ?
Or glows thy bosom with another flame?
Oh, no ! too sure, while I remain unblest,
All joys are strangers to thy anxious breast.

" Soon shall the gods resume the life they gave,
Nor can thy prayers thy parting lover save ;—
But sure the gods might grant this small demand,
At least to perish in my native land,
Where pious hands my cold remains might burn,
And seal my ashes in th' unconscious urn,—
'Twere better than in foreign lands, alone,
To perish thus, a fugitive unknown,
Had death at once th' unerring weapon cast,
And one misfortune been my first and last !
Not death itself can now afford relief,
And life is lengthen'd to prolong my grief.
Yet well I know the last, sad, closing day,
With all its horrors, is not far away,
And I must die upon a foreign shore,
Nor see that face, nor press that bosom more ;
Give up my spirit on this lonely bed,
No friendly arm beneath my languid head ;
Nor with my closing eye's last trembling beam
Behold the tears of sorrow round me stream ;
Nor pour my latest sighs, with faltering sound,
In blessings, on my sobbing friends around :
And when, at last, my soul reluctant flies,
No hand to close my sunk and sightless eyes ;
Vultures and wolves shall on my body prey,
And my bones whiten in the blaze of day !

" At the sad news I see thy frenzied air,
Thy hands outstretched to Heav'n in fruitless pray'r ;
I hear thee call my name and tell our loves,
Wild rushing through resounding vales and groves ;
But, ah ! to wound that snowy breast forbear,
Nor scatter to the winds that flowing hair ;
And think scarce less from other each was torn,
When my first absence thou wert doom'd to mourn :
'Twas death itself to wander far from thee,
And more, far more than this, a death to me !
But that I knew thy breast could ne'er obey,
I could command thy fruitless griefs away ;
Nay, bid thee joy that all my ills are o'er,
And grief, disease, and exile, vex no more ;

At least with firmness meet relentless fate,
Nor sink at once beneath a lessening weight;
With patient meekness all thy woes endure,
Which time may soften, though it cannot cure!"

In August, 1797, Johnson was prevailed upon to return to New York, and thence he went over to Jamaica, on Long Island. Here his old friends again flocked around him. Joseph Osborn and his brother, Charles Osborn, were unremitting in their attentions. " In my acquaintance with the world," observed he, " I have seen no parallel to their friendship and generosity." Of his Southern friends he spoke with enthusiasm to the last; and especially of the frank and liberal treatment he met with in every respect from his partner, Dr. Brownfield. His eyes, it is believed, were closed by Joseph Osborn, in whose handwriting there is the following simple inscription upon a page of a manuscript book which had been the property of his friend: " Wm. M. Johnson died at Jamaica, L. I., Tuesday morning, five o'clock, the twenty-first of September, 1797." His tombstone may still be seen in a graveyard at Jamaica. His age did not exceed six-and-twenty.

Such was the obscure career of one of the earliest of our neglected poets. That he was " a poet born" there can be no doubt, on a consideration of his character and temperament as evinced by his life, and attested by those who knew him, and of the genius manifested in those of his writings which a happy chance has preserved and placed in my possession. Notwithstanding the difference of fashion in poetry between our day and that of the subject of this memoir, all readers, capable of appreciating that essential spirit of poetry which is independent of the exterior fashion of phrase and style, will recognize, even in some of the specimens which I have quoted, a delicacy of sentiment, combined with a passionate ardor; an enthusiasm for natural beauty, with that deep yearning after the good, the true and lovely in moral nature which most strongly characterizes spirits of the highest order,—with, at the same time, a melody of language, and graceful ease of style, united to strength and directness,—abundantly sufficient to establish his claim to a high place among the poets of our country. His writings have never been published, and his name is an unknown sound to the present generation. His life was passed in obscurity, and that perpetual and exhausting struggle with penury which has so often and so sadly withered the noble promise of young genius; and by the time that his superior talents and excellence of character had raised him to a social position, which promised a more prosperous future career, we see him sinking beneath a premature blight of disease. In the preceding sketch I have attempted to make the narrative tell at once the story of Johnson's genius and qualities of character. To render him justice in both points of view, his attainments and conduct must be compared with his chances; and, when we consider his nameless origin, the desultory scraps of education which his early circumstances permitted him, the many temptations to which he was subjected, both from his poverty and the society into which he was necessarily often cast, the former must be acknowledged to have been such as to entitle his memory at least to this slight and tardy attempt to rescue it from oblivion.

JOHN HOWARD PAYNE

AS

A DRAMATIC CRITIC.

EDMUND KEAN AS SHYLOCK.
TALMA AS A MAN AND AN ACTOR.
HAMLET.

SELECTED FROM HIS WEEKLY JOURNAL, ENTITLED "THE OPERA-GLASS."
LONDON, 1816.

PAYNE AS A CRITIC.

[Anything that can be told relating to Edmund Kean is of great interest to the history of the stage, and, therefore, we have especially selected the following criticism on this child of genius, written by Mr. Payne, and published in "The Opera-Glass," on Kean's performance of *Shylock*, at Drury Lane Theatre, on Monday evening, January 7, 1827. The occasion was the first performance of his masterly rendition of the wily Jew, after his return from America. As a dramatic critic, Mr. Payne was far above the average. He always understood the meaning of the character, and while he did not illustrate his criticisms with any startling revelations, still he is always acceptable to the reader. He was perfectly honest in giving his judgment and opinion; friend or foe fared the same. He was able to describe the actor's work and to analyze the difficulties the actor has to surmount in the fine rendering of a character like *Shylock*. But Payne had not that graphic descriptive power as a critic like Doran, who by his keenly felt appreciation of the actor's genius makes us see the very workings of the actor's face, hear the qualities of his voice, feel the emphasis of the words, and mentally join in the applause that greets the actor at the time when the deception is given. Doran's account of Kean's first performance in London of the character of *Shylock* is one of the finest things in English literature. In fact, his work on "The British Stage" deservedly should stand at the head of all works on the subject of dramatic history and biography.]

KEAN AS SHYLOCK.

There is no play which has undergone more singular adventures upon the stage than this. It was for many years the victim of the alterers, and Lord Lansdowne's "Jew of Venice," which was acted at Lincoln's Inn Fields in 1701, kept it out of sight for forty years. His lordship introduced a feast, in which the Jew had a separate table, and drank to his money as his only mistress; he added spectacle and music; and Dogget performed *Shylock*, which was shorn of its grandeur, and turned into a low-comedy part. It is to Macklin the stage is indebted for the restoration of the original, on the 14th of February, 1741; and the boldness of the attempt attracted a thronged house, principally for the purpose of laughing at a man whose sterling talent was only surpassed by the systematic persecution it underwent throughout his long career. But it is the attribute of true talent not to be disheartened by

377

insult or injury. Macklin felt that he was right in his present experiment, although it was attempted to jeer him out of it, and would not give up his point. For the first time for many years, when he appeared, he was received with silence. It continued till the speech

> " How like a fawning publican he looks !"

This seemed suddenly to arouse the audience to a sense of the correctness of his view of the character, which increased as the character itself increased in interest and the acting in power till it ended in the completest dramatic triumph ever known. The play was repeated nineteen nights successively,— the last for Macklin's benefit. It was on one occasion that a gentleman in the pit, being forcibly struck by Macklin's acting, uttered the expression so often quoted since,—

> " This is the Jew
> That Shakspeare drew;"

which Macklin himself always ascribed to Pope, understanding the panegyric on himself as a satire against Lord Lansdowne ; but the state of Pope's health at the time sufficiently corrects the error of the veteran's recollection. Cooke appears to have made the first great hit in *Shylock* after Macklin. The first appearance of Mr. Kean, since his return from America, in this character, was, as we hoped and expected it would be, a complete triumph over the ferocious attempt to drive him from the British stage. The house was crowded. There were very few ladies in the pit ; it presented a dense mass, rendered peculiarly sombre by the general mourning under which the performances recommenced. In the impatience to atone for past severity, all civility to the other actors was forgotten. There was one unbroken yell for Kean, which drowned all other sounds ; and even the fair faces of Mrs. Orger and Mrs. West could not subdue the storm to silence. On *Shylock's* appearance, of course, the burst was tremendous. The clapping, and bravoing, and rising up, and waving of hats and handkerchiefs, and huzzaing of the audience detained the actor for some time bowing in silence, and putting his hand to his heart and to his head, as though, when his feelings were rendering the one grateful, he would correct them by recalling to the other what *Coriolanus* says to the populace,—

> " Hang ye ! Trust ye ?
> With every minute you do change a mind ;
> And call him noble, that was now your hate,
> Him vile, that was your garland !"

When Kean was permitted to begin to act, he appeared worn and weaker than when he left ; but the diminution of his physical force seemed to have thrown him more entirely upon the resources of his genius. Hence he was better than ever, from not being capable of his customary faults, and preserving all his power of subtile and intense expression. The whole of his first scene, in the third act, was a continued blaze of varied beauties. The differ-

ent ways in which he repeated the " Let him look to his bond." now with a
tone of threatful decision, now with a malicious chuckle, and the torrent of
passion with which he poured forth the magnificent speech which follows,
giving its fullest effect to every change in the coloring, were felt and acknowledged by most enthusiastic applause. The best part of the passage, because
an improvement upon himself, was his manner of saying, "Shall we not revenge?" There was nothing of rant or fury in it. It was dignified, but
mighty. It seemed the denunciation of a spirit whose nod could "shake the
spheres." Then his running from the one passion to the other, in the next
dialogue with *Tubal*. Could anything be finer? Then the intenseness of his
ejaculation, " I thank God ! I thank God !" on hearing of *Antonio's* misfortune, and the little fiend-like laugh which preceded the eager question which
follows on it, " Is it true? is it true?" There is no such acting to be met
with nowadays, except in Kean. The whole of the court-scene was exquisite.
There was no instance in which he left the epigram of the short speeches
without its keenest point. His emphatic and downright way of putting,—

> " If every ducat in six thousand ducats
> Were in six parts, and every part a ducat,
> I would not draw them ; I would have my bond !"

was very warmly applauded ; so was his

> " On what *compulsion* must I ? tell me that."

But the fine by-play of Cooke, during the passage in which *Portia* replies,
was entirely omitted by Kean. There was no reverential bow when *Portia*
says of mercy,—

> " It is an attribute of God himself :"

at the name of the Supreme Being, which would not be heard by a Jew
without such acknowledgment, nor that admirably conceived, rejecting
shake of his head and waving of his hand at,—

> " We do pray for mercy ;
> And that same prayer doth teach us all to render
> The deeds of mercy,"

with which his great predecessor in *Shylock* disclaimed the application of the
Lord's prayer to his creed, and consequently to himself. But even Cooke was
never finer than Kean was in the exulting exclamation,—

> " A Daniel come to judgment ! Yea, a Daniel !"

in the clinging to the young doctor, when he found him so strongly support-
ing his side of the question,—in the haste to show him by the bond how right
he was,—and the tone of cajolery with which he uttered,—

> " An oath, an oath, I have an oath in heaven ;
> Shall I lay perjury upon my soul ?"

25

and the wheedling eagerness with which he darted to his bond when *Portia* asks if she shall tear it, replying,—

"When it is paid according to the tenour!"

and the keen and quiet triumph which he supposes he has obtained over the lawyer on hearing the demand of a surgeon to be hard-by to stop *Antonio's* wounds, when, with a sort of half-laugh at him, he looks over the parchment, asking,—

"Is it so nominated in the bond?"

and adds, in the same spirit,—

"I cannot find it; 'tis not in the bond!"

The quick flinging out of the scales which *Shylock* wore concealed, on the instant scales were called for, and the sudden and utter change of deportment on finding himself foiled, although without in the least forgetting his dignity, were expressed with great felicity. The final speech,—

"I am not well: send the deed after me,
And I will sign it,"

was better given by Cooke. There was a choking in his voice, and a desolateness in his manner, when he said, "I am not well," which even made those sympathize with the sufferer who exulted in his fall.

The exit of Kean, by merely rousing up from the apparent unconsciousness of all the bantering which was going on against him, and flinging his whole soul into one fierce long look at the laughers, without any of those overstrained attempts at pantomime, which we have often seen made in the situation, was the conception of a master. It was followed by as tremendous applause as we ever heard in a theatre, and it was with some difficulty the remaining performers could proceed. It appeared intended by some to stop the play at that point, as a marked compliment to the actor, but the cries for "Kean!" were at length discontinued, and not resumed till the end of the play, when, after having coquetted awhile for the continuance of the cry, he made his appearance in his own dress, and had the good sense not to accompany it with a speech. Nothing could have been more hearty than the acclamations of the house. The same scene was gone through which began the evening, and, when he had finally retired, the ceremony of reception was wound up by three cheers.

The celebrated performers of *Shylock* appear to have varied in their manner of understanding the character. Mossop seems to have been sullen and ferocious; Cooke was bitter and sarcastic; Kean is sly, subtile, intense, and epigrammatic. He certainly never performed it more thoroughly than he did on Monday evening.

TALMA.

An Extract from Payne's Notice of Talma.

IT is a fact that those accustomed to the drama of this country were seldom much struck at first by Talma. Some, whom we ourselves have known, have openly declared that they thought him overrated; and others, who have been a little afraid of committing their reputation for good taste, have passed him by in silence; but we have never known an instance in which opportunities of studying him did not change this indifference into enthusiasm. There is no great difficulty in explaining this. The English performers, especially the tragedians, generally think only of making what they call " points;" they throw all their power into some few explosions, and fancy that any further effort would be thrown away. But the acting of Talma was even. He had his moments of surpassing brilliancy, too; but they were so thoroughly interwoven with the character that they were only remembered with it, and would have been marred in being detached. The beauty of the fragment was nothing in comparison with the beauty of its proportion to the form; and so admirably did each particular harmonize, that there was nothing sufficiently beyond the rest in any one to detain observation, because the whole was perfect. You could always perceive in Talma, when he came upon the stage, that he was in the middle of his character. He did not then begin it. Every look and tone "denoted a foregone conclusion." It was not the mannerist settling his part into his own peculiar style, and that style never varying, whatever might be the part. The tone, the look, the air, were different as he appeared as different heroes. He endeavored scrupulously to possess himself of their personal appearance and habits. But, in adopting these, he, in some degree, qualified them. We heard him argue once upon the hump and unequal legs of *Richard.* He then expressed at large his decided conviction that there was absolute bad taste in carrying the imitation of ignoble peculiarities into anything like caricature. He would temper the picture to the *beau idéal.* He might give a hint of *Richard's* deformity if he acted him on the French stage, but no more. In *Sylla*, however, where there was nothing repulsive in a close copy, he was scrupulously exact. He thinned his hair, and heightened his brow by a band of flesh-colored leather. As Napoleon had been aimed at in the character, and Talma himself introduced into the play as Roscius, he was encouraged in his accuracy by its bringing him nearer to the look of the emperor. We have heard him say that the deep, abrupt, and decided tones in which he spoke through *Sylla* were adopted from the manner of its prototype.

We will select one instance from a multitude of recollections, in order to give a notion, if possible, of his mode of study to our readers. As most of them will best understand us by comparing him with some one they know, we cite a parallel passage of " Orestes" by Macready and Talma.

Orestes, as a pretext for seeing *Hermione*, gets himself sent by the other courts of Greece to that of *Pyrrhus*, to induce him to give up *Astyanax*, whom he protects for the sake of the boy's mother. *Orestes* appears as an

ambassador, and speaks, though firmly, the language of persuasion. In discussing the question he becomes warmed into something bordering on a threat,
and says to *Pyrrhus*,—

> "The father draws their vengeance on the son—
> The father, who so oft in Grecian blood
> Has drenched his sword—the father, whom the Greeks
> May seek e'en here:"

and then, suddenly recollecting himself, he adds, "Prevent them, sir, in
time;" or, as it is better expressed in the original, "Sire, prevenez les!"
Macready raised his voice in the first three lines and a half to the highest
pitch, then abruptly pausing and changing to his lowest note, with a fierce
look, and still fiercer nod, finished the sentence. Talma, on the contrary,
in the spirit of one sent to prevail by remonstrance, and reluctant to appeal
to arms, changed his manner when he checked his impetuosity, and, with a
look, seemed to supplicate the prince, in consideration of the ruin he would
draw upon himself, to yield,—a look of respect and interest more than defiance, he pursued, "Sire, prevenez les!"

Had *Orestes* attempted to provoke the haughty and irascible *Pyrrhus*, it
would at once have betrayed his secret desire for the mission to be unsuccessful. It would, besides, have been untrue to the purpose he was sent upon;
and his sense of duty would not permit him, ere he was wrought up to madness, to bury his embassy in his love. Besides, a dogged threat to a king, in
his own court, would have been coarse; and *Orestes* was neither that nor a
braggadocio.

This trifling instance will show how keenly the one looked into all the
subtler and more delicate shades and bearings of the character he personated,
while the other was satisfied with mere stage effect, too superficial in its conception to bear the slightest scrutiny. There was another point in Talma's
performance of this character so exquisite, that we cannot deny ourselves the
pleasure of naming it. When *Hermione*, through jealousy, wishing to make
Orestes the instrument of her revenge on the slight of *Pyrrhus*, encourages
him to expect her love if he will destroy the prince, whom, she says, she now
hates, *Orestes* promises to accomplish her will that very night; on which
Hermione, in her impatience, betrays her real motive by exclaiming,—

> "But now,
> This very hour he weds Andromache!"

In the French play (there is nothing said in the English) Talma exclaimed,
on hearing this, "Eh bien, madame!" with an accent which so thoroughly
expressed the sudden revulsion of his excited hopes,—the surprise, the agony,
the despair, which had been flung back upon him by that one remark,—that
it told the whole story of the character, and made the whole house shiver.
Never did we hear applause so tremendous as on one occasion, when those
words were spoken by Talma. No other actor ever made them noticed.

Talma's face was by no means remarkable when not in action; but when excited it was amazing. He once told us " he had been twenty years educating his face." On a particular occasion we saw him give ample evidence of its power. There was a play attempted at the Français upon the subject of ·King John. *Hubert* was given to Talma. The play was in the course of turbulent damnation, when Talma rushed in from the murder of *Arthur*. He sunk into a chair, his elbows on a table, and his hands covering his face. The uproar was what our friend Dominie Sampson would call "prodigious," till Talma withdrew his hands and displayed a countenance of such ghastly horror that the tumult changed instantly into shouts of " Bravo, Talma!" which continued until he left the stage, when the damnation recommenced. He could " wet his face with tears" whenever he liked, but they sprang from feeling more than art. In passages of his last, " Charles VI.," he did this with great effect. His voice was deep and full, but a little inclined to what the French call *la voix voilée*, which can only be rendered in English, and that not distinctly, by the phrase " a muffled voice." It was sweet, strong, and flexible. He had nothing of the "respirative drag, as if to catch breath," with which the old " Dramatic Censor" taxes Garrick, and which most of our English performers have, Macready, for example, to a most distressing degree. Talma used to say it was as much an actor's duty to learn to manage his breath as his words, and certainly he did it to perfection. His person was much under the standard of the hero. It had, from our first knowledge of him, a little of the aldermanic tendency. It must have been not unlike that of Garrick, which is represented as " in many respects, particularly about the hips, formed like a plump woman." Some of his action was very like what Macklin describes of Garrick. Like him, Talma " hung forward, and stood almost on one foot, with no part of the other on the ground than the toe of it." He had the same way, Macklin says, Garrick had, of, as he coarsely terms it, "pawing" the characters he acted with; but this he had in common with the French school. He was much given to patting the breast of the person to whom he spoke; and he had the convulsive shake of the hand peculiar to the actors of his country. We once mentioned this last to him. " Yes," observed he, " it is wrong; it ought to be corrected."

Talma used to regret that the prejudices of the French obstructed the improvements he wished to make in their style of declamation. To this day he is censured for having broken the monotony of their verse, by running the lines into one another, and thus evading the rhyme. His delivery was more elaborate than ours; perhaps the difference in the nature of their drama requires it should be so; for they have more to do with words than we have. Hence Talma *acted* words. We heard him recite *Hamlet's* "Soliloquy on Death" in English. He colored every syllable with his voice, and gave

> "The oppressor's wrong, the proud man's contumely,
> The pangs of despis'd love, the law's delay,
> The insolence of office, and the spurns
> That patient merit of the unworthy takes,"

with a different, but finely characteristic expression to every phrase. We once heard him, in the phrase where *Othello* describes *Desdemona*,—

"Whereof by parcels she had somewhat heard;"
But—*not intentively*,"

express the "not intentively" in a manner perfectly inimitable; but con-
veying a fulness of meaning of which we never, had we not heard it, could
have dreamed it were susceptible.

We have heard Talma observe that he never acted a part without obtaining,
in the course of the performance, some new notion about it, which he never
forgot, but could always add to the next. But though we have been much
with him, we never saw him study. On mentioning this to him, he replied,
with a smile, " My dear, I am studying now." He had the faculty of instantly flinging himself into his part. He would stand talking at the side
scenes of the theatre in English, and upon matters which interested him, and
suddenly break off on hearing his cue, and spring into *Nero* or *Hamlet*.

The letter written by him in English, of which we last week gave a *fac-
simile*, explains, in some degree, his theory in acting. Lest it should be mis-
laid, we repeat it here: " I could not point out the principles which ought
to guide you in the study of declamation better than did Shakspeare himself.
In a few lines he has laid down the bias, and true standard of our art; therefore I refer you to what *Hamlet* says (Act III., Scene II.) respecting the
means of personating the various characters which are exhibited by human
life. It will unfold to your view my own principles, and evince, at the same
time, my veneration for the great man."

We have another English letter of his before us. It contains passages still
more remarkable, which we have underscored. It was written to a young
gentleman who had been counselled to take lessons from D'Egville, we believe,
in stage deportment, because D'Egville had given lessons to John Kemble.

" You know how I live, perpetually engaged, some way or other,—always
busy, without doing anything, and continually pestered with idle visitors; so
that hardly any time is left to me for my private affairs. . . . As you are absent from London, I don't forward you the letters to ——. I suppose you will
apprise me of your return there; then I will send them to you, written in the
manner you desire. If you take any lessons from the latter, it ought to be upon
the stage, and not in a room, that you may give a full scope to your steps and to
your motions; but, my dear friend, the first rule is to be deeply impressed.
*Impregnated with the character and the situation of your personage, let your
imagination be exalted, your nerves be agitated,—the rest will follow,*—your arms
and legs will properly do their business. The graces of a dancer are not requisite in tragedy. *Choose rather to have a noble elegance in your gait, and
something historical in your demeanor.*—Dixi."

It is scarcely fair to judge of Talma's power in composition from these
specimens. He himself says, in a postscript to one letter, " make allowances
for my Frenchification." But they are by no means ordinary letters for a
foreigner. They infinitely surpass Garrick's French letters to Le Kain, and
Voltaire's English ones when in London. In French he wrote delightfully,
and particularly letters. Madame de Staël told him, to our certain knowledge,
that he was " the best letter-writer, for a man, she had ever known; that she
had always supposed epistolary talent the exclusive distinction of her own sex

till he had proved to her the contrary." That she was convinced he had even higher powers in the same way we have her written testimony. In a letter to him, which we have read, dated Lyons, July 5th, 1810, she says, " You must write and become the sovereign of thought, as you are of sentiment; you require only the will, and possess the power." His only published work is an " Introduction to the Memoirs of Le Kain," in which he makes some excellent observations on the art of acting. He mentioned to us a few months since that he had material in his mind and *memoranda* for extending this sketch into a work of five hundred octavo pages. It is deeply to be regretted that he died without fulfilling his design. All that he did he gave us, and we intend, when we can, to lay it before our readers in a translation.

In private life the habits of Talma were altogether domestic. He was never so happy as when he had the day to himself, disencumbered of visitors, by whom he was sometimes badly persecuted. We have heard him say, with a momentary impatience, when one after another gossiping idler has been announced, "*Il y a des jours maudits*" (" There are days with a curse upon them"). But he instantly gave way, mastered his impatience, and gave himself up freely wherever he could be useful. His easiness of disposition made some consider him as weak. But he was too well aware of the strength of his own character to waste it upon ordinary occasions, and he never put it forth but when he could do so to some purpose. He saw too far to let trifles operate upon him as they do on ordinary minds, and would even sometimes allow persons to imagine they were controlling him, merely not to deny their vanity, and a gratification which he well knew could do him no harm. His pervading characteristic was a spirit of benevolence, and he did not care for his own indulgence, when, by resigning it, he could give pleasure to others.

Of late years his mind was entirely absorbed in a passion for building. He had a beautiful country-seat near to Brunoi, about sixteen miles from Paris, and for some time this was his hobby. Every season he made some alteration in it; one wing would be removed, and while a new one was erecting the one which remained would come down. We were once praising some part of his country-house. " When did you see it?" "It is two years since." "Oh then, nothing remains of what you praise. It is never two years the same." Here he had extensive grounds, and suites of apartments for numerous visitors. He used to pass all the time he could spare from business here, and for many years only kept an apartment in Paris, whither he went twice, or sometimes oftener, a week, to perform. Within the last five years he took a piece of ground at the back of the Rue St. Lazare, in La Rue de la Tour des Dames. Mademoiselle Mars, Mademoiselle Duchesnois, Horace Vernet, and some others clubbed with him to make a very little town of their own there, which they called La Nouvelle Athenes. Nearly all the houses of the street are occupied by distinguished artists. They are generally built upon the models of their occupant. That of Talma was his passion. He had furnished and arranged it beautifully. His classical taste was to be seen in every part of it. He had fitted up a room splendidly, after antique models, and called it his Roman room. The bed in the chamber where we last saw him was draperied *à l'antique*. He was stretched out in great pain, but pleasant and full of chat. He said his disease was inflammation of the stomach and bowels. The bulk of the conversation fell upon the idea of an English theatre in Paris. He was of opinion it never could succeed to an extent sufficient to pay that first-rate talent, without which it would not only fail, but encourage disrespectful notions of English dramatic genius. This unceremonious mode of reception he used with all his friends. Indeed, to dress or use any sort of etiquette perplexed him. He never was so happy as when undisturbed by strangers and in his dressing-gown. He would sit so, when he could, all day ; but business often hurried him out about twelve, and he usually arose early. He never dined when he acted, but took something light at an early hour. After he had been playing, his dressing-room was the resort of the *beau esprits*. We have seen ladies as well as gentlemen there while he was disrobing, which he would do and talk the while, and was then always in his pleasantest moods. When told he had acted well, he would often say, and with perfect *naïveté* and no touch of vanity, " You think so ?—Yes, you are right." We once introduced a party to his room after a remarkably fine performance of *Sylla*. A lady who had been unusually intent upon the acting, gazing at him and drawing in her breath, unconsciously exclaimed, " *Eh bien, monsieur! Vous voila donc abdique!*" (" So, sir, you then have abdicated !") He said it was the highest compliment he could receive.

His income, though, we think we heard him say, about five thousand pounds (country engagements included), was inadequate to support the numerous claims upon it. His building mania was a very impoverishing one; and we fear he did not die rich. When seized with his last illness, he was perplexed with pecuniary engagements, which he found it difficult to fulfil at the moment ; and the consciousness could not have diminished a disease of that nature.

When his wife attempted to see him on his death-bed, her anxiety may not have been reduced by a wish to set him easy on that score: her companion had bequeathed her his whole fortune. Madame Talma, however, not disconcerted in her plans by the denial of an interview (not, we are persuaded, on the part of Talma himself), immediately gave public notice of her resolution to provide for his children.

PAYNE'S CONCEPTION OF HAMLET.

WE some time ago promised to give our conception of the character of *Hamlet.* We said we did not agree with Mr. Young in his notion of the character; and therefore we shall now, as briefly as possible, express our view of it, and the reasons upon which that view is founded. We look upon *Hamlet* as a being of the gentlest disposition, goaded by the sense of an imperative duty to execute a bloody act of retribution, for which his nature unfits him, and to which he is continually endeavoring to stimulate himself, but in vain. The opposing influences which are struggling within sometimes work him up to a frenzy, driven by which he dashes into deeds of desperation. In one of these paroxysms he stabs, as he supposes, at the king, and kills *Polonius* by mistake; while he turns from every cooler opportunity of destroying the king, though he has one very remarkable one; and eventually kills him from the impulse of the moment. It is upon the spur of an unexpected circumstance that he converts the mission of *Rosencrantz* and *Guildenstern,* which was intended for his destruction, into their own; and equally unpremeditated in his attack upon *Laertes,* when, suddenly, on returning to England, he sees him the only emphatic mourner at the funeral of *Ophelia. Hamlet's* intense affection for the ill-fated girl rouses a "towering passion" in him at the view of her "married rites," and at the implied assumption in *Laertes,* by "the bravery of his grief," to be almost the only mourner on an occasion where he conceived his own feelings gave him a claim to lament more deeply than any other:

> "Forty thousand brothers
> Could not, with all their quantity of love,
> Make up my sum!"

His morbid sensibility takes fire at what it regards as an intrusion and usurpation. In his excitation he treats *Laertes* ill. Of this he instantly repents. He tells *Horatio* that he feels he has "forgot himself," and acknowledges that, as the slayer of *Laertes's* father, he stood to *Laertes* in the same position as the king did to himself; and, of course, *Laertes* could not be blamed for the fury of his recognition and the fierceness of his repulse to the unceremonious attack. He explains to *Laertes* himself that his conduct to him arose from one of those paroxysms to which we have alluded, as produced by his situation operating a transient change upon his natural character, and, with much earnestness, asks his pardon. But, though we admit that he was occasionally lashed, by being "perplexed in the extreme," into frenzy, we can by no means think him more mad than any one who is driven into violent but momentary passion. We have alluded to *Hamlet's* conduct towards the king. This, to us, seems the distinct key to his character. From the first he suspects the king. He longs to be assured. His suspicion is presently cleared up by a full disclosure from his father's spirit. He is now decided. There is no doubt. He will kill the king. He assumes madness as a mask, under which he may act more freely. But no sooner does he put on this mask than he begins to reason away his conviction. He determines to try the effect of a play, in which the murder shall be represented before the murderer. He does not like to take the ghost's word without " grounds more relative," because

> "The spirit that I have seen,
> May be a devil; and the devil hath power
> To assume a pleasing shape; yea, and, perhaps,
> Out of my weakness and my melancholy,
> (As he is very potent with such spirits,)
> Abuses me to damn me."

And, before the play is acted, so wretched is he in the confusion produced by a conscientious shrinking from anything like the deliberate shedding of the blood of others, that he enters into a regular argument with himself as to whether it would not be better to shed his own. But the play is acted. All his doubts are cleared. The king is guilty, and deserves to die. Almost instantly a remarkable opportunity to kill him arises. He finds the king alone, at prayer. He claps his hand to his sword, and says,—

> "Now might I do it, pat, now he is praying;
> And now I'll do it;"

but here, what he does not know to be his nature, again resists what he feels to be his duty. He devises excuses to avoid striking the blow, and flatters himself that he delays merely because he should not have adequate revenge, as his father was killed when unprepared; and, if the uncle were taken when praying, he might go to heaven, and so be better off than his father. These are the words of the author:

> "And so he goes to heaven:
> And so am I revenged? That would be scanned.
> A villain kills my father; and, for that,
> I, his sole son, do this same villain send
> To heaven.
> Why, this is hire and salary, not revenge.
> He took my father grossly, full of bread;
> With all his crimes broad blown, as flush as May;
> And, how his audit stands, who knows, save Heaven?
> But, in our circumstance and course of thought,
> 'Tis heavy with him. And am I then revenged
> To take him in the purging of his soul,
> When he is fit and season'd for his passage?
> No.
> Up, sword; and know thou a more horrid bent,
> When he is drunk, asleep, or in his rage;

> Or in the incestuous pleasures of his bed;
> At gaming, swearing; or about some act
> That has no relish of salvation in't:
> Then trip him, that his heels may kick at heaven;
> And that his soul may be as damned, and black,
> As hell, whereto it goes."

That *Hamlet* himself understands that he is cheating himself by this sort of special pleading is evident from what he says of the player,—

> "What's Hecuba to him, or he to Hecuba,
> That he should weep for her? What would he do,
> Had he the motive and the cue for passion,
> That I have? He would drown the stage with tears
> And cleave the general ear with horrid speech;
> Make mad the guilty, and appal the free,
> Confound the ignorant, and amaze, indeed,
> The very faculties of eyes and ears:
> Yet I,
> A dull and muddy-mettled rascal, peak,
> Like John-a-dreams, unpregnant of my cause,
> And can say nothing; no, not for a king,
> Upon whose property, and most dear life,
> A damn'd defeat was made. Am I a coward?
> Who calls me villain? breaks my pate across?
> Plucks off my beard, and blows it in my face?
> Tweaks me by the nose? gives me the lie i' the throat,
> As deep as to the lungs? Who does me this?
> Ha!
> Why, I should take it; for it cannot be,
> But I am pigeon-livered, and lack gall
> To make oppression bitter; or, ere this,
> I should have fatted all the region kites
> With this slave's offal. Bloody, bawdy villain!
> Remorseless, treacherous, lecherous, kindless villain!
> Why, what an ass am I! This is most brave;
> That I, the son of a dear father murdered,
> Prompted to my revenge by heaven and hell,
> Must, like a whore, unpack my heart with words,
> And fall a cursing like a very drab,
> A scullion!
> Fie upon't! foh!"

And, more remarkably, where he names, in his soliloquy after meeting Fortinbras, the very proneness of which we have spoken, to argue away his conviction of what he ought to do, on seeing such decision all around him upon a mere trifle, notwithstanding it involves the lives of thousands, when his tremendous duty only requires the death of one,—

> "How all occasions do inform against me,
> And spur my dull revenge! What is a man,

> If his chief good, and market of his time,
> Be but to sleep and feed? a beast, no more.
> Sure he that made us with such large discourse,
> Looking before, and after, gave us not
> That capability and godlike reason
> To rust in us unused. Now, whether it be
> Bestial oblivion, or some craven scruple
> Of thinking too precisely on the event,—
> A thought, which, quartered, hath but one part wisdom,
> And, ever, three parts coward,—I do not know
> Why yet I live to say, *This thing's to do;*
> Sith I have cause, and will, and strength, and means,
> To do't. Examples, gross as earth, exhort me.
> Witness, this army of such mass and charge,
> Led by a delicate and tender prince,
> Whose spirit, with divine ambition puffed,
> Makes mouths at the invisible event;
> Exposing what is mortal and unsure,
> To all that fortune, death, and danger, dare,
> Even for an egg-shell. Rightly to be great,
> Is not to stir without great argument;
> But greatly to find quarrel in a straw,
> When honour's at the stake. How stand I, then,
> That have a father killed, a mother stained,
> Excitements of my reason, and my blood,
> And let all sleep? while, to my shame, I see
> The imminent death of twenty thousand men,
> That, for a fantasy, and trick of fame,
> Go to their graves like beds; fight for a plot
> Whereon the numbers cannot try the cause,
> Which is not tomb enough, and continent,
> To hide the slain?—O, from this time forth,
> My thoughts be bloody, or be nothing worth!"

Yet notwithstanding the resolution with which he concludes, his thoughts are not "bloody." The event which brought about the catastrophe was not one of his seeking, and though he kills the king, he does it from the provocation of his mother's sudden death and the treachery practised upon himself, not from the mandate of his father, whence his duty and his determination had taken rise in the beginning of the play. In short, the whole conduct of the story seems an illustration of the beautiful remark *Hamlet* makes to *Horatio*, in one of the scenes omitted in representation,—

> "Our indiscretion sometimes serves us well
> When our deep plots do pall; and that should teach us
> There's a divinity that shapes our ends,
> Rough-hew them how we will."

The only reason to be alleged against our impression that gentleness is the characteristic of *Hamlet*, and the waspishness and bitterness with which it is generally given its antipodes, is his treatment of *Ophelia*, just before the play. Upon this subject we conceive that every objection may be destroyed by an explanation of what we imagine to be the true meaning of that remarkable interview.

Hamlet's love of *Ophelia* arises from his confidence in her perfect artlessness and sincerity. Thorough truth and simplicity alone could attach a character like *Hamlet.* He turns from his soliloquy and discovers her in the hall, with a prayer-book in her hand, walking to and fro by herself; a situation so unusual with her, that her father thinks a device requisite to "color her loneliness." At first *Hamlet* suspects nothing. He is a little surprised at meeting her, but merely observes,—

> "Nymph, in thy orisons
> Be all my sins remembered."

To which she replies by a cold inquiry after his health, "for this many a day," though she has but a short time before seen him, to which *Hamlet* answers (and, we take it, he should answer in a sort of half laugh and half wonder),—

> "I humbly thank you; well."

But *Ophelia* abruptly follows up her first extraordinary speech by, in the most uncalled-for manner and unsuitable moment, handing him back his presents, and saying,—

> "My lord, I have remembrances of yours,
> That I have longed long to re-deliver;
> I pray you, now receive them."

This offends *Hamlet,* and he somewhat indignantly puts back the casket, declaring,—

> "No, not I;
> I never gave you aught."

Upon which *Ophelia,* perhaps galled by his manner, without considering the cause, replies, partly from feeling and partly from the lesson she has received,—

> "My honored lord, you know right well, you did,
> And, with them, words of so sweet breath composed
> As made the things more rich; their perfume lost,
> Take these again; for to the noble mind,
> Rich gifts wax poor, when givers prove unkind.
> There, my lord."

Here *Hamlet,* already excited by the oddness of the appeal of *Ophelia* to a suspicion of some trick, exclaims aside, "Hah!—Hah!" and, turning suddenly upon her, emphatically asks,—

> "Are you honest?"

or, in other words, "Is this sincere; or, are you in the plot with the rest? You, whom, when all around me are spies, I supposed incapable of guile?" *Ophelia,* evidently disconcerted, exclaims,—

> "My lord?"

Upon which *Hamlet*, more nettled at the evasion, repeats the question in plainer terms, and in the altered phrase of,—

"Are you fair?"

not meaning, "Are you handsome?" as generally understood; but, "Are you dealing fairly with me; or, are you, my last and only hope of sincerity and artlessness in the world,—are you turned hypocrite with the rest, to play upon me, to fool me to the top of my bent?" *Ophelia* is still more perplexed by this iteration of the question. She can only repeat,—

"What means your lordship?"

She is mortified at the suspicion of *Hamlet*, and still more mortified at knowing she deserves it. At this crisis it would be but natural for the king and *Polonius*, who are both listening, to be drawn a little forward by their eagerness,—*Polonius* especially. He sees his daughter puzzled, and becomes alarmed for the success of the experiment in which he is so deeply enwrapt, not only because suggested by himself, but from its involving state affairs, and touching him still more nearly as a matter of intense domestic interest. *Hamlet* here might catch a glimpse of the intruders. Indeed, we see no way in which the scene can be understood without. To *Ophelia* he had begun by a downright question. He was dealing directly with her. But now the case is altered,— he knows he is watched and overheard. He instantly changes his course, and turns his questions of "honest and fair," which were by far too clear-sighted and pointed for the madman he would be supposed, into a quibble, which bears him off wide from the point at which the listeners would have seen that he was aiming. Thus is the imputed unfeelingness of his subsequent speeches to *Ophelia* fully explained away by action. The speeches themselves grow out of the quibble, and of the determination to puzzle the detected lurkers, while, at the same time, they keep up a covered censure upon the girl who has allowed herself to be made a tool in the plot against him. For instance, what else can be meant by, "That if you be honest and fair, your honesty should admit no discourse to your beauty"? And, "The power of beauty will sooner transform honesty from what it is to a bawd, than the force of beauty can translate honesty to his likeness; this was some time a paradox, but now the time gives it proof." "Virtue cannot so inoculate our old stock, but we shall relish of it." "We are arrant knaves, all; believe none of us."

Surely this is talking at *Ophelia*, though from the purpose toward which it was expected he would tend; and, so full was *Hamlet* of the discovery he had just made, that he suddenly turns upon her again, with the question more pointed than all the rest,—

"Where's your father?"

And she, faltering again, answers by the direct untruth,—

"At home, my lord."

Which shocks *Hamlet*, and he makes the remarkable reply,—

" Let the doors be shut upon him; that he may play the fool nowhere but in his own house."

Evidently meaning, " Let him not play the fool, as he is now doing, by acting the spy upon me in this house;" and instantly bids her farewell, and seems to take, for the first time, a resolution not to marry, because now convinced there was no one to be found deserving implicit confidence. He even flings upon her the direct reproach of dissembling, to him the worst of crimes, in saying,—

"Wise men know well enough, what monsters you make of them." " I have heard of your paintings too, well enough. God hath given you one face, and you make to yourselves another."

All this to *Ophelia* seems unintelligible; but there is no ground for not supposing, while she thought *Hamlet* distracted, that her delicacy should have inflicted upon her a degree of discontent with herself at having practised thus upon him she loved; which might have powerfully contributed to the subsequent wreck of her own reason. But if *Ophelia* and her father were deceived, the wary king was not. He plainly saw that—

> " What he spake, though it lacked form a little,
> Was not like madness;"

and, convinced that the mind of the prince was on the alert, that he knew too well what he was about, adds,—

> "There's something in his soul,
> O'er which his melancholy sits on brood;
> And, I do doubt, the hatch, and the disclose,
> Will be some danger."

But he has not observed that his and *Polonius's* presence were perceived by *Hamlet*, and therefore cannot unravel the mystery of his pregnant phrases. We are persuaded that any one studying the scene, with reference to the new view of it suggested in these hints, will not only agree with us, but find our impression strengthened by every line, and the character vastly improved by the interpretation, which an able actor can readily make intelligible to any audience. The fate of *Polonius*, which presently follows the passage, confirms our notion. *Hamlet* has just before been listened to; but when he finds the same system of espionage carried into his own mother's closet, he is goaded to an act of sudden vengeance by the thought, and stabs through the arras, exulting in the expectation of at once ridding himself of a duty and of an intruder.

There are one or two other points which we think worthy of being attended to. We have never seen a *Hamlet* who seemed to comprehend the proper mode of giving the passages preparatory to the play scene. When *Rosencrantz* replies to his question, " Wherefore they smiled when he said man delights not me,"—

"To think, my lord, if you delight not in man, what lenten entertainment the players shall receive from you,"

it is at that moment that *Hamlet*, whose perceptions and plans are as rapid as lightning, determines on the whole business of the play; it is at that moment an unwonted exultation comes over him, and the speech of *Rosencrantz* is no sooner ended than the delighted prince exclaims, rejoicing in his secret project,—

"He that plays the king shall be welcome; his majesty shall have tribute of me."

And so evident is this sudden brightening in his whole manner to *Rosencrantz* and *Guildenstern* that when the king and queen question them on the result of their interview, they say expressly,—

"It so fell out, that certain players
We o'er-raught on the way. Of these we told him;
And there did seem in him a kind of joy
To hear of it."

Now Mr. Young, and everybody else we have seen in the part, after having settled the whole affair of the play long before, and having let pass the first intimation of the coming of the players, without the slightest expression of joy, either in their by-play or deportment, in the concluding soliloquy of the act suddenly change from the violent explosion of self-upbraiding, and come forward and whisper to the pit,—

"I'll have these players
Play something like the murder of my father,
Before mine uncle."

As if it were a bit of news, and *Hamlet* had but then settled it in his mind! Such, we grant, are the words; but when the simplest change in the emphasis will get over their absurdity as they stand without the commentary of the stress as we would wish to hear it placed, all censure upon the sentence must fall upon the actor, not the author. The merely saying, "I'll have," so as to denote a "foregone conclusion,"—that is, "all these reflections convince me that my plan is a good one,—the more I think, the more I am persuaded, such is the surest course,—it shall be so,—I'll have the play acted, for by no other means can I hope effectually to catch the conscience of the king."

It is evident that our conception of the part of *Hamlet* cannot be expressed in the present state of the play upon the stage. The great elucidating passages, the keys of the character, are, by absurd custom, omitted; and in the scene with *Ophelia*, some other disposition of the stage might be necessary to evade a laugh at the listeners, and to render the situation picturesque as well as obvious. Established error, says some writer, as slowly gives way to acknowledged truth as the recovered blindman quits his staff. But if we have, from reading, or our own observation, been able to offer any hints which may be hereafter made the means of producing a clearer view of this admirably drawn part, in performance, we shall feel proud of having thus rendered our humble mite of homage to one of the noblest works of its great author.

A LIST

OF

PAYNE'S DRAMATIC WORKS.

TRAGEDIES.

BRUTUS; OR, THE FALL OF TARQUIN.

ROMULUS. (Written for Edwin Forrest, but never performed. MS. in W. P. Chandler's possession.)

VIRGINIA; OR, THE PATRICIAN'S PERFIDY.

OSWALI OF ATHENS.

RICHELIEU; OR, THE BROKEN HEART.

THE ITALIAN BRIDE.

MAHOMET. (Altered and adapted from Miller and Garrick's "Tragedy of Mahomet," with the character of *Mahomet* rewritten for Edmund Kean.)

THE ROBBERS. (Adapted from Schiller's play, and reduced to three acts, and produced by Payne at Sadler's Wells Theatre.)

PERICLES, PRINCE OF TYRE. (Altered from Shakspeare's play, and reduced to three acts. MS. in W. P. Chandler's possession.)

THE WANDERER. A play in five acts; written when at the age of fourteen.

LOVERS' VOWS. A play in five acts, altered from the translation of Messrs. Inchbald and Benjamin Thompson. Mr. Payne made the adaptation in 1809, when a young Roscius, and performed the part of *Frederick*.

COMEDIES.

CHARLES THE SECOND; OR, THE MERRY MONARCH.

PROCRASTINATION.

MARRIED AND SINGLE.

PLOTS AT HOME.

ALL FOR THE BEST.

THE TWO SONS-IN-LAW. (MS. in the possession of Thomas J. McKee.)

THE LAST DUEL IN SPAIN. (MS. in the possession of Thomas J. McKee.)

THE BORROWER. (See Irving's "Life and Letters.")

WOMAN'S REVENGE. (MS. in the possession of Gabriel Harrison.)

DRAMAS.

THE SPANISH HUSBAND.

THÉRÈSE; OR, THE ORPHAN OF GENEVA.

26

NORAH; OR, THE GIRL OF ERIN.
ADELINE; OR, SEDUCTION.
THE TWO GALLEY-SLAVES.
THE RIVAL MONARCHS.
PAOLI.
SOLITARY OF MOUNT SAVAGE.
ALI PACHA.
MAID AND MAGPIE.
ACCUSATION.
THE GUILTY MOTHER.
MAN OF THE BLACK FOREST.
MADAME DE BARRI.
THE FESTIVAL OF ST. MARCK.
THE BRIDGE OF KEHL.
THE JUDGE AND THE ATTORNEYS.
THE MILL OF THE LAKE.
MAZEPPA.
NOVIDO, THE NEAPOLITAN.
THE FALL OF ALGIERS.
THE PRISONER AND THE ORPHAN.
THE MILLER'S MAN.
THE DUEL; OR, THE VETERAN'S REPOSE.
TSMAZL AND MARZAM.
JACONDE.

OPERAS.

CLARI, THE MAID OF MILAN.
THE WHITE MAID (or the White Lady).
THE TYROLESE PEASANTS.
VISITANDINES.
ENGLAND'S GOOD OLD DAYS.
AZENDAI. (See Irving's " Life and Letters.")
OLD ENGLAND'S MERRY DAYS. (See Irving's " Life and Letters.")

FARCES.

FRICANDEAU; OR, THE CORONET AND THE COOK.
THE POST-CHAISE.
'TWAS I.
LOVE IN HUMBLE LIFE.
THE LANCERS.
GRANDPAPA.
PETER SMINK.
NOT INVITED.
THE BOARDING-SCHOOL; OR, LIFE AMONG THE LITTLE FOLKS.
MRS. SMITH. (MS. in the possession of Gabriel Harrison.)
   Sixty-three pieces in all.

INDEX.

27

www.ingramcontent.com/pod-product-compliance
Lightning Source LLC
Chambersburg PA
CBHW020239110726

47898CB00004B/1325